A SCRAPBOOK FOR SUMMER

A SCRAPBOOK FOR SUMMER

Alan Flitcroft

Matador
9 Priory Business Park,
Wistow Road, Kibworth Beauchamp,
Leicestershire. LE8 0RX
Tel: 0116 279 2299
Email: books@troubador.co.uk
Web: www.troubador.co.uk/matador
Twitter: @matadorbooks

ISBN 978 1784624 132

British Library Cataloguing in Publication Data.
A catalogue record for this book is available from the British Library.

Printed and bound in the UK by TJ International, Padstow, Cornwall
Typeset by Troubador Publishing Ltd, Leicester, UK

Matador is an imprint of Troubador Publishing Ltd

For Alison and Emma

A portion of the proceeds from every sale of a copy of A Scrapbook for Summer *will be donated to Cancer Research UK.*

scrap'book (*noun*): a blank book for pasting in scraps, cuttings, etc.

The Chambers Dictionary

Battersea

Saturday 18 May 2013

'Manu.'

One glance at the caller ID and I feel sick. Summer's mobile sings out from the kitchen table with its familiar ringtone: 'Walking on Sunshine' by Katrina and the Waves. I am about to pick it up when his name flashes on the screen and now my hand hovers above the phone, groping air.

The red button says 'Decline'. The green button says 'Accept'. What does he want? Why can't Manu leave us alone?

Katrina launches into the upbeat chorus, her voice cutting through the gloom that permeates the flat. It's a sunny afternoon, but the blinds and curtains are closed and the rooms are cast in shadow. I only have to wait a few more seconds and the phone will divert to voicemail.

I make up my mind. If there is one thing I have learned over the last year, it's that avoiding problems doesn't make them disappear.

I reach for the phone and press the green button.

Battersea

Sunday 19 May 2013

One day later. I study the silver-framed photograph of the two of us that she keeps by the side of the bed. We are in a capsule at the top of the London Eye and she is leaning towards me, whispering into my ear. Whatever she is saying makes me laugh, as I am sporting a huge grin. Behind us, England's capital city is spread out beneath a clear blue sky and there is no sign of the clouds to come. I wish that time could have stopped at that moment.

Next to the photograph is an old scrapbook. A slice of London's history lies within its faded red cover, a jumble of events that may or may not have happened the way I imagine them. Summer inspired me to start the scrapbook when we first met and her presence is a watermark that soaks through every page.

She started looking through the scrapbook again just before she fell ill for the last time, but now her eyesight is failing and she is too weak to concentrate for more than a few minutes at a time. I have taken over, reading a few pieces to her every day, although I'm never sure how much she hears as she drifts in and out of sleep. We are half way through our book of memories – last night I read one of her favourites, the tale of the Deadly Purple Sapphire – but I do not expect us to get to the end.

I stand by the bed, holding a package that I opened after it arrived for her this morning. We have no more secrets from each other and besides, her weak fingers would struggle to break the sealed flap. Inside is a letter confirming her entry into the Shine Walk at the end of September, together with a purple T-shirt and a number. Black figures on white paper; number 4372.

Only a few months ago, it had seemed a good idea for her to walk around London in aid of Cancer Research, giving her a purpose and something to aim for. Looking at her now, lying between the sheets with wretched breaths grating in her throat, the notion that she could walk twenty-six miles feels like a cruel joke.

I sit on the edge of the bed, stroking the brittle bones in her hand and causing the charm bracelet on her wrist to rattle. The curtains are closed to protect her eyes from the glare of sunlight and the air in the room is stale.

She has been confined to the bed since she left hospital five days ago, defying her doctors.

'I want to die in my home,' she announced, in a moment of lucidity. The senior oncologist dragged me to one side to persuade me otherwise, but I wasn't in the mood for listening. This was one last thing I could do for Summer.

I am bitterly aware that it is not the cancer that will kill her, but us – her doctors, her family, and above all me – because between us, we turned off the taps that kept her alive. After the doctors huddled together and decided they could do no more, we nodded in silent understanding and stood by as the plastic tubes were removed. We knew that this act condemned her, but at the same time, it set her free. With no tubes or wires tying her to drips and machines, there was no reason for her to stay in hospital; all she needed now was a supply of morphine to ease the final few days.

We left the cancer ward and its sickly sweet smell in a little convoy, with me pushing her in a wheelchair and staring straight ahead, ignoring the disapproving looks from the white-coats. When we arrived home, I carried her fragile frame into the flat and laid her in the bed, next to the photograph in the silver frame where I am laughing at the top of the London Eye. I knew this would be her final resting place.

The door creaks open and Buster slinks in, his ears flat against his head and his jaw scraping on the carpet. The nurse says that we shouldn't allow him into the room, but I can't see how Buster can make things any worse. He jumps on to the end of the bed and rests his chin between his front paws, staring at his mistress with sad, black eyes.

She stirs and her eyelids flicker open; her irises are still the colour of roasted coffee beans but the whites of her eyes are now stained nicotine-yellow.

'Your Shine T-shirt has come,' I say. 'Do you want to see?'

I push wisps of hair away from her face and pull the T-shirt from the bubble-wrap envelope. It looks ridiculously large now that her body has shrunk to folds of paper-thin skin and jutting bones. She gives a half-smile and then her heavy eyelids fall.

I drop the T-shirt on to the duvet and hold her hand. Her fingers close over mine and she mumbles something that I can't hear. I lean closer and smell the sourness of her skin.

'Was it him?'

I don't want to answer.

'It was him.' Her voice is stronger, more insistent.

'Yes.' It is all I need to say. I have never been able to resist Summer.

She sighs. 'It's over then.'

'No. It will be alright. Everything will be alright.' The words tumble out of my mouth and are sucked into the airless room.

'Kiss me,' she whispers.

I hesitate and her grip tightens, urging me on.

I press my lips to hers and she opens them slightly to let me in. I can feel her fingers loosening and I breathe gently into her mouth, as though this might give her a few more precious moments of life. When I pull away, her grip is gone.

Buster steals forward and licks her lifeless hand. I reach over to the photograph in the silver frame and turn it face down on the bedside table. I do not want to see a picture of myself laughing.

Battersea Power Station

'What the hell am I doing here?'

I am muttering to myself as I survey the sea of neon and Lycra gathering beneath Battersea Power Station. I have been transported into a nightmare world of hyperactive do-gooders in garish colours and fancy dress, accompanied by a soundtrack of high-pitched chatter. They collect in groups on the tarmac wasteland that one day will be the bedrock for executive apartments and manicured gardens as another area of London's South Bank succumbs to redevelopment.

I scowl at an orange-wigged woman wearing a tinsel ra-ra skirt that might conceivably have looked good on someone thirty years younger. I shake my head in disbelief, but she is blissfully unaware of my disapproval, waving glow sticks above her head and dancing a jig to the delight of her friends.

It is the night of the Shine Walk – Saturday 28 September 2013 – and of course I know why I am here. I am doing this for the memory of Summer and frankly, what is my alternative? Another night in front of the TV, eating a glutinous take-away from plastic containers and getting mildly drunk on supermarket lager.

Autumn is closing in and a cool breeze brushes through the crowd. The weather girl on the television with the frog-like mouth and stick-on smile warned that there may be showers overnight, so I have my rain gear in my backpack, along with water, energy bars, plasters and a tea-cosy hat that my mum gave me last Christmas. In the meantime, I am comfortable and inconspicuous in my old jeans and trainers. My only concession to the Shine Walk vibe is to wear the gaudy purple T-shirt that they sent through the post. For some reason, Summer had ordered a large size, so it fits me well enough, even with a layer on underneath to keep me warm. It was as if she knew that she wouldn't make it, and that I would walk in her place. I have pinned my number to the front of the T-shirt. Number 4372.

The four chimneys of Battersea Power Station are bathed in spotlights and stretch high into a violet sky. I associate them with a Pink Floyd album and a helium-filled inflatable pig, and when I found out the walk started here, I did my usual research. Back in 1976, during the photo shoot for the *Animals* album cover, the balloon broke loose from its moorings causing air traffic control chaos. Several helicopters tracked the flying pig to Kent where it eventually came down on a farm. I like to imagine the farmer standing in his field holding a comedy pitchfork, scratching his head and wondering what a giant porker is doing in his field with a fleet of Westlands descending from above.

For those of us who like curious coincidences, the opening track on Pink Floyd's *Animals* album is pleasingly entitled 'Pigs on the Wing'. Perhaps I will write up the episode sometime; I haven't written much in my scrapbook since our final kiss that May evening.

An over-excited man leaps about on a temporary stage in front of us. He is the warm-up act and his mission is to whip us into a ferment of enthusiasm. According to him, there are 16,000 of us on the walk, all with our own causes, our own memories, all in aid of Cancer Research. Tonight, we will create havoc, not in the air like the Pink Floyd pig, but on the streets – the streets of London.

The man on the stage, a DJ from a commercial radio station that I never listen to, addresses us in a language where the letter 't' has largely been erased from existence.

'Hello, everybody! Give me a shou' out on this wonderful Sa'urday evening.'

There are murmurs from the crowd.

'Com'on now! I wanna hear ya! How y'all doing?'

A few people cheer around me.

'Again, Shine walkers! Make some noise!'

I join in now, along with most of my fellow participants, as we realise that he won't shut up unless we scream loud enough. There are twenty-six miles ahead of us and we are worried about whether our bodies will stand up to the rigours of the walk. False bonhomie from a Z-list celebrity is not helping.

'Bonkers,' he yells, '... all of you... bonkers! Wha' are you?'

'Bonkers!' He has beaten us into submission now and we will shout anything he wants. Placated, he turns his attention to one side of the stage.

'So, let's give a big, warm Shine welcome to Fitness Fran. Fran, come up 'ere!'

A woman with mop-top curly hair and a body encased in turquoise spandex bounds up from the wings.

'So, wha' ya gonna do for us, Fran?'

The DJ hands her the microphone and Fran addresses the crowd.

'Shiners. Are you ready for a warm up?'

There is no response but she is oblivious to our lack of enthusiasm.

'You are? Wick-ked! Let's go!'

Music thumps from the speakers alongside the stage. Fran claps her hands exaggeratedly in time to the beat and sways from side to side. Around me, some of my fellow walkers join in half-heartedly.

I groan.

'Hi. You don't look like you're enjoying this.'

A girl sidles up to me. She has a plain face and mousey hair tied back beneath a rainbow beanie hat. A pink glow stick hangs around her neck, giving her features a rosy sheen. She smiles. She has a nice smile.

'A bit cheesy, hey?' She indicates the stage where Fran is now doing star jumps.

She seems inoffensive, like she doesn't scare many geese with loud boos.

'I just want to get on with it, don't you?' I reply.

'Yes. I'm a bit nervous actually. Not sure I'll get round. Have you done much training?'

'No. None at all. I shouldn't be here, really.'

She tilts her head and looks confused. I feel the need to add an explanation.

'I'm... I'm taking someone else's place. They couldn't make it.'

Embarrassed, I look down at my well-worn trainers and notice she is wearing sturdy walking shoes – Little Miss Sensible.

'Well, well done you. I'm Annie by the way. Pleased to meet you.' She offers a hand which I shake limply.

'Ben.' My mouth is dry and my response is little more than a croak.

'Are you OK, Ben?'

'Yeah, sure.' I recover myself and lift my head back up.

'I'm on my own,' she says. 'A bit scary. You?'

'Yes – just me I'm afraid. Billy No-mates.'

'Want to walk together? Twenty-six miles is a long way on your own.'

I look her up and down. She has twiglet legs. I want to get this night over with and I could do without her holding me up.

'Well, let's see,' I say.

Her blue eyes narrow and I realise that she has taken this as a snub. Summer would tell me to stop being a toerag. The girl is nice enough and all she wants is some company.

'No harm in starting together, though,' I say in what I hope is a cheery tone. 'Do you know where we go?'

'Over there, I think.' Her face softens and she gestures in the direction of a stream of Day-Glo that is shuffling its way around the far side of the power station. I remember from the map on the website that the walks starts by looping around to the river and then on to Battersea Park. The crowd is so dense that everyone walks as if they are wearing leg irons.

'Come on then. At least we will get away from this palaver.'

I glance back at Fitness Fran, who is whoop-de-whooping along to the music. She has the crowd, and her reluctant DJ sidekick, doing leg extensions. Disgust must have been etched on my face as Annie laughs. 'Are you always this miserable?'

I hunch my shoulders. 'Sorry. I'll try to brighten up.'

'No worries. If it helps, you can tell me your story as we go round. I'm a good listener.'

'What story?'

She looks straight at me.

'We all have a story, Ben. That's why we're here.'

Battersea Park

Sunday 4 July 2010

It was a sunny, cloudless day and London was overcome with the shock of fine weather. Sun-starved bodies lay strewn around Battersea Park like wet rags as the combination of sunshine and a Sunday brought out the local residents in the same way that a rain shower brings out worms. A day like this might not happen again for years. It should be made the most of.

Summer and I were no exception. We had woken up slowly – when she stayed over on a weekend we were never quick to jump out of bed – but then Summer opened the curtains and squealed.

'Ben, it's a gorgeous day. Let's go to the park.'

I snorted, 'Yes, babe,' and rolled over.

She was on top of me in a flash. Once Summer had an idea, a goal, there was no stopping her. It was one of the things I loved about her. Summer never let an opportunity pass her by.

'Oh no you don't, sleepyhead. You are getting up now.'

She flicked her long, dark hair across my face and I could feel myself getting aroused.

'OK, OK,' I laughed. 'But first, I want to play.'

I made a grab for her but she was too quick, jumping from the bed and whipping off the duvet in one easy movement.

'No time for that, you naughty boy. We have rays to catch.'

It was late morning when we got to the park, armed with tubs of salad sourced from our Sainsbury's Local. Summer was on a health kick and had us eating coleslaw, pasta and edamame beans. I hankered after sausage rolls and a Scotch egg, but Summer had a way of bending others to her will, especially me. With previous girlfriends, I resented making compromises, however small, but it was never that way with Summer. It was enough just to be with her.

Fortunately, alcohol was exempt from her regime and wine

was allowed. We sat on a tartan picnic blanket and drank warm Chardonnay from plastic glasses. Summer wore a flower-print dress, her long legs stretched out beneath its short, flared skirt. I had brought the *Sunday Times* but reading was too sedentary an activity for Summer on such a beautiful day. She flicked off her sandals and danced barefoot on the grass, pirouetting like the ballerina she once was with her arms curved gracefully in front of her. She executed one perfect circle after another and it was obvious that she had danced a lot as a child.

I put the paper down and watched. Summer thrived in the heat and her caramel skin glowed in the sunshine. She flipped into cartwheels, her skirt flapping around her waist as she spiralled around us, and I could sense several pairs of men's eyes straying from their own partners and wandering in her direction. I wanted to shout out to them all.

'Summer is my girlfriend. Do you hear me? She is mine!'

Except that a spirit like Summer could never be a possession. Trying to snare her would have been like catching smoke, so it was better not to try. Instead, I let myself go with the flow of her energy and marvelled at her imprint on the world. We had been together for four years, yet still I lived in a two-tone world of love and fear: love for Summer and fear that one day her smoke would escape my grasp.

'Come on, let's get an ice cream.'

Summer dragged me up from the rug and she was off, running towards a van she could see in the distance. I started after her, not because I particularly wanted an ice cream, but because I knew that Summer would have no money, and she would need me to pay. Summer hardly ever carried money. It was one of life's burdens that she cared to do without.

Summer asked for a strawberry Cornetto and I ordered a Magnum, which seemed a more masculine choice, presumably because it is named after a gun, or as I prefer to believe, a private investigator from an eighties television series with a terrible moustache. We decided to walk around the park and eat as we went, but we had only gone a few hundred yards before Summer skipped away down an overgrown path that curved away from us.

'Summer,' I shouted after her, 'where are you going?'

'I've no idea. Let's see,' she called back.

I followed obediently. The path was in shade as it cut through trees and bushes that the sun couldn't penetrate. It felt like a mugger's alleyway to me and I quickened my pace instinctively, so much so that when I turned a corner I almost careered into her.

'Ooh, Ben, we must get a dog. We must.'

Summer was pointing to a moss-spattered plinth in front of her bearing the statue of a small, moth-eaten dog, if dogs can be moth-eaten. It was an ugly-looking mongrel, twisted on itself, with a stupid look on its face and tufts of hair torn from its body. It reminded me of Piglet from the Winnie-the-Pooh books.

'It's so cute, Ben.'

'Cute? That thing?'

'Yes. Look at its face. I want one. I want one.'

She gave me the big eyes and licked her Cornetto suggestively.

'And where's it going to live? Who's going to take it for walks?'

Summer didn't answer. Instead, she tipped her head to one side.

I decided to try something.

'I tell you what. We'll get a dog if you move in with me. Then we can walk it together.'

I had been pestering Summer to live with me since we had left university, but she refused to leave her mother's house in North London. It was a rare source of irritation between us.

Summer stiffened.

'Please don't ask me that, Ben. You know I can't move in with you. I've told you so many times.'

I kicked my feet in the dust.

'I just don't understand.'

Summer kissed me on the cheek with ice cream lips.

'I'm sorry, Ben. I'm sure it will happen one day, but not just yet.'

I knew that it was best to let the matter drop. Whenever I had pushed this issue too far before, Summer had dissolved into tears and abandoned me for days or even weeks. Instead,

I contemplated the statue and resolved to find out about it. What was it doing there? What did it represent? No doubt there was a story behind this sorry animal, an entry for my scrapbook.

'So, can we get a dog, Ben?' Summer pleaded with me again.

The little dog statue was leaning over with one ragged ear cocked, as if he were waiting for an answer. I took a bite out of my Magnum and felt the tingle of ice on my teeth. I could never resist Summer.

Battersea

Thursday 10 March 1910

Joseph buttons his coat against the chill. It is early spring, warm enough during the daytime, but certainly cold enough at night to warrant his greatcoat.

Frank growls beside him, a crowbar over his shoulder.

'Bloody ridiculous if you ask me. I mean, look at 'em. All over a bleedin' dog.'

'Not even a real dog,' chips in George, leaning on the cart. 'Just a ruddy statue of one.'

'Now, now, Frank, George. We just do what we have to do. And we have the bobbies here to make sure there's no trouble.' Billy is their foreman – an old lag who likes the quiet life, a veteran of thirty years working for the council keeping his head down. Then along comes this shenanigan.

Joseph observes the scene. He has some sympathy with Frank. There must be over a hundred policemen present, the smoke from their cigarettes mingling with swirls of breath clouds in the frosty air. Most of them wear blank expressions on their faces, no doubt dreaming of warm beds and mugs of cocoa, quietly cursing the powers that be that had sent them on this fool's errand. Joseph thinks of his wife, Clara, curled up between the sheets. They had married three years ago and until recently, Joseph considered that they had both been happy with the arrangement. A baby was yet to come along, but Clara did not seem to mind and he told himself that they had time. They were both still in their early twenties but recently, Clara had changed. Instead of the shy girl he married, she had become headstrong and less attentive to his needs. Now, often he would come home and find his meal was not on the table.

'I haven't had time today, Joseph. There's bread and cheese in the pantry.'

And last weekend, she even refused to press his shirts for the week, telling him there was no reason for ironing to be woman's work. Joseph had confided this incident to Frank who was unimpressed.

'You need to get a hold of that one, lad. She's got ideas and them's dangerous.'

Joseph thinks Clara changed when she started attending those suffragette meetings in the evenings, as she always returned from them in an argumentative mood. He could hear her now.

'Men have suppressed women for generations. It's time we stood up for ourselves. And don't think you're going to stop me, Joseph Patterson, by keeping me chained up in this house.'

Joseph is bemused by these unprovoked verbal attacks. He has no intention of subjecting Clara to enslavement – he just wishes she was not so angry these days, particularly with him. After all, he isn't in government, he doesn't make laws. Politics is for the bosses. He is content to be a council labourer earning enough to put food on the table and a roof over their heads. And tonight should be a good little earner, a nice bit of overtime pay for him and the other lads. Perhaps he will treat Clara to a new Sunday dress with the extra money. That should get him back in her good books.

An officer walks towards them.

'Are we all set?'

'All set, sir,' says Billy, touching his cap.

'Right. Let's get this thing over with, shall we?' The officer turns to his men. 'Sergeant! Let's move out.'

Orders are barked and cigarettes dropped to the ground and stamped upon. The policemen organise themselves into lines.

'In the middle, lads,' barks the officer. 'Safer that way.' It sounds to Joseph more like an order than a suggestion.

The bobbies part to let the four of them through. Frank has his crowbar, Billy a sledgehammer and Joseph a shovel. George pushes the cart carrying more implements.

The policemen at the front begin to move, and the rest of the group shuffles after them. It is only half a mile to the

14

estate, but it takes them fifteen minutes to complete the journey. George's cart keeps banging into the bobbies in front, who yelp with pain and indignation.

'Oi! Watch what you're doing with that thing, will you?'

'Why don't you walk a bit faster?' protests George.

'Enough of your lip, sonny. We can only go as fast as the men in front of us.'

Billy steps in. 'Easy, George. We might need them on our side later.'

Joseph shivers. The air is still and the streets are empty, the good citizens of Battersea sound asleep in their homes. It is hard to imagine an army of violent protesters waiting to ambush them.

When they reach the statue, the policemen fan out, creating two circles around the memorial. Any troublemaker would have to breach two lines of men to get through to the workers.

The officer speaks sharply.

'There you go, boys. Make it snappy, won't you? We want to get away from here before there's any trouble.'

Two bobbies edge sideways, creating a path through. Another two shine flashlights on to the statue so that the four men can view their task. Billy ushers them forwards and George sets the cart down. He assesses the structure, contemplating which implements will be suitable for the job.

'Poor little mite,' he says. 'Seems a shame to get rid of him.'

'Ours is not to reason why, George,' replies Frank. 'We're the workers, we just do what we're told.'

Joseph examines the bronze figure of the dog, sitting defiantly on top of a cold, square plinth. It looks like a Jack Russell cross. Their neighbours have a Jack Russell, a friendly little thing called Stomper. This dog had never had a name. Everyone knows it as 'The Little Brown Dog'. He wonders what suffering it endured.

Billy swings his sledgehammer at the base of the statue.

'Come on, boys. Let's not get sentimental.'

It takes them an hour and a combination of crowbars, sledgehammers and pickaxes to dislodge the statue from its resting place. They work undisturbed. No massed ranks of students, doctors or suffragettes descend upon them. Towards the end, a tramp stumbles drunkenly past and is sent on his way with a kick of a policeman's hobnailed boot. *Over a hundred policemen, all on overtime, to deal with one tramp*, thinks Joseph. *That's a good use of council money.*

When they are done, a few of the bobbies help them to haul the statue on to the cart. It is remarkably heavy for such a small dog.

'Where to, Billy?' asks George.

Billy scratches his chin and it is clear that he hasn't thought this far. He doesn't have a plan as to where to store the newly homeless memorial.

Frank butts in.

'There's an old shed near our place, George. Let's take it there and then the bosses can work out what to do with it later.'

'Alright. I'll need a hand though with this cart. This bugger's too 'eavy for me.'

A few more policemen jump forward and grab hold of the cart handles, eager for something to do on a night that had otherwise consisted of inactivity and boredom.

Joseph stands to one side, his eyes taken by the inscription that faces upwards towards the heavens. They have been so focused on their work that they have not stopped to read it before now.

'Do you mind?'

Joseph nods at the torch held by the constable next to him, who obligingly aims the light at the plaque. Joseph mouths the words silently.

'In Memory of the Brown Terrier Dog Done to Death in the Laboratories of University College in February, 1903, after having endured Vivisection extending over more than Two Months and after having been handed over from one Vivisector to Another Till Death came to his Release. Also in Memory of the 232 dogs Vivisected at the same place during the year 1902.'

And the final line that had led to all the trouble:

'Men and Women of England, how long shall these Things be?'

The Brown Dog Riots

On 2 February 1903, two Swedish anti-vivisectionists, Louise Lind af Hageby and Leisa Schartau, infiltrated a lecture at University College London given by the eminent physician William Bayliss. The lecture involved the dissection of a brown terrier dog. The Swedish women subsequently claimed that no anaesthetic was used and that the dog was struggling in pain throughout, a claim strenuously denied by Bayliss. Bayliss sued for libel and won.

Three years later, in 1906, anti-vivisectionists commissioned a bronze statue as a memorial to the little brown dog. The statue was to be erected in the Latchmere Estate in Battersea, an area that at the time had a reputation as a centre of radicalism and was home to some notable institutions sympathetic to the anti-vivisectionist cause; Battersea Dogs Home, for example, refused to allow any of its dogs to be donated to medicine for experimentation purposes.

The inscription on the statue was provocative, particularly the last line: 'Men and Women of England, how long shall these Things be?'

The memorial became subject to regular attack by medical students and other pro-vivisection sympathisers, leading to a twenty-four-hour police guard for the little brown dog. The police commissioner wrote to Battersea Council requesting that it contribute to the £700 per annum costs of protecting the statue. The request was rejected.

There was also a series of demonstrations, including a 1,000-strong march in December 1907 by anti-doggers, as they had become known. The march culminated in a pitched battle in Trafalgar Square between the marchers, 400 police and a group of anti-vivisectionists, suffragettes and trade unionists who formed a natural anti-establishment association, brought together by the brown dog cause.

A new Conservative council in Battersea, elected in November 1909, determined to remove the statue, despite the creation of a brown dog memorial defence committee and a 20,000-signature petition in its support. The statue was removed quietly overnight on 10 March 1910 by four council workers, protected by some 120 policemen. Nine days later, 3,000 anti-vivisectionists staged a protest in Trafalgar Square, demanding the return of the statue, but to no avail. The statue may even have been destroyed by the time of the protest; after being stored initially in a cycle shed, it is believed to have been melted down by a council blacksmith.

The story of the little brown dog and the resultant social unrest even crossed the Atlantic. The New York Times wrote that 'it is not considered at all probable that the effigy will ever again be exhibited in a public place'. However, seventy-five years later, a new statue by the sculptor Nicola Hicks was unveiled in Battersea Park, hidden away almost apologetically on a little-used path that runs behind the ornamental Old English Garden. The new brown dog is a representation of Hicks' own terrier, and has faced its own criticism. Whereas the original brown dog sat upright and defiant, Hicks' version appears confused and submissive.

The original 1906 inscription is repeated on the plinth, along with the following commentary:

'Animal experimentation is one of the greatest moral issues of our time and should have no place in a civilised society. In 1903, 19,084 animals suffered and died in British laboratories. During 1984, 3,497,355 animals were burned, blinded, irradiated, poisoned and subjected to countless other horrifyingly cruel experiments in Great Britain.'

Ironically, the gates to the Old English Garden bear very clear signs which state in no uncertain terms, 'No dogs allowed'.

Battersea Park to Vauxhall Bridge

'Did you get a dog?'

'Sorry? What…'

'Summer wanted a dog. Did you get one?'

'Of course. When something got into Summer's head, there was no stopping her.'

We are walking through Battersea Park. Through the gloom, I notice the entrance to the ornamental garden and the path that Summer and I had bounded down all those years ago, but there is no time for a sentimental detour. Despite my initial misgivings, Annie is setting quite a pace, and it is me who is struggling to keep up, even though we are only in mile one of twenty-six.

'What did you get?'

'Just a mongrel. He has some spaniel in him, but apart from that his pedigree is dubious. Buster won't be winning any prizes at Crufts, that's for sure.'

'He was a rescue, I suppose?'

'Yes, from Battersea Dogs Home. I thought we would be there for ages, with Summer cooing over every dog and agonising over which one to save. I was worried we might end up taking half a dozen home, but no. She saw Buster and he saw her and that was it. He licked her hand and she was smitten.'

Ahead of us, a Cancer Research volunteer is shepherding the walkers around the corner so that we double back on ourselves and head back into the park. I know from the map that we have to meander around the park for a couple of miles before we exit to cross Albert Bridge.

The volunteer is dressed in the Shine Walk purple T-shirt and a trilby with a salmon-pink ribbon around the rim. She waves her arms like a windmill and grins fanatically, as if this is her favourite way to spend a Saturday evening.

'This way. One mile done. Well done, everybody!'

I turn to Annie.

'Do we have to put up with another twenty-five of these?'

Annie smiles. 'Relax, Grumpy, we're all doing this for charity.'

Are we? I have a list of donations on my JustGiving page – I am both surprised and proud that it adds up to £2,380 at the last count – but I know that I am putting myself through this ordeal for reasons other than simple money raising.

The park is eerily dark, except for the luminous walkers who shine like glow worms amongst the trees and bushes. A woman in a crimson shell suit and scuffed trainers staggers ahead of us. I worry for her if she is struggling at mile one, but then I notice that she is clutching a bottle of Smirnoff. She takes a swig, wipes the back of her mouth with her hand and turns round.

'Wotcha, darlin'. Fancy a bitta rough?'

She wiggles her bum in my direction and winks, before veering off the path and flopping down on the grass, cackling. The Shine Walk will be some entertainment for her tonight. I turn back to Annie.

'Funny thing about Buster. He lived with me and I used to feed him, walk him, take him to the vet, but he was always Summer's dog. As soon as she walked into my flat, his floppy ears perked up and his tail wagged. And the two of them would cuddle up on the sofa together – no room for me.'

'Are you sure she didn't keep a secret stash of doggie treats in her pocket?'

I smile at the thought. 'Summer didn't need doggie treats. That was the effect she had on everyone she met, and Buster was no different. It sounds corny, but she was just like her name. Whenever she walked into a room, she brought sunshine and flowers with her. Everyone loved Summer.'

'Especially you.'

I stop and Annie keeps going for a few strides before she realises.

'Sorry,' she says. 'I didn't mean to upset you.'

'No. I… you're right. Of course. Especially me.'

Annie holds out a hand. 'Come on. Let's get a step on. I love Albert Bridge.'

My thighs are already beginning to ache by the time we leave the park via the Albert Gate. It had felt like a long drag through Battersea Park and yet we have barely made a dent in the twenty-six miles.

Annie is right though. The sight of Albert Bridge – pastel pinks, blues and greens, lit up in all its Victorian suspension bridge glory – is uplifting, and crossing from south to north of the river feels like real progress. To me, Albert Bridge has always seemed the most fragile of London's bridges. We pass the sentry box with the sign that says in upper case, rust-coloured lettering: 'ALL TROOPS MUST BREAK STEP WHEN MARCHING OVER THIS BRIDGE.' I have always loved this sign, imagining a paranoid bridge engineer fearful that a troop of clodhopping squaddies will bring the monument to Prince Albert's name crashing down into the Thames. At least the Shine walkers aren't marching in time, so we are relatively safe tonight.

A group of cyclists crosses the bridge alongside us, cheering and waving. One of them, an Asian boy, wears sunglasses and has a boom box behind him strapped to his panier rack and pounding out Jessie J's 'Price Tag'. They may be part of the Shine Walk entertainment but I prefer to think that they are a random bunch of good-timers who cycle around every night assaulting the ears of Londoners with violently loud pop music.

Annie and I reach the end of the bridge and turn right along the Embankment. A band of well-wishers stand at the corner applauding and urging us on. A sign says that we have completed three miles. The first pit stop is a mile away, just before Tate Britain.

Tate Britain

Saturday 10 April 2010

I had tickets for the Henry Moore retrospective at Tate Britain. I thought Summer would enjoy it, as she had taken me to Tate exhibitions before.

London was cloaked in a miserable grey sky, but there was little threat of rain and we planned to cycle along the Embankment to the gallery. Summer compensated for the dullness of the day by wearing a lemon jacket with bright green buttons. A sparkle of silver flashed on her wrist: the charm bracelet that I gave her as a present when we first got together. She always loved that bracelet and I felt a sudden urge to kiss her as we left the flat. Summer's lips tasted of the fresh peach she had eaten for breakfast.

'I love you.'

She wriggled away from me and beamed a smile.

'I know. It's because I'm so loveable!'

We rode along in convoy: me, weaving painfully through the fume-coughing traffic, hunched over the drop handlebars of my road bike, pushing pedals that felt as if they were stuck in treacle; Summer, sailing serenely on her rickety old 'sit up and beg' contraption as if she were on a country excursion. She never deviated from her line and somehow the cars and lorries moved aside to let her through. The world made way for Summer. That was how things were.

By the time we reached the Tate, the crowds were thick around the entrance. We found a convenient bike rack and slalomed through the throng to the side entrance. Despite our timed tickets, there was a small queue for the Henry Moore. We joined at the back and Summer grabbed my hand.

'Tell me about him, Ben. Henry Moore.'

'You know about him. Big sculptures. A bit weird. Usually have holes through the middle.'

'I know who he is, silly.' She punched me playfully in the arm. 'I mean, tell me about *him*. What does his work mean to you?'

'I er... I'm not sure. I've never really thought about it.'

'I don't believe that. You always look these things up. Come on... just say something. First thoughts are usually the best.'

I pictured a rotund woman, reclining with her arm bent behind her head, all curves and twisted limbs, chubby fingers and facial features that could have been sculpted by a child.

'I don't know. Big mamas. Like they want to flaunt their bodies, but actually they're grotesque figures. Distorted. Perhaps they reflect that something is wrong with the world?'

Summer leaned her head to one side and looked at me with her brown eyes.

'That's not bad. And there was I thinking he just wasn't a very good sculptor.'

She gave my arm a playful punch and laughed.

We entered the first room of the exhibition. Room 1: World Cultures.

Visitors were maintaining a respectful hush as they regarded the pieces. The humidity-controlled air was punctured only by the click of heels on the stripped pine floor and the occasional mumble as a couple discussed an exhibit. I contemplated a work of a half figure clasping her hands above her head. She had an anguished expression, or possibly she was just yawning. The exhibition guide informed me that with this work Moore 'embraced the stoniness of pre-Columbian culture'.

Summer stared at a faintly disturbing stone mask for at least ten minutes. It had two deep holes for eyes and a skewed nose comprising slits reminiscent of Voldemort in the Harry Potter films.

'That gives me the creeps,' I said, nestling up and breathing in the smell of her. Lime and mandarin. Jo Malone. One of her favourite scents. Summer was citrus flavours that day.

'I think it's a sad face,' she replied. 'It looks like it has lost something.'

She floated away and I followed her into Room 2: Mother and Child. There was a bordering-on-the-obscene charcoal study of the torso of a woman breastfeeding a baby, and a series of sculptures that were vaguely recognisable as mothers holding infants.

Summer was staring at one of the sculptures, her eyes glistening.

'Summer. What's up?'

'Don't you see, Ben? Look at them.'

She could barely choke out the words.

'I'm sorry, Summer. I just see statues. Women with children. That's what the room is about.'

Summer put her hands on either side of my face and turned my head to one particular work. 'Look,' she pressed me. 'What is she looking at?'

A few heads turned in our direction at the sound of Summer's raised voice and I felt the heat rising in my cheeks. The mother in the sculpture didn't seem to be looking at anything specific to me. Her pinhead features were turned away from her child so that she was gazing at the ceiling. Presumably, Moore hadn't intended her to be contemplating the light fittings?

'I don't know, Summer,' I whispered. 'I don't think she's looking at anything.'

'That's just the point, Ben.'

The tears were tumbling down her cheeks now. I reached down and wiped them away with my hands.

'Summer, what's the matter? It's just a statue.'

'I have to go, Ben. I'm sorry. I love you.'

She ducked away from me and started to run, barging into a woman whose handbag was sent skittling across the polished wooden floor.

'Hey!'

Summer didn't stop. She ran back into the first room and out of sight.

I picked up the handbag and returned it to the woman.

'I'm sorry. I don't know what's got into her. I hope you're OK.'

The woman looked darkly at me before turning away and tutting to herself. I didn't have time to humour her. She would have to stew in her own irritation. I dashed for the exit.

I was only seconds behind, but Summer was a fast runner and by the time I returned to the lobby area there was no sign of her. Outside, her bike was still in the rack. I ran up the ramp and gazed desperately up and down the Embankment. I thought I saw a flash of yellow turning the corner by Vauxhall Bridge, but I couldn't be sure. It didn't matter. Summer was gone.

Tate Gallery

Wednesday 16 February 1938

J.B. slams his glass down on the mahogany desk. Brandy slops over the rim and forms a pool on the wood. He makes no attempt to mop it up. The desk is stained already; another mark will make little difference.

'Blow the man,' he curses. 'Damned impudence!'

He reads the letter one more time.

> *My Dear Manson,*
>
> *I will of course be delighted to accommodate your request and make a loan of the Despiau work to the gallery. In return, I wonder if you could do me the small favour of agreeing to display a piece by my friend, Henry Moore. As you are aware, he is an artist I greatly admire and who has deservedly gained a reputation of some standing. Many of influence in the art world (of whom I dare to presume I am one) are of the opinion that it is time the Tate recognised Moore's talent. I have taken the liberty of enclosing a photograph and description of the work in question, entitled Mother and Child.*
>
> *Yours Ever,*
>
> *Sainsbury*

J.B. takes a gulp from the glass. Seething anger mixed with very special old pale makes his face burn.

Who is that charlatan Sainsbury to determine what he should display in the gallery? J.B. would not presume to advise him on whether to stock peas or carrots in his cheap stores. He is as bad as the rest of them. It wasn't J.B.'s fault that they didn't acquire the Matisse in '35 when the trustees refused to allow him the funds. And frankly, the Roger Fry works that he passed over were second-rate and not worth their place. If he had accepted them, he would have been accused of favouritism, and if there was one thing J.B. stood for, it was artistic integrity. Never would he allow his personal feelings towards an artist affect his professional judgment.

It is always J.B. who bears the criticism. He is a lightning rod for the Tate's detractors. Like the blasted court case tomorrow. J.B. will be the one in the dock, even though it was a dolt of a museum staffer who wrote the Utrillo catalogue. How could the idiot not have known the mad drunkard was still alive? That he was still peddling his anodyne landscapes to fools with more money than taste? The lawyers were even suggesting that as part of the court settlement, the Tate should offer to buy one of Utrillo's abject paintings. The embarrassment is insufferable.

J.B. tops up his glass and catches his reflection in the half-empty bottle. A shock of snow-white hair falls over his forehead, contrasting with the scarlet hue of his face. The stress of his position has turned his once-auburn locks white. In truth, he should resign now for his health, but he doesn't wish to give his enemies the pleasure. The worms would crawl out of the establishment woodwork, led no doubt by that poisonous dwarf, Bell, and he can only imagine their vile letters to *The Times*.

'A tenure that will rank as one of the poorest of any Director in the history of the Tate Gallery, characterised by an underwhelming acquisition policy, and dull and uninspiring exhibitions. His hapless leadership can be summed up by the fact that his most significant achievement will be viewed as the installation, not of seminal works of art, but of more lavatories.'

The brandy scorches the back of his throat. His adversaries are all philistines. Had he, J.B., not represented Britain at the Biennale? And was it not J.B. who was responsible for the Burne-Jones and Constable centenary shows? It is true he has installed more toilets for the comfort of visitors, but what is so terrible about that? And no one mentions the electric lighting he has introduced in all the rooms, allowing the gallery to stay open later in the long winter evenings.

He examines the photograph of the Henry Moore sculpture that Sainsbury has sent him and shudders. A hideous, twisting representation of a mother and child, a clichéd Moore and, like the man himself, ugly and devoid of any artistic merit. J.B. knows that he must draw the line. The sculpture of Eve by Despiau would be a valuable addition, but the gallery's standards must not be compromised.

He drains his glass, picks up his fountain pen, and scribbles over the photograph. He will reply to Sainsbury in no uncertain terms tomorrow evening after he is finished with the Utrillo case.

The clock on the mantelpiece ticks towards 6pm. Time for one more brandy and then he will leave the office.

★

When the cleaner finds him two hours later, his head is on the desk and he is snoring gently. She carefully removes his fingers from his glass and places the tumbler on a tray to be taken down to the kitchen, along with the empty bottle she found in the wastepaper basket. She doesn't want to wake him as he looks so peaceful, so she will leave his office this evening and give it a thorough going over tomorrow. She will throw open the windows in the morning as well to give the room a good airing and rid it of the liquor fumes. She is not concerned though. This is not the first time that she has come upon the Director asleep in his office at the end of a tiring day.

She picks up a black and white photograph that he has pushed to the edge of the desk and examines the picture. It appears to be a statue of a mother and a baby, but it is not lifelike at all. She doesn't like the modern art. She prefers her pictures and statues to look like the people and objects they are supposed to be. The Director has scrawled across the photograph and she wrinkles her eyes to read his daddy-long-legs handwriting. She makes out four words:

'Over my dead body!'

James Bolivar Manson

James Bolivar Manson was Director of the Tate Gallery from August 1930 to March 1938, a period when there was no government funding for acquisitions. Partly due to the lack of funding, partly due to his own artistic preferences, his tenure as Director was characterised by a conservative acquisition policy and a series of unexceptional exhibitions. In one infamous episode, Manson asked Sir Robert Sainsbury, a well-known patron of the arts, if the Tate could borrow a study of Eve by the French sculptor, Charles Despiau, from his private collection. In return, Sainsbury requested that the gallery also displayed Henry Moore's 1932 Mother and Child. *Manson's withering response was, 'Over my dead body!'*

Manson suffered from alcoholism and depression and is generally recognised as one of the least successful of the Tate's directors. His last few months as director were particularly difficult. He was named as the defendant in a libel case brought by the French artist Utrillo, after a Tate staff member wrote in a catalogue that Utrillo was both dead and a dipsomaniac. Neither statement was true, and the first one patently not so. On 17 February 1938, a court settlement was reached which included the purchase of a Utrillo painting by the Tate.

Only a fortnight later, Manson disgraced himself at a dinner at the Hotel Georges V in Paris, hosted by the Ministre des Beaux Arts *to celebrate the British Exhibition that was taking place at the Louvre. Manson turned up drunk and proceeded to disrupt the ceremony with cat-calls, obscene insults and, bizarrely, cries of 'cock-a-doodle-do', supposedly mimicking a Gallic cockerel. He is also reported to have harassed Lady Phipps, the wife of the British Ambassador, throughout the evening; it is unclear whether this was as a result of lustful intent or otherwise.*

The art critic Clive Bell attended the dinner and wrote of the events in a letter to his wife. He concluded by writing: 'I hope an example will be made, and that they will seize the opportunity for turning the sot out of the Tate, not because he is a sot, but because he has done nothing but harm to modern painting.'

Following a request from the Foreign Office after the Paris incident, Manson was compelled to resign his Directorship 'on health grounds'.

One year later, in 1939, the gallery acquired its first Henry Moore sculpture and now boasts a significant collection of the artist's works. The gallery's most recent Moore exhibition, in 2010, featured the 1932 Mother and Child *sculpture, rejected by Manson seventy-two years earlier.*

Vauxhall Bridge to Horseferry Road

'There.' I point to the corner of Millbank and Vauxhall Bridge Road. 'That's where I thought I saw her yellow coat disappearing. I didn't see her for a week.'

'A week? Where did she go?'

'I always assumed she went home to her mother's. It wasn't the first time it had happened. She would just take off and there was nothing I could do except wait for her to come back. She wouldn't answer her phone, respond to texts, anything. And she never took me to her mother's house, so I didn't know where they lived. Only that it was somewhere in Muswell Hill.'

Annie looks puzzled.

'It wasn't the first time? Did she disappear often?'

I shrug. 'What do you mean by often? Three or four times a year, usually for a few days at a time, but the longest was about a month. Would you say that was often?'

'I would say that was odd. She never said why she went?'

'No, and after the first time, I learnt not to ask. She begged me not to question her. She was so upset. I remember her bawling her eyes out telling me how much she loved me. Over and over again.'

'It's a funny way to show you love someone. To disappear for a week with no explanation.'

'I know, but Summer was an enigma. I had to accept that there were closed doors in her life that she didn't want me to walk through. Otherwise, our relationship wasn't going to work.'

We have passed the first pit stop where we both grabbed a bottle of water and an energy bar. The Tate Britain gallery stands to our left followed by the drab Millbank Tower. A small group of walkers has stopped to attend to one of their number who is sitting against the Embankment wall, one foot stripped of its shoe and sock. A blister by mile five is not a good sign. I wriggle my toes. So far so good for me.

A Shine volunteer wearing an outsize foam glove points the route out for us. We are to turn up Horseferry Road towards Victoria.

'Brilliant stuff, everybody! Let's walk all over cancer!'

She hops from one foot to another as if she is dancing on hot coals, high-fiving walkers with her foam glove as they pass. Annie and I give her a wide berth.

'They'll grow on us by the end,' Annie comments.

'Like bacteria?' I ask.

'Grumpy again! Tell me more about Summer. Cheer yourself up.'

It is true. I like talking about Summer. I haven't really had a chance to let my feelings out until now.

'She had a burning sense of right and wrong. She wanted to fight injustice whenever she saw it. I used to think that democracy was about putting a cross on a voting slip once every few years, but to Summer it was so much more than that.'

'Like…?'

'Protests, marches, petitions. Once, the local council refused planning permission for a new primary school at the end of our road. All the locals were against it. They didn't want yummy mummy 4x4s clogging up the street twice a day.'

'And Summer thought that was wrong?'

'Completely. For her, the interests of the kids came first, even though we didn't even have a child. She knocked on every door of every neighbour trying to persuade them to write to the council supporting the school.'

Annie is sceptical. 'I bet that was a hopeless cause. Not in my back yard, and all that.'

'You would have thought so, but Summer in full flow was a fearsome force. Eventually, the council got enough letters to re-open the decision. They still might not build the school, but at least she made them think again.'

'Impressive. Perhaps if more of us were like Summer the country might be a better place.'

'Maybe, although I'm not sure Tony Blair would agree. She used to write to him and his ministers on a regular basis about all sorts of things. The wars in Iraq and Afghanistan, student loans, fox hunting, renewable energy, bird flu. You name a cause, and Summer would take a stance on it.'

I smile at the recollection. Sometimes, Summer would receive a reply from Downing Street, never directly from the Prime Minister, but from an important-sounding civil servant. 'Thank you for your letter dated blah, blah. The Prime Minister has asked me to reply on his behalf to assure you that we take the issue you raise extremely seriously blah blah.'

'They're just designed to shut you up,' I used to say to Summer, as she filed another 'From the Office of the Prime Minister' letter away. Summer was proud of these replies. She saw each one as a little victory and kept them all as evidence of her various campaigns.

'They'll carry on doing what they want to, you know. Your letters won't make a difference.'

Summer would wag her finger at me.

'Shame on you, Ben. On my own, I may be a little ant, but little ants can form powerful armies.'

'Well,' says Annie, upping the tempo of her walking, 'I admire her actions. Democracy needs people like Summer.'

My thighs protest as I increase my own pace. Is it my imagination or has Annie just got annoyed with me? I catch her up in a few strides, and manage to speak through my heavy breaths.

'I still have her file, you know. With all those letters.'

Annie turns her blue eyes on mine, and there is a ferocity in her gaze that stops me in my tracks.

'You should keep it going. Start filling it up with your own replies from the Prime Minister.'

'Well, maybe I'll just knock on his door when we go past tonight,' I reply sarcastically. 'Ask him what he's doing about cancer research.'

'That would be a start,' she says evenly, and accelerates away.

I let her go. I am approaching a place with horrible memories that I can't face up to right now, so it is better for me to walk alone, if that is possible amongst the throng of walkers and overly cheerful volunteers. The Victorian façade of Number 65 Horseferry Road looms out of the darkness. It is a building with plenty of ghosts, but there is one in particular who is mocking me from within its red brick walls.

I look straight ahead, quicken my pace and take slow deep breaths, but it is only as I turn into Victoria Street that I start to relax again. I am heading towards Parliament Square now, leaving Horseferry Road and my personal ghost in the past. The air feels damp but it isn't raining; the tears of the Gods, as Summer called them, might come later. I look up and see a slice of white moon sidling out from behind a charcoal cloud. The moon shines bright compared to the insipid glow of the London streetlights. *Just like Summer*, I think. She always shone.

Parliament Square

Wednesday 27 February 2013

Ray sets down his cart and surveys the square. It is a brass monkeys evening and he is grateful for the thick gloves provided by Westminster City Council, or more accurately, provided by Veolia Environmental Services, the company which employs Ray and holds the contract to clean Westminster's streets. It seems to Ray that no one works directly for the council any more. Street cleaning, council tax payments, parking fines – everything is 'outsourced' to someone else.

Ray is pretty sure that Veolia is a French company. When he was at school, all the kids used to say that the French were dirty and smelly, so it was a funny turn of events that a French company was now responsible for cleaning the heart of England's capital. Even if it was true, Ray thinks, you probably can't call the French dirty any more. That would be racist and that weren't allowed these days, not now there are so many foreigners in the country.

Ray doesn't begrudge the immigrants coming over to Britain. Altaf, who supported Egypt in the Olympics even though he was born in Acton, says that Britain is a land of opportunity. So far, Altaf's opportunity has been to work evening shifts with Ray emptying litter bins and picking up rubbish, but that doesn't stop him bollocking on in the pub about Britain being the best country in the world. The way Ray looks at it, it is obvious that foreigners want to live in a better place than where they come from, and that is OK by Ray if they work hard and don't cause no trouble.

Like the Polish. He knows a couple of Polish lads from the Nag's Head. Pav and Boris always put in a shift – regular twelve-hour days painting before they knock off for a pint. They work in places like Wimbledon or Barnes where people can afford to pay for decorators, and whenever Ray asks, Pav tells him, 'we are painting a yuppie house from the basement to the loft conversion.'

'All they ever want is cream,' moans Boris over his beer, like he is desperate to paint bright colours.

And the Polish did their bit in the war as well. Ray had heard someone on the telly say that Polish pilots shot down more German planes in the Battle of Britain than the RAF. Yes, the Polish were alright, although their food tasted like shit. Ray had stopped by a Polish deli one night when it was the only place open and he had nothing in the fridge, and had bought a couple of dodgy-looking sausages which hadn't agreed with him. His gut had given him gyp for days. The next time his fridge was empty, he stopped at the chippie. You couldn't beat a bit of English cod and chips with salt and vinegar.

No, Ray wasn't going to vote National Front or nothing like that, although that Nigel bloke from the Independence Party who nearly bought it in a plane crash speaks a lot of sense, even if he does look like a shirtlifter. Ray has seen him once or twice in the square, strutting the politician walk like he has a poker up his arse. Ray sees a lot of politicians and most of them walk stiff straight, marching along like they are so important and they have to get to some place fast to save the world. As far as Ray is concerned, there isn't much that can't stand to wait a while. Like cleaning. If he doesn't clean a pavement today, he can always do it tomorrow. It isn't such a big deal.

Ray remembers that time eighteen months ago when they all got a day off because the union went on strike about pensions or something. There was a big march but Ray wasn't going to waste his free day joining that. Instead, he enjoyed a good few hours in the Nag's Head and when they all went back to work, they just cleaned up two days' worth of crap rather than one. Other than that, nothing changed.

He takes out a brush from his cart and engages in some less than enthusiastic sweeping. It is amazing how much rubbish gets dropped in the square by all the tourists: fag ends, Cornetto wrappers, sweet packets. In his time, Ray has come across a few odd things as well. Used condoms were pretty common – that would be no surprise to any street cleaner –

but finding an old toilet dumped in the middle of the green one day had him flummoxed. Luckily, none of those peace protesters had used it. That would have been too disgusting. Armitage Shanks it had been, Ray remembers it clearly. That's a good British company that everyone knows about because everyone pisses and shits on the Armitage Shanks logo every day of their life. The ceramic toilet was too heavy for him to lift into his cart, so he had phoned in and they had sent down a couple of blokes in a van to pick it up. One of the sods probably picked up a few quid for it down his local scrap yard.

And then there had been that row of shop dummies plonked on the pavement. They were naked, if that was the right way to describe human-shaped bits of plastic, and both Ray and Altaf felt a bit Moby Dick looking at them. Two men and two women, although you could only tell the difference by the size and shape of the curves and bumps as shop dummies didn't have bits and bobs like real people.

They loaded two each into their respective carts. Altaf insisted that he would only take the male dummies, muttering something about Allah which Ray didn't quite catch, but which he knew was crap as Altaf drank lager and didn't pray to Mecca like he was supposed to if he was a real Muslimist. The female dummies just seemed to make Altaf particularly queasy, which Ray suspected was because Altaf wasn't that experienced with women, either real or plastic.

In a show of chivalry, Ray took his coat off and grabbed Altaf's as well, wrapping them around the female dummies in his cart.

'To protect their modesty,' announced Ray proudly, as they wheeled the carts back to base. Altaf nodded appreciatively.

Ray is on his own this evening. An extra shift has been added to the rota later tonight and Altaf has volunteered to earn himself a bit more cash as the company pays higher hourly rates after 7pm. Ray isn't so bothered about the money. He prefers to get his shift over with so that he can get down the Nag's Head for a couple of hours later. He prods a scuffed-up sleeping bag with the handle of his brush. It is empty; he knew it would be. No one has slept in it for days. It is too cold for the protesters now. Further on, there are a couple of ragged tents, a few cardboard boxes and discarded signs on the pavement and he can see a group of fold-up chairs and an old gas stove as well. This sad little lot is all that is left of the peace camps that have been in Parliament Square for years.

Ray has seen lots of them come and go, starting with Brian, who became a bit of a celebrity. He was a decent bloke in the early years and used to offer Ray a smoke of an evening. Brian started camping there in a protest against the war, although Ray always suspected that it was also an excuse for Brian to get away from his wife. For the life of him, Ray couldn't remember which war it was now and to be honest, he wasn't sure that Brian could tell you by the end. Every time there was a new war, Brian would protest about that one as well, so after a few years they all blurred into one big protest. No, Ray never minded Brian. After all, free speech was what the World Wars were all about, so that people like Brian could protest outside the House of Commons if they wanted to.

Altaf didn't agree. He thought Brian and the ones that followed him messed up the square with their cheap tents and crappy signs. As far as Altaf was concerned, the police or the army should have used tear gas and rubber bullets to get rid of them.

'No way this would happen back home,' he said, by which Ray assumed he meant Egypt, rather than Acton.

Altaf did have a point at times. At least Brian cleaned up after himself. Some of the others were filthy bastards and occasionally, Ray had to sweep up mess from the green, but overall it wasn't too bad. When the camp got bigger, they brought in straw bales to use as toilets, which Ray avoided on the grounds that he was paid to clean streets not public conveniences.

The politicians complained that the protesters were a health hazard, saying that they encouraged rats and mice and stuff, but Ray thought that was a made-up argument to get rid of the noisy demonstrators and their tents. It was true that sometimes he saw a rat scuttling along the gutter, but then that could happen on almost any street in London. And, the protesters weren't anywhere near as vicious as the snot-nosed students who had wrecked Whitehall a couple of years before and turned the square into a war zone. That took some fucking cleaning up afterwards. Ray knew he had to do it.

The first time the protesters were evicted was in 2010 after Boris Johnson had said something on the telly about the camp being an eyesore. The bailiffs moved in overnight and Ray saw the pictures on the news the following day, with the protesters chaining themselves to railings, waving their rainbow flags and gobbing at the bailiffs in their hi-vis jackets. It made no difference. The bailiffs won in the end.

When Ray returned for his shift the following evening, Heras fencing had been put up around the green and most of the protesters had given up and gone home, although a few had simply moved on to the pavement. For some reason, Brian was allowed to keep his tent on the grass, which by now he was sharing with an angry Aussie woman who Ray didn't much care for. She seemed to have a bad influence on Brian, as he wasn't friendly any longer and there were no more fags for Ray. Barbara, her name was. She wore a patchwork quilt jacket and screamed through a megaphone so loud that your ears hurt.

There was a sign on the fence that listed all the items the bailiffs had taken: tents, sleeping bags, chairs, sound systems. There was even a sailboat on the list. Ray wondered what anyone had wanted with a friggin' sailboat in the middle of Parliament Square. And a beer barrel. Bastards. None of them had ever offered Ray a drink when he was doing his rounds, although he was sure Brian would have done if it wasn't for the Barbara woman.

It was a funny thing but there didn't seem to be much peace within the peace camp. Brian and Barbara were always getting pissed off with the others and there were loads of arguments, usually about them not protesting loudly enough or talking to someone from the papers who Brian didn't like. And Barbara could certainly eff and blind with the best of them when she wanted. Ray could tell that many of the protesters were scared of her.

One evening about five or six years ago, Ray turned up for his shift and a tardis had landed on the pavement, like Doctor Who had arrived from another galaxy. In fact, it wasn't Doctor

Who but a woman called Maria who told Ray that she came from Switzerland. Barbara especially hated her.

Maria looked like a bloke, with short dark hair that needed a brush and a threadbare navvy jacket, but she always spoke nicely to Ray. After Brian left, Maria seemed to become the new leader as Barbara didn't have the same influence anymore, possibly because she had pissed all the other campers off over the years or possibly because they just wanted a bit of peace and quiet and were fed up with her wailing through the megaphone.

Ray was involved himself in the next eviction. It was a miserable windy evening in January last year when they were all summoned in to work for a late session, which hacked Ray off as it meant he couldn't get down the Nag's Head. Some bloke from the council waved a bit of paper at them saying they had authority to remove all the tents and other crap from the pavement and the police would accompany them in case of any trouble. They didn't need bailiffs this time though, just the cleaning team.

They were standing in the corner of the square about to start the clean-up, all wearing white overalls like you see the police forensic teams wear at crime scenes on the telly, when the council man told them they had to leave the tardis alone. Apparently, the court had decided that Maria could stay. Perhaps the judge was a Doctor Who fan, thought Ray. That really hacked Barbara off, whose tent was dumped on a truck along with the others. She bawled at Ray at one point, screaming that he was 'a fucking collaborator' and her spit pebble-dashed his face. He felt the rage rising in his belly, and clenched his fist instinctively, but a policeman put a hand on his arm and led Barbara away before Ray could punch her. Altaf was next to him and shouted after her.

'Fucking...' he paused, thinking what to say, '... fucking... convict!'

Ray looked blankly at him.

'She's Australian, man,' he said, as if that explained it.

Maria didn't last much longer in any case and Ray watched as a lorry with a robot-like crane removed the tardis a few months later. The tardis was suspended in the air for a few minutes, lopsided, with a grinning skull and crossbones on the side and words that said something about 'Oil' and 'Death'. When they finally lifted it on to the lorry, Ray climbed up and took a peep inside. Disappointingly, it was the same size on the inside as it looked from the outside.

That was about a year ago now. Since then, a few protesters had come back with tents and sleeping bags and every so often the police had moved them on. There was no leader no more and the whole protest camp thing was fizzling out. It had lasted twelve years, which wasn't a bad effort, but all things come to an end. Brian would have been disappointed but then he couldn't really expect people to stay there forever, could he?

It is obvious what the extra shift is about tonight. Over the last two days, Ray has seen a couple of council workers poking about in the remains of the camp, peering into the tents and coming back every few hours or so to see if any protesters are there. He'd heard a rumour back at base that the council thought it was all over now and that they could take down the fencing and re-open the green. That would be a right pain in the arse, as he would have to start cleaning up after the daytrippers and tourists again, who left all sorts of crap behind them – a different sort of crap from the protesters, but still crap that Ray has to pick up.

He looks at his watch. Time to get a move on; there is a pint of Special waiting for him in the pub. He will think about Altaf and the others that evening clearing up the remnants of the peace camp and have a drink for them. Suckers. He rubs his gloved hands together. Who wants to be out on a night like this when you could be down the pub in the warm having a few beers with your mates?

Parliament Square Peace Protest Camp

The first peace protester to start camping out in Parliament Square was Brian Haw, who commenced his vigil in 2001 in protest at the United Nations sanctions against Iraq, which ultimately led to the invasion of Iraq by coalition forces in March 2003. Brian was subsequently joined by several other activists, most notably the Australian Barbara Tucker in 2005 and the Swiss-born Maria Gallastegui in 2006. Barbara Tucker particularly was known for her aggressive campaigning, frequently using a megaphone to broadcast her messages across the square and gaining a reputation for haranguing other protesters who didn't share her views. In her seven years as a member of the peace camp, she was arrested nearly fifty times.

Over the years, the peace camp developed from Haw's one-man protest against economic sanctions to encompass protests on a number of foreign policy issues, although the core protests remained directed against the UK Government and its allies for their military actions in Iraq and Afghanistan. The Greater London Authority ('the GLA') and Westminster City Council fought a longstanding legal battle to remove the protesters from Parliament Square. As Mayor of London and Head of the GLA, Boris Johnson won a High Court ruling to evict the protesters and more than sixty bailiffs, assisted by police, cleared the camp on 20 July 2010. Fencing was erected around the green to prevent the protesters from returning, although Brian Haw was allowed to stay as his occupancy had pre-dated the law that had been relied upon in court.

Many MPs and local politicians were infuriated, however, when a number of protesters simply moved their camp from the green to the pavement. As the pavement was under the control of Westminster City Council as opposed to the GLA, the council had to undertake further action to remove them. This was achieved in January 2012 following the passing of a council by-law in December 2011, itself made possible by Parliament's Police Reform and Social Responsibility Bill receiving Royal Assent the previous September.

Even in January 2012, Maria Gallastegui obtained a last-minute injunction preventing the removal of her tardis-like hut from the site. Ms Gallastegui stayed on until May 2012 when her tardis was winched on to the back of a lorry and removed from the square. Unlike Barbara Tucker, Maria Gallastegui adopted a more peaceful approach to protesting, and reportedly even assisted the council workers in lifting her tardis on to the truck.

Despite the council's action, a number of protesters continued the peace camp on the pavement, but the final clearance came in February 2013, almost ten years after the start of the Iraq war. The Westminster street-cleaning team removed the final collection of sleeping bags, tents and other items after officials observed the camp for forty-eight hours and confirmed that it was no longer occupied. At the same time, the fencing around the green was taken down and the square was fully returned to public use.

Brian Haw, a lifelong chain smoker, was diagnosed with lung cancer in September 2010. He subsequently left the camp on New Year's Day 2011, nearly ten years after he started his protest, for treatment in Berlin. Haw died in Germany six months later on 18 June 2011. He was sixty-two years old.

There is now a campaign to erect a statue of Brian Haw in Parliament Square to enable the veteran peace campaigner to continue his vigil, even in death. After years of trying to evict him, the authorities now face the prospect of a permanent Brian Haw in the square.

Victoria Street to Parliament Square and Whitehall

I walk on my own along Victoria Street towards Parliament Square. Victoria Street is a soulless part of London, epitomised by the dull block of glass that is the DTI building – a characterless building to house characterless civil servants. In contrast, Westminster Abbey and the Houses of Parliament glow bronze as I enter the square and the face of Big Ben shines like a full moon. It is approaching 10pm and we have been walking for nearly an hour and a half. I hear a 'click, clack' and turn round to see two earnest walkers with poles, their faces creased with concentration, focused on each step. Click, clack. Click, clack. Click, clack. I will be driven mad if I walk the remaining twenty-odd miles with the clickety-clackers, so I increase my pace to get away and before long I see Annie in front of me.

When I set out from my flat this evening, I thought I would speed round the twenty-six miles on my own and get the walk over and done with as quickly as possible. Now, I am struck by the realisation that I don't want to walk alone. There is so much I want to talk about. I catch Annie up in a few strides and tap her on the shoulder. She turns round and fixes her gaze on me. A few seconds earlier and the words were ready to spill out of me. The sight of her face and I am suddenly tongue-tied.

'Hey,' is all I can muster.

'Hey,' she replies.

We walk a few more steps into the square. There are no peace protestors anymore. Brian Haw and his encampment are gone, as is the fence around the green, and Parliament Square seems empty without them.

'Mind if I walk with you again?'

Annie shrugs.

'If you like. It's better to be with someone.'

'I know. I'm sorry about what happened back there. You're right of course. I should carry on with the letters.'

Annie sweeps strands of her hair back with a pale, bony hand. She is incredibly thin and looks far too fragile to walk twenty-six miles overnight. I resist an urge to hug her.

'It was my fault,' she sighs, a deep sigh as if life is too hard to live. 'I'm sorry. I just think that when you find someone who is so precious, you should cling on to them for as long as you can.'

'I… I think that is what I'm trying to do.'

'I know.'

We are turning into Whitehall. Another purple-clad volunteer stands on a box clapping his hands over his head.

'This way, folks! Keep it going. Good job.'

It is a long time since I was last in Whitehall.

Whitehall

Thursday 9 December 2010

The cold snap of the previous week had given way to milder temperatures and it was a bright day when we set off for central London. For a month now, Summer had been agitating over the student loan demonstrations. She had missed the action at Millbank when 200 students scaled the roof of the Conservative Party's headquarters building, which left her feeling both guilty and frustrated. At least it also left her without a criminal record. One adrenaline-fuelled kid was charged with attempted murder after throwing a fire extinguisher off the roof at the police below. He was lucky that it missed everyone, otherwise they would be locking him up in the Tower of London and throwing the key into the Thames.

There had been a couple of other demonstrations since, and I had somehow persuaded Summer not to go. I was worried about the violence as it was obvious that there were hotheads bent on causing trouble amongst the mainly peaceful students. But today was the big one and Summer wouldn't be deterred.

'I would never forgive myself, Ben. It's too important not to be there. This is the future of our kids at stake.'

I was taken aback by this as the subject of children was a touchy one between us. I had mentioned it before, along the gentle lines of, 'Have you ever thought about whether you want kids?' only to have Summer burst into tears, run to the bathroom and lock herself in for three hours.

When she eventually emerged, she had given me a kiss and a warning.

'We're too young, Ben. Please don't mention that again.'

I had felt as if she was saying that we would always be too young, yet here we were, on the day that Parliament was going to vote through an increase in tuition fees, and Summer was using our future offspring as justification for joining the demo in Trafalgar Square.

I packed water, snacks, gloves, jumpers, woolly hats. I packed for both of us as Summer insisted on wearing a flimsy scarlet top – 'The colour of revolution,' she argued. I did convince her to take a raincoat, which she wrapped reluctantly around her waist.

'It's a waste of time, Ben. I won't wear it. I want to stand out from the crowd.'

The stories in the chat rooms about the police tactics were gruesome. A new word had crept into the political debate: *kettling*. The police had been penning demonstrators into Trafalgar Square, Parliament Square or Westminster Bridge until the combination of the cold, lack of food, water and toilets, and sheer boredom dampened their riotous spirits. Exhausted and deflated by just being kept standing around, when the police eventually released them the students slunk off to wherever they had come from. If we were going to be kettled, I wanted us both to be ready.

We arrived at the south side of Trafalgar Square a few minutes before twelve. It was already a seething mass of humanity with chanting students packed around Nelson's Column. They wore muted colours and some covered their faces with scarves or pulled down the hoods on their hoodies. A triple line of hi-vis-jacketed police stood ready by Admiralty Arch with riot shields, shiny helmets and ebony-coloured batons. The threat of violence gripped everyone like a vice; Trafalgar Square was a powder keg waiting to be lit and there were plenty of protestors in Guy Fawkes masks who looked ready to emulate their gunpowder plot hero and do just that.

Placards were thrust into the air reading 'F**K FEES' in white letters on a socialist red background. I had no idea why they bothered with the asterisks; their message was clear. A group standing on the edge of one of the fountains orchestrated the crowd in a repeated chorus of, 'No Ifs, No Buts, No Education Cuts.'

Summer grabbed me by the arm, her face alive with excitement.

'Come on, let's go to the Houses of Parliament.'

We joined the hordes of demonstrators making their way down Whitehall. The aim was to demonstrate in front of the Houses of Parliament as Cameron, Clegg and the rest of them voted on the bill. If Summer and her friends were going to go down on this issue, they wanted to go down fighting on the front line.

We were carried along down the middle of the road, our feet hardly touching the ground. A group of Glasgow University students next to us screamed, 'Nick Clegg, full of smeg,' in poetic unison. Ahead, a guy with long dark hair and a black overcoat swung from a Union Jack on the Cenotaph. The crowd cheered his antics – another student thumbing his nose at the establishment.

A police van was abandoned in the centre of the street and a protester stood on its roof wearing a mask, fists raised into the air. I could see graffiti daubed onto the sides of the van: 'Tory Scum' and 'PIGS' in spray-paint scrawl. A kid in a navy puffa jacket jumped up and kicked at the windows. Another grabbed a pole and smashed it down on the windscreen, which cracked like an egg and showered splinters of glass over the students nearby.

One guy held a professional-looking camera over the heads of the crowd and from my vantage point he looked like press. A few people put their hands in front of his lens and shoved him backwards, but he had his pictures that would be front page the day after. *Daily Mail* readers would be suitably outraged by the image of unruly students vandalising a police van. The photographer was lucky they didn't smash the camera.

We pressed on. Around us, people were banging dustbin lids and everyone seemed to be screaming. There was a pop, and a flare shot into the grey sky, quickly followed by another. Red smoke drifted over our heads and the sting of cordite burned my throat. Summer clutched my hand and I was suddenly grateful for her scarlet top. She stood out amongst the khaki, grey and black favoured by everyone else in the crowd.

A few yards further and we came to a scrunching halt, my face jammed into the back of the person ahead of me. The smell of stale sweat made me gag. Word came back from ahead that the police had formed a line and were not allowing any more demonstrators into Parliament Square. A chant started up – 'Shame On You, Shame On You' – and next to me Summer joined in with gusto.

I stood on tiptoes and over the heads of the demonstrators I could make out the dark blue helmets of a line of riot police twenty yards ahead of us, batons raised. Suddenly, the police parted and the crowd surged backwards. Summer stumbled and I grabbed her arm and manhandled her to the side of the road. Just in time. A huge grey horse thundered past us. The mounted police were charging the demonstrators. One kid was sent spinning to the ground and when he was pulled up, blood oozed from a gash in his head.

The students were pushed backwards and I dragged Summer with me, despite her protests.

'Parliament is that way, Ben.'

Police whistles shrieked through the hubbub of the crowd. Two students had climbed on to traffic lights and people were handing them bottles and lumps of rock to throw at the police, who were now following the horses into the crowd. They raised their riot shields to protect themselves and the debris bounced off them. Everyone was holding up phones taking videos for uploading to the internet later. One of the guys on the traffic lights was ripped from his perch by three policemen and hauled away. He kicked and screamed, 'Fascist scum!' but it would be a night in the cells for him. The other jumped down and disappeared into the throng before he suffered the same fate.

I looked across the sea of heads, seeking an exit route, but the crowd was too dense and there was no escape. A few metres away from me, a policeman was pulled from his horse and his boot caught in the stirrup. He thrashed around as demonstrators descended on him like flies around a rotting corpse. A posse of yellow jackets came storming through, swinging their batons indiscriminately, followed by another police horse, its massive hooves carving through the crowd. When one of their mates was in trouble, the police wouldn't hold back. I heard the crack of metal on bone and the boy next to me fell to the ground, clutching his jaw, blood pouring from his face.

Across the road, a fire was blazing and I covered my mouth and nose with my hand as the stench of burning rubber filled my nostrils. A group of students in balaclavas emerged from the smoke and began to smash windows in the office building next to us with sticks, boots and rocks. Summer wriggled away from me and grabbed a pole from a placard lying on the ground. She joined in with the group, lashing a window in a mad frenzy.

The police were on us in a flash. One of them held her by the waist and she flailed her arms, but he had her fast. I made a grab for her, but as I did so I was knocked off my feet by a member of the balaclava gang as he fell to the ground, shielding his head from a policeman raining blows on him. By the time I recovered my balance, Summer was gone. I peered desperately through a forest of bodies and then I saw a flash of scarlet amidst the mayhem. I sprinted towards it, shoving people out of my path and in an instant I was there, in the policeman's face, screaming, so close that my spit spattered his visor. I had no idea what I was saying but he dropped Summer and lifted his baton. I pounced, swept Summer up in one movement and staggered out of there, pulling her along with me. A heavy blow connected with my left shoulder but I didn't dare look back. The ranks of the demonstrators closed around us and I dragged Summer into an alleyway where there was relative calm.

Her face was flushed and her eyes were wild.

'You stupid…'

She wrenched my head towards her and kissed me. She kissed me hard, jamming her tongue into my mouth and pulling at my hair. She bit my lip and I tasted blood. Just as I felt I couldn't breathe anymore, she snapped my head backwards, panting heavily.

I pressed her against the wall to protect her and closed my eyes. My shoulder throbbed with pain and my heart was thudding wildly. All I wanted was to shut out the pandemonium on the street and pretend that we were in our own little bubble. Finally she caught her breath and whispered into my ear.

'I love you, Ben.'

London Student Demonstrations and Riots

In November and December 2010, there were a series of student demonstrations in the UK, mostly centred on London. The focus of the demonstrations was student tuition fees, which had in fact been introduced twelve years earlier by the Labour government, but at that time were subject to a cap of £3,290 per annum. The new Conservative-Liberal Democrat coalition government planned to increase the cap to £9,000 per annum. Nick Clegg, Deputy Prime Minister and Leader of the Liberal Democrats, was especially targeted, as he and his party reneged on a pre-election promise not to vote to increase tuition fees.

The first major demonstration took place on 10 November when a reported 50,000 demonstrators marched down Whitehall and into Parliament Square. The police were completely unprepared for these numbers and only a few hundred policemen were initially on duty. The march ended with a rally in the afternoon in front of Tate Britain. Following the rally, a group of protesters massed outside the Conservative Party headquarters at 30 Millbank and some 200 of them stormed the office building. Riot police were deployed to supplement the police numbers and employed the technique known as kettling, trapping the demonstrators in Millbank Square. Approximately one hundred protesters made their way on to the roof of 30 Millbank, pelting the police below with glass, banners, eggs and rotten fruit. One eighteen-year-old student, Edward Woollard, threw a fire extinguisher off the roof and was subsequently arrested for attempted murder, a charge which was later reduced to violent disorder. Woollard was sentenced to thirty-two months in a young offenders' institution in January 2011.

Further demonstrations took place on 24 November and 30 November, again centred on Trafalgar Square, Whitehall and Parliament Square. The police were better prepared for these events, with greater numbers, riot police and mounted police deployed from the outset. There were several violent clashes between police and protesters, with injuries on both sides and many protesters arrested.

The controversial kettling technique was used in a number of areas. The Metropolitan Police Commissioner Sir Paul Stephenson insisted that kettling was a legitimate police tactic adding that it was 'quite shocking seeing young kids out there in that sort of situation, engaging in acts of crime… it was thuggery, it was disgraceful'. Simon Hardy of the National Campaign Against Fees and Cuts called the police actions 'outrageous' saying 'we were stuck for five or six hours, not allowed to leave, intimidated by hundreds upon hundreds of riot police, treated very badly, when all we were doing was exercising our democratic right to protest'.

The final major demonstration took place on 9 December, the day that Parliament voted on the proposed reform. Police kettled protesters in Parliament Square and Whitehall. It was during this demonstration that Charlie Gilmour, a Cambridge undergraduate and the adopted son of Pink Floyd guitarist David Gilmour, was photographed swinging from a Union Jack flag on the Cenotaph. He was subsequently arrested and jailed for sixteen months, although not for his actions at the Cenotaph, but instead for throwing a bin at a convoy of cars containing Prince Charles, sitting on a protection officer's car and smashing a window. The Prince of Wales and the Duchess of Cornwall had been on their way to attend a Royal Variety Performance at the London Palladium when their Rolls Royce and other vehicles in the convoy were caught up in the demonstrations and attacked by protesters in Regent Street.

Charlie Gilmour apologised for his actions, explaining that he was intoxicated by drink and drugs and saying that he did not realise the significance of the Cenotaph war memorial. Despite the fact that the charges against Gilmour did not relate to his disrespectful behaviour at the Cenotaph, Judge Nicholas Price QC, perhaps motivated by the court of public opinion, felt compelled to refer to the matter in his summing up, saying that 'you have shown disrespect to those who gave the ultimate sacrifice, to those who fell defending this country'.

Trafalgar Square

Saturday 19 March 1910

Clara wore a long black skirt and a starched white blouse. Frills and bright colours were for frivolous girls, not high-minded women engaged in serious affairs. She stood straight-backed on the steps of Nelson's Column and thrust her pole into the air. Her arms ached – she had been holding it for over an hour now – but she couldn't allow Emily to think she was weak. Emily was a few steps away from her holding the pole at the other end that, along with hers, held up their banner: 'Battersea Protests the Removal of the Brown Dog'. Above them, a large square cloth was draped across the plinth at the base of the column with the words 'Animal Defence and Anti-Vivisection Society' scrolled around an eight-pointed yellow star.

The cause was a just one, supporting their sisters to stand up against acts of cruelty to animals. And that was how men treated women today: like dumb animals with no feelings or independent thought. It was time for change, and women like Clara and Emily had to stand together to make that change happen.

The removal of the Brown Dog statue was the last straw for Clara. She had known Joseph was working a night shift, but it was only three days later that she realised that her own husband had been involved in the scandalous action.

'I earned a few extra bob the other night, moving that statue.' He grinned at her stupidly, standing in the doorway clutching a flimsy, sky-blue chiffon dress with a delicate lace trim at the neck. 'Thought you might like this.'

At that moment, she saw him for a buffoon. There she was, a committed member of the Women's Union, an organisation steadfastly opposed to cruelty to animals and her own husband had been instrumental in removing one of the great symbols of the cause. She could bear it no longer.

Clara packed a case that night. She wasn't sure where she would go, but she knew she had to leave the house. As it turned out, Emily had been happy to help out a sister in need and put her up for a few days.

When Clara left, she had turned back to take a last look at the front room. Her husband sat limply in the chair by the fire, cradling the blue dress in his hands.

'Goodbye, Joseph,' she said, bluntly.

He did not reply. Instead, he stood up and tossed the dress on to the flames, and as she closed the door behind her, she felt a surge of heat from the chiffon flaring in the grate.

Trafalgar Square to Buckingham Palace

'Did you get away?' Annie asks.

'Yes, but only about four hours later. The police kept us there for ages.'

'Lucky you had your food and water.'

'That was fine, but Summer lost her coat in the skirmish with the policeman, so I lent her mine. I was frozen numb by the end.'

'Well, the things you do in the name of democracy.'

'Or stupidity. We should never have gone. There were too many troublemakers there.'

She frowns at me and I feel the need to explain.

'Well, look what good it all did. Tuition fees still came in, students are leaving university in massive debt, nothing changed.'

Annie's forehead wrinkles. 'Maybe not, but the politicians know that it was unpopular and they might think twice before upping the fees again. If no one ever did anything, then the government would have free rein to trample all over us.'

'Only until the next election. Then they would be voted out.'

'That assumes the other lot would be better.'

I concede that she may have a point and we trudge on. Nelson looks down on us from his column and I wonder what he would have thought of the undignified stream of Day-Glo and Lycra marching around London's streets. But then, Nelson has seen a lot over the years, even with only one eye. We pass through Admiralty Arch and on to the red tarmac of The Mall and I take some time to consider my companion.

She is of slight build and medium height – I guess 5 foot 5 or 6 – and despite her painfully thin legs she walks with a determined stride. She wears a grey fleece and khaki walking trousers and her only concession to bright colours is her rainbow-striped beanie hat. Her light-brown hair is tied into a ponytail which escapes from beneath her hat and falls down her back. As with many of the walkers, she has a sign pinned to her fleece. It says 'I am walking for… Peter'. I wonder who Peter is. A husband, boyfriend, father, friend? Perhaps even a son?

'What do you think?'

Annie is smiling at me.

'I'm sorry?'

'What do you think? You've stared at me for the last two minutes. Am I up to scratch?'

I laugh.

'I'm not sure how to answer that.'

She points ahead and I can see the hustle and bustle of activity around stalls where volunteers are handing out goodies. Behind them is a cluster of green plastic temporary toilets, which will spoil the view for the Queen if she decides to step out onto the Buckingham Palace balcony tonight.

'Well, you're saved by the bell,' she says. 'Here's the next pit stop.'

Buckingham Palace

Friday 26 August 2011

I took the day off work to take Summer on the Buckingham Palace tour.

'I want to see where the most famous woman in England lives,' she had declared a fortnight earlier, out of the blue. All it took was a few clicks and I had secured two tickets online. Summer wore a leaf-green peaked cap which made her look like a pixie. The sun shone and the roses in the beds outside the Palace were in full bloom. Summer was in high spirits, skipping across the forecourt behind the Victoria Memorial, attracting several glances from admiring male tourists as her skirt flapped in a gentle breeze.

Inside, we joined a small group with our official guide, a lank-haired woman in a navy suit and black soft-shuffle shoes, with an unfortunate scab on her chin that made her look as if she had cut herself shaving that morning. I tried desperately to put this uncharitable thought to the back of my mind. According to her Buckingham Palace badge, our guide's name was Julia.

Julia led us along a lush magenta carpet between alcoves of marble statues to the Grand Staircase, where she pointed to a series of full-length portraits adorning the walls.

'These pictures,' she announced authoritatively, 'were commissioned by Queen Victoria. They form, if you will, a family album.'

Summer fidgeted next to me.

'They are fusty,' she declared, waving her hand dismissively at a scarlet-jacketed soldier wearing an ostrich-feathered hat and thrusting his jodhpur-encased loins forward. 'And that one,' she added, loudly, 'he is arrogant.'

'That one,' said Julia frostily, fingering her scab, 'is a portrait of the Duke of Kent, Queen Victoria's father.'

'Well, he doesn't look very kind,' replied Summer. 'Was he the king?'

Julia's face brightened. Summer had clearly given her an opportunity to display her expertise.

'In fact, no. The previous king was Victoria's uncle, William the Fourth. He is in the picture on the right. And before him, we had King George the Fourth, the former Prince Regent who eventually came to the throne at age fifty-eight.'

I had visions of Hugh Laurie in *Blackadder* and couldn't stop myself from smiling. Julia glared at me, unaware that she had said anything funny. I doubted whether Julia had ever seen *Blackadder*; she would prefer historical dramas and David Attenborough wildlife documentaries.

'You will, of course, have noticed that there is no portrait of King George the Fourth.' She arced her arm around the wall and we all nodded knowledgeably. I was sure none of us would have recognised a portrait of George the Fourth if it was staring us in the face, unless George the Fourth looked remarkably like Hugh Laurie.

Julia paused for dramatic effect, desperate for one of us to ask the obvious question.

'Why is there no picture of your King George?' asked Summer sweetly, putting her out of her misery.

Julia picked up her cue enthusiastically.

'Well, it is a striking omission, certainly. We believe that there is no portrait of the king due to a family dispute. Victoria's mother was German, from the Saxe-Coburg family, and George the Fourth disliked that branch of the family. So much so, that he deliberately ignored his young niece, Victoria, an act of rejection which she never forgave. Consequently, when she became Queen, she refused to include his portrait within the family album.'

Julia stood back and folded her arms, a look of smug satisfaction on her face.

Summer stamped her foot. 'That is horrible. Why must families fall out?'

Julia was taken aback by Summer's reaction. She had expected her audience to murmur in quiet appreciation of her historical knowledge.

'Well,' she said, 'I suppose it can happen to all families, even the Royal Family.'

Summer's face turned thunderous. I laid my arm around her shoulder to calm her down but she pushed me away.

'I am not sure I like the Royal Family,' she muttered, so that only I could hear.

★

Summer's favourite room was the Throne Room, where reds, golds and dusky pinks predominated. To my taste, the room was gaudy, but Summer loved the thrones set on a pedestal at the head of the room. The two in the middle 'were chairs in the Jacobean style' according to Julia, made for the current Queen and the Duke of Edinburgh at the time of her coronation. They were embroidered with their initials: one with ER for the Queen and the other with P for Philip. I wondered if he ever sat in her chair for a giggle. I wouldn't have put it past him.

As Julia led our group out of the room, Summer grabbed my arm and dragged me back.

'Ben, come on. I want to sit on a throne.'

'Summer, you can't. Look, there are ropes.'

She glanced around. A sleepy-eyed official stood to one side overseeing the room.

'Go and distract him, Ben.'

'Summer... no.'

She stroked my hand.

'Please, Ben.'

As ever, my resolve crumpled.

I walked over to the man and coughed gently. 'Excuse me,' I asked politely, 'I wonder if you could tell me who this is.'

I steered him towards the bust of a man on a plinth in the corner, so that we both had our backs to the room and Summer had her chance. The official looked at me blankly. Compared to the thrones, the bust was a mere immaterial detail and it was plain that he had never been asked about it before.

'I'm sorry, sir. I just look after the room. I'm afraid I don't know.'

'Do you think it's a god of some sort? Greek or Roman perhaps?' I tried to buy some more time.

'Hey!'

'What are you doing?'

There was a commotion behind us and we both turned. A group of visitors were staring at Summer, sitting serenely on the Queen's throne. One of them flapped his guidebook in her direction and Summer waved back, a short little wave as if she were the Queen herself.

The official reached the thrones in three bounds.

'Off there now, young lady,' he growled.

Summer smiled innocently at him, stood up and stepped away from the throne.

'I'm sorry,' she said, tilting her head slightly beneath her green cap, 'I wanted to feel like a queen. Was that not allowed?'

I could see the official melt. His features softened but he knew that he had to treat this blatant breach of Palace rules seriously.

'I should have you locked up in the Tower,' he said, stifling a smile. 'Get out of here before I call the guards.'

Summer reached up and kissed him on the cheek. He blushed as pink as the thrones and the group who took exception to Summer's antics grumbled amongst themselves. Summer threw them a withering look, took me by the hand and we hurried out of the room.

Our tour finished with the White Drawing Room, although contrary to its title my overriding impression of it was yellow. Two bright yellow chaises longues dominated the centre of the room underneath a take-your-breath-away crystal chandelier which dropped from a John Nash ceiling. There was a marble fireplace, its mantelpiece supporting an elaborate white-faced clock featuring two cherubs and a gold relief. All the walls bore large mirrors and the reflections made the room appear bigger than it was.

'Can you spot the secret door?' asked Julia, touching her scab. Again, she knows something that we don't.

We all made a show of looking around to satisfy Julia, knowing that if a door were truly secret, then we wouldn't be able to find it.

'It's over there,' exclaimed a portly man with an American accent, pointing to one of the mirrors. He had a guidebook in one hand which had obviously given him some help. Julia looked disappointed, but recovered herself sufficiently to reply.

'Yes. Well done. The mirror and the cabinet open up to the Queen's private rooms behind. I understand that many visiting dignitaries have been surprised by her sudden appearance.'

Julia grinned, as if the Queen were the world's greatest practical joker.

Summer hopped from one foot to another. Despite her initial enthusiasm for the Palace, she was now desperate to be outside. She couldn't bear to be caged for too long at any time, let alone on a hot summer's day.

Julia had a script to finish, however, and she was not to be deflected.

'The White Drawing Room is used by the monarch for formal receptions. If only its walls could speak, it could tell us some fascinating stories. I understand, for example, that this is the room where the Prime Minister, Stanley Baldwin, advised King Edward VIII that he would be compelled to abdicate if he pursued his wish to marry the American divorcee, Wallis Simpson.'

Summer stopped hopping. 'What is that story, please?' she asked.

Julia coughed. 'It was 1936 and attitudes were different at the time. Edward VIII came to the throne in January and was not a popular king. He interfered in politics, and was against many of the traditions of the monarchy, but worst of all, he conducted an affair with an American Catholic, who was in the process of divorcing her second husband. The Constitution did not permit the monarch to marry a divorcee. In December, when he had been king for less than a year, Edward abdicated in favour of his brother, so that he could marry Wallis Simpson.'

'So he chose love over rank?' Summer was wide-eyed.

'That is one interpretation,' Julia said tight lipped. 'Another is that he chose his lover over his duty.'

It was obvious that Julia did not have a high regard for the king's choice. Summer gave her a venomous look.

61

'What he did was brave. Duty is an excuse exploited by bad people to further their own ends.'

Julia was ruffled by Summer's outburst.

'Well, I...,' she stumbled, '... there are two sides to every story.'

'Not in this case,' Summer said stoutly. 'Love should always win over duty.'

And she turned on her heels and strode out of the White Drawing Room.

'Oh dear,' observed Julia, sneering at me, 'your friend is rather...' she sought the appropriate word, '... rather emotional.'

'And all the better for it,' I replied.

★

When I finally caught up with her, she was sitting outside on the steps of the terrace that overlooked the Buckingham Palace gardens. She was holding her head in her hands. I touched her shoulder and she leant against me.

'Summer, what's up?'

'Ben,' she raised her head and kissed me, 'you know that you are love for me, not duty.'

I was confused. 'Of course. What–'

She held a finger to my lips.

'Please remember that. Always.'

Buckingham Palace

Monday 16 November 1936

David adjusts his tie, taking time to compose himself. He lifts his head and nods at the footman, who pushes open the heavy, mirrored door. David walks through into the drawing room, confidently, but without swagger. The Prime Minister stands awkwardly in front of him. Baldwin is a heavy-set man, with a square face and thinning, slicked-back hair. This is his third term as PM and David senses that Baldwin is becoming weary with the burden of office. Well, that burden is about to become somewhat heavier to bear.

The two men shake hands and David invites Baldwin to sit down on one of the two yellow couches facing each other in the centre of the room across a glass table. The couches are hard and lumpy. Perfect, in other words, for meetings of short duration. David sits opposite the Prime Minister. He will not offer tea or engage in small talk. He wishes to get to the matter in hand, but before he does he needs a moment to assess the man sitting opposite him. He takes a silver cigarette case from his jacket pocket, opens it and offers Baldwin a Chesterfield.

'No, thank you, Your Majesty. I don't.'

David's forehead creases. In his experience, one is best advised not to trust a man who doesn't smoke. He extracts a cigarette, taps it on the case and considers the Prime Minister. Baldwin is undoubtedly experienced but David has never rated him. He sees him as a plodder, a political tortoise who has climbed to the top more by virtue of outstaying his rivals than any innate talent. He is a politician who has a distaste for controversy and David believes he can exploit that trait to his advantage. The Prime Minister's eyes are watering. He must know why he has been summoned to the Palace and he is nervous. David finds a box of matches in his pocket, lights up and takes a drag on his cigarette. He blows the smoke into the air and watches it wind around the chandelier hanging from the ceiling.

'My dear Prime Minister,' he starts. His voice rings as clear as the chimes on the drawing room clock. It is critical that Baldwin senses no weakness in his resolve.

'Your Majesty.'

'I have summoned you here today to address one matter, and one matter only. I believe you are aware as to the matter in hand.'

Baldwin shifts uncomfortably on the couch.

'I believe I am, Your Highness.'

'Prime Minister. There is no easy way to say this so it is best if I come straight to the point. I think you will agree.'

Baldwin nods. 'I agree, Your Highness.'

David sits forward, hands clasped.

'You and I have spoken of my relationship with Mrs Simpson before, have we not?'

'We have indeed, Your Highness, only last month.' Baldwin's upper lip curls slightly at the mention of her name. The impertinence of the man.

'And you are aware that Mrs Simpson has commenced divorce proceedings in the courts?'

Baldwin nods again.

'I am here to tell you, Mr Baldwin, that Mrs Simpson has become an indispensable part of my life. So much so, that I cannot conceive of a future without her by my side.'

David takes another pull on his Chesterfield and lets the words hang in the air amongst the curls of cigarette smoke. The vulgar Regency clock ticks on the mantelpiece and Baldwin runs a finger around the inside of his wing collar. When he speaks, his voice is barely audible.

'As you know, Your Highness, I was aware of your feelings for the lady in question, although I was not aware that your feelings ran so deep.'

David is irritated by Baldwin's refusal to utter Wallis' name.

'No matter. You are now. And you should know, as Prime Minister of this country, that it is my intention to marry Wallis Simpson as soon as she is free to marry me.'

David's voice rises in pitch betraying his own trepidation and he curses himself for the lapse. He has slapped a metaphorical silk glove across the Prime Minister's jowls and now it is for Baldwin to respond. He does not want the Prime Minister to sense his uncertainty and take advantage.

A cloud passes across Baldwin's features, but otherwise the Prime Minister remains stone-faced. David feels the need to fill the silence.

'I wish to do so as king, in which case I believe I will both be a happier man and a better servant to my country.'

David puffs on his cigarette and inhales the nicotine deep into his lungs. The air between the two men is thick. A jewel of sweat escapes from under Baldwin's greased hair and crawls down his forehead. It is the only sign that the Prime Minister is feeling any discomfort.

The clock on the mantelpiece marks time. Tick. Tick. Tick. Tick. David sits back. He has said his piece for now and his fate lies in the hands of the man opposite him. A vein in Baldwin's forehead pulses as the Prime Minister gathers himself to speak. Tick. Tick. Tick. Finally, Baldwin clears his throat

'Your Highness, your queen becomes the queen of the country, and in the choice of a queen the voice of the people must be heard. It is my duty as Prime Minister to advise you that I do not believe the people of this country will accept your choice of queen. I know our people. They will tolerate much in private life, but they will not stand for this in a public personage.'

David feels the anger welling up inside him. How dare the man pretend to represent the opinion of the British people better than his own king? He grinds his half-smoked cigarette into an ashtray on the table.

'What exactly are you saying, Mr Baldwin?'

'I am saying, Your Highness,' Baldwin's gaze drops to the floor, 'that Your Majesty's government will be unable to support the marriage.'

David recovers himself and sits forward again, his palms together now as if in prayer. He had wagered on a more conciliatory response from a Prime Minister desperate to avoid a scandal. 'And that will mean?'

'My government will resign, Your Highness. There will have to be an election. The British public will have their say.'

David slumps back into the chair. A fight with the government was one thing, but subjecting himself to judgement by the people was another. It suddenly occurs to him that his Private Secretary, the insufferable Hardinge, was right. This affair has been the talk of Westminster and Baldwin has rehearsed this response, no doubt in consultation with his closest ministers. What lily-livered souls they are. Handing responsibility for determining the matter over to the electorate, rather than taking on the decision themselves. But even in his despair, David knows that it is a clever move, backing him into a corner from which there is no easy escape. He has clearly underestimated the man, although two can play at that game. He will throw the conundrum back to the Prime Minister.

'If you were in my shoes, Mr Baldwin, what would you see as my options?'

The Prime Minister's face flushes, but his voice remains calm. With a sense of foreboding, David realises that he is prepared for this question as well.

'In my view, Your Highness, you have three options. Firstly, you can give up the idea of the marriage.'

David shakes his head vigorously but Baldwin has his gander up now and he continues, undeterred.

'Secondly, you can pursue the marriage against your government's wishes.'

'And provoke a constitutional crisis, Mr Baldwin, when your government resigns? That is not a realistic option.'

The Prime Minister leaves David's observation unanswered and instead presses on. 'Or thirdly, Your Highness, you can exercise your right to abdicate.'

David hears Baldwin's words as if through a dense fog. They float towards him out of a gloom, fuzzy and indistinct. It takes him a minute for his brain to process them. A minute that feels like an eternity.

Tick. Tick. Tick. Tick.

The words detach themselves from one another and leap around inside his head, before his brain succeeds in rearranging them into a coherent sentence.

'Or thirdly, Your Highness, you can exercise your right to abdicate.'

The veneer of self-assurance that David has worn since entering the room melts away as the dregs of confidence drain from his soul. He is exposed for what he is. An ordinary mortal tortured by the conflict between love and public office. He sighs and passes his hands wearily across his face. His heart is heavy, but his choice is clear.

'If that is your counsel, Prime Minister, I must take your third option. I am prepared to go.'

Edward VIII – The Abdication

Edward Albert Christian George Andrew Patrick David Windsor (known to his family as David) became King of the United Kingdom on 20 January 1936. Despite a string of relationships and affairs, he remained unmarried at the age of thirty-nine. At the time of his accession to the throne, he was engaged in a relationship with the married American, Mrs Wallis Simpson, who he had met some years earlier. Wallis Simpson was not only married, she was also a divorcee, having split from her first husband in 1927 before marrying the businessman, Ernest Simpson.

Edward's relationship with Mrs Simpson was well known in society circles, but the British public were kept largely in the dark due to the refusal of the Fleet Street newspapers to publish any stories related to the affair in deference to the King (a self-imposed restriction not replicated in Continental Europe and the US). The first meeting between Prime Minister Stanley Baldwin and the King on the subject was held on 20 October 1936 after Wallis Simpson had commenced divorce proceedings against her husband. The Simpsons' marital relationship had by then broken down and in order to facilitate the divorce, Ernest Simpson arranged to be caught in a hotel suite with another woman; actually a friend of the Simpsons who had been a bridesmaid at Wallis Simpson's first wedding, Mary Kirk. Ernest Simpson went on to marry Mary Kirk in November 1937, but it is not clear whether he was conducting an affair with her before his divorce from Wallis. At the time, it was not unusual for couples to stage-manage adultery in order that the woman could successfully pursue divorce and, in this case, it was also essential to Edward that Ernest Simpson was seen as the guilty party and not Wallis Simpson.

Baldwin requested that the King persuade Mrs Simpson to give up the divorce proceedings, clearly sensing the inevitable consequences. The King rejected this request, arguing disingenuously that the divorce between the Simpsons was a private matter for them and that it was not his place to interfere. One week later, on 27 October, Wallis Simpson was granted a decree nisi *at Ipswich Assizes.*

The second meeting between Baldwin and Edward was precipitated by an extraordinary letter sent to the King by Alexander Hardinge, his Private Secretary, on 13 November. In that letter, Hardinge warned the King that the continued silence of the British press could not be maintained and that the Prime Minister was discussing the matter of his relationship with Mrs Simpson directly with senior ministers. Hardinge suggested that the King persuade Mrs Simpson to 'go abroad without further delay'.

The letter prompted Edward to summon the Prime Minister to Buckingham Palace on the following Monday, 16 November. It was at that meeting that Edward finally made it clear to the Prime Minister that he intended to marry Wallis Simpson when her divorce was finalised. Baldwin advised that such a marriage would be unacceptable to the British public. Wallis Simpson was a divorcee, with two surviving former husbands, and at the time the Church of England was opposed to remarriage when former spouses were still alive. As king, Edward was Defender of the Faith and Head of the Church of England, and therefore it was inconceivable that he could marry a divorcee and remain on the throne. Baldwin set out the three options for the King: give up the marriage; marry Wallis Simpson against the advice of the government, who would then resign; or abdicate.

There was a groundswell of sentiment against Wallis Simpson, much of it unfounded and some of it fanciful, which no doubt also served to influence Baldwin's view. As an American, she was treated with some suspicion and was perceived as only wishing to marry the King for his position and wealth. In fact, Wallis Simpson attempted to deflect the King from his course in a series of letters in the autumn of 1936, offering to abandon her divorce from Ernest Simpson and 'steal quietly away'. However, the King was determined to go through with the marriage.

Another accusation levelled at Wallis Simpson was that she was sympathetic to the Nazis. She was rumoured to have had an affair with the Nazi Joachim von Ribbentrop, when he was Ambassador to Britain in 1936. Von Ribbentrop supposedly gave her seventeen carnations every day – one carnation for each time they had made love. To the extent that Wallis Simpson had pro-Nazi sympathies, these were shared by Edward, and the two of them were high-profile guests of Adolf Hitler on a visit to Germany in 1937.

There were also claims that Wallis Simpson exercised sexual control over the King, having cured him of a form of sexual dysfunction. She was certainly domineering, sufficiently so that Edward VIII's official biographer, Philip Ziegler, refers to 'some sort of sadomasochistic relationship' between them, but there is no evidence that Edward ever suffered from any sexual abnormality.

Following the 16 November meeting, Edward suggested a further solution to the crisis, proposing a morganatic marriage, whereby Wallis Simpson would not become queen and any offspring from the marriage (which was unlikely) would have no rights to the throne. Baldwin agreed to consult on the proposal but it was subsequently firmly rejected by both the British government and those of Australia and South Africa.

The rejection of this proposal left the King with only one realistic choice of action and Edward confirmed his intention to abdicate to Baldwin on 5 December 1936. Five days later, Edward signed the abdication papers in front of his three younger brothers, one of whom, Albert, Duke of York, was to succeed him as King, taking the title George VI. The following day, on Friday 11 December 1936, King Edward VIII, King of Great Britain and Ireland and the British Dominions Beyond the Seas, Defender of the Faith, Emperor of India, committed his final act as king, granting assent to the abdication bill. That evening, he addressed the nation in a radio broadcast, saying that, 'I have found it impossible to carry the heavy burden of responsibility and to discharge my duties as King as I would wish to without the help and support of the woman I love.'

His reign had lasted 325 days and he was never crowned.

Edward married Wallis Simpson in a private ceremony in France on 3 June 1937. No member of the Royal Family was present. Less than seventy years later, in a different era with different attitudes, Prince Charles, Prince of Wales and heir to the throne, married the divorcee Camilla Parker Bowles in a civil ceremony at Windsor Guildhall on 9 April 2005. A crowd of over 20,000 well-wishers lined the streets to cheer the royal couple.

Buckingham Palace to Hyde Park Corner

We make our way up Constitution Hill towards Hyde Park. We are past mile seven and we are now lumbering rather than striding along. The pit stop on The Mall was a welcome break, an excuse to stop putting one foot in front of another for a few minutes. It was also an opportunity for me to take off my right shoe and readjust my sock which was twisted between my toes. I didn't take the sock off; if I don't see the beginnings of a blister, I can deny its existence.

Alongside me, Annie munches an apple that she grabbed off one of the volunteers. I stick with water thinking that if I bite into an apple I will get some skin caught in my teeth and it will irritate me for the rest of the walk. Constitution Hill is slick with the sheen of an earlier rain shower, and the yellow light from the streetlamps bounces off the wet tarmac. I quicken my pace as I can hear the clickety-clack of the dreaded pole walkers behind us, and Annie matches my step.

We cross Hyde Park Corner under Wellington Arch with the statue that looks like Boadicea in her chariot but isn't. It is 10.30pm and Hyde Park Corner is busy with Saturday night traffic. The Shine walkers all bunch up and cross en masse when the lights go red.

'Click, clack, click, clack.' The poles catch up with us again. Damn.

Annie leans over to me. 'I hate those people with walking poles,' she whispers. 'Drives me nuts.'

I smell her apple-flavoured breath and laugh.

'Let's speed up again when we get to Hyde Park.'

Hyde Park

Saturday 9 July 2011

I put my arm around Summer's waist and Buster hared off to chase a squirrel up a tree, or to sniff another dog's bottom – who knows? Buster loved Hyde Park as there was so much activity for him to thrust his wet nose into. The sun was high in the sky, the roses were in their last summer flush and we were walking alongside Rotten Row heading towards the Park Lane end of the park. That day, we were on more than just a Buster dog walk, we were on a mission.

In the distance, the buildings of Whitehall were visible on the skyline and rising above them was the arc of the London Eye.

'One day, I would like to go on the Eye,' Summer said. 'I would like to see all of London laid out before me – like a carpet.'

'I'll look into it,' I promised, giving her a squeeze. 'Just another thing to do before we die.'

She dug her elbow into my ribs.

'Don't talk like that. I'm going to live forever.'

I whistled for Buster and our stupid but loveable dog emerged from behind a clump of trees, shook his head at me, and then bounded off again, weaving between people enjoying the sunshine.

Summer looked amazing in a simple white T-shirt, with crimson skinny jeans and bright-white pumps. She wore a necklace of black and silver beads – one of her favourites – and in her hand, she held a small bunch of red and white peonies. She had dressed to match her flowers. I had gambled on shorts and was pleased to see a number of others had done the same. There was something reassuring about not being the only one exposing his legs to public view.

We turned left when we reached the Queen Mother's Gate

and before long we came across the memorial: a collection of steel pillars, each approximately 10 feet high, arranged in four clusters on a gravel base. A group of four or five tourists were slaloming their way through the memorial and we followed them, Buster sniffing around our heels. Summer ran her hand over the first three steel pillars.

'Each one feels a bit different,' she observed. 'They have different textures.'

'They were all individually cast,' I said. As ever, I had done my research in advance. Summer lived the moment; I planned it.

I read the inscription on the side of one of the pillars: '7 July 2005. 08:50. Edgware Road.'

This was the memorial to the 7/7 bombings. Fifty-two pillars representing the fifty-two victims, set in four groups according to the number who died at each of the four locations: Edgware Road, King's Cross, Aldgate, Tavistock Square. I knew that the terrorist attack on London in 2005 had affected Summer badly. Her father was a strict Muslim from West Bengal, while her mother was English, and when there was trouble between the West and Islam, she felt it personally.

The memorial had been unveiled two years earlier on the fourth anniversary of the bombings, and I could tell this visit was going to become an annual pilgrimage for Summer.

'Remind me, how many pillars are there, Ben?'

'Fifty-two.' I recalled the number instantly. 'One for each of the victims.'

Summer's eyebrows knitted, as if she were struggling to fit two pieces of a jigsaw together.

I walked to the far side of the memorial where there was a granite plaque set on the grass, engraved with the names of those who had died. I was always struck by the diversity of the names, people from all cultures who lost their lives on that day. This had not been an attack on white, middle class, Church of England, *Daily Mail* readers. This had been an attack on multi-cultural London.

Summer slid up to me and held my hand.

'Weren't there fifty-six victims?' She had solved her conundrum.

'Fifty-two victims,' I responded, 'and four bombers. Fifty-six dead.'

'Like I said,' she squeezed my fingers, 'fifty-six victims.'

I knew what she meant.

'I don't suppose it would have been acceptable to have pillars for the bombers,' I said evenly.

'It all depends on your perspective, doesn't it?' she replied. 'That is why these things happen. People don't see things from the point of view of others.'

She knelt down and laid her posy of peonies by the plaque, allowing her fingers to run over the inscribed names as Buster sniffed the scent from the flowers. When she stood up, she took my hand and began to read the names out loud in a rhythmic chant. Next to us, the group of tourists stood still and silent as she spoke.

'James Adams, Sam Badham and Lee Christopher Harris, Lee Baisden...'

By the time she had read out the last name, a crowd had gathered. There must have been some twenty people around us, heads bowed, hands clasped, hypnotised by her voice. Even Buster had appreciated the solemnity of the situation, sitting quietly by Summer's feet, gazing up at her as she spoke.

'And Gladys Wundowa,' she said, pausing for a deep breath. 'May they all rest in peace.'

'Amen,' I said instinctively.

'Amen,' the crowd chorused around us.

The July 7 Bombings

In total, fifty-six people died in the 7/7 bombings, including the four bombers. The fifty-two victims were from a diverse range of backgrounds and included many foreign-born nationals and Muslims. Three of the bombers (Mohammad Sidique Khan, Shehzad Tanweer and Hasib Hussain) were British-born sons of Pakistani immigrants. The fourth bomber, Jermaine Lindsay, was Jamaican born and a convert to Islam. The people who died on Thursday 7 July 2005 were as follows:

Aldgate:

Lee Baisden (34) – a carer for his widowed mother, who had multiple sclerosis, with plans to marry his long-term partner.

Benedetta Ciaccia (30) – Italian-born business analyst who was due to be married two months later; she was buried in Rome in her wedding dress.

Richard Ellery (21) – described by his flatmate as having 'a knack of making you feel better just by talking to him'.

Richard Martyn Gray (41) – a father of two whose children watched him play cricket for the Ipswich and East Suffolk Hockey Club that he helped set up in 1986.

Anne Moffat (48) – head of marketing and communications for Girlguiding UK; when she died, she had a 'Make Poverty History' booklet in her handbag.

Fiona Stevenson (29) – a lawyer who worked mainly on criminal cases and was, in the words of her boss, dedicated 'to representing those ensnared in the criminal justice system, but unable to defend themselves'.

Carrie Louise Taylor (24) – her mother, June, travelled with her to Liverpool Street station every day where they kissed each other goodbye. Carrie would then walk to the tube, stopping every few steps to turn and wave. June would watch her until she was out of sight, saying: 'I'm so very glad that the last picture I have of her is smiling and waving at me.'

Shehzad Tanweer (22) – bomber; his family were shattered by his involvement in the bombings. His uncle said: 'He was proud to be British. He had everything to live for. His parents were loving and supportive. He was a very kind and calm person. He was respected by everyone.'

Edgware Road

Michael Stanley Brewster (53) – a civil engineer who worked for Derbyshire County Council; encouraged his daughter to go to university but never got to see her graduate.

Jonathan Downey (34) – he and his wife were members of the Woodlands Trust. A group of fifty relatives and friends planted trees and shrubs in his memory.

David Foulkes (22) – worked in Manchester and travelled to London that day to meet a colleague; was planning to move in with his girlfriend and start a family.

Colin Morley (53) – an advertising and marketing executive committed to making the planet a better place; his latest project, 'Be The Change', encouraged people and organisations to find ways to improve ethically, socially, environmentally and personally.

Jennifer Vanda Ann Nicholson (24) – music was her passion; a talented pianist and singer, she worked as an advertising sales executive for a music publishing company. She had plans to marry her boyfriend, James, and study for a PhD.

Laura Susan Webb (29) – was in Peru with her boyfriend at the time of the 9/11 attacks on New York when she emailed her family saying: 'I heard the horrific news yesterday of the terrorists in America. Those poor people. I hope that things in London will stay safe.'

Mohammad Sidique Khan (30) – bomber; left a pregnant wife in hospital and a fourteen-month-old daughter.

King's Cross

James Adams (32) – a church deacon whose support for an orphanage in Southern India led to a building being erected there in his memory. His parents issued a statement after his death: 'We do not know who is ultimately responsible for our loss but we do not hold any religion or faith accountable.'

Samantha (Sam) Badham (35) and Lee Christopher Harris (30) – partners who lived in Tottenham and caught the tube together that day; they were found lying on the track with their legs entwined. Samantha died at the scene; Lee was in a coma for eight days before dying on 15 July.

Philip (Phil) Beer (22) – an outgoing and fun-loving personality;

his family asked mourners to wear brightly coloured clothes to his funeral and he was cremated in a pink coffin.

Anna Brandt (41) – Polish and a mother of two daughters; one daughter arrived in London on the day of the bombings to visit her mother.

Ciaran Cassidy (22) – a shop assistant who had been saving for several months for a planned trip to Australia.

Rachelle Chung For Yuen (27) – a married accountant from Mauritius; she only travelled on the Piccadilly Line that day because of disruption on the Northern Line, with all southbound trains being routed via the Bank branch. The last time she saw her family was at her sister's wedding in Mauritius one month earlier; her husband said 'she always cherished her family above anything else'.

Elizabeth (Liz) Daplyn (26) – an administrator who worked at University College Hospital in the neuro-radiology department. Her sister commented: 'When thinking about what she might have done in the future… it could have been everything and anything.'

Arthur (Soul) Frederick (60) – retired to London after more than thirty years in the Royal Montserrat Police Force; he also had a music career and his hit song 'Signs of Christmas' is still played on Montserrat radio.

Karolina Gluck (29) – Polish, she had been in London for three years; she was due to travel to Paris that evening with her boyfriend for a romantic weekend.

Gamze Gunoral (24) – on a year's break from her job in finance in Turkey, studying in London to improve her English.

Ojara Ikeagwu (56) – a mother of three and social worker who moved to London from Nigeria in 1976. She worked with adults with learning difficulties in Heston and in 2003 started a programme to provide free books, pens, pencils, rulers and uniforms to 500 schoolchildren in her home village in Nigeria. Her husband continues to fund the programme today and the school has been named after her.

Emily Jenkins (24) – an adoring aunt to two nieces. Her mother said: 'She was the last person who would always be digging sandcastles on the beach and babysitting at every opportunity.'

Adrian Johnson (37) – married his childhood sweetheart and in the five years before his death supported her through cancer. His wife Catherine said: 'It was so ironic that I would lose Adrian. We were saving a bottle of champagne to celebrate my five-year milestone in 2006, but I could not bring myself to drink it alone.'

Helen Katherine Jones (28) – her former neighbour said: 'She was a very lively person, she had lots and lots of friends and was a fantastic friend and neighbour. She also used to throw great parties!'

Susan Levy (53) – commuted regularly to work with her younger son, Jamie, who had alighted from the Piccadilly Line train at Finsbury Park; her older son, Daniel, lived in Australia and, speaking on his behalf her husband said 'the most important part of his day was to open his computer in the morning and find a message from his mother waiting for him'.

Shelley Marie Mather (26) – a New Zealander who loved travel. Her mother said 'she wanted to circumnavigate the universe'.

Michael Matsushita (37) – Vietnamese-born and brought up in New York, he had recently moved to London after eighteen months as a tour guide in Vietnam and Cambodia to start a new life with his girlfriend.

James Mayes (28) – his parents and sister issued a statement: 'One of the greatest and most tragic ironies of the manner of his death was that he believed passionately in human rights and freedom of expression and belief.' An annual award, sponsored by his family and The Open University, has been established in his name to be given for the best student project on the 'Islam in the West' course.

Behnaz (Nazy) Mozakka (47) – Iranian-born, she had lived in Finchley for thirteen years and worked as a biomedical officer at Great Ormond Street children's hospital. After her death, her father, son and daughter sold the family home. Her daughter, Saba said: 'The three of us now live separately, and while we are still very close to the family and love each other dearly, our glue has been taken away from us.'

Mihaela Otto (46) – born in Romania, but liked to be known as Michelle. According to her sister, she saw London as 'simply the best city in the world'.

Atique Sharifi (24) – an Afghan Muslim who came to London to escape the Taliban. He worked in a pizza parlour to earn money to send back to his sister in Kabul, their parents having been killed in the Kabul war.

Ihab Slimane (24) – from a French family of Tunisian origin, Ihab had come to London for the summer to improve his English.

Christian Njoya Diawara Small (28) – a talented hurdler who in May won gold in the Middlesex County Championships. Christian had recently returned from a trip to Africa which had inspired him to change his name from Christian Small to Christian Njoya Diawara Small, Njoya Diawara meaning 'strong in spirit'.

Monika Suchocka (23) – an accountant from Poland who had arrived in London two months earlier; she played the piano and had joined a choir.

Mala Trivedi (51) – born and brought up in Kenya, but moved permanently to the UK in 1979. Mala worked in the X-ray department at Great Ormond Street children's hospital.

Jermaine Lindsay (19) – bomber; married to a white convert to Islam with a son. A baby daughter was born after his death. After the bombings his wife, Samantha Lewthwaite, gave interviews where she apologised for the actions of Lindsay, describing him as a 'loving husband and father'. She added: 'My whole world has fallen apart and my thoughts are with the families of the victims of this incomprehensible devastation.' Samantha Lewthwaite is now a wanted terrorist herself, being linked with various terrorist attacks and believed to be a member of the Somali militant group, Al-Shabaab. She has been dubbed the White Widow.

Tavistock Square

Anthony Fatuwi-Williams (26) – born of Nigerian parents, his cousin told the congregation at his funeral that Anthony 'didn't handle sadness very well', going on to say: 'Tears and sadness don't do anything for Anthony at this point. Only joy and happiness is the way he should be remembered.'

Jamie Glenbucket Gordon (30) – lived with his fiancée in Enfield but on the night before the attacks stayed at a friend's house. His route to work the next morning led him to take the ill-fated number 30 bus.

Giles Vernon Hart (55) – married to a Pole, with two children, Giles was a prominent supporter of the Solidarity movement which was instrumental in overthrowing communism in Poland. After his death, he was posthumously granted one of Poland's highest honours, the Knight Cross of the Order of Merit of the Republic of Poland, for his services to democracy. His daughter said: 'He believed in justice, liberty and freedom and hated oppression, fundamentalism and totalitarianism.'

Marie Joanne Hartley (34) – mother of two who worked for a greetings card firm in Altham, Lancashire; she had travelled to London to try to recruit new artists at an art fair in Islington.

Miriam Hyman (31) – *a freelance picture editor, born in London, who raised money for a cancer charity and worked to bring greater understanding between Palestinians and Jews. Since her death, the Miriam Hyman Children's Eye Care Centre has been set up in Orissa, India.*

Shahara Islam (20) – *the oldest of three children born to Bangladeshi parents; in a statement, her family said: 'She was an Eastender, a Londoner and British, but above all a true Muslim and proud to be so.'*

Neetu Jain (37) – *born in Delhi, but moved to London when she was only one year old. She was about to get engaged and had just started a new job in computer software. A work colleague remembered that one of her last acts was trying to get some friends together for dinner. 'I can't believe there was always one of us too busy to meet up. What a waste! Why do we always believe there will be another day?'*

Sam Son Ly (28) – *born in Vietnam, but brought up in Australia; Sam was on a two-year working holiday to London with his long-term girlfriend. He went to the UK to earn more money to pay for his father in his old age.*

Shayanuja Niroshini Parathasangary (30) – *Sri-Lankan born, but lived in the UK since she was one; Shayanu, as she was known, was planning to move out of her parents' house to a property she was renovating with her sister – only two doors away.*

Anat Rosenberg (39) – *passionate about the piano and ballet, Anat moved to London in 1990 to study modern dance. Her boyfriend said that 'she was afraid of visiting Israel because she was scared of suicide bombings on buses'.*

Philip Stuart Russell (28) – *his twenty-nineth birthday would have been a few days after the bombings; on the day, he was still classed as missing and optimistic friends gathered in the hope that he would turn up to the birthday drinks that he had organised. He never did.*

William Wise (54) – *on the morning of the bombings, William forgot to pick up his glasses as he left the house. He returned home, collected them and kissed his wife, Christine, goodbye. As a consequence, he was later than usual. Christine never kissed her husband again.*

Gladys Wundowa (50) – *had already completed a shift as a cleaner that morning at University College London and was on her way to Hackney. She and her husband had plans to move back to their native Ghana where they were building a house.*

Hasib Hussain (18) – bomber; his family were said to be devastated by Hasib's actions. In a statement, they added: 'We are having difficulty taking this in. Our thoughts are with all the bereaved families and we have to live ourselves with the loss of our son in these difficult circumstances. We had no knowledge of his activities and, had we done, we would have done everything in our power to stop him.'

'Any trouble between the West and Islam always hit Summer hard,' I explain. 'She said that sometimes she felt like an elastic band stretched to breaking point between the two cultures.'

'What did she think of the 7/7 bombings?' Annie asks.

'She thought they were terrible, of course. She hated the idea that anyone could twist her religion to justify killing and injuring people, but she saw the other side too. She was convinced that Tony Blair lied to justify the invasion of Iraq and, for her, that was unforgiveable.'

'She was a Muslim then?'

'In name, but not in practice. She was Muslim in the same way that I'm Church of England. But you would never see Summer in a burkha or praying six times a day to Mecca. A headscarf sometimes, that was as far as she would go.'

'It must have been difficult for her growing up then, with a religious father. Did he approve of her English boyfriend?'

I take a heavy breath. Annie is getting into difficult territory.

'I never met him,' I say truthfully. 'He left Summer's mother before we got together and went back to India. Summer didn't even have any contact with him.'

I had assumed that we would walk in the park but instead our route takes us along the pavement that runs beside Knightsbridge. Lost in thoughts for a few moments, I am sharply brought back to real time by the shouts of a volunteer.

'Head for Harrods,' he barks at us. 'It's not open though!'

Harrods is a beacon in the distance, lit up like an adult fairground. Annie looks at it wistfully before tossing her apple core into a bin.

'You know, every Christmas I go into Harrods and walk around. I never buy anything – it's all ridiculously expensive – but I just love the feel of that shop.'

'Well, one day...' I say.

'One day, when I'm rich,' she continues my thought, 'I will buy all my Christmas presents from Harrods.'

I am doubtful. 'Wouldn't you be better getting them online from John Lewis?'

'Then you wouldn't get any Harrods green bags. I want everyone to see their present comes in a Harrods bag.'

I think about it. 'You could just buy the bags in Harrods. I'm sure they sell them. Then you can pretend to everyone that their presents come from Harrods, when really you've got them cheaper on the internet.'

She regards me disappointedly.

'That's not the point, Ben.'

'I know, I'm just messing.'

I am thinking about the one time I shopped at Harrods.

Harrods

Saturday 9 December 2006

I was light-headed as I chained up my bike in Hans Crescent. It felt like a breath of wind could lift me into the air and carry me off along Knightsbridge. I had spent the previous night with Summer and I knew with complete and utter certainty that she was my destiny. I knew the instant she turned her oyster shell eyes in my direction and locked her gaze on me. We were in a club frequented by UCL students and I would like to say that I asked her to dance but that wasn't true. I knew if I tried to find some words to say to her, they would come out all wrong. So, instead, I walked up to her, took her hand, and led her on to the dance floor. I don't know where I found the confidence. I was usually shy around girls until I got to know them, but somehow I knew that was the moment. We had shared a few guilty minutes on a sunny October day and since then I had skulked around college, stealing glimpses of her, planning my routine so that I might bump into her around campus, throwing a few lines of inane conversation in her direction whenever I could. I was the nerd who hung around on the edge of her at college. Our October encounter in the Main Quad was scored on the slate of my memory, but I didn't know if she even remembered it and I was surprised when she noticed me in the club. I wasn't going to hold back. *Carpe puella.* Seize the girl.

Summer danced like silk. Smooth, supple, her eyes half-closed, lost in the music. She wore a shimmering turquoise dress with a high neck-line, and her hair flowed across her shoulders and down the small of her back like treacle oozing from a jar. Her honey-coloured skin was dusted with silver glitter that sparkled in the strobe lighting.

I jigged along self-consciously next to her, dazzled by the arc lights bouncing off the shine of her dress, but she didn't seem to notice my feeble attempts at rhythm. She was in a trance.

When the music slowed, I hesitated, unsure if we should slide off the floor and find a drink and avoid that awkward romantic dance, but Summer took my hands and placed them around her neck. She nuzzled my cheek, thrust her hips into mine and we pirouetted around the dance floor. It seemed to me as if we were the only ones dancing, as if everybody else appreciated that we were the show and had obligingly stepped aside. I twisted the curls of her hair in my fingers and licked salty pearls of sweat from her shoulder.

When the music stopped she leant back and held my face between her hands. Her eyes held mine for a few seconds before she tipped her head to one side, leant forward and kissed me. I tasted sweet strawberry lip gloss.

'Let's go to bed.' She said it matter-of-factly, as if it would be the most natural thing for us to do in the world.

We went back to my room, a rectangular student room with custard-cream walls in a tired-at-the-edges purpose-built block on Charlotte Street. The college had obviously been skimping on the maintenance costs for years. It was not especially romantic but with Summer anywhere would have been perfect. We kissed a long, slow, passionate kiss and fell gently onto the bed. She tugged off my shirt and traced circles on my chest with manicured fingernails. She wore vivid blue nail polish that matched her dress.

She lifted herself on top of me and I stared up at her, trying to etch a picture of her into my brain. The last flakes of glitter twinkled on her arms as she reached behind and undid her zip. Her dress fell away like apple peel and I took her small breasts in my hands, my fingers rubbing gently across her dark nipples. She threw her head back and moaned quietly, and then fell forward again to kiss me, splaying her hair across my face. She kissed me on my shoulders, my nipples, my stomach. Little pecks that gave me goosebumps. Slowly, she made her way down my body and I squirmed in anticipation.

She tugged at my belt and unzipped me and I wriggled out of my trousers and my Calvins, struggling to contain myself. Summer was naked now and I traced the patterns of her body with my eyes: the shadows of her cheekbones, the slope of her shoulders and the curve of her breasts, her ribs visible beneath her golden skin, rising and falling with her quick breaths. I made to roll over so that I would be above her, but she resisted me, raising her finger to her mouth to tell me to be still. She leant down, kissed me gently on the lips one more time, and then lowered herself on to me. I shuddered violently and let myself go.

When I woke in the morning, the light from a watery sun was filtering through the curtains. Summer lay next to me, lying on her side, her left arm stretched up above her head. I propped myself up on an elbow and gazed at her as she slept. A lock of hair fell across her face and wafted endearingly over her nose every time she took a breath. Her long lashes curled upwards from her closed eyelids like fine teeth on a comb. I pulled a sheet over her to keep her warm and the movement woke her up.

She shook her head a little, and blinked, adjusting herself to the surroundings.

'Hi, I'm Ben,' I said, with embarrassing ineloquence.

She looked up at me.

'I know. The man with the magic hands.'

'You remember that day?' I asked anxiously.

She smiled.

'I remember that day every day.'

We made love one more time before Summer said she had to leave to meet a friend. I was frantic with worry that that was it – one night of passion and no more.

'Can I get your phone number?' I asked timidly, as she hovered by the door. 'It would be nice to see you again.'

Summer howled, as if I had just cracked the funniest joke in the world.

'You don't get off that easily, Ben,' she said. 'I'm not a one-night-stand kind of girl. Give me your arm.'

I held out my pale forearm and she took a pen from my desk and scribbled a number on it.

'Call me,' she growled, 'or you're toast.'

Her eyes fell upon my scrapbook, which was lying open on the desk. I had been working on a piece about Jeremy Bentham.

'What's this?' she asked, turning over a page.

'It's a…' I didn't really know how to explain it.

'It looks like that story you told me about. The one about the head.'

'It is,' I confessed. 'After I met you, I decided maybe I would start writing things like that up.'

She looked up from the pages of the book and stared at me.

'You did this because of me?'

'Well… I… I suppose so.'

There was silence in the room. I stood there, rigid. She was obviously not sure what to make of this.

Summer smiled. 'That's really sweet of you. You'll have to let me read it sometime.'

'Of course.' I relaxed. At least she didn't think I was a psycho. Suddenly emboldened, I had a thought.

'Are you doing anything tonight?'

She thought about it for a second. 'Yes, I am.'

'Oh.' I was deflated. 'Well, maybe…'

'Actually,' she stopped me, 'I'm going out to dinner with my new boyfriend… so long as he's paying of course.'

'Your new…'

She held up her hand and smiled.

'I'll meet you at the Portico. 8 o'clock. Don't be late.'

As soon as she had closed the door, I chucked on some clothes and left the room. I don't know what came over me, but I knew that I wanted to buy her a gift for that evening and it had to come from Harrods in one of their famous green bags. Only the best was good enough.

I entered the store by the side entrance and I was a little boy lost, completely bewildered by the scale of the place. There was a festive theme everywhere: garlands of green, silver and gold tinsel, stacks of shiny parcels tied with silk bows, giant snowflakes suspended from the ceilings, Christmas carols piped through the speaker systems.

At the escalator, I passed a lurid green elf with Prince Charles ears who was directing parents and children to 'Santa's toy kingdom on the third floor'. I headed instead for 'Fine Jewellery' on the first floor and immediately spied a beautiful pear drop amethyst necklace that would look gorgeous against Summer's throat.

'How much is that one?' I asked, innocently.

'This one, sir,' sneered the assistant, scanning me up and down, 'this one is £3,300.'

'Oh.' I tried not to sound surprised.

The assistant wore a stiff white blouse and too much blusher. I was wearing ripped jeans and my hair hadn't seen a brush or a comb that morning. She gave me a haughty look.

'Perhaps sir would prefer something like this?'

She opened another glass case and pulled out a simple loop of yellow gold. I shook my head.

'I was looking for something a bit more... a bit more special.'

The assistant stifled a gasp. 'This necklace is a Marco Bicego, sir. It is 18 carat gold, studded with diamonds.'

I squinted. It was hard to make out the diamond chips.

'How much...'

The assistant stopped me before I could finish.

'£2,450, sir.'

I looked her squarely in the face.

'It's just not special enough,' I said.

She replaced the necklace and leant over towards me.

'Sir. This is our Fine Jewellery department. Do you think you may be better off in our jewellery department on the Lower Ground Floor?'

'Will they have something special there?' I asked, vacantly.

'I am sure they will, sir,' she replied, barely disguising the disdain in her voice. 'I am sure they will.'

I descended into the depths of Harrods to find another jewellery department that was clearly the more affordable option. I agonised over whether gold or silver would look better against Summer's light brown skin and then I remembered how the silver glitter sparkled like magic dust on her arms. My mind was made up and I picked out a silver link charm bracelet which I felt had a degree of understated elegance. Then I had to add a charm from a whole range of options. London icons: buses, taxis, phone boxes, Big Ben. Animals: cats, dogs, horses, butterflies, bees. Lucky symbols: clover leaves, keys, horseshoes.

More prosaically, they had letters. I asked the assistant to select an 'S' and a 'B' and she laid them on a cloth on the glass-top counter. Two letters seemed a little clinical, and I worried that it was presumptuous. We had only spent one night together, after all. Something glinted and caught my eye. A love heart charm, with a diamond chip. I pointed to it and it was laid down between the 'S' and the 'B'. The three charms together reminded me of teenage lovers scratching their initials on the bark of a tree with an arrow through a love heart. It was a bit cheesy but then I felt as if I was caught up in young love like a teenager, although unlike transient teenage love I intended to stick around for some time and I hoped the letters would send that message to Summer. And then the tiny diamond in the heart caught a light, and its sparkle reminded me again of the previous night, of the shimmering turquoise dress and the sprinkles of glitter on her skin.

'OK. I'll take all three,' I said quickly, before I prevaricated any longer.

The assistant attached the charms to the bracelet and gift-wrapped it for me. I spent over £200 in the end, not quite in the Marco Bicego league, but still a hefty sum to add to my credit card debt, so I was entitled to some fancy Harrods gift-wrapping. I had been in the store for nearly two hours when I finally emerged from the artificial light into a bright, cold afternoon in December, holding on tightly to a small Harrods green bag containing a precious package.

Knightsbridge

'Sorry,' I say, 'probably a bit too much detail at times. It's just that I remember everything about that night.'

'It's OK. I'm not a nun,' Annie smiles. 'Did she like the bracelet?'

'She loved it. I told her I had worried about the letters, that she might think I was being a bit over the top after just one night.'

'And?'

'She said they were the best bit. That they meant we were together. She wore that bracelet all the time. In all the years we were together, I never got her a better present.'

Harrods

Wednesday 27 December 2000

Baz watches as the bright yellow cherry-picker snakes upwards into the grey sky. Luckily, there is no rain, but he is glad of his oversized puffa that is keeping him warm. Gerry on the other hand, is wearing some weird shit hippy jacket that looks all wrong on a sixty-year-old bloke. Baz wonders if Gerry's missus is happy letting him go out like that. Gerry says they were childhood sweethearts and have been married forever, so maybe she even helped him choose the jacket. One thing's for sure, though. They didn't buy it at this place. Harrods. Too snooty for people like Gerry and Baz.

'Here, take this.'

Gerry hands him a hi-vis jacket which he puts on awkwardly over his puffa. The guys on the crane have reached the first window and are fiddling around with the big crest that is attached to the railing outside. Baz tips his baseball cap back and stares upwards, but he can't make out what they are doing. They look pretty heavy those things though. A few passers-by stop to look, curious as to what is going on.

'What exactly are we doin' here, Gerry mate?' asks Baz.

'We're taking them things down, dozy. Isn't it bleedin' obvious?'

Baz ignores Gerry's insult.

'I can see that, but what are they? Some kind of crest? Like you get on football shirts.'

'They're Royal Warrants, Baz,' Gerry says, sounding like he knows it all. 'You know, the kind that say 'By appointment to'. It means the Queen shops 'ere.'

'Does she?'

'Well, if she does, she won't be doing after we take down her crest, that's for bloody sure.'

Baz leans back further, still peering upwards. 'There are four of them though. Are they all the Queen's?'

'Nah, they're for other members of the Royal Family. Like, one of them's Prince Philip, I think.'

A bald man comes out of the store in a camel coat and a silk scarf, accompanied by three hangers-on in black overcoats. They all gaze up at the men on the crane who are now lifting the first crest on to the platform of the cherry-picker.

'That one looks like a bunch o' feathers,' observes Baz. 'Who's that one belong to then?'

'No fuckin' idea. What do you think I am? Bleedin' brain of bleedin' Britain? We're just here to hump them things into the van.'

Gerry points a stubby finger at the white transit parked on the high street. Traffic cones and tape have been laid out to keep pedestrians off the pavement and away from the cherry-picker. One lane has been blocked off to traffic so people can walk on it and the van can park there, and if one of the crests is dropped, at least it won't fall on anyone's head. The whole set-up is causing chaos, with cars backing up along Knightsbridge, their drivers hooting their horns in frustration. *Tough shit*, thinks Baz. They can beep all they like but it's obvious the crane and the van aren't moving until all four crests are down.

The bald bloke smiles and claps his hands. He chats to one of the men next to him and then turns to Gerry and Baz, giving them two thumbs up.

'Good work, boys,' he says, and walks back into the store, followed by the rest of his group.

'That bloke owns the place,' announces Gerry, 'and Fulham Football Club.'

Baz knows who he is now.

'Ah, yes. Al-Fayed, ain't it? Thought the geezer had a dodgy accent. Why's he taking these things down then? If he hates this country so much, why don't he just bugger off back where he came from?'

Gerry thinks for a moment. 'You know. I think he likes it over here. He don't want to go home. Considers himself proper British now. What with owning Harrods and Fulham an' all that.'

'Ah yes,' Baz remembers now. 'He wants a British passport, don't he? Only they won't give him one.'

Baz looks up to see that the crane is being lowered, the first crest jammed into the platform at an odd angle and held by two of the men.

'No way he'll get that passport now,' he adds. 'Queen's going to be proper pissed off when she finds out he's done away with her badge.'

'I don't think he's bothered about that,' replies Gerry. 'He's pretty hacked off with them royals.'

'Why's that then?' asks Baz. 'What have they ever done to him?'

'He thinks Prince Philip did in his son, don't he? You know, in that car crash with Princess Diana.'

'Did he?'

'Did he what?'

Baz sighs in frustration. 'Did Prince Philip knock off Diana and Al-Fayed's son? What was his name?'

'Bambi or summat. And no one knows, do they?'

Mohamed Al-Fayed and the Royal Warrants

Mohamed Fayed was born in Alexandria, Egypt, adding the prefix Al to his surname in the 1970s at about the same time as he moved to the UK. His exact age is unclear; most reports state that he was born in 1929, while Al-Fayed himself claims to be have been born four years later.

Al-Fayed was already a successful businessman when he arrived in the UK, but his profile increased significantly when, in 1985, in partnership with his brother Ali, he acquired control of the House of Fraser group and its flagship store, Harrods, in controversial circumstances. One year earlier, Al-Fayed had acquired 29.9% of the group from Lonrho. Roland 'Tiny' Rowland, the head of Lonrho, had a burning ambition to acquire Harrods, but Lonrho was blocked from doing so by the Monopolies and Mergers Commission (MMC) in 1981. The official reason, which now seems laughable, was that Lonrho also owned Brentford Nylons and together with the House of Fraser group would have too dominant a share of the bed linen market. The real reason for the block was probably because the company had been accused of breaking trading sanctions with apartheid Rhodesia only eight years earlier, leading Prime Minister Edward Heath to call Lonrho 'the unacceptable face of capitalism'.

The MMC barred Lonrho from acquiring any more shares in the House of Fraser group. In an attempt to get round this hurdle, Rowland agreed to sell Lonrho's 29.9% stake to Al-Fayed. The plan was that the sale would help persuade the government to release the restrictions, at which point, Lonrho would then be free to acquire House of Fraser, including repurchasing the 29.9% from Al-Fayed.

Rowland did not believe that Al-Fayed had sufficient funds to purchase House of Fraser. In this, he was mistaken, as the Al-Fayeds acquired control of the House of Fraser group for £615m in 1985. Rowland was furious, convinced that the Al-Fayeds' funds had come from the Sultan of Brunei and not, as claimed in the official offer document, from their business interests.

This led to a long-standing feud between the two men, with Rowland persuading the DTI to launch an inquiry into the matter. The DTI's report, published in 1990, stated that 'we are satisfied that the image [the Al-Fayeds] created between November 1984 and March 1985 of their wealthy Egyptian ancestors was completely bogus'.

Despite this criticism, the Al-Fayeds' takeover of House of Fraser and Harrods stood.

Tiny Rowland would not lie down, however, and subsequently made a bizarre allegation that Al-Fayed had broken into his safe deposit box at the store and stolen papers and other items of value. Al-Fayed was arrested but no charges were brought and this dispute was only concluded after Rowland's death, when Al-Fayed reached a financial settlement with Rowland's widow.

In 1994, Al-Fayed made his first application for a British passport which was refused. His feud with Tiny Rowland was cited in the press as being a contributory factor to the refusal, although the findings of the 1990 DTI report were almost certainly more instrumental in the decision. At the time, Al-Fayed stated: 'Why won't they give me a passport? I own Harrods and employ thousands of people in this country.'

After this refusal, Al-Fayed told journalists that he had paid two Conservative ministers, Neil Hamilton and Tim Smith, cash to ask questions on his behalf in Parliament, much of it delivered in brown paper envelopes. This became famously known as the cash-for-questions affair. Both resigned from the government. Al-Fayed also disclosed that the Conservative MP, Jonathan Aitken, had stayed free of charge at Al-Fayed's Ritz Hotel in Paris at the same time as a group of Saudi arms dealers. This disclosure ultimately led to Aitken bringing a libel case against The Guardian, which in turn resulted in Aitken being imprisoned for perjury in 1997.

While Tim Smith admitted guilt, Neil Hamilton always protested his innocence and sued The Guardian, which published the original story, for libel. Hamilton reached a settlement with The Guardian the day before the trial was due to take place. Hamilton then went on to sue Al-Fayed himself for libel for comments he made in a Channel 4 Dispatches programme in 1997 where Al-Fayed repeated his assertions that he had given money and other payments-in-kind to Hamilton to ask questions in the House of Commons. It was at this trial in 1999 that Al-Fayed accused the Duke of Edinburgh of leading a conspiracy to kill Princess Diana and his son, Dodi, by engineering the car crash that killed them in Paris in August 1997. Despite attempts by Neil Hamilton's barrister, Desmond Browne QC, to denigrate Al-Fayed's character, accusing him of being a bully and a liar and having 'an evil habit of vindictively pursuing those who he regarded as his antagonists', Hamilton lost the libel case and a subsequent appeal.

Royal Warrants of Appointment are granted in recognition of those who have provided goods or services to the royal households of the Queen, the Duke of Edinburgh, or the Prince of Wales, and when she was alive, the Queen Mother. The warrants are typically granted for five years at a time to a named individual at a senior level within the company concerned, and signify that the company has delivered high standards of service and products to the named royal for at least five years. The company is then permitted to display the relevant Royal Arms with the words 'By Appointment' on their buildings, products, stationery and vehicles.

Until the year 2000, Harrods had the relatively unusual distinction of holding all four Royal Warrants. However, in January 2000, the Duke of Edinburgh's Royal Warrant was not renewed. Newspaper reports at the time suggested that this was because the Duke was angry at the accusations by Al-Fayed that he had been responsible for the deaths of Diana, Dodi and their driver, Henri Paul, in the Paris car accident. Buckingham Palace denied this, explaining that the removal of the Royal Warrant simply arose out of the standard five-yearly review and was as a result of there no longer being a trading relationship between the Duke and Harrods. In accordance with standard practice, Al-Fayed was given twelve months to remove the Duke's coat of arms from the building and all stationery.

The Royal Warrants of the Queen and the Prince of Wales were due to expire on 31 December 2000. In a pre-emptive move, Al-Fayed announced in July of that year that he would not be applying for renewal of the warrants, saying that it would be hypocritical and misleading for Harrods to continue to hold them as none of the British Royal Family had shopped there for years. He did invite members of the Royal Family to spend 'any of their vast fortune' in Harrods if they so wished, with the exception of the Duke of Edinburgh who he banned from the store.

The Queen Mother's Royal Warrant had no expiry date, as her warrants are no longer reviewed following her death. Despite this, on 27 December 2000, workmen removed all four coats of arms from each of the corners of the store. It was the first time since 1913 that Harrods was not in possession of a Royal Warrant.

Nearly ten years later, Al-Fayed funded a documentary entitled Unlawful Killing. The documentary was made by director Keith Allen and concerned the deaths of Diana, Dodi and Henri Paul and the subsequent 2008 inquest which returned a verdict of 'unlawful killing', blaming the driver Henri Paul (who was found to have alcohol in his bloodstream over the legal limit) and unspecified following vehicles.

The final scene of the documentary showed footage of Al-Fayed burning the Royal Warrants in the garden of his home in Surrey, believed to be sometime the previous year (2010). In the film he says: 'There was a clear verdict of unlawful killing, so why has nobody been arrested? What is at the core of all this racism?'

He goes on to refer to 'powerful people in this country', adding: 'They wouldn't accept me or my son, and when he fell in love with Diana they murdered him.'

The film was never shown in the UK on legal grounds, but details were reported in the press and online, along with pictures of the Royal Warrants burning. Comments posted online reacting to this story included, 'Isn't it time we got rid of this loathsome man?'

Since he has been in the UK, Al-Fayed has paid millions of pounds in taxes, provided employment for several thousands of people, generated millions of pounds for charity through donations and fund-raising activities, and taken a historically small South-West London football club to the Premier League, keeping it there for over ten years.

In 1999, Al-Fayed was refused a British passport for the second time by the Home Office. It is very unlikely that he will ever apply again, and even more unlikely that if he does, his request will be granted.

Knightsbridge to the Natural History Museum

We are walking along the Brompton Road towards that curious area of London where there is a concentration of museums: the V&A, the Science Museum, the Natural History Museum. It is as if London is challenging you. You can wallow in the expensive frippery of Knightsbridge's high-end shops and department stores or you can choose to walk five minutes to South Kensington and immerse yourself in culture, science and natural history.

What will make you feel better about yourself? Spending a fortune on a new designer outfit, or spending a few hours improving your mind? I know what Summer would say. Why do you have to choose? You can do both. But despite her lightness of being, if forced to decide I know Summer would always have opted for a museum tour over a shopping trip.

Until I got to know her, I might have assumed that Summer's favourite would be the V&A, the museum of art, design and culture, and we did go to see the Fashion Galleries at the V&A after they opened. Summer was particularly entranced by one of Princess Diana's ball gowns, a sparkling, white dress, studded with pearls, that she set off with a glittering tiara. As part of the exhibit, there was a picture of Diana wearing the outfit at the London Fashion Awards, clutching a bunch of delicate white and pink flowers.

'She looks unhappy,' Summer observed, contemplating the picture. It was an odd comment. Diana had a broad smile and her skin glowed.

'She is fragile,' explained Summer, 'like the flowers she is carrying. Her smile is for the cameras.'

I examined the date. It was 1989, eight years before Diana died in a car crash, and she must have still been married to Charles at the time. I wondered if her private life was already in tatters, or whether she had a premonition of the tragic events that would befall her. And then I thought that maybe

Summer felt the same and that, perhaps, Summer's smiles had become false.

No – despite our trip to the V&A, Summer's favourite was the Natural History Museum, that gothic cathedral to the natural world that sits between Queen's Gate and Exhibition Road. Summer and I made an annual pilgrimage to the Wildlife Photographer of the Year exhibition which always featured stunning images, but it wasn't unusual for Summer to jump out of bed and simply declare: 'I know, let's go to the museum today.' And I knew that *the* museum was always the Natural History Museum, and not the others, which she would refer to by name. I remember the last time we went to *the* museum. It was the week before things changed.

Natural History Museum

Saturday 10 March 2012

Summer woke up early and excited. The Natural History Museum had a new exhibit – a piece of a meteorite from Mars – and we had decided to go and see it. A shower of Martian meteorite fragments had fallen in the Moroccan desert the previous year, rendering them of particular value because the dry conditions meant that they were relatively uncontaminated. Actual rock from Mars is rare – no human has been there and back to collect any samples – so the museum scientists thought they had died and gone to geological heaven.

We arrived at the museum at about 10am, after I forced Summer to stop for coffee and a muffin in Starbucks on the way. As far as I was concerned, a meteorite that had spent several gazillion light years travelling to Earth could wait a little longer for me to get a caffeine fix and something inside my stomach. The lump of meteorite was on display in the Vault, a Fort Knox-like strongroom at the end of the mineral gallery, where the museum stored its more valuable geological treasures. Summer stared at it for nearly fifteen minutes – an unprepossessing lump of grey rock encased in what looked like a pyrex dish.

'Just think, Ben, it is so far from home. What must this rock have seen on its journey here?'

'Darkness, probably.'

Summer punched my arm. 'Stars, planets, moons, galaxies, alien flightcraft, who knows?'

I thought it unlikely that the meteorite had passed a fleet of extra-terrestrial starships on its journey to Earth but I let it pass.

'I thought Mars was supposed to be a red planet,' Summer mused.

'It is.' I had read up on this stuff in the museum guide.

'Iron oxide. It's like the planet is covered in a layer of rust. But underneath, the rocks are black, brown, grey, like this one.'

'So Mars is like people,' she said. 'What you see on the surface is often different from what is underneath.'

She looked at me provocatively, but I was not going to be drawn.

'I guess that's one way of looking at it,' I replied.

We wandered around the other display cases. Summer loved a cluster of gold rock that came from an Australian mine.

'It looks as if you can eat it, like the inside of a Crunchie.'

'That would be a very expensive bar of chocolate,' I observed drily.

Further on there was an eye-catching collection of diamonds, presented together on little cocktail sticks. Summer read the sign: 'The Aurora Pyramid of Hope. 295 naturally coloured diamonds.'

She fingered her charm bracelet and the heart with its small chip of winking diamond and gave me a squeeze.

'One is enough for me, Ben,' she laughed.

I felt rather cheated by the presence of another Martian meteorite in the collection, albeit a smaller piece of slick grey rock, that fell to Earth in 1911. The sign said there were less than seventy Martian meteorite rocks in the world, and here were two of them within five yards of each other. Summer saw me frown and instantly knew why.

'This one can't be as important as the one from Morocco, Ben. It's not in a glass dish.'

I comforted myself with the thought that she must be right.

Finally, we stopped by a display case that included a large purple stone set in a tarnished silver ring, decorated with symbols that looked like signs of the zodiac. It was an ugly piece of jewellery, possibly a bracelet, but I couldn't really tell. The text on the case stated that this was the Deadly Purple Sapphire, also known as Edward Heron-Allen's Cursed Amethyst. It was in fact, an amethyst, not a sapphire, plundered by a British soldier, Colonel Ferris, from India over 150 years ago.

Ever since Ferris removed the stone from its rightful

home, it had apparently brought bad luck to all those who had touched it. Ferris himself suffered financial ruin and ill health, and the text detailed a litany of other unfortunate events that had befallen its various owners. Heron-Allen, the last man to possess the stone, was convinced it was cursed and kept it locked in a bank vault for nearly forty years, bequeathing it to the museum after his death.

Summer read the story of the stone as we gazed at it in its display cabinet. When she finished she sighed, and shook her head.

She stroked my hand as she spoke.

'Ben, nothing good ever comes out of taking something from its home.'

Chichester

Saturday 7 July 2001

The Head of Micropalaeontology at the Natural History Museum is pleased with the way the evening has gone. Yes, Dr John Whittaker, a cheery soul with wire-rimmed spectacles and an unruly sweep of grey hair, can definitely assert that the First Symposium of the Heron-Allen Society has been a success. Some fifty-odd attendees, which was a few more than he had dared hope for, listened attentively to the seminars and chatted amiably over drinks for a couple of hours afterwards. In fact, his wife Christine practically had to shoo them out of the door of the West Sussex Record Office at 9pm.

The highlight of the symposium, even though he was saying so himself, had been John's own talk on foraminifera. Although a polymath of his day, Heron-Allen was, as everyone knew, mostly renowned for his studies of foraminifera – or to describe the most fascinating and complex class of fauna in oversimplistic layman's terms: tiny, amoeba-like creatures, mostly marine based, such as plankton. As such, the foraminifera session was the most important one of the day.

John had decided to lead it with a presentation of his own latest findings, partly because he was, after all, the museum's leading expert on the subject, but mostly because, as Chairman of the Heron-Allen Society, he wanted to ensure that the First Symposium went well. And, as Christine had said to him when he expressed concern over the gathering one evening, the best way of doing that was 'to get off your backside, John, and do it yourself'.

He was aware that there had been some muttering amongst members about him hogging the limelight, but snide comments from academic rivals were an occupational hazard. Afterwards, everyone he spoke to had congratulated him heartily on his presentation and so, as he drives away from

Chichester, he is flushed with a warm glow of satisfaction. Even his harshest critic, Christine, who came along to give him support and now sits in the passenger seat next to him, is moved to faint praise.

'Well, that could have gone a lot worse.'

He had finished the day's programme with a curio: a strange artefact bequeathed by Heron-Allen to the museum known as the Delhi Purple Sapphire. It was of no particular scientific, historic or geological significance – in fact, it wasn't even a sapphire, it was an amethyst – but the stone was said to have been cursed when it was looted from a tomb in India by a British soldier in the mid-nineteenth century. The tale of the stone and its various owners who had, almost without exception, fallen on hard times or illness or even death – at least one had committed suicide – made for a light-hearted finale to what had otherwise been a serious day of academic learning and discussion.

Heron-Allen himself had believed the stone to be cursed and consigned it to a bank vault for the last forty years of his life, hidden inside several boxes and reputedly protected by charms. At first, John had not believed this story, as Heron-Allen was a man of science and surely did not believe in the supernatural. However, his colleague Peter, who unearthed the artefact in the archives when John was just a fresh-faced youngster on the museum staff, had shown him the note that Heron-Allen had enclosed with it, warning anyone who came into its possession of its cursed nature.

He chuckled to himself as he recalled his party piece at the end of the day. John had, with permission from the museum of course, taken the stone to the symposium and laid it out for the members to view, while he recounted its colourful history. At the end of his short speech, he had produced a pair of white gloves and challenged members to defy the curse and come up and hold the blighted amethyst themselves.

Christine had asked him not to do this. She was wary of the stone.

'Don't meddle with what you don't understand, John,' she had scolded him. But he couldn't resist a bit of fun and, as he had predicted and much to his amusement, his challenge had caused a degree of discomfort. Members were torn between their faith in logic and science and their trepidation of the unknown. There was a lot of uneasy shifting in seats until one of the American contingent stood up, put on the glove and held the amethyst gingerly for a few seconds for the audience to see, before replacing it on the table with a triumphant grin.

'Nothing to it, folks,' the American boomed out as he made his way back to his seat, but despite his bravado John had detected a film of sweat on the man's forehead when he had come up to the front. A few more followed, before John called a halt to the exercise, at which point he saw a number of distinguished academics, whose working lives had been built on concrete pillars of study, evidence and proof, exhale sighs of relief.

Well, no harm had come to anyone as far as he could tell, so perhaps the First Symposium of the Heron-Allen Society has finally put the notion of the cursed amethyst to bed. It is now secured safely in its box, which in turn sits in the boot of his car on its journey back to London.

Darkness has closed in and fat drops of rain begin to fall on the windscreen. John can see the trees by the side of the road bending in the wind. They are in for a storm.

'Careful, John,' says Christine, 'it looks filthy ahead.'

John eases off on the accelerator as the rain drives down harder. He switches the wipers to the fast setting and they hammer backwards and forwards – thunk, thunk – clearing sheets of water from the windscreen.

A tree branch lies in the road and John swerves to avoid it. Christine says nothing, but huddles down in the passenger seat. A lorry on the other side of the road crashes through a deep puddle sending up a curtain of rainwater that drenches their small hatchback.

Thunk, thunk. The wipers are working overtime.

A crack of lightning splits the sky turning everything white, and even before the lightning has faded, a timpani roll of thunder shudders above their heads. The storm is upon them. The air in the car turns icy cold and the pelting rain gives way to battering hail. It is as if a skipload of gravel is being tipped on to their windscreen. Hailstones. John can hardly believe it.

The Gods are throwing hailstones at them in West Sussex in July.

The sky is black and he can hardly see the road. He can't stop himself from thinking of the Purple Sapphire in the boot, stolen all those years ago from the Temple of Indra, the Hindu God of Rain and Thunderstorms. Perhaps discretion is the better part of valour.

'I think I should pull over, love. Let the storm pass,' he says to his wife, who has shrunk even lower into her seat.

'It's that bloody stone,' she screams over the deafening noise of the hailstones. 'Why did you have to bring the damned thing?'

The Deadly Purple Sapphire

The Deadly Purple Sapphire is actually an amethyst, set in a silver ring decorated with unusual alchemical and astrological signs. Attached to the ring at one end are two mauve scarab stones which complement the deeper purple of the larger amethyst. At the other end is an unusual druid-like symbol. The stone is not in itself rare or valuable but it has a history that makes it particularly interesting.

The stone was looted by a Bengal cavalryman, Colonel W. Ferris, from the Temple of Indra in Cawnpore some time around 1855 or 1857 (records vary on the date), during the Indian Mutiny. The temple was dedicated to the Hindu God of War and Weather, and the stone is rumoured to have been subject to a curse ever since it was stolen. Misfortune is believed to befall anyone who touches the stone.

Ferris himself lost nearly everything he owned, including his health. He passed the stone to his son who suffered similar misfortune and gave the stone to a friend. The friend committed suicide and bequeathed the unwanted artefact back to the son.

Edward Heron-Allen was a polymath: an author, palm-reader, violinist, collector, celebrated scientist and, oddly, a friend of Oscar Wilde. He acquired the amethyst in 1890 and was immediately beset by a series of disasters. He too passed it to a friend, a singer who suddenly lost her singing voice and never sang again. The stone was returned to Heron-Allen who threw it into the Regent's Canal to be rid of it. Three months later, a dealer recognised it and handed it back to him, after the stone had been rescued from the depths by a dredger.

Heron-Allen's first daughter was born in 1904, fourteen years after the amethyst came into his possession. Convinced that the amethyst was bringing bad luck to the family, and desperate to shield his new-born daughter from its influence, Heron-Allen locked it in seven boxes, cast protective charms around it and secured the stone in a bank vault. He left instructions that the boxes were not to be opened until at least thirty-three years after his death, that it should be bequeathed to the Natural History Museum and that under no circumstances should his daughter be allowed to touch the stone. Heron-Allen died in 1940 and in 1943 his daughter duly donated the amethyst to the museum. It lay undisturbed for thirty years, until it was discovered in the museum's mineral cabinets in 1973 by Peter Tandy, a junior curator, and subsequently put on display in 2007.

Dr John Whittaker, former Head of Micropalaeontology at the Natural History Museum and Chairman of the Heron-Allen Society, is himself said to have been affected by the curse. He took the stone to the Society's First Symposium and on the way home encountered 'the most horrific thunderstorm I have ever experienced', so bad that he and his wife considered abandoning their car.

The night before the Second Symposium, he fell violently ill with a stomach virus, and he was unable to attend the Third Symposium due to a kidney stone.

Perhaps Dr Whittaker should have heeded the warning in Heron-Allen's handwritten note that was found with the stone when it was unearthed by Peter Tandy.

'Whoever shall then open it, shall first read out this warning, and then do as he pleases with the jewel. My advice to him or her is to cast it into the sea.'

Natural History Museum to Kensington High Street

'Do you want to talk about it? You know, how things changed?'
I can't bring myself to answer. The truth is that it is still raw. Annie interprets my silence as a 'No'.

'That's fine,' she says. We walk a few more steps along Exhibition Row before she has a thought.

'You know, if you ever do want to talk about it, I'd be happy to listen. People say that I'm a good listener.'

I smile at her. She said that to me at the start of the evening and I can see that people talk to Annie. She has an innocence about her that suggests she understands what it is like to be vulnerable. That she will be non-judgmental. Perhaps it is the freshness of her pale skin dashed with freckles, or possibly the wide sky-blue eyes that invite you in.

'Thanks,' I say, 'I may take you up on that offer sometime.'

A few drops of rain dapple the pavement and it is definitely getting colder. We have just passed mile nine so we have managed a third of the way around in the dry. We stop at a bench to get out our rain jackets and cover up before a real downpour, as it will be tiresome dragging a wet body around another seventeen miles of London. I put on my mum's woolly hat, not so much to keep me warm as to be able to tell her that it came in useful, and munch on a cereal bar that I collected at the last pit stop.

We pass the monolith that is the Royal Albert Hall on our left and then the Royal Geographical Society opposite the park, where I take a second to look at the statues of Shackleton and Livingstone that adorn its walls. I wonder what stories they would tell if they were around today.

Although not quite as adventurous as those two explorers, we take our lives in our hands and cross Kensington Gore. It is eleven in the evening, the London traffic is still flowing, and another volunteer sees us across the road, blaring out instructions through a megaphone.

'Stay on the pavement. Stay on the pavement. Right, cross now. Cross... now!'

He is drowned out by a beatbox thumping out dance music. I turn to see where the sound is coming from and recognise the cyclist who passed us before on Albert Bridge, which seems a lifetime away now. He is still wearing his sunglasses, even though we are close to midnight and the rain is now falling steadily, and the beatbox remains strapped resolutely to his panier rack. Half a dozen other cyclists ride alongside him and give us a collective cheer as we go past.

'Buster and I come here a lot.' I point in the direction of Hyde Park. 'I love this bit of the park: the Albert Memorial, the Serpentine, Diana's fountain. So does Buster. Always chasing after a duck or a squirrel.'

'I like the middle bit,' Annie says, 'where the lake is. I used to take Peter there when he was ill. We would sit in the deckchairs and watch the model boats.'

'Oh God,' I groan. 'Don't remind me. Buster went after one of those once. It was a model clipper with fancy rigging that looked like the Cutty Sark. Or at least it did until Buster got hold of it. The bloke was furious.'

Annie smiles but there is a tremor in her voice. 'Peter and I saw a few dogs jump into the lake. It always caused mayhem. It made Peter laugh, though, and that was good because...' she falters, 'because not much did... towards the end.'

Her face is blank, as if all expression has been sucked from her features, and we lapse into silence. It doesn't seem right to intrude into her grief. I still don't know who Peter is but I figure that we have another six hours or so together and if she wants to tell me she will.

Shards of rain are lit up by the lights of cars along Kensington High Street and a few drops creep down my neck. I can feel the blister developing between my big toe and the one next to it on my right foot. My thighs are aching and my walking partner has gone silent on me. I tell myself to remember this moment if I am ever stupid enough to think of doing the Shine Walk again.

Hyde Park

Sunday 10 June 2012

It had been nearly three months since Summer left me; three months when all I did was go through the motions. Get up, take Buster for a walk, have breakfast, go to work, make small talk with colleagues, go home, eat dinner, go to bed. At weekends, I moped around trying to fill the days with something useful, like food shopping or washing, but often just resorted to lazing on the sofa in front of the TV. Buster sloped around after me with his jaw sunk to the floor and when I was stretched out in the sitting room, he curled up in his basket by the fireplace and glowered in my direction. He missed Summer more than I did and refused to climb up on the sofa next to me the way he used to with Summer. Buster was punishing me for screwing up. Still, in just over a month I would be leaving for New York, so Buster would be rid of me then, my parents having agreed to take him for however long I was abroad.

I decided to take Buster to Hyde Park as we hadn't been there for a while and it would get me out of the flat. We used to go to Hyde Park a lot with Summer so I hoped it would remind Buster of happier times. I parked the car on a meter in Queen's Gate near the museum and Buster pulled at the lead as we walked towards the park gates. He knew where we were going.

We entered the park through the wrought iron gates on Kensington Gore and as soon as I let Buster off the lead, he raced off, tail swishing, ears flapping. Buster is mostly spaniel, but the people at Battersea Dogs Home were not especially specific.

'A spaniel cross,' was all they would commit to.

Buster is adorable. Curly, charcoal hair and big, round inky-black eyes that we fell in love with instantly. You can always tell Buster's mood, though, from his ears. If he is down, they hang limply like soggy washing on a line. If he is happy, he lifts them up so they stick out comically from his head. Summer and I used to joke that perhaps he was a Prince Charles spaniel. I remember one particularly earnest friend of ours who failed to appreciate the reference.

'You mean a King Charles spaniel, Ben. And, you know, I don't think so. He is the wrong colouring.'

I couldn't resist. 'No, but he has the royal spaniel ears, don't you think?'

Summer laughed about that for days.

I walked in the direction of Kensington Palace. Buster engaged in a routine of careering off into the trees, then after a minute or so, running back to me, circling around my legs and, satisfied that I hadn't disappeared, haring away again to frighten the living daylights out of another squirrel. It was a cloudless day in June, but the summer heat hadn't yet kicked in and I wore an old leather jacket. The park was full of joggers, cyclists, rollerbladers and plain old walkers like me. I planned to head for the north side of the park and then loop back, but I would have to be careful with Buster at the boating lake. I was still scarred by the abuse I got from one enthusiast after Buster belly-flopped on top of his multi-masted pride and joy bringing an abrupt end to its mini-voyage. We didn't hang around to see him fish it out of the water and so I never saw the full extent of the damage, but I still have visions of ripped sails and broken masts. To Buster, a model boat is simply a different shaped squirrel, and much easier to catch.

We negotiated the boating lake without incident this time; there were only a couple of boats on the water and Buster was distracted by a pack of Yorkshire terriers who he found much more interesting.

'Buster, come here,' I shouted, always embarrassed when my dog sniffed the bottoms of other canines.

Buster ignored me and charged off again, and not for the first time I wondered if we would have been better getting a dog with less energy. But then, that dog wouldn't have been Buster, so as always, the thought quickly passed.

And then I saw him stop in his tracks. He stood like a gundog, nose twitching, before suddenly tearing off in a different direction, barking madly. Buster only ever barks when he is truly excited. People scattered from the path of this crazy animal travelling faster than Usain Bolt.

'Buster. Here, boy! Buster!'

I shouted in increasing desperation, rather like the guy who became an internet phenomenon running after his dog in Richmond Park, trying to stop it chasing deer. There are no deer in Hyde Park though and I couldn't think what had gripped his attention.

Buster disappeared from view behind a small copse of trees and I started after the silly mutt. Perhaps there was a particularly attractive spaniel bitch on heat that had got him so excited. I rounded the copse and scanned the park; he had stopped barking now so I had to rely on my eyes to find him.

And then I saw it. Not Buster, but a flash of lemon-yellow close to the exit at the top of the park. I had seen that colour before. And then I was running, spinning my legs as quickly as I could, pumping my arms, bursting my lungs.

She was bending down and I saw that Buster was with her and she was talking to him, ruffling his coat, fiddling with his collar, kissing his wet nose. She was a hundred yards away but it felt like a hundred miles.

I was panting, a stitch was driving a knife into my ribs; I had to keep running.

I bawled out her name.

'Summer! Sum… mer!'

She stood up, looked at me for a second and with a drop of her shoulders she turned away. Buster started to walk after her, but she stopped him, pointing back at me. I could tell that Buster was confused.

'Summer!' I tried to shout again, but I was so breathless by then that my voice was hoarse.

Buster turned in my direction and in that second Summer was gone. The lemon-coloured coat slipped through the park gate and on to Bayswater. A bus pulled up at a stop and then rolled away, and I knew there was no point in chasing after her anymore.

When I reached Buster a few moments later, he was

standing stock still, tongue lolling, tail between his legs, ears flat against his head. Bewildered, he knew his mistress had gone again. Something glinted at his neck and I knelt down to see what it was. Attached to Buster's collar, sparkling in the weak sun, was a silver charm bracelet.

Kensington Church Street to Bayswater Road

A woman in a Cancer Research T-shirt holds her left arm out straight while furiously making circles with her right hand. At the same time she is yelling at the top of her voice.

'Ten miles gone! Nearly halfway, folks! Brilliant job!'

Even my shaky maths tells me that ten miles isn't half of twenty-six, but I suppose 'Not quite halfway, folks!' is a glass half-empty way of looking at things and not so motivating to the bedraggled mob of walkers that follow the direction of her left arm into Kensington Church Street.

At least we have stopped walking west as Kensington Church Street climbs northwards from Kensington to Notting Hill in a gentle curve. It is a narrow street and the shops and houses feel like they are closing in on us on both sides. We pass several expensive-looking antique shops and I imagine a number of the Georgian houses in the neighbourhood have been renovated at considerable cost over the last twenty years or so.

Still in silence, Annie and I emerge into the wider thoroughfare that is Notting Hill Gate, and after the suffocating darkness of Kensington Church Street it is like coming up for air. The rain is easing off, so perhaps we are lucky and it was only a shower. My spirits are rising as we turn east and Annie is obviously inspired by where we are.

'The film *Notting Hill*,' she says, 'have you seen it?'

'Yes, I thought it was a male fantasy.'

'Male fantasy?'

'You know. Bump into a beautiful Hollywood actress in the street, she falls in love with you, happy ever after.'

'Mmm,' she thinks for a second, 'is that your fantasy?'

'Well, I suppose now you ask, no. It's not.'

'I always thought that film was spoilt by Hugh Grant,' she says. 'There's no way Julia Roberts would fall for him in real life. It didn't make sense.'

'I have news for you, Annie,' I say, 'it wasn't real life. It was a movie.'

She punches my arm, laughing. I wince.

'Sorry. Did that hurt? I thought I was being gentle.'

'No, it's fine,' I mumble. It is painful, but not in the way Annie thinks. Summer used to punch me exactly like that.

We walk a few more steps before I try another gambit.

'You know, I preferred *Love, Actually*. I'm a real softie. I always watch it at Christmas.'

'Which is your favourite?'

'Sorry?'

'Which story is your favourite? Hugh Grant as Prime Minister and Martine McCutcheon, or Colin Firth and the Portuguese girl? I love it when the pages of his novel go flying into the lake.'

I consider this for a second.

'I like the Liam Neeson one. With the boy who plays drums and runs through the airport after the girl.'

'Ah,' she says. 'Where the mother has died.'

'Yes. I suppose so.' Now I thought about it, I suppose it made sense that I related to that plotline. I turn back to Annie. 'Which one do you like?'

'Well, the bit that always makes me cry is when Emma Thompson finds the necklace in her husband's pocket. But then all she gets for Christmas is a lousy CD and he's given the jewellery to a girl from the office.'

'Alan Rickman.'

'Sorry?'

'Alan Rickman was the husband. Also Professor Snape in the Harry Potter films. He must play nasty people.'

'But he wasn't nasty in *Love, Actually*,' she says, 'just misguided for a while.'

I laugh. 'Is that the term for infidelity now? Misguided?'

'A lot of people would take that definition,' she says.

'Actually,' I say, 'now I think about the film, the one I really loved...'

'... was the Keira Knightley one.' Annie finishes my sentence for me.

'Yes. How did you guess that?'

'Because you remind me of the guy. Standing in the snow with his cards declaring his love for her. It's the sort of romantic gesture I could see you doing.'

I look at her. I have always loved that scene in the film.

'I'm not sure whether that's a compliment or not.'

She tips her head to one side and her lips crease in a hint of a smile.

'Besides,' she says, 'all men fancy Keira Knightley.'

We are coming back up to Hyde Park now, along its northern perimeter. We pass the Russian Embassy with its red, white and blue flags; the same colours as the Union Jack, but a different arrangement, which perhaps sums up our two countries. Soon we will be at the gate where I saw Summer leave the park that time. In all the years since we first got together, even during those horrible months when we were apart, I was never misguided. No one ever came close to Summer. Not even Keira Knightley.

Soviet Embassy

Friday 4 September 1970

Mikhail Nikolayevich Smirnovsky sits back in his leather armchair and cradles his tumbler of Scotch. His long fingers run pleasingly over the dimples in the crystal glass as he contemplates his surroundings. Three of the study walls are lined with heavy wood panelling, while the fourth is dominated by a floor-to-ceiling leaded window pane. It is dark outside, but from his chair Mikhail can still make out the shadowy outline of Kensington Palace beyond the embassy gardens. An austere, rectangular desk sits solidly against the window. On the desk are a blotting pad, a telephone and an Anglepoise lamp that casts a soft, yellow light over the room. A carriage clock ticks on the mantelpiece above the fireplace. In winter, Mikhail will have the staff fix a fire in the grate every evening, but in London in early September, it is still warm enough to do without. It is one of the advantages of his posting; the British weather is pleasantly temperate.

Mikhail is a thin-faced man, approaching his fifties, and old enough now to appreciate the privileges of his position. In his earlier years, he had been a passionate communist, working long hours to gain advancement within the Party and publically supporting those who he thought would progress and whose ideas he admired. It was a risky strategy, as Communist Party officials slipped easily in and out of favour, but he had been lucky enough to hang on to the coat tails of sufficient successful politicians to gain his reward – a sought-after assignment as the Soviet Ambassador to the United Kingdom, with a comfortable residence next to Hyde Park – and now he is content to leave active politics to the younger generation.

He swirls the glass under his nose, breathing in the fumes of the earthy whisky, and when he takes a sip, the Scotch slips down his throat like honey. He gives a sigh of quiet satisfaction. It has been an excellent night. The Kirov Ballet's performance of *Sleeping Beauty* at the Royal Festival Hall was exquisite. He had arrived early to meet the cast beforehand backstage – a meeting that had been choreographed in as much detail as any ballet. The Director, Sergeyev, had guided him down a line of dancers to shake hands and exchange pleasantries, and the dancers mumbled and stared at the floor as he passed. Sergeyev himself had regarded Mikhail with suspicion. The Ambassador's presence was a gesture of support, but more importantly, it was a reminder to the members of the company that their government was watching them.

Mikhail had been slightly disappointed that the beautiful prima ballerina, Natalia Makarova, was not performing and was not at the theatre. He had been looking forward to seeing with his own eyes her famous porcelain skin and razor-sharp cheekbones, and most of all, watching her dance. People who had seen her told him that she shimmered and floated across the stage like liquid mercury. His disappointment was short-lived, however, as the rest of the company danced majestically leaving the audience in rapture. Irritatingly, this included the traitor, Nureyev, who sat a few seats along from him in the auditorium, and who rose first to lead the applause at the end.

He had been briefed that Nureyev had attended every performance given by the Kirov in London and so would most certainly be at the Festival Hall that evening. Mikhail had been careful not to get close to him at the reception beforehand for Moscow would be deeply unhappy if the Soviet Ambassador were photographed next to the Motherland's most notorious lost soul. Mikhail grimaced. The memory of Nureyev's defection was still painful. Now, his presence in the audience at the Kirov Ballet, the company who he deserted almost a decade ago, was tantamount to a public thumbing of his nose at the Soviet Union. It was intolerable behaviour and Mikhail had left directly after the performance to avoid the embarrassment of an unfortunate encounter. The embassy car was outside the theatre within five minutes of the curtain to whisk him home to Bayswater.

Still, he could understand why Nureyev was there. There

was no doubt that the Kirov Ballet was greatly superior to Western ballet corps and, in Mikhail's view, any dancer choosing to leave the company was surely misguided. There were many excellent things associated with Britain, such as the fine single malt he was rolling around his mouth, but while he enjoyed the Royal Ballet, watching their performances was like eating an insubstantial meal – sour bread and thin soup, compared to the Kirov's prime cut fillet steak and Mouton Rothschild claret. Like him, Nureyev must miss the Kirov; not everything was better in the West.

He takes another mouthful of whisky and replays scenes from *Sleeping Beauty* in his head. The Tchaikovsky score soars through his brain. Heaven. He is in heaven.

Somewhere in the distance, he hears a ringing sound and for a few moments, he ignores it, lost in his reverie. The noise is insistent, however, and he shakes his head and comes to. The telephone on the desk is ringing which is not good news. It is the hotline from Moscow.

Mikhail stands up and walks slowly across the room. He places his glass on the desk and picks up the receiver as if it is a scorching coal.

'This is the Ambassador.'

'Smirnovsky,' a heavily accented Russian voice growls at the end of the line. 'What is going on?'

Mikhail is confused by this. Moscow has rung him. He plays for time.

'Who am I speaking to?'

'Andropov.'

He gulps involuntarily. Andropov. Head of the KGB. Something serious is happening.

'Smirnovsky, are you there?'

'Yes, sir. Sorry, it is late over here. I was preparing for bed.'

'Late! You damn fool. Have you spoken to the British Foreign Office?'

The Foreign Office? On a Friday night? He hesitates.

'Er, no…'

'Well, get hold of them, man. Tell them we have her mother who wants to speak to her. If we can find her before this gets out, we may be able to stop this. I have our best agents in

London tracking her down now. Your job is to get the British to cooperate. If we don't find her, we will need them to give her up.'

'I'm sorry…' The soothing Tchaikovsky in his brain has now been replaced by clattering confusion.

'For God's sake, Smirnovsky,' Andropov splutters at the end of the line. 'You were supposed to be with them this evening. Did you see her or were you asleep? Do you have any idea what's happening?'

Mikhail recovers himself.

'I am afraid not, sir. Perhaps you could enlighten me.'

'It's Makarova, you dolt. She's defected.'

The defection of Natalia Makarova

On the evening of 4 September 1970, Leningrad's Kirov Ballet performed Tchaikovsky's Sleeping Beauty at the Royal Festival Hall. It was the first of three farewell performances at the end of the company's UK tour. Their prima ballerina, Natalia Makarova, considered to be the outstanding ballerina of the time, did not perform her role as Princess Florine that night. Instead, she went to dinner with friends in London, who suggested that she contact the British police and request political asylum. With unusual haste, she was granted asylum the following day and taken into hiding by Scotland Yard to evade the KGB. She was the first ballerina to defect from the Soviet Union, following in the footsteps of Rudolph Nureyev, who famously defected in Paris nine years earlier in 1961.

Her stated reasons for the defection were artistic, rather than political. She felt constrained by the conservative repertoire of the Kirov, which stuck rigidly to classics and communist propaganda pieces and she feared that she would lose her spontaneity. She yearned for more freedom to develop as an artist, saying, 'I felt the urgency to use the gift that God had given me to the fullest extent.'

Makarova went on to dance with the American Ballet Theatre and the Royal Ballet and never regretted her decision, commenting that her spontaneity saved her. When asked if she had planned the defection, she replied, 'No, absolutely not... I had no plans at all and then I cried. All my life was in front of my eyes. And it was the turning point.'

Lancaster Gate to Edgware Road

We turn away from the park at the Royal Lancaster Hotel and head north-east along Sussex Gardens. It is no longer raining and Annie and I stop to take off our raincoats and stuff them in our backpacks. My mum's woolly hat has also done its bit now and is packed away. I sit down, remove my shoe and sock and contemplate the blood seeping out from between my toes. My blister has burst, so I rescue a plaster from my basic first aid kit and place it carefully on the affected area. Annie stands over me with a concerned look on her face.

'Are you OK?'

'Sure,' I say with bravado. 'It will take more than a poxy blister to stop me doing this.'

'I wasn't talking about that,' she says. 'It must have been difficult for you when Summer left.'

'Oh, I see.' I go quiet, concentrating on putting my sock and shoe back on without disturbing the carefully positioned plaster.

Annie looks ahead.

'Ahh,' she says, changing the subject. 'The twelve-mile post. Still not halfway. Just another couple of miles though to the next pit stop, then we've broken the back of it.'

'It's alright, Annie. Just give me time and I'm sure I'll talk about it. We still have a good few hours.'

'If you can keep going, Hoppity,' she laughs. 'That blister looked a bit nasty.'

I look up and realise that Paddington Station is just a few hundred yards away. I need to get away from here. I jump up and start to walk again.

'Just try and stop me,' I say.

Paddington Station

Thursday 19 July 2012

The Heathrow Express opened for business in 1998, providing Londoners with a super-quick transport service to Heathrow Airport. Every fifteen minutes, a shiny new train whisks passengers from Paddington to Heathrow and within half an hour they are queuing up at their check-in desks.

I stood next to the train. Its doors were gaping, inviting me in, but my feet were stuck to the platform. All I had with me was a rucksack, my hand luggage for the flight. In the rucksack, I had stuffed my scrapbook, a fully-charged iPad, a bar of Lindt chocolate – Summer's favourite – Sebag Montefiore's tome, *Jerusalem,* that I had been plodding through for months now, a spare T-shirt, Calvins and socks. And a silver charm bracelet, which I carried with me everywhere.

The rest of my essential possessions had been packed into crates and shipped over to New York a week ago. In theory, they would be waiting in a Greenwich Village loft, provided for me by the company. I would have to find a place of my own within six months though; the company's relocation package only went so far. On the back of previous bitter experience, I had packed the T-shirt and underwear in case my crates took a detour and I beat them to Greenwich Village.

My other crap, detritus accumulated over several years and superfluous to requirements for a one-year secondment to New York, had been shifted to a windowless box in a Big Yellow storage hangar in Southfields. These items would probably never see the light of day again.

I stared at the train. It was yellow and silver and blue, and due to leave in five minutes. A number of passengers had already boarded: a mix of sober-suited businessmen with smart carry-ons and even smarter phones and holiday makers wearing flower-print tops and flapping around like fish out of water in a busy London station. A family appeared next to me, loaded with heavy suitcases and too many kids.

'Get on, now. It's leaving,' screamed the mother.

Two bored teenage boys, with earphones jammed into their ears so that they probably couldn't hear her, mooched on to the train. Their mother carried a young baby in her arms, who gurgled happily and stuck a chubby finger up its nose.

'Come on, Kev. Shift your arse.' She boarded the train leaving her red-faced husband with three enormous suitcases and no help. Behind him, a young girl tapped away on a mobile phone, oblivious to her father's struggles.

'Here, let me give you a hand.' I lugged one of the suitcases on to the train, convinced that it was heavier than the 20-kilogram allowance. It would certainly merit one of those orange 'Heavy' tags that are attached accusingly on to your luggage by disapproving check-in staff.

'Hey, thanks, son,' wheezed Kev as he lifted another one.

'Pandora, what the bloody hell are you doing? Get on the damn train,' he barked at his daughter, who sniffed and strode on to the carriage, her eyes never shifting from her phone.

'Alright, Dad. No panic. Two minutes to go.' She threw the words disdainfully over her shoulder.

Kev looked at me and rolled his eyes. Between us, we picked up his last suitcase and shoved it through the train doors.

'Cheers, lad. Are you not getting on?'

The train was silver and yellow and blue and it left in two minutes.

'No. I think I'll wait for the next one.'

'Suit yourself.' Kev looked at me as if I was short of the full deck.

Inside the train, the baby started to bawl.

''Arry, look what you've bleeding done now? I told you not to mess with her.'

'Weren't me, Mum.'

'Well, who was it then? Peter soddin' Pan?'

'Calm down, everyone. We're on holiday.' Kev entered the fray to broker peace.

'But, Dad, it weren't me. It were Josh.'

'Josh, what are you playing at?'

'Oh, that's right, Dad. Take Harry's side. Like always.'

'I am not taking anyone's side.'

'You do, Kev. You're always picking on Josh.'

'I do not, love. That's not fair.'

'But Josh was poking her, Dad.'

'Weren't.'

The baby gave a full-throated scream and drowned the rest of her family out.

Somewhere behind me a whistle blew and the train doors swished shut. I was left stranded on the platform with my rucksack. No matter. There would be another train in fifteen minutes and my flight wasn't for a few hours yet.

The next train was on the adjacent platform. I turned round to see an identical open carriage door on an identical train. A languid man in an Italian designer jacket, blue jeans and loafers observed me from inside. He had a pinched nose and an intense stare that made me feel uncomfortable. I picked up my bag and moved down one carriage. The train was yellow and silver and blue.

I cast a glance back to the barriers. A train had just pulled in from Swansea and a flood of passengers swamped the concourse. A girl squealed and ran over to a boy carrying a holdall and swinging a guitar case over his shoulder. He just had time to drop the holdall before she jumped into his arms and slathered him with kisses. The guitar case bounced on his back as they embraced each other and a pang of envy sliced through me.

People pushed past me on the platform. They all had an unshakeable purpose: to board the train and get to Heathrow. I looked at the digital clock above me to see that departure time was in ten minutes. Someone once told me that if you have a difficult choice to make between two options, then you should assign one option 'heads' and the other 'tails' and flick a coin into the air. The trick is that before the coin comes down your brain tells you which side up it wants the coin to fall. Hey presto! Your decision is made before the coin lands, regardless of whether it actually turns up heads or tails.

I mentally tossed a coin into the air. Heads, New York.

Tails, London. But as the coin was spinning in my mind, I realised that was not the choice I was making. Boarding the train was not about New York or London. Instead, it was all about Summer. Apart from a glimpse of a sunflower-yellow coat in Hyde Park, I hadn't seen her now for four months and I missed her terribly. Without Summer, I was a shell of a human being.

I stood there immobile and the minutes slid by. Somewhere close by, someone's phone started to ring. A guard sauntered along the platform and signalled the platform indicator.

'Four minutes, mate. You going to hop on?'

'Yeah, thanks.' I picked up my rucksack and took a step towards the train, but it felt like leadweights were attached to my shoes. The phone I could hear was still ringing and I realised with a jolt that it was my ringtone. I dug into my pocket and pulled out my mobile, just as the caller hung up. I didn't recognise the number.

I stared at the phone, then at the train, then at the phone again.

I tapped the number and called back, and after two rings, a female voice answered.

'Hello.'

'Hello,' I said. 'Who is this?'

'This is Fiona Chandra. Is that Ben?'

Fiona Chandra. I knew the name from somewhere but couldn't place it.

'Ben, yes. Sorry,' I stumble, 'you called me.'

'I did. I think you are friends with my daughter.'

And then I remembered. The back page of Summer's passport with details of who to contact in an emergency. Mrs Fiona Chandra, Summer's mother.

There was a beat as neither of us spoke. Fiona broke the silence.

'Ben, I think you should know something.'

'Mrs Chandra, where is Summer? Can I see her?'

'She's here with me, Ben,' she said quietly. 'I'm afraid we're in hospital.'

'Hospital. What... why?'

'I'm sorry to tell you over the phone but...'

I was rigid with panic.

'But what? What's happened?'

'Ben, Summer has cancer.'

Behind me the guard blew his whistle, but it sounded miles away. The train doors closed in front of me with a pneumatic sigh. I dropped my rucksack and it seemed to float gently to the ground.

'Ben, are you still there? Are you alright?'

The train left the station. It was silver and yellow and blue.

Edgware Road

We reach the busy Edgware Road and Annie and I bunch up with other walkers as we wait to cross the street, ignoring the Joe Strummer subway that runs underneath the junction. I wonder if the lead singer of The Clash envisaged a smelly, graffiti-smeared underpass as a memorial to his musical genius when he and Mick Jones wrote 'London Calling'. Fifty yards on and I see the statue of the window cleaner outside the tube station, a Norman Wisdom figure, in hobnail boots and overalls, carrying his ladder awkwardly over his shoulder and tilting the peak of his cap upwards with a vexed expression on his face. It is only when you look up that you see what is bothering him: an impossibly tall office building with banks of glass windows that stretch to the clouds. The statue's 6-foot ladder is woefully inadequate.

I point the window cleaner out to Annie and she laughs. The humour in the statue jars against events that I associate with Edgware Road tube station.

Edgware Road

Thursday 7 July 2005

Sid fingers his beard nervously. He has found a position by the sliding doors in a carriage near to the front of the train. The carriage is packed and he is squashed against the perspex screen with his rucksack on the floor between his legs. His body is rigid with anticipation. He checks his watch as the train moves off. 8.42am. They synchronised watches on the train down to London. Just a few minutes now.

The man standing next to him looks Sid up and down and his eyes fix on the rucksack. Sid turns away. It is as if the man knows, but surely the mission cannot fail now. The train pulls into a station, the doors open, and a few passengers escape. Sid squeezes against the perspex to let them past, gripping his rucksack with his calves. They do not know it but they are the lucky ones. As they are replaced by more commuters Sid edges round to a vacant seat, hauling his heavy pack behind him. Everyone is staring at him as he sits down and he can see distrust in their faces. It is hot in the carriage and sweat prickles his chest. The sign above his head says that he should give up the seat to the elderly or infirm or pregnant women. He has no intention of giving up his seat.

A large man with a briefcase takes the seat next to him, his stomach spilling over his waistband and invading Sid's space. Sid shrinks involuntarily and studies a young woman opposite him. She is pretty, with dark hair that falls to her shoulders. She is reading a book, but she looks up from her page for a moment and catches him watching her. She smiles at him and Sid is embarrassed. He turns his head away and focuses on somebody's armpit, their arm stretched up to hold on to the rail in the ceiling. The girl's head should be covered of course, but Sid still hopes that she gets out of the train at the next stop.

He checks his watch again. 8.46. He loosens the drawstring

around the top of his rucksack, reaches inside and caresses the button that he will soon be called upon to press. The others will press their buttons at the same time, they will complete their mission and the glory of the one true god, Allah, will be upon them. Western governments will understand that this is a war, and that Allah has many soldiers, and the British and American people will understand that as long as they support the governments that kill and maim Muslims, they are also guilty. The people on the train are not innocent; they are stained with the blood of his Muslim brothers and sisters.

Sid is proud to be a soldier. He will be spoken of in the same breath as Sheikh Bin Laden and Dr al-Zawahiri. His children will grow up in the knowledge that their father is a hero of Islam and Allah will reward him, because martyrdom will be the supreme demonstration of his faith.

An arm stretches out above him and, without thinking, he raises his hands to protect himself.

'It's alright, son.' A black man grins at him. 'Just opening the window for some air.'

He lowers his hands slowly as the man flicks open the slat window. He must calm down. Sid wonders what it will be like. He imagines a blaze of dazzling white light and warmth flowing through his body as Allah puts his arms around him and welcomes him to Jannah.

He looks at his watch one more time as the train pulls into a station. 8.50. The appointed time. The others should be detonating their packs now, but Sid has to wait; they all agreed that they should explode their bombs in a tunnel for the blasts to have their maximum effect. He is on edge now, but surely it is too late for anyone to stop him. His head throbs as he scans the people in the carriage one last time, the people who are about to pay for their government's actions. His eyes meet those of a grey-haired man with a square face and wire-rimmed spectacles who sits on the other side of the carriage. Sid turns his head to avoid the man's gaze. Everyone is still looking at him. They know. They must know.

The man standing by the doors makes as if to move and Sid stiffens, but then the train doors close and the man settles back to stay where he is. He glares at Sid with suspicion written across his face. Sid looks away and sees that the dark-haired girl is still sitting across from him, reading her book, which makes Sid sad. He reminds himself that war involves casualties, and even pretty girls with nice smiles are guilty.

The train moves out from the station and Sid thinks of his wife, Hasina, back home in Dewsbury. He hopes that she is doing fine. He is doing this for her, for their beloved daughter, Maryam, and for their unborn child. For his mother. For his brothers and sister. For the young people at the Centre. For all Muslims. And above all, for Allah.

Sid doesn't need to look to know that they are closing in. The man by the door takes a step towards him. The black man is staring straight into his face. The fat man next to him is stretching for something in his briefcase. He must act now before it is too late.

He reaches inside his rucksack and pushes the button. The carriage fills with brilliant white light.

Edgware Road

Thursday 7 July 2005

Kris watches him board the train. Short black hair peaking out from underneath a baseball cap and a neatly trimmed beard and moustache. He has light brown skin and wide hazel eyes. Asian. Probably Indian, or possibly Pakistani. Kris wonders if he is high on drugs. He wears a dark blue hoodie over a white T-shirt, with baggy tracksuit trousers and scuffed trainers, and struggles with a large olive-green rucksack. Everyone else is going about their business with briefcases, handbags or small packs. This man looks as if he is equipped for a hiking expedition. Kris thinks about offering to help, but other passengers pile on and he is pushed backwards. By the time he regains his balance, the man has made it on to the train and settled by the doorway.

The train starts to move and the man puts a protective hand on his rucksack. He leans against the screen by the doors breathing heavily and perspiration glistens on his forehead. Kris looks him up and down. He doesn't want to be rude but there is something about the man's demeanour which draws him in. The man seems ill at ease, shifting from one foot to another, constantly looking down at his pack as if to check it is still there. His vigilance seems unnecessary; the rucksack is so obviously heavy that it is inconceivable that any other passenger could sneak off with it.

The man looks up and catches Kris staring at him. Undeterred, Kris holds his gaze and the man turns away. The train is full with morning commuters. A girl reads *The Kite Runner* by Khaled Hosseini. Beside her, two large men are shoehorned into seats next to each other. Kris winces – it looks uncomfortable – as the men's bellies and thighs jostle against each other for space.

The train pulls into a station and the doors open. Kris

moves aside to allow some passengers to get off. The Asian man takes his opportunity and moves to a seat that has just been vacated, taking his rucksack with him and placing it between his knees. One of the large men gets up and moves across to the adjacent seat, where he will have more space. He brings a briefcase with him that he sets on the floor next to the olive-green rucksack. The Asian man looks momentarily startled at this.

The carriage fills up as more passengers board the train and Kris is clamped tight between a tall, white man with earphones swaying his head to his music, and two bleached-blonde American girls who chatter about visiting Buckingham Palace. Kris tunes them out. He finds Americans loud and brash; they act as if they own the world.

Kris's mind starts to wander to the day ahead. He has a meeting at 9.30 and glances at his watch. It is coming up to 8.50 and he should be on time, provided there are no unforeseen delays on the tube. The train emerges into a station and Kris leans down to read the signs through the windows. They are at Edgware Road.

A number of passengers bump and barge their way off the train and only a few get on, so Kris suddenly has some breathing space. The two American girls are still next to him, squealing in his ear. He half turns away from them, thinking that he might try and find a seat, but the train jolts forward and he decides to stay put until the next stop. He finds his gaze alighting on the Asian man again. The man is fiddling with the top of his rucksack, reaching in for something, and then, as if in a dream, the floor of the train rises up and Kris is blinded by a burst of white light.

Mohammad Sidique Khan and the 7/7 London bombings

Mohammad Sidique Khan, known widely in his local Yorkshire community as Sid, was reputed to be the ringleader of the group of four men who perpetrated the terrorist attack on London on the morning of 7 July 2005. At thirty, he was the oldest of the four. The other three bombers were Shehzad Tanweer (twenty-two), Jermaine Lindsay, also known as Jamal (nineteen), and Hasib Hussain (eighteen). Khan was a youth worker and former teacher who lived in Dewsbury with his wife and fourteen-month-old daughter. He was viewed by many in his community as a mentor and role model. At the time of the bombings, his wife, Hasina, was pregnant, although she suffered a miscarriage later that day.

On the morning of the bombings, Khan, Tanweer and Hussain drove from Leeds to meet Lindsay (who lived in Aylesbury) at Luton train station. From there, they took a train to King's Cross station in London, where they were seen hugging each other in a state of euphoria on the concourse. They each carried heavy rucksacks containing explosives.

Khan boarded a westbound Circle line train, Tanweer an eastbound Circle line train and Lindsay a southbound Piccadilly line train. It is thought that Hussain intended to catch a northbound tube train, but perhaps due to delays or possibly an issue with his detonator (Hussain was seen buying a new nine-volt battery at WH Smith in King's Cross), Hussain is instead thought to have caught a number 91 bus to Euston before switching to a number 30 bus travelling east from Marble Arch.

At about 8.50am the three tube train bombers detonated their packs. Khan killed six people soon after his train left Edgware Road station. Tanweer killed seven people between Liverpool Street and Aldgate stations. Lindsay killed twenty-six people between King's Cross and Russell Square. The deeper, narrower tunnel of the Piccadilly line compared to the Circle line concentrated the blast leading to the higher number of fatalities. Approximately one hour later, at 9.47am, Hussain detonated his pack on the top deck of the number 30 bus in Tavistock Square, killing 13 people.

Nearly two months after the bombings, a video was broadcast by Al Jazeera where Khan explains his motivation. It is thought that the tape was recorded during a three-month trip made by Khan and Tanweer to Pakistan in late 2004/early 2005, during which it seems that the two linked up with representatives of Al-Qaida. *Speaking directly to camera in a Yorkshire accent, Khan reads from a pre-prepared statement and justifies the attack with the following words:*

'Your democratically elected governments continuously perpetuate atrocities against my people all over the world. And your support of them makes you directly responsible, just as I am directly responsible for protecting and avenging my Muslim brothers and sisters. Until we feel security you will be our targets and until you stop the bombing, gassing, imprisonment and torture of my people we will not stop this fight. We are at war and I am a soldier. Now you too will taste the reality of this situation.'

A further video came to light, recorded by Khan in November 2004, before his trip to Pakistan. He is seen cradling his baby daughter, Maryam, and it appears that Khan was not originally planning to return to the UK from this trip, as the video is a farewell message to her. Khan says:

'I absolutely love you to bits and you have been the happiest thing in my life... I just wish I could have been part of your life, especially these growing up... these next months, they're really special with you learning to walk and things. I just so much wanted to be with you but I have to do this thing for our future and it will be the best, inshallah, in the long run... Look after your mother, she needs looking after, Maryam, keep strong. Learn to fight. Fighting is good.'

One survivor of the Edgware Road bombings, John Tulloch, was famously photographed emerging from the tube station with his head bandaged, his face bloody and burnt, and wearing a mauve blanket around his shoulders. Tulloch was sitting within a few feet of Khan when he detonated his backpack and went on to write a book about his experience, entitled One Day in July: Experiencing 7/7. In the book, Tulloch writes a letter to Mohammad Sidique Khan.

'On 7 July 2005, you tried to kill me. You personally killed six others in my carriage and your accomplice 'soldiers' killed many more. I recall three images of you. One is only in my memory, because, despite my uncertainty when I gave the police my report of the explosion you caused, I am now fairly certain we looked at each other across the second carriage of that train.'

Marylebone Road

We are walking along the Marylebone Road, past Baker Street tube and the Globe Tavern. It is gone midnight, but Saturday night drinkers are still spilling out of the pub onto the pavement. It is dry now, but I get the impression a few drops of rain wouldn't have sent them inside, as most of them are puffing away on cigarettes. I could forego the cigarette but I would love to stop for a beer. Annie reads my mind.

'No time for that. Besides, it will make you feel worse for the second half. Still thirteen miles to go you know.'

'Thanks for reminding me,' I say.

At least the plaster has eased the pain from my burst blister and I am walking a bit easier now. I decide to plunge in with Annie.

'I'm sorry. I must be boring you banging on about Summer all the time. Do you want to talk about Peter?'

Annie turns to me and passes her hands across her face. There is sadness in her blue eyes and I can tell that she is wondering whether to open a Pandora's box of painful memories.

'It's OK if you...' I start.

'That's very sweet of you, but I should talk about it. I haven't really spoken to anyone since he died. Not about what I feel anyway.'

'And what do you feel?'

'Peter was my twin brother, but he was more than that. He was my best friend. We spoke to each other every day.'

'Twin. Wow! That must be especially hard.'

'He liked to call me his little sister. He was born a few minutes before me.'

'And I suppose he used to look after his little sister?'

'Always. In the playground, at school, whenever we were out together. It was annoying sometimes and I was convinced it used to put off boyfriends, having Peter hanging on my shoulder, but I knew he was only looking out for me. Sometimes, even now, I turn round and expect to see him – in the street, in a bar, in a shop, in my sitting room – but he's never there. All I see instead is a big Peter-shaped hole where he should be standing.'

'When did he die?'

'Last Christmas. On Christmas Day. We sat by his bed and opened presents. He was so weak we had to open the parcels for him and hold them up for him to see. It was a charade really. Buying him presents when we all knew he only had days or weeks to live, but it had been his goal – to see one final Christmas – so we had to do it properly.'

'What did you get him, if you don't mind me asking?'

I can see her face hardening with the effort of talking about her brother.

'No, that's fine.' She struggles to speak. 'I put together a photo book. Pictures of our family, his friends, the people who he knew best in life. I spent weeks getting it all together. On the last page, there was a picture of the two of us celebrating our twenty-first birthday. It was one of his favourite photos. We were drinking champagne and we each had one arm around the other. It was nothing special. We looked goofy.'

'That sounds like a wonderful present.'

I cannot begin to fathom the pain of losing a twin.

'You know, it was as much a present for me as for him. Something for me to remember Peter by.'

'I think that makes it even more special. And I'm sure he understood that.'

'I wasn't there when he died. I had gone to the hospital café to get a coffee and when I got back, my mum just got up and gave me a hug and I knew he had gone. I felt terrible. I was with him when he was born, but not when he died.'

'That wasn't really your fault.'

'I know, but it doesn't make it any better. The photo album was on the bed, open at the last page, the two of us grinning like idiots for the camera. I like to think that picture was in his head when he closed his eyes for the last time.'

Her shoulders begin to shake and I put my arm round her.

It feels like the right thing to do. She wipes the tears from her cheeks with her sleeve.

'Come on,' she urges, 'almost halfway. Peter would tell us to stop being mushy and get on with it.'

I don't answer. We have passed Madame Tussauds and the mess of a road junction at the top of Great Portland Street and now we are approaching Warren Street tube station. In the process, the thirteen-mile halfway marker has come and gone. I had expected much whooping and hollering from various purple-clad volunteers at this milestone, but instead it was just a number on a lamppost that we plodded past without ceremony. Ahead of us are the sea-green windows of University College Hospital.

University College Hospital

Tuesday 24 July 2012

I loitered nervously in the atrium of University College Hospital, clutching my small bunch of pink and white freesias as if my life depended on it. The reception area was full and the plastic seating provided was inadequate for the number of visitors and patients milling around. Occasionally, a member of hospital staff in green overalls would identify a patient and help them to the lifts or the exit doors, presumably depending on whether they were pre- or post-treatment. Their overalls bore badges denoting them as 'Patient Transport'.

I walked unsteadily up to the perspex-fronted reception desk. It had been nearly four months now and I was scared. The perspex was the colour of runny sick. The receptionist peered over her spectacles and tapped on her keyboard.

'Thirteenth floor, room 1311,' she said matter-of-factly.

I felt like I was glued to the floor.

The receptionist adjusted her glasses.

'You can go up.' She gestured to the lift.

'Er, OK. Thanks.'

She frowned at me and I jolted my heavy feet into action. It was a hot day and despite their T-shirts and shorts people were sweltering in the glass atrium; summer had arrived. The thought spurred me on, and I walked purposefully to the lift lobby.

My resolve faltered as I approached room 1311, which was more of a wide corridor than a room. My grip was so tight that I must have been crushing the life out of the freesias. I had purposely got the pink and white flowers to match the posy held by Princess Diana when she wore the dress that Summer and I saw in the V&A. The reference was a bit obscure, but in my mind it gave my offering additional meaning. I gulped some air, which smelt strongly of disinfectant, and walked forward.

There were six beds, and a woman sat by the nearest one wearing a hijab, gaily decorated with birds of paradise, and an electric blue trouser suit with a satin sheen that reflected the glare of the hospital lights. I could see at once where Summer got her love of bright colours. She turned a pale face towards me and her mouth creased into a smile.

'Hello,' I mumbled, holding my flowers pathetically. 'I'm Ben.'

She pointed to the bed and I looked over in trepidation. Summer was propped up with her dark hair splayed across the crisp white pillows. A drip was attached to her left arm. She had lost weight and her cheekbones were even more prominent than before. She looked at me and my legs gave way, so that I half stumbled towards her and had to reach for the bed to support myself, dropping the flowers on to the floor as I did so. Her lips parted and she broke into a huge, white-toothed Summer smile.

'Well, you took your time,' she said.

I took her hand in mine and felt the bones in her fingers. Her fingernails were perfectly manicured with purple nail varnish. It was typical of Summer to make an effort, even when she was in hospital for an operation.

'Are you going to say something?' she laughed.

I held her skinny hand to my cheek.

'Summer, I'm... so... sorry.'

It was inadequate, but there was nothing else to say.

Summer squeezed my hand.

'It was me that ran away, silly.'

'I know, but I could have stopped you. I just... I just wasn't thinking straight.'

'I never blamed you, Ben.'

Behind us, I could hear her mother rising from her chair.

'I should introduce you,' Summer said. 'Mum, this is my idiot of a boyfriend, Ben.'

My heart leapt. Summer still referred to me as her boyfriend.

I lowered Summer's arm gently on the covers and stood up to shake her mother's outstretched hand.

'It's good to meet you after all this time,' she said. 'Summer never stops talking about you. At least, now I can see what all the fuss is about.'

I hung my head, embarrassed.

'It's good to meet you too, Mrs…'

'Chandra,' she finished my sentence for me. 'I'm afraid I never had Summer's confidence to change my surname. But you can call me Fiona. At least I kept my English first name.'

I nodded. I felt inadequate in front of this woman. I had abandoned her daughter when she needed me most.

'I'll go and get a glass of water or something,' she said. 'Leave you two for a while.'

She leant over and kissed Summer on the forehead.

'Just ten minutes, darling. You still need to rest.'

Summer smiled at her.

'I love you, Mum.'

When she was gone, I rescued the flowers from the floor and put them on a table at the foot of the bed.

'They're like the Princess Diana flowers,' Summer said, and I felt a warmth inside me. Summer and I always thought the same thoughts. 'They're lovely. We'll ask a nurse to get some water for them later.'

I pulled up a chair and stared at her for a few seconds. Her long, glossy hair. Her chocolate-drop eyes. Her honey-coloured skin. Apart from the thinness in her face, it was hard to believe that she was so ill.

'Do I look OK?' she asked, tentatively.

'You look amazing,' I replied. 'How are you?'

'As well as can be expected for someone who has had half her right breast removed.'

'It doesn't matter to me,' I reassured her. 'All that matters is that you get better and come back. Will you do that? Will you come and live with me?'

Summer's face sagged.

'You know it's not that simple, Ben.'

I was ready for this.

'I've been thinking about it ever since you left. I want you to come and live with me. I need you to come and live with me. You and everything that comes with you.'

She looked at me suspiciously.

'Everything?'

'Everything.' I fumbled in my pocket and pulled out the bracelet that she had attached to Buster's collar that day in Hyde Park, setting it down on the table by her bed. The silver letters – S and B – spread out either side of the tiny heart.

'And I want you to have this back. It belongs to you.'

I leant over to kiss her and suddenly she had her arms around my neck, pulling me down on to her. The movement ripped the drip from her arm, but neither of us cared. I fell on to the bed and kissed her more passionately this time. I remembered the taste of fresh peaches.

Behind us, someone gave a dry cough.

'Now, now.' I rolled off the bed and was confronted by a concerned-looking nurse.

'Sir, Miss Meadows is recovering from an operation. We do need to be gentle with her.'

She spied the drip hanging loose and grimaced at me.

'These things are here for a reason,' she said, moving round to the side of the bed to attach it to Summer's arm again.

And then she noticed that Summer was crying. Fat, Asian monsoon tears flopping down her cheeks.

The nurse scowled at me.

'Is everything alright, Miss Meadows?' she asked.

Summer choked back the tears.

'Everything is wonderful, nurse.'

'I had never met her mother before that day. Summer was always very secretive about her family life.'

'What was she like?'

'She was amazing. I had a coffee with her after I left Summer in the hospital. She should have been annoyed with me that I'd let her daughter down, but she was the opposite. One of the kindest, gentlest people I have ever met.'

'You were the guy her daughter loved. You had to have something about you.'

I am not so sure.

'Maybe. It didn't seem so obvious at the time but I suppose it was her who called me, so it wasn't as if she didn't want me to see Summer again. She found my number on Summer's mobile.'

'And told you which hospital she was in?'

'Yes. And what was happening and when to visit. I owe her everything.'

A blaze of light and a throng of people mark the next pit stop and I am on familiar territory. Through the wrought iron gates that mark the Gower Street main entrance, between the two lodges and into the Main Quad of UCL. In the dark, it is hardly recognisable as the elegant cloistered courtyard I remember from my student days. The Octagon dome of the Wilkins Building is silhouetted against the night sky and in front of the famous portico is a row of temporary stalls bearing gifts for the Shine walkers.

Rhianna blares out from a pair of speaker stacks to our right and a group of dancers are performing a routine with umbrellas, complete with exaggerated furling, twirling and unfurling. They look disappointed that we haven't had more of a downpour.

To the left of the stalls is a U-shaped block of temporary toilets and Annie and I head for those. The Shine walkers have bunched up at this pit stop and there must be 200 or so milling around the Quad, looking faintly disturbing with their glow sticks and coloured wigs. We have to queue for the toilets, behind a group of pink-wigged women of a certain age who take photos of each other in various poses before Annie offers to take one of the four of them together. They stand there grinning and holding two fingers up in Churchillian style, looking proud as punch, with a row of green plastic toilet cubicles in the background.

After we have relieved ourselves, I sit on a bench and take a look at my feet. The plaster is still in place on the toe of my right foot and the blister throbs, but I think it should be fine. My left heel is beginning to feel sore as well, rubbing on my trainer. It looks a little red, but I can't see a blister forming as yet, so I decide to leave it for now.

Annie returns from the various stalls with Tracker bars, water and apples. I take a swig of water and bite into an apple, risking the skin-stuck-in-the-teeth outcome. It is one in the morning and I don't feel like eating a lot – just something to keep my energy levels up. We sit in silence for a few minutes amongst the hubbub of the Shine crowd and I scan the buildings around the Quad. It is seven years since I stepped into this space as an eager history undergraduate. I thought I was grown-up, leaving my family home to make my mark on the world but, of course, I still had a lot of growing up to do.

University College London

Monday 18 September 2006

It was the first day of term and as a keen freshman, I was up early for two worthy but dry lectures on eighteenth-century imperialism and modern international politics. Now it was lunchtime, and overwhelmed by the crowd of students buzzing around the counters in the Refectory, I grabbed the first pack of sandwiches I could see. I felt as if everyone but me knew what to do, where they were going, who they were with. I paid for the sandwiches – tuna and sweetcorn – and a can of Coke, and looked desperately around.

I was relieved to spot a group of first years I recognised from the Freshers' Fair and I wandered over. Four or five of them were lounging on and around one of the red plastic-effect sofas and as I approached I could see that a girl was holding their attention. She was Asian, or mixed race possibly, with light brown skin and dark, dark brown hair – almost black – that tumbled down her shoulders and back. She wore an orange top and a bright pink skirt that on anyone else would have clashed horribly, but on her seemed to be made to wear together. Her vibrant colours contrasted strikingly with the dull blues, blacks and browns that the rest of us were wearing. She was talking animatedly, her hands waving in front of her to emphasise her points. I couldn't hear what she was saying but the small group of first years were captivated. I tapped the nearest boy on the shoulder who swivelled around and with immense sophistication I managed to say, 'Hi.'

'Hi,' he responded, before turning back to the girl, who was now getting up to leave. She flashed a smile and for a moment I kidded myself that she was directing it at me, even though I had only just broken into the group.

'Anyways. Got to hurry people. See you all later.' She swung a rucksack on to her back and the group parted to let

146

her exit. Several pairs of eyes, including mine, watched her sashay across the room.

'Hey, Ben, how was your morning?' One of the students recognised me and I remembered his name was Chas.

'Fine, yeah, thanks, Chas. The lecturers won't be winning anything at the Comedy Awards but they were OK. You?'

'Just one lecture. Then we've been hanging out here.'

My eyes flicked back to the girl who was now almost out of sight.

'She's quite something, hey?' Chas noticed my glance.

'Who is she?' I asked, trying to sound nonchalant.

'Summer Meadows. She's studying politics. I'm surprised you don't know her.'

'Summer Meadows?' I laughed. 'Is she for real?'

'Absolutely.' Chas was deadly serious. 'Everybody's talking about Summer.'

University College London

Monday 2 February 1903

Henry stands stiffly to one side of the room, between Ernest Starling and Scuttle. He estimates that there are fifty students observing the experiment, mostly eager young men not much younger than Henry himself, who hang on to Bayliss' every word and movement, but also a few women who appear equally interested. Two ladies in particular, sitting on the second row, are taking copious notes. They wear oversized hats in the modern style and the people behind them have to crane their necks for a view.

Henry can tell that the experiment is not going well. Bayliss has been fiddling with his electrodes for twenty minutes or so to little effect, the dog squirming and whimpering as he does so. Henry is pleased the dog is fitted with a muzzle as it mutes the sounds of the unfortunate animal. They had injected the dog with morphine earlier in the day, and are topping this up with alcohol and chloroform during the procedure, but Henry still has the uncomfortable sensation that the dog is in pain. He reminds himself that this is in the interests of scientific progress, but judging by Bayliss' fumblings and frustrated grunts, it seems that there is little progress being made today. The dog, a scruffy, tan-coloured mongrel, has certainly suffered in the name of science. Henry is aware that Starling operated on the animal two months previously, examining its pancreas, since when the dog has been confined to a small cage in the lab. Strictly, Bayliss should not be performing a second procedure on the same animal.

Bayliss gives a great sigh and disconnects the electrodes. He stands back, drawing himself up to his full height – he is not a tall man – and faces his audience from behind the operating table.

'Ladies and Gentlemen, I am sorry but this is the end of

our experiment today. I apologise, but I have been unable to demonstrate my theory regarding the nervous system. However, I assure you that this in no way means the theory is incorrect, merely that I was unable to prove it today. I will now hand the dog over to Mr Dale, who will put it out of its misery.'

There is a murmuring amongst the students as Bayliss pushes the board holding the dog across the operating table in Henry's direction.

'Over to you, Dale,' he says quietly. 'Do what you have to do.'

Henry edges past Starling, who whispers in his ear.

'The pancreas, boy.'

Henry stands over the dog. He wants to end it there and then but first he has to comply with Starling's wishes. He selects a thin, surgeon's scalpel from the instruments on the table in front of him and carefully unclamps the wound Starling had made earlier.

The dog wriggles and lets out a low moan.

'For pity's sake!' A voice rises in the audience, but Henry ignores it and focuses on his work. He removes the dog's tiny pancreas and sets it in a bowl, then glances up at Starling who gives him a nod of approval.

Henry looks down at the poor dog. Underneath the muzzle, it is panting heavily, straining for breath. He had planned to put the dog slowly to sleep by increasing the flow of anaesthetic, but when he looks into its dull eyes, Henry knows that he should finish everything now. He puts down the scalpel and picks up a larger, butcher's knife. There is a small gasp from the audience and he hesitates.

'Go on, boy,' Bayliss urges from his side.

Henry closes his eyes in a moment of reflection, then opens them and thrusts the knife into the dog's heart.

University College London

Monday 2 October 2006

I was standing in the South Hall contemplating Bentham's auto-icon when I heard a voice.

'I don't know about you, but that thing gives me the creeps.'

A shiver of excitement shimmied through me as I realised that Summer Meadows was standing next to me. Better still, she had dropped her backpack to the floor and was obviously going to stay and talk.

'It fascinates me,' I replied. 'The history of it, and everything.'

The auto-icon is a macabre object. The philosopher, Jeremy Bentham, decreed in his will that his body should be dissected in the name of science and that, once all the soft parts had been dealt with, his skeleton should be dressed in his clothes and topped off with his head, preserved in the manner of the 'New Zealanders'. The ensemble was then to be placed on one of Bentham's wooden chairs, along with his walking stick – which he called 'Dapple' – and showcased in an appropriate box. Bentham envisaged that his friends and followers might organise regular meetings to celebrate his memory, at which he instructed that his auto-icon, a name he coined, should be present. In modern parlance, we might conclude that Bentham was a bit up himself.

In any event, things didn't quite pan out in the manner he envisaged. The doctor entrusted with the various tasks was a friend of Bentham's, Dr Southwood Smith, who in accordance with the terms of the will was forced to carry out a public dissection of Bentham's body, after first delivering a lecture to the medical students present while standing over the corpse. According to accounts, during this ordeal, Southwood Smith was as white as the sheet that half-covered the dead Bentham in front of him.

After the lecture, Southwood Smith went on to preserve the head. However, he botched this, and quickly concluded that the gruesome result – bloodied, blackened and with the skin stretched so taut that the head had less expression than an ageing Hollywood star with one too many facelifts – was unsuitable for public display. Hence, he commissioned a wax replica of the head which he attached to the top of the skeleton. Bizarrely, Southwood Smith seems to have wrapped the real mummified head in cloth and left it inside the trunk of the skeleton, presumably thinking that two heads were better than one, even if one of them did look like a chargrilled toffee apple.

The skeleton and wax head were then dressed in Bentham's clothes, stuffed with straw and topped with an oversized hat, as per the stipulations of the will, and placed on a chair with Dapple, the carved walking stick, inside a wooden cabinet. Bentham's auto-icon was thus created.

Presumably, the annual convention of his followers that Bentham had foreseen did not come to fruition, for Southwood Smith kept the auto-icon in a corner of his rooms for some eighteen years, first in New Broad Street and then Finsbury Square, before eventually offering it to UCL in 1850. Now instead of his 'Disciples', as Bentham had modestly called them, being the beneficiaries of the philosopher's gift to posterity, Bentham was subject to permanent scrutiny by a never-ending stream of passing students in the corridors of UCL.

'You know it's not his real head, don't you?'

'Ooh,' Summer grabbed me by the arm and shudders, 'does that mean it's his real body?'

I quivered involuntarily at her touch. She smelt faintly of orange blossom.

'Yes, it's him alright. Or at least, his bones. The clothes are his too, filled out with straw. But the head is wax.'

'What happened to his real head?'

'The body was left to a doctor on condition that he create this auto-icon with the skeleton and preserve his head to go on top. Unfortunately, he made a right Horlicks of it. By the time he finished, the skull looked more like a scorched walnut than a human head.'

'Ooh,' she giggled, 'so he went for a wax version instead.'

'Yes, although, believe it or not, the real head is still around. In fact, it's here at UCL, locked away in the archaeological department. You don't want to see it though. It's pretty disgusting.'

'Errgh.' She let go of my arm and I felt a tinge of disappointment. 'How do you know all this?'

'It's just something I do. I look things up, research them, find out their stories. I love the unusual stories. I like to imagine how things were, what people felt, what they said. I guess that's why I'm studying history.'

'What else do you know about him?' She gestured towards the figure.

'Bentham? He was a philosopher, a utilitarian. Very famous in his time. You would probably know his principle of the greatest good. That a state should strive for the greatest happiness of the greatest number. He also believed that education should be for all, regardless of creed, race, gender, which was radical in those days. The college was founded on his principles, although the funny thing is he personally had nothing to do with UCL.'

'So, why is he here?' She tipped her head seductively. I knew I was babbling on, but she seemed interested.

'Just one of those things. The doctor kept the auto-icon in his rooms for years; I like to picture him seeing patients with this thing staring at them over his shoulder. Must have been a bit disconcerting. Perhaps he had too many complaints because eventually he grew tired of having Bentham as a roommate and donated it to UCL.'

'I'm not surprised. He must have put off a lot of patients. I would have found another surgery.'

'You know, the doctor was a friend of Charles Dickens. They used to discuss the social issues of the East End in front of this thing. Wouldn't you have loved to be a fly on the wall at those sessions? Fascinating.'

She laughed. 'I think it would have been funny to see the look on the doctor's face when he turned his friend's head into, what did you say, a scorched walnut?'

'Maybe. He must have had one of those moments when he looked at it and just thought... well, you know...'

'Fuck!' She grinned as she finished my sentence and I was oddly aroused by her using the F word. It made her seem real, less like a fairy-tale princess. 'You should write all this down, you know,' she continued. 'The stories, how you imagine things happened.'

'Should I?' I shrugged my shoulders. 'Who would read it? It's a bit obtuse.'

'I would read it. I think it's interesting.'

'I might test you on that one day.'

She leant over and pecked me on the cheek.

'I like to be tested,' she said, picking up her bag and swinging it over her shoulder. She walked away without looking back. I remained rooted to the spot, rubbing my cheek and catching make-believe flies in my gaping mouth.

Webb Street

Monday 11 June 1832

Southwood Smith clamps the head in place. The skin feels waxy through his surgical gloves, but decay has not yet set in. Since dismembering the body on Friday, he has kept the head packed in ice.

He moves to the front to check the positioning and grinds his teeth in distaste. As a doctor, he is used to corpses, but they are usually intact and do not generally belong to his good friends. To see Bentham's disembodied face, floating unsupported by any neck or trunk and gazing at him with black holes where his eyeballs used to be, renders him a little uneasy.

His mind drifts back to the horrors of the previous Friday when he had been required to dissect the body during the course of a lecture. He had agreed to all this, of course, when he and Bentham had concocted their plan two years earlier and it had seemed a sterling idea at the time. Bentham would bequeath his body to the advancement of medical science, and in so doing would give the lie to the misguided argument that cadavers should not be available to doctors for study. Southwood Smith was all in favour; medical professionals required real human specimens to work upon in order to further their knowledge of the workings of the human body. How else would medicine progress?

Nevertheless, the reality of performing a lecture over the corpse of his friend and subsequently dissecting the body in front of an audience of students had tested him greatly. He stumbled over his oration on a number of occasions, fighting back the bile that threatened to erupt from his throat. When he performed the vivisection, he insisted that Bentham's face was covered to give himself the illusion of carving up the organs of an anonymous donor. He placed the heart, liver, kidneys and lungs in glass receptacles, holding them up for inspection by the audience. He would seek to preserve them later.

When it came to the head, he could not perform the procedure. Instead, he bade his assistant to saw through the spine, while he discreetly took a position at the rear of the platform, turning his back to the audience to retch at the rasping sound of the saw teeth on bone.

There was no avoiding the next step, however, and so here he is, seeking to preserve the head according to Bentham's wishes. The chosen method of preservation is that of the style of the ancient New Zealanders, who drained the fluids from the heads of the deceased. Southwood Smith has constructed an apparatus to hold an airpump over the head, which he will use to draw out the fluids through a hole drilled into the skull. To aid the process, the head is clamped over a saucer of sulphuric acid.

He operates the airpump by hand, like a set of bellows. Placing a mask over his head to dilute the smell of camphor – after death, Bentham's whole body had been doused in the stuff in an effort to delay the onset of decay – he begins to squeeze the pump handles together in a gentle rhythm. A tube leads from the pump to a large, ceramic bowl, and after a few seconds, a fatty, clear liquid starts to drip into the basin.

Smith keeps this up for a good ten minutes, and then stops to examine his handiwork. He tentatively probes Bentham's left cheek, but it still feels squashy. He knows from his studies that the New Zealanders rendered their heads as hard as nuts, so he resumes his pumping with increased vigour.

The process takes all morning, during which Southwood Smith stops several times for a rest and to check the head. He is a little disconcerted; the flesh is becoming increasingly marked as it dries, and the skin is tightening, rendering Bentham expressionless. He continues, however; it is important to drain all the fluids otherwise rot will inevitably set in.

Eventually, just before lunch – not that Southwood Smith feels like eating after his gruesome morning's work – the flow of liquids falling from the tube into the basin as he pumps slows to occasional drips. He prods the skin one more time – it is as tight as a drum – and he is satisfied that his work is done.

He sets the airpump and the apparatus holding it in place to one side, and moves to the front to view the preserved head. He can't restrain a sharp gasp when he sees the results.

'For the love of God!' He speaks aloud, even though there is no one in the room to hear.

Bentham's head is shrivelled to half the size it was, but worse, it is as if it has been subjected to a furnace hotter than hell itself. The skin looks burnt, a macabre patchwork of black and red scorchmarks, and Bentham's face is fixed forever into a tight-lipped grimace. A few remaining wisps of grey hair straggle the top of the skull, which is otherwise bald.

Southwood Smith pulls a tray towards him and picks up two false eyes of deepest blue. They were selected by Bentham himself for the skull, who used to delight in bringing them out at dinner parties to amuse his guests. Southwood Smith hopes that, when in place, they will make the preserved head a little more presentable. He slots them into the eye sockets with some difficulty, as the holes have shrunk along with the rest of the head.

He stands back once more. The blue eyes bulge from Bentham's deformed face and it is as if the ghost of Bentham is accusing him from beyond the grave. Without warning, his chest begins to heave, and he turns away from the head just in time. He vomits – a gush of olive-green sick that rises from the depths of his stomach and splashes on the laboratory floor.

University College London

Sunday 15 October 2006

It was an Indian summer of a day and UCL students had spilled out on to the grass in the Quad. I was sitting on my own, making notes from Parsons' *The British Imperial Century* and catching a few sunbeams. It was not a day to be confined to the library. Around me, my fellow students were spread out in small groups, chatting, making out, eating, drinking, smoking. I seemed to be the only sad single but I was OK with that. I had an essay to write and I could do without wasting a few hours in inane student conversation, invariably a futile exploration of the meaning of life.

I was three weeks into my college existence and was beginning to find my feet. I had joined the History Society and was turning out in the undistinguished left back position for the college fourth football team. Played three, won one, drawn one, lost one; so mid-table mediocrity – a pretty accurate description of my time so far at UCL. The myriad of people I had met in Freshers' Week had been whittled down to a core group of friends who shared a similar sense of humour and view on life. We had discovered the college film club and a few of us were planning to see *Breakfast at Tiffany's* that evening – at least, I would join them if I could get my essay out of the way. I loved the timeless romance of those old classic movies. And further afield, Bar Andalucia in Whitfield Street was a popular meeting place, where we cash-strapped students grazed on shared plates of tapas rather than commit to three-course meals at London prices.

I was captivated by London. It was a city full of infinite possibilities and I was inspired by its history. Every building, every square, every street, every park held a story, and new stories were added every day. London was a place that gave me hope, that its future would be even more incredible than its past, where amazing people would achieve amazing things. UCL was full of bright-eyed students looking to stamp their own imprint on the world and I was daunted by the notion that so many brilliant people had passed through the college's cloisters. I only hoped I would make a decent fist of life so that I didn't fail their legacy totally.

I scanned my book. After this chapter I would start my response to the question 'Was British colonialism in the nineteenth century a force for good?' The answer, of course, was 'yes and no', but I needed to flesh out that trite response into four or five pages of A4.

'Do you mind if I sit with you?'

I looked up to see Summer Meadows standing over me, wearing a rainbow-striped bikini top and a cream linen skirt that showed off the deep bronze colour of her legs. She eased a hessian bag off her shoulder, put it down on the grass, and smiled. No one could resist that smile – not even a dedicated student with an essay to write.

'Sure,' I said, pathetically. I wished I was more eloquent, but the words didn't come.

She curled her long legs underneath her and lowered herself gently to the grass.

'Are you studying?' She glanced at my book.

'Yes. Essay crisis, I'm afraid.'

'Oh,' she frowned, 'I can go away if you like.'

'No, no,' I said, quickly. 'Please, stay. It's good to have a distraction.'

She smiled again, with her beautiful straight teeth.

'Is that what I am? A distraction?'

'No, that's not what…' I stopped. 'Well, actually, you are. A welcome distraction.'

'Thank you,' she said. 'I will take that as a compliment. I'm…'

'Summer, I know. We talked in front of Jeremy Bentham.'

'Aah. I wasn't sure you would remember that.'

I blushed. Of course I remembered.

'Would you do me a favour?' she asked.

'Absolutely. Within reason.'

'Oh no. You can't qualify. It's either a yes or a no.' She was teasing me.

'OK then.' I folded my book and took up her challenge. 'Yes.'

She rummaged in her bag and pulled out a bottle of sun cream.

'Do you mind rubbing this into my back?'

I rocked backwards.

'It's alright,' she said, 'I don't bite.'

'It's just that...'

'Well, if you'd rather not do it, I can find someone else, although you did say...'

'No, no, it's fine. I was... it's just a bit... well, you hardly know me.'

'Are you saying that you're a bit weird?'

'I...'

She was laughing. Well, if that's how she wanted to play it, I was game if she was.

She lay on her front and I squeezed some lotion on to the small of her back. She flinched as the cold cream dropped on to her in an untidy splodge. I leant over and began to smooth it gently into her skin. It crossed my mind that her olive colouring meant that she probably didn't need protection against the last embers of a dying English summer, but I quickly suppressed the thought.

'I think you need to straddle me,' she muttered into the grass, 'then you can knead it in properly.'

I hesitated and she sensed this immediately, turning her head slightly.

'Unless you feel awkward about it.'

'No, no,' I spluttered, swinging my left leg over her back so that I was now on top of her, one knee on the grass either side.

I squeezed another blob of sun cream into my palms, and as I did so, her hands snaked round and undid the strings of her bikini top. All of her back was now exposed and, as her top fell away, I saw the tantalising swell of her breasts to each side. I tried to ignore the stirrings down below and concentrated on my task. I spread the sun cream by running my hands lightly down her shoulder blades and performing palm circles on her lower back. I gradually increased the pressure and then I placed both hands on her and dug my thumbs into her flesh. As I moved them upwards, I pinched her muscles between my thumbs and fingers and she squealed.

'Is that OK?'

'That's more than OK,' she mumbled. 'Please, go on. Make sure you get the sides.'

I stroked the tops of her shoulders and compressed the shoulder muscles at the base of her neck. I ran my hands down the sides of her back, my fingertips brushing the fleshy slopes of her breasts and sending a shimmer of ecstasy through my body. She groaned and I traced my fingers back up her spine. I climbed off her, aroused, my skin tingling, decidedly uncomfortable.

'Oh, that was wonderful, thank you,' she breathed into the grass.

I heard a clatter of voices behind me.

'Hey, Ben. You dog. What are you doing to Summer?'

It was Chas, with a couple of other first years. I was suddenly desperately conscious of the bulge in my jeans and my face turning aubergine. I picked up Parsons and tried to focus on the words swimming before me.

'Just doing her a favour,' I mumbled into the book.

Summer turned her face towards me and winked.

Chas and the others sat down around us. They had brought a bottle of sparkling wine and plastic glasses.

'A beautiful day, we are beautiful people, we deserve a glass of bubbly,' announced Chas.

'Oh, sorry.' I was still embarrassed. 'I really must go, I have an essay to write.'

Chas was amused by the situation, the corners of his mouth turning upwards in a half-smile.

'Well, if you must be a swot. See you later, yeah, for the film.'

I stood up, stuffing my book into my bag.

'Yeah, hopefully. If I can get the essay done.'

I walked off slowly, my face still burning.

I could hear laughter behind me and then the pop of a cork as Chas opened the bottle.

University College Hospital

Tuesday 6 October 1953

John takes a step backwards when he sees her. She has the face of a skeleton, with bloodless skin stretched taut over her bones. Her hair is limp and pressed flat against her scalp and her irises have faded to a dull grey. Her painfully thin arms rest on the bedclothes, blotched red with sores. She notices him falter and smiles.

'Do I look that terrible, J.B.?'

He recovers himself and steps forward.

'I brought you these. I hope you like them.'

He thrusts forward a bouquet of ox eye daisies.

'They are lovely, J.B. Thank you. I will ask the nurse to put them in water later.'

'How are you, darling?' he asks, setting the flowers on the bedside table.

'Bored, J.B. Bored of being confined to this bed. But apart from that, I am fine. Bernie is an angel and deals with all my correspondence. And Win is a rock, of course.'

He sits down on a stool next to the bed.

'That is good, that is good.'

'And how about you? Do you have something for me for when I am well? I fancy singing the Chausson again.'

He picks up her hand; it weighs no more than his conductor's baton.

'Dearest Kaff. I will always have a piece for you to sing, you know that. And I would very much love to hear you sing the Chausson one more time.'

She laughs. A child-like laugh.

'Oh J.B., you are hopeless. I am not sure that I will ever get out of here. I am tired, very tired.'

He doesn't know what to say. The spectre of her death hangs over the room. It is not fair that this disease should claim such a wondrous gem as Kathleen.

'You know,' she continues, 'wouldn't it be lovely if I could just go to sleep and not wake up again?'

'You mustn't talk like that, Kaff. You will get better, I know it.'

She regards him with tired eyes.

'You always were a terrible fibber, J.B.'

'I'm not... I mean...' His words fade away. And then a thought rises within him. Would it be possible? 'Kaff? May I ask you something?'

'Don't be silly, J.B. You are one my closest friends. You may ask me anything, but I am afraid I am not in much of a state to...'

'Kaff,' he rushes his words, 'will you sing for me one more time?'

'What?' She looks at him as if he is a madman. 'Sing? Here? Now? In this room?'

He hangs his head. 'I'm sorry, Kaff. Insensitive of me. I shouldn't have asked.'

But even as he speaks the words, he sees a touch of colour flush in her ivory cheeks, and then she opens her mouth and begins to sing. Her voice fills the small room. It is hard to believe that her frail body can produce such a rich sound. She sings the first part of the 'Poème: La fleur des eaux'. John closes his eyes and imagines he is back in the Free Trade Hall, conducting Kathleen Ferrier and the Hallé Orchestra. He can hear the solo violin – *lento e misterioso* – and then with a point of his imaginary baton, he summons the flutes to enter, trickling like a mountain stream over the top of the violin strings. He raises his hand and the deep tones of the rest of the woodwind section rise up with it. A flick of his wrist and he adds the smooth notes of the horns and the trombones. Above them all floats the voice of the contralto – Kathleen Ferrier – effortless, controlled, achingly beautiful.

We pass through the gates and turn left down Gower Street. A sense of loss pulses through me at leaving UCL behind, but we are over halfway now and that thought cheers me somewhat. And Annie is still by my side; I haven't completely alienated her yet with my ramblings.

'So that was how your scrapbook got started?' she asks.

'Yes. All because of Summer. The story of Southwood Smith botching the preservation of Bentham's head was my first piece.'

'And you did others?'

'Loads. Usually when we visited somewhere. I liked doing the research.'

'I think that's beautiful.' Annie tips her head to one side. 'I would love someone to keep a scrapbook like that for me.'

'Maybe it sounds a bit more romantic than it was.' I hunch my shoulders, embarrassed. 'It's a bit of a hotchpotch of stuff. I looked up the definition of the word scrapbook once. "A collection of cuttings, scraps etcetera," the dictionary said. I guess my stories are in the etcetera category.'

'Well, I think you're underplaying it. I bet Summer loved it.'

'Yes, you're right.' I picture Summer now, sitting up in bed reading the book. The curse of the Deadly Purple Sapphire, the defection of Natalia Makarova, the story of the little brown dog that always made her cry. I turn back to Annie. 'I'm afraid I haven't written much since… well, since… you know.'

Annie says nothing. She knows.

'So what did you do when you left uni?' she asks after a few more steps, casually changing the subject.

'I started in an ad agency. It wasn't one of the big ones – those jobs were impossible to get – but a small one, with offices off Fleet Street.'

'How does a history degree get you into advertising?'

'Well, it doesn't really. But then history doesn't lead you into anything. I blagged pretty well in the interview, I think.'

'And did you enjoy it?'

'Yes – for a while. I was an account executive, which basically means dogsbody, running around doing the photocopying and getting the teas and coffees from Starbucks. I didn't do much creative stuff, which was disappointing, but we were a subsidiary of a bigger US company and so at least I worked on some big consumer brands.'

'Like?'

'Like… I don't know… like Meaty Beaty.'

'Meaty Beaty?'

'Kids' food. There was a jingle. "*Mea-tee, Bea-tee, it's a real trea-tee. Mea-tee, Bea-tee, kids love it for their tea*".'

Annie looks sceptical.

'I hope you didn't write that.'

'I wish I had. The bloke who did made a lot of money out of it. "*Mea-tee, Bea-tee, it's a real trea-tee.*" Kind of catchy if you're seven years old.'

Annie laughs. 'I'll take your word for it.'

We pass through Bedford Square with its uniform Georgian architecture around all four sides that somehow makes it seem squarer than other London squares. Beyond the square, the hulking flank of the British Museum rises alongside us and soon we are turning left into Great Russell Street.

British Museum

Tuesday 24 May 1983

The Greek Minister for Culture stubs out her cigarette, nods at the grey-suited Museum Director, and the delegation shuffles into the gallery. A reverent hush falls across the group as the friezes come into view, and all Raj can hear is the clacking of Melina Mercouri's shoes on the grey marble floor. He is towards the rear, notebook in hand, jostling with fellow journalists for position. In theory, the Director is hosting this staged event, but it is Mercouri that takes the lead, and the group fans out like an arrowhead behind her. She has spent her life putting on performances, and this is no different. The Director makes no attempt to hide his lack of enthusiasm, walking listlessly alongside one of his colleagues in Mercouri's shadow, staring down his long, thin nose at the floor. Raj read somewhere that he has described this visit as allowing the burglar to case the joint in advance.

After two more rows of Greek dignitaries and museum officials, comes the media. Television to the front with two crews from rival broadcasters pushing and shoving each other like thirsty drinkers at a crowded bar. Then comes the press. Broadsheets first – Raj recognises hacks from *The Times* and *The Telegraph* – behind them the redtops and finally, a smattering of lesser journos, mostly freelancers, desperate for the crumbs of a story that they can sell to keep the wolf from kicking down the door for another week. Raj has been commissioned to write a feature for a monthly news magazine; he needs to find an angle, as by the time the mag comes out the story will have been covered to death.

The photographers are not allowed into the gallery, the excuse being that the flashes of their cameras might damage the marbles, although as light floods unchecked through the high-windowed ceiling Raj suspects that the museum simply wishes to avoid pictures in the press of the Minister cosying up to a section of frieze and claiming it for Greece. The paparazzi stand as a dejected mob outside the doors, shoulders hunched in disappointment, cameras hanging limply from their necks. Raj thinks they have no need to worry. Melina Mercouri is a former actress, and she knows how to stage a show. They will get good pictures.

The group moves painfully slowly. Mercouri is examining every minute detail of every piece so there is no mistaking the importance of these artefacts to her and, of course, to Greece. Raj stares at one of the sculptures: a man, or possibly a god, with a muscular torso, a vacant expression and a pudding basin haircut. His hands and feet are missing. Raj is not sure whether the absent appendages are due to the ravages of over two millennia, carelessness on the part of Elgin and his men, or shoddy custodianship by the British Museum.

In any case, this is what all the fuss is about. The friezes and sculptures depicting an ancient Greek pageant and various battles are impressive given that they were chiselled out 500 years before Jesus Christ was born, but they do not really stir Raj's senses. Heads and limbs are missing, the marbles are discoloured and damaged, and the friezes are incomplete.

Raj has done his research. Approximately half of the surviving Parthenon pieces are housed here, in the British Museum. Of the rest, most are in Athens, but others are scattered around museums in various corners of Europe. It is one of the arguments against returning the marbles: that the Parthenon would not be made whole in any case. And surely it is better to exhibit them here, at eye-level in a pollution-free gallery that millions of people visit each year, than have them exposed to the acidic Athens air that will rapidly eat away at the stone. By most accounts, the marbles here in London are in considerably better condition than those that Elgin left at the Parthenon.

Mercouri stoops over the head of a horse. She mutters something to the Director, who purses his lips in a thin smile and nods. Mercouri traces her fingers lightly over the horse's head. Raj knows that she is feeling the smoothness of the marble, a privilege not afforded to the public who are banned from touching. The smooth whiteness of the marble is not good, however. Instead, it is the product of a disastrous renovation of the marbles in the thirties, when museum staff became over enthusiastic with their cleaning and polishing. In fact, the original horse had veins that stood out from the stone and a honey-coloured patina over its white marble base. Mercouri brings this unfortunate episode up on a regular basis. The British Museum claims that it is a better home for the preservation of these precious artefacts, she says, but just look at the vandalism perpetrated in the name of restoration, simply to make the marble silky smooth and milky white to appeal to sensitive visitors.

Mercouri finishes her examination and throws her head back. Her thick haystack of straw-coloured hair flips and twirls in the air, before settling back on her shoulders. By contrast, the Museum Director has a high forehead, receding grey hair and wire-wool eyebrows. He shakes his head despondently and moves on. Mercouri turns to the media scrum and grins with nicotine-stained teeth.

Raj writes two words in his notebook.

'No contest.'

The delegation continues around the gallery. Raj is squeezed between an overweight, tousle-haired veteran from *The Spectator*, sweating slightly in a shapeless mac, and a younger journo he doesn't recognise, who has a mop of floppy dark hair and scribbles profuse notes on each section of the frieze and every sculpture. Raj thinks he must be a freelancer, new to the profession, keen to make an impact. He has not yet become jaded by the relentless pursuit of the next story.

It occurs to Raj that there is little reason for them to be in the gallery at all. Mercouri is clearly not going to make any public statement in here, and none of the hacks, with the possible exception of the young, keen one, are in the least bit interested in the marbles themselves. They might as well be walking around a room decorated with flock wallpaper.

Mercouri drags the visit out for another forty-five minutes, and then leads the group out of the gallery. Immediately, she reaches into her bag and pulls out a packet of Marlboros, the signal for one of her aides to flick a lighter. She puts a cigarette between her lips and leans over to catch the flame. Raj notices the wrinkles around her mouth, her skin dry and stretched taut over her skull, the result of a lifetime of hot Mediterranean sun and sixty a day.

The Spectator hack takes his cue and pulls out a green and gold Rizla tin from the depths of his coat pocket. He opens the lid and fishes out a roll-up that he made earlier. Raj's nose twitches as the acrid stink of cigarette fumes fills his nostrils, with most of the other members of the media lighting up at the same time. They have endured nearly an hour without a drag and are gasping.

Ahead of them in a neighbouring gallery, Raj sees a microphone has been set up on a small platform with a recreation of a Greek temple as a sympathetic backdrop, or a provocative one, depending on your point of view. The pack of salivating photographers is already there, set to one side, lenses trained on the Culture Minister. She is wearing a simple white dress with a high neckline that will make her appear business-like on the television news reports and in tomorrow's papers. Mercouri makes her way towards the makeshift stage, followed almost incidentally by the Director and the other officials. The media scrum pursues them like an amorphous blob and the hacks take up their station next to the photographers.

Raj levers the young journalist out of his path with his elbow, so that he can get a better view of the two protagonists. *The Spectator* man blows cigarette smoke into his face and mutters.

'Christ! What a bloody circus this is,' he says to no one in particular.

Mercouri steps up to the microphone and sweeps her hair to one side in an extravagant gesture. She draws on her cigarette, throws her head back, and exhales disdainfully into the British Museum air. Cameras click furiously and the plume of smoke is caught in the flashlights as it wafts towards the ceiling.

A television camera homes in on the Culture Minister and a phalanx of microphones are thrust in her direction. The museum microphone is insufficient for the journos, who want to record her words on their mini tape-recorders for transcribing later. Raj can't be sure, but it looks as if she has tears in her eyes. She is an actress after all. Mercouri begins to speak, her voice cracking with emotion, or possibly the effects of years of smoking. As you would expect from a professional, she has learnt her lines well.

'First, I would like to say thank you to the British Museum for inviting me here today...'

Pause.

'... and for looking after our marbles, the *Parthenon* Marbles, for nearly 170 years.'

She emphasises the word 'Parthenon'. Melina Mercouri does not recognise the role of Lord Elgin in the history of the marbles. To her, Elgin was a thief, a fraudster, a cultural vandal. They are the Parthenon Marbles and in no sense did Elgin lay claim to these artefacts.

Mercouri continues.

'Greece understands that the Parthenon Marbles mean much to the people of Great Britain. But in turn, Britain must understand how much the marbles mean to the people of Greece. After all, we cared for them for over 2,000 years. They are our pride. They are our noblest symbol of excellence. They are the essence of Greekness. That is why we have asked the British government, in the name of fairness and morality, to take the honourable course and return the Parthenon Marbles to their rightful home, to Greece.'

Apart from Raj, all eyes, all cameras are focused on Mercouri. Raj, though, is studying the Museum Director, who stands rigidly to attention behind her. The Director is ignored. He is not the story. He never starred in risqué movies. His face, which is growing redder the longer Mercouri speaks, will not sell papers.

He must endure further torture, however, for Mercouri has not yet finished.

'One argument for keeping *our* marbles here in London, over 1,500 miles from their home, is that the pollution in Athens will damage these precious artefacts. I wish to announce today, that I will be launching a competition to design a new purpose-built museum at the Acropolis, with controlled air conditioning and lighting, to provide the best possible showcase for the Parthenon Marbles and to preserve the marbles for generations to come. The friezes and other objects still in Athens will be carefully removed to this new museum and, of course, we hope in time…'

She twists and smiles at the Museum Director, who remains grim-faced. Undeterred, Mercouri turns back to face her audience.

'We hope… in fact, we expect… that the beautiful marbles we have seen today, created by Greek craftsmen for a Greek temple, will be returned to their home and take their place alongside their counterparts, from whom they were so brutally… and may I say, illegally… separated nearly 200 years ago. They are our soul and we wish to have them back. Thank you.'

She puts her cigarette to her thin lips and sucks hard. The theatrical tears are now dribbles on her sun-parched cheeks. Cameras click furiously and Raj is momentarily blinded by the flashlights. He stumbles as he is shoved in the back and when he regains his focus and his footing, he sees that Mercouri has stepped forward and is now surrounded by hungry journalists. The TV cameramen are standing on tiptoes, their cameras tilted over the heads of the mob. Questions are being fired at her from all sides. Raj has missed the moment; there is no way he can get through the wall of bodies.

He looks around and sees the Museum Director, standing to one side, a forgotten soul, shaking his head slowly. Perhaps this is the angle Raj needs. He walks over and coughs.

The Director starts and considers Raj with steel-grey eyes.

'Excuse me, sir. I wonder if you wouldn't mind answering a few questions?'

'Certainly. I would be delighted to.'

The man is tense. He is a kettle about to boil.

'Sir, can I ask you what you think of the proposed restitution of the marbles to Greece?'

The Director breathes deeply.

'Well, obviously I am against it.'

'And can I ask why?'

'Why? Why?' His face is now the colour of an overripe plum. 'Because, young man, ripping the Elgin Marbles from the walls of the British Museum would be a greater disaster than if the Parthenon were to be blown up.'

Raj jots notes down at speed. It is at times like this that he is grateful he learnt shorthand.

'Is it even feasible,' he asks, 'to return the marbles to Greece?'

The Director ponders his answer for a second.

'Well, in theory it is possible. Anything is possible,' he says. 'But that was the Mussolini argument, when he got the Italian trains to run on time.'

Raj is taken aback. Surely the Director is not comparing the proposed removal of the marbles to the propaganda of a fascist dictator?

'Are you saying...' But Raj is not allowed to finish.

'I am saying that this would be cultural fascism. Enormous national danger. If you start to destroy intellectual institutions such as the British Museum, you are culturally fascist. It's like Hitler burning books.'

'Like Hitler?' First a reference to Mussolini, now the Führer himself. Raj cannot believe what he is hearing.

'Like Hitler. And you can write that for your readers. Goodbye.'

The Director clicks his heels and walks away, leaving Raj dumbstruck. Behind him, he can still hear the chatter of the journalists surrounding the Culture Minister, and he knows that if he turns to look, he will see Mercouri preening for the cameras.

The Elgin/Parthenon Marbles, Melina Mercouri and Sir David Wilson

In the early nineteenth century, the British Ambassador to Constantinople, Lord Thomas Elgin, removed large quantities of sculpture from Athens, shipping the objects back to the UK. Principal among these were marbles taken from the Parthenon. These included fifty-six of the remaining ninety-six frieze panels, seventeen life-size figures and fifteen metopes – sculpted panels originally displayed above the Parthenon's columns.

In order to remove the marbles, Elgin had obtained a firman, or written authority, from the Ottoman court. In theory, this authority meant that Elgin acquired the objects legally. However, this has been the subject of much debate, with commentators arguing that Elgin used bribery and deception to acquire the firman, that it was not properly authorised by the Sultan, and, in any case, its wording was unclear and did not envisage removal of the marbles. Only an Italian translation survives which suggests that the firman was intended to provide access to Elgin's team of artists, allowing them to view, contemplate and draw the antiquities, to make moulds and to excavate inscribed blocks which may have been buried in the rubble. Almost as an afterthought, it adds: 'and when they wish, to take away some pieces of stone with old inscriptions, and figures'.

At the time, the Acropolis was not the Greek national monument that it is today. The Parthenon was in a dilapidated state, having been ruined in 1687 when a Turkish gunpowder store in the temple suffered a direct hit from a Venetian cannonball. A small garrison and town had subsequently grown up on the slopes of the Acropolis around the Parthenon and much of the original sculpture and building blocks had been used for housing or ground down for cement. Nevertheless, in removing and transporting the marbles, there is no doubt that Elgin inflicted further damage.

The marbles suffered further deterioration in storage at Elgin's London home, Burlington House, where they were supposedly stored in a damp shed for several years, partly due to Elgin being detained in France following the resumption of hostilities between the French and the British, but mostly because the British government refused to meet Elgin's asking price for the marbles (in 1815, Elgin sought £73,600 for the collection, being the total of his expenses plus twelve years' interest).

There was much debate in Parliament and elsewhere over the

marbles. Some championed Elgin, arguing that he had saved the marbles for posterity. Others contended that he was little more than a thief and a vandal. Curiously, two contemporary poets took opposite sides and were moved to record their opinions in verse. John Keats composed a sonnet, 'Seeing the Elgin Marbles', celebrating their display in the British Museum, while Lord Byron wrote that the marbles had been 'defac'd by British hands'.

Eventually, in 1816, the marbles were acquired for the museum at a cost of £35,000, some £4,000 less than the expenses Elgin had incurred in acquiring the marbles.

Melina Mercouri was a successful and glamorous Greek actress. Her most famous role was that of a prostitute in the 1960 film Never on Sunday, for which she won the Best Actress award at the Cannes Film Festival. As well as being an actress, she was a political activist. Greece was under a military dictatorship for seven years from 1967 and Mercouri was one of the most prominent critics of the regime. As a result, she lost her precious Greek citizenship and had her property confiscated. She was also the subject of an assassination attempt. When democracy was restored in 1974, Mercouri continued her political activities as a founder member of the Pan Hellenic Socialist Party and she was elected to the Greek parliament in 1977. In 1981, at the age of sixty-one, she became the Culture Minister for Greece, and in that role she campaigned vigorously for the return to Athens of the Parthenon Marbles, as she insisted on calling them. A highlight of this campaign was a four-day trip to London in May 1983, including a visit to the British Museum where she famously cried on viewing the marbles.

During her tenure as Culture Minister, Mercouri launched a competition to design a new museum for the marbles (actually in 1989 and not in 1983 during her London visit). The winning entry was beset by problems and stalled completely when the ruins of an ancient town were unearthed on the proposed site, causing building work to cease. A new competition was launched in the year 2000, won by the Swiss architect Bernard Schumi. Eventually, on 21 June 2009, the New Acropolis Museum was opened to the public, a spectacular and airy glass and steel construction, with views of the Parthenon. The museum now houses the Athens-based marbles, alongside copies of the London-based marbles. Many, particularly in Greece, believe that it is only a matter of time before these copies are finally replaced by the originals and the marbles are reunited.

Sadly, Melina Mercouri did not live to see the opening of the New Acropolis Museum. A chain smoker, she died of lung cancer in New York on 6 March 1994 at the age of seventy-three.

Unsurprisingly, a succession of directors of the British Museum have vehemently argued that the marbles should remain in London. The Museum Director at the time of Mercouri's visit in 1983 was Sir David Wilson, who described the visit as allowing a 'burglar to case the joint in advance'. The comments made to Raj are based on observations made by a clearly irritated Sir David in a subsequent interview given to the BBC two years later in June 1985.

Sir David's cultural fascism comments aside, the arguments for restitution or otherwise of the marbles generally revolve around the following themes: the legal argument – both the legality of Elgin's original acquisition of the artefacts and the current position (the trustees of the British Museum are prevented by law from permanently disposing of objects such as the marbles); the context argument – whether it is preferable to reunite the marbles so that they can be seen as a whole in the context of their original environment, albeit that they will never be replaced on the Parthenon, or whether it is better for half the marbles to remain in the British Museum where they can be seen in the wider context of other artefacts from both Greek and other ancient civilisations; the floodgate argument – whether returning the marbles will lead to the mass return of artefacts and works of art from museums around the world to their original homes; and the 'If Elgin hadn't saved them, they would have either been destroyed or in a terrible condition, and we have looked after them better than you would have done for nearly 200 years, so we deserve to keep them' argument versus the 'Thank you very much but can we have them back now, please? And by the way, you didn't do that great a job of looking after them' response.

Wednesday 10 October 2007

University College London
Gower Street
London WC1E 6BT

Right Honourable Tessa Jowell MP
Secretary of State
Department for Culture, Media and Sport
2-4 Cockspur Street
London SW1Y 5DH

Dear Ms Jowell,

This afternoon, my boyfriend and I enjoyed a wonderful visit to one of our country's national treasures, the British Museum. One of the highlights of our visit was the Duveen Gallery which houses the Parthenon Marbles. I am sure you will agree that the marbles are magnificent works of art of unparalleled cultural and historical significance. It is truly a privilege for us to have custody of these wonderful objects here in London.

However, I believe that the pieces exhibited here in London should now be reunited with the pieces that remain in Athens, so that admirers such as myself and millions of others can contemplate the spectacle of the Parthenon friezes and sculptures in their entirety, in a manner intended by Phidias and others when they were created 2,500 years ago. The whole must surely be greater than the sum of the parts and will undoubtedly be a thing of beauty for the world to cherish.

For this reason, and with a heavy heart as a British citizen and a Londoner, I urge you, please, to find a way to return the marbles to Greece. The imminent completion of the new museum at the Acropolis with views over the Parthenon, designed specifically to house the Athens Marbles, will provide the ideal setting for the marbles to be reunited, and is the perfect opportunity for our government to demonstrate that not only is it above petty nationalism, but also that it acts with the grace, altruism and righteousness for which the British people are renowned.

Please allow me to raise some specific examples which reveal the sadness in the current situation: the head of a centaur lies in Athens, while its hooves gallop in London; a Lapith woman remains in Athens, deprived of her foot which rests in London; the goddess, Iris, is cruelly severed at the neck, with her head in Athens and her leaping torso removed to London.

When Lord Elgin removed the marbles from the Parthenon, it was like tearing a child away from its mother. The British Museum has cared for this child lovingly for nearly 200 years, but now, I humbly submit, it is time for the family to be reunited.

I look forward to hearing your views on the matter.

Yours faithfully,

Summer Meadows (Ms)

Tuesday 23 October 2007

Department for Culture, Media and Sport

Ms Summer Meadows
University College London
Gower Street
London WC1E 6BT

Dear Ms Meadows,

The Secretary of State has asked me to thank you for your letter dated 10 October regarding the sculptures from the Parthenon, often referred to as the Elgin or Parthenon Marbles, that are in the possession of the British Museum.

As you are no doubt aware, the status of the sculptures is a complex legal, cultural and historical issue. Her Majesty's Government is of the view that the question of restitution of any or all of the sculptures is a matter for the trustees of the British Museum, acting with due consideration for their duties under the British Museum Act 1963. It is the Government's understanding that the trustees have no current plans to permit the sculptures to be removed from display at the British Museum. A fuller explanation of the trustees' position on this issue is set out on the British Museum website and can be accessed via the following link: www.britishmuseum.org.

I trust this is a helpful response to the points raised in your letter.

Yours faithfully,

Dame S– S– DCB
Permanent Secretary

Annie is indignant. 'Well, that was a first-class fob-off if ever I heard one.'

'Of course. Summer wasn't daft. She knew that she would get responses like that more often than not. But her thinking was that the more letters she and others like her wrote, the more these issues wormed their way to the front of politicians' minds, and the chances of them actually doing something about them increased. One letter would not change anything, but 1,000 letters might.'

'It is the old dichotomy, I suppose,' Annie says, drily. 'Why does anyone bother to vote in an election when their single vote will never alter the result?'

'Exactly. But if no one votes, we all undermine democracy and end up with dictatorship.'

We pass the gates of the British Museum and its colonnaded entrance wreathed in shadows – ironically built in the Greek Classical style and looking remarkably similar to the Parthenon – before we emerge, blinking, on to Southampton Row. Southampton Row and, beyond it, Kingsway, are beacons of bright light compared to the darkness of Great Russell Street. With disregard for the time of day, cars and lorries roar up and down the dual carriageway, and people cluster on the pavements, phones clamped to ears as they plan the rest of their night.

We join a line of Shine walkers who are ushered across the road by a volunteer with a wide-brimmed straw hat and an even wider grin. Half a dozen leather-jacketed lads, with drainpipe jeans and designer trainers, eye us suspiciously. Suddenly, the purple T-shirted, neon-lit charity walkers look vulnerable in the hard-nosed reality of a Saturday night in central London. We are daytime creatures who have shifted time zones and are now caught in a nocturnal world. We are people used to being tucked up in our beds at this time. We are not London nightlife crawlers. To our right is Covent Garden, where London's highbrow mingle with tourists, shoppers and drunks. I have never considered myself to be especially sophisticated, but I do remember one trip to the ballet.

Royal Opera House

Saturday 15 August 2009

It was Summer's official birthday. Her real birthday was 15 February, but Summer liked to have an alternative celebration six months later on a Saturday during August, when she didn't have to go to work and the weather was invariably better. She justified it by reference to her name, arguing that it was ridiculous for a girl called Summer to be stuck with a winter birthday. In all the years I had known her, the sun had inevitably danced to Summer's tune by always shining on her official anniversary and this year was no exception.

It was a muggy evening and I was sweltering in my dinner jacket with a tightly knotted bow tie crushing my throat. I waited for Summer in Drury Lane, concerned that she might not turn up. The phone call was bothering me.

One advantage of the Official Birthday concept was that it gave me another excuse to buy Summer a present, and I had splashed out this year, buying two tickets for the Mariinsky Ballet at the Royal Opera House. They had set me back a small fortune, but ever since their tour had been announced, Summer had wanted to go. In any case, we had both graduated one month earlier and now we had jobs to go to that would pay us actual money, so I felt we deserved the extravagance. And I wanted to ask her something important.

I had woken her with a cup of tea and a slice of toast in bed.

'Mmm.' She was half asleep.

'There's a letter for you,' I said casually.

Summer occasionally directed letters and correspondence to my address, so it was just about believable, particularly when she was still drowsy. She propped herself up on the pillow and took a sip of tea, before fumbling with the envelope. The tickets slipped out on to the duvet, the Royal Opera House crests facing upwards.

'Ben, what are these?'

'Happy Official Birthday, babe,' I smiled.

'Are these…?' She was suddenly wide awake.

'Tickets to the ballet. Tonight. I hope you're free.'

She threw her arms around my neck and suffocated me with kisses. I fell on top of her, kissing her shoulders, caressing her breast through the sheet. My passion was cut short though. The ringtone on her phone – 'Walking on Sunshine' by Katrina and the Waves – sliced through the moment.

'Leave it,' I tried, but Summer had reached over and looked at the screen.

Her face hardened when she saw who was calling.

'I have to get this, Ben,' she said. 'Sorry.'

I wanted to know who was more important than me and craned my neck to see the caller ID. 'Manu.' The name meant nothing to me. Someone from Summer's work perhaps, although it was a Saturday.

Summer accepted the call and rolled out of bed.

'Just give me a second,' she said into the phone. And then to me. 'Sorry, Ben. Can I take this in private?'

I was jolted. Such formality was just not Summer. And what conversation could she possibly be having with anyone that I couldn't listen to?

I left the room and sat in the kitchen, chewing on a slice of toast. Buster eyed me lazily from his basket. Manu? I wondered if I had heard that name before, but couldn't place it. As I swallowed my last mouthful of toast, I felt Summer's arms encircling my neck. She kissed my cheek and sat down next to me.

'I'm sorry, Ben. I've got to go and do something.'

'Because of that phone call?'

She looked down at the table. 'Because of that phone call, yes.'

'What…' But she put a finger to my lips and shushed me.

'Please don't ask, Ben. I will see you at the ballet tonight. I promise we will have a beautiful evening.'

And there I was, dressed in a penguin suit, standing self-consciously on the pavement, wondering if she would make good on her promise. The ballet was Tchaikovsky's *Sleeping*

Beauty and it had particular resonance because it 'belonged' to the Mariinsky – still better known by their Soviet name, the Kirov – who first performed it in Saint Petersburg in 1890. It was also special as it was the ballet that reopened the Royal House in 1946 in its new Covent Garden location. And frankly, that was about the extent of my knowledge of ballet. Other than knowing the basics of the *Sleeping Beauty* story – bad fairy curses baby, baby grows up to be beautiful princess who pricks her finger and sleeps for 1,000 years, handsome prince cuts through forest and wakes princess with a kiss, everyone lives happily ever after – I was lost. It would have been ridiculous for me to see this on my own.

I needn't have worried though. After I had been waiting ten minutes, a black cab pulled up, and out stepped Summer looking like a film star in a spangly red full-length dress that flowed across the curves of her body. Summer had learnt ballet when she was a child and kept it going through school, and she still loved it. Seeing the Mariinsky in the flesh was a delight for her.

She gave me a huge smile and performed a twirl in front of me. A couple of lads cheered from across the street.

'So, what do you think?'

'You look fabulous,' I said.

She walked up to me and adjusted my bow tie, before giving me a deep, long kiss. I could dimly hear the boys across the street cheering again, but it was like they were calling from another room. When she broke away, she looked me in the eyes.

'I'm sorry about today,' she said.

'Is everything OK?'

'Everything is OK. But please don't ask me about anything.'

'Why…?' I started.

'Please,' she said quickly. 'Let's not spoil the evening.'

I relented. 'Come on. Let's go inside.'

It was an hour before the start of the performance and we sat at a small table in the bar underneath the huge Crystal Palace-style glass roof. I bought two glasses of champagne and tried not to think about the cost. The atrium dripped money with patrons in glamorous evening wear and glittering jewellery – at least I wasn't the only one done up in a monkey suit.

'Thank you, Ben.' She raised her glass to me. 'I am so looking forward to tonight.'

'Happy Birthday,' I responded. 'You will tell me what's going on, won't you?'

She frowned. 'I said please don't ask me anything.'

'No,' I said quickly, appalled that she had misunderstood, 'I meant in the ballet. Like when there's a *pas de deux* or something?'

'Oh.' Her face instantly softened. 'Of course. The *pas de deux*, the *en pointes*, the *paso dobles*... all of them.'

I put my glass to my lips and swallowed a mouthful of champagne. The bubbles tickled the insides of my cheeks.

'The *paso doble*? That's bullfighting right?'

She laughed. 'You see, you are not so ignorant after all.'

'So how long did you do ballet for?' I asked.

'About ten years. Until I was sixteen. I was quite good, you know.' She winked at me.

'I can imagine.' And I could also imagine that her ballet training was largely responsible for her lithe body.

'Why did you stop?'

'Oh, you know.' She looked down at her glass. 'Stuff.'

'Stuff?'

'Stuff,' she repeated. 'Growing up and all that. It just got in the way.'

I thought back to my late teenage years. Angst about girls, brain-freezing exams, terrible fashion taste, grunge and house, cheap lager and barely drinkable wine, wacky cigarettes, fraught relationships, disfiguring acne, angst about girls. Yes, there was a lot of stuff to get in the way at that time in your life.

'The dancers here,' she continued, 'have had no distractions. The principal ballerina tonight is Evgenia Obraztsova. She will have trained full time at the Vaganova Academy in Saint Petersburg since she was ten years old. She has been caged like a bird and I could never imagine doing that.'

'I guess that you need that level of dedication to be a professional.'

'And talent,' she added. 'They say Obraztsova dances with a shimmering lightness. She will be exquisite tonight, you will see.'

'But not as exquisite as you,' I said, taking another gulp of champagne. 'Summer, can I ask you something?'

Her eyes screwed tight.

'It's OK,' I added quickly. 'It's not about today.'

'What is it, Ben?'

I shifted uncomfortably in my seat, but fortified by the champagne, I ploughed on.

'It's just… it's just that I move into my new flat next week and I wondered if…'

She held a finger up before I could finish.

'Ben, you are the most wonderful person and I love you more than life itself. Please understand that. But I can't move in with you.' There was an anxious tremor in her voice.

My shoulders sagged. I had expected this.

'Why not, Summer? We love each other, we've been together for nearly three years now, is it not time we gave living together a go?'

'Ben,' her eyes dropped to the table and she clasped and unclasped her hands, 'I am just not ready to burden you with me, and everything that comes with me.'

'Summer,' I protested, 'you won't be a burden, I promise.'

'And everything that comes with me, Ben.' She repeated the words slowly.

I was perplexed. 'And everything that comes with you?'

'Ben,' she leant over and kissed me lightly on the cheek, 'one day, we will discuss this again. And maybe then it will be time, we will see. But not now. I cannot move in with you now. And if you love me, please let's forget about it tonight. Let's not ruin a beautiful evening.'

I stared at her, rigid with disappointment. Summer took a sip of her drink and kissed me again, on the mouth, so that I tasted the buttery champagne on her lips. As she pulled away, I shook myself, suddenly struck by the reality that I was sitting with a gorgeous girl in a stunning dress in magnificent surroundings. Even if she wasn't ready to move in with me, she was still my girlfriend and she loved me. I trusted her on

184

that, and she was right: I shouldn't spoil a magical evening. I drained my glass and came to my senses.

'Would you like another one?' I said. 'After all, a girl only gets two birthdays a year.'

She placed her own half-empty glass on the table and smiled. 'Did you say I was exquisite? Like a prima ballerina?'

'I did.'

'Well then, I guess it would be rude to deny such a gentleman the pleasure of buying me another drink.'

Lincoln's Inn Fields

Past Holborn station, we turn left into the huge square that is Lincoln's Inn Fields. We are entering lawyer land now, where London's legal machinery cranks and grinds on a daily basis, with Lincoln's Inn itself on the far side of the square and the Royal Courts of Justice beyond. Lincoln's Inn Fields is also home to the headquarters of Cancer Research UK and our route has obviously been deliberately designed to pass this point. A projector has been set up to display the Cancer Research and Shine logos on the wall of their Head Office building.

Annie stops and fumbles with her rucksack.

'Sorry,' she says, 'do you mind taking a picture?'

She takes off her hat, undoes her ponytail and shakes her head, so that her hair fluffs up. She thrusts a digital camera in my direction, stands in front of the wall with the projections behind, and smiles self-consciously. She looks attractive, I think, as I click the shutter.

Perhaps I should have a memory too. I hand Annie her camera back and dig out my phone from my pocket.

'Do you mind?' I ask, awkwardly.

Annie laughs. 'Not at all.'

'Here, would you like me to take one of the two of you together?'

A man with a Shine T-shirt stretched over his paunch steps from the darkness and holds his hand out to Annie.

'Oh, er, it's OK... we're not, we're not...' I stumble over my words.

'Nonsense,' he says, taking the phone off Annie. 'Now, where do I press?'

Annie shows him what to do and then sidles across to join me. We stand apart from each other with fixed grins.

'Oh, come on, lad,' urges our photographer. 'A pretty girl deserves an arm around her. What's wrong with you, son?'

It is not worth protesting. I drape my right arm around Annie's shoulders and we stand stiffly to attention, like guards outside Buckingham Palace.

'Say cheese,' he says.

Annie and I grimace and force the word out.

'Che... eee... ese!'

Lincoln's Inn Fields

Tuesday 23 September 2008

Summer had asked me to meet her in the North Cloisters at seven thirty.

'What's up? What are we doing?' I asked.

'Something important,' she replied. 'I'll explain later.'

With Summer I had learnt to go with her flow so I didn't question her any further, but I realised something serious was up when she arrived in a black headscarf. She was carrying a wicker picnic basket and the charm bracelet that I had bought her in Harrods twinkled on her wrist. She moved her scarf momentarily to one side to give me a kiss and I breathed in the scent she was wearing: lavender and orange blossom. As she pulled away, she pressed the basket into my hand.

'What's in here?' I asked innocently.

'Food.'

'Food?'

'Food,' she confirmed.

It was the holy month of Ramadan when Summer fasted during daylight, but it was evening now and the sun had set. I had assumed that we would grab a meal somewhere, not bring our own picnic into the centre of London.

Summer squeezed my hand.

'Bear with me, Ben. This matters.'

I squeezed her hand back and said nothing. Summer led the way down Gower Street, across into Southampton Row and down to Kingsway. I heard the buzz of a crowd but it was only as we turned into Lincoln's Inn Fields that I saw the throng of people.

'What's going on, Summer?' I asked.

'Iftar,' she said. 'We are breaking our fast with the homeless. We're all supposed to bring food.'

She gestured to the basket I was carrying.

Now I knew, I could make sense of the scene. Tables had been set up, with pots of food simmering on small gas stoves. Curry aromas floated across the square: saffron, cinnamon, garlic. Behind the tables were young Muslims, the men with dark hair and tidy beards, the women dressed like Summer in hijabs or headscarves. They were ladling out curry, rice and samosas on to paper plates.

A queue had formed in front of each table, each one a microcosm of London's shameful underbelly. Men and women with black teeth and dirty skin, clothes caked with filth from the streets, clinging on to supermarket carrier bags that held their precious possessions. They edged forward waiting patiently for the hand-outs. I was aware that Lincoln's Inn Fields was known for its soup kitchens, but I had never seen this before.

An earnest-looking man with a penetrating gaze walked over to us and bowed his head.

'Welcome, brother. Welcome, sister,' he said. 'My name is Miqdad. Thank you for coming tonight.'

Summer smiled and the man's shoulders visibly relaxed.

'No, thank you,' she replied. 'It is a wonderful thing that you do.'

I had understood what was happening now and I held up the picnic basket.

'What would you like me to do with this, Miqdad?'

He turned and made a sweeping gesture with his hand.

'We encourage you to share your food with the people here. Eat together. Drink together. Listen to each other's stories. If you need to heat anything up we have stoves.'

'Oh, I'm sorry,' Summer interrupted. 'I didn't know about that so I only have pastries and cakes. I hope that's OK.'

'That is very much OK, Miss...?'

'Meadows. Summer Meadows. Call me Summer.'

'Summer?' He thumbed his chin as he contemplated the name. 'What a beautiful name. Thank you for bringing some sunshine to us here tonight.'

'And I'm Ben.' I figured I should volunteer this as he was unlikely to ask. I was used to people being so distracted by Summer that I was left in the background.

'Ben. We are pleased to welcome all faiths here. May Allah smile on you.' Miqdad bowed again and backed away.

Summer grasped my hand and walked me over to a vacant patch of pavement. I set down the basket and she opened the lid. It was full of paper-towel parcels which Summer and I carefully unwrapped to reveal pastel-coloured cupcakes, pains aux raisins and chocolate croissants. Before long there was a line of people in front of us and it seemed that we were providing the dessert after they had finished their curry main course. The cupcakes were particularly popular. Several times, I picked up a croissant or a pain aux raisins, only for the person in front of me to shake their head vigorously and point at a cupcake with a grubby finger. I could tell that Summer had baked and iced these herself at home, whereas the pastries looked suspiciously as if they were fresh from the Refectory that morning.

After only twenty minutes, we had nearly run out. Our friend, Miqdad, wandered over to see how we are doing.

'I'm sorry, sir,' said Summer. 'But I didn't bring enough. It's all gone so quickly.'

'Even one cake would have been enough,' said Miqdad, graciously. 'But please, you must eat something yourself before you run out completely.'

Summer protested.

'No, we can't possibly do that. These people need the food more than we do.'

'No,' Miqdad wasn't to be dissuaded, 'this is an important part of iftar. That we eat together.' He picked up the last two cupcakes from the basket and handed one to Summer and one to me. I noticed the beady eyes of the man next in the queue fixed on the cupcakes.

'Thanks,' I replied, 'but I'll take a croissant.'

'OK, if you insist. Although they do look exceptionally good.' Miqdad turned and gave my cupcake to the man in the line, who tipped his battered fedora to me appreciatively and wandered off to sit on a bare patch of grass.

I picked up a chocolate croissant and leaving Summer to hand out the remaining pastries in the basket, sat down next to the homeless man to eat with him. He ate quickly, crumbs from the cupcake falling into his wiry beard. Apart from the fedora on his head and the clothes he was wearing, his possessions were confined to the contents of two orange Sainsbury's plastic bags.

'I'm Ben, by the way,' I said, through a mouthful of croissant.

'Percival,' he replied. 'Very pleased to make your acquaintance, sir.'

He extended a hand and I shook it gingerly. Percival had an accent cut from crystal and I wondered what twists and turns there had been in his life for him to arrive at a food station in Lincoln's Inn Fields.

'Thank you for the er…' He lifted the remains of the cupcake in his dirt-encrusted fingers. 'Very kind of you.'

'No problem. Is this a regular thing for you?'

He finished the cupcake and rubbed a grey tongue across his lips.

'I come here every week, if that's what you mean,' he said. 'But these Muslim wallahs, they're new. They arrived two weeks ago, like angels from the Lord.'

'It's Ramadan,' I explained. 'Their holy month.'

'Ahh, that would be it, then,' he said. 'Well, their food is fit for a king and they are hospitable people. Us vagabonds are used to feeding on scraps thrown at us from the back of a van, like we are wild dogs. Whereas, these people treat us with… you know… a bit of…'

'Dignity?' I offered.

'Absolutely, sir.' He slapped his thigh. 'You have it on the nail. Dignity. That is it, sir. And respect. We people of the street appreciate a modicum of respect.'

I chewed my croissant slowly and across the grass I saw Summer giving her cupcake to a man in a baggy tracksuit. He took the cake in one hand and remonstrated at her with the other. I wondered if I should go and help her out but Percival spoke again and distracted me.

'You're not one of them, are you?' He was pointing to a corner of the park where a group of about twenty Muslims were kneeling down to pray. 'Why, may I ask, are you here?'

'Because I love a girl who is one of them,' I said unhesitatingly. 'And she wanted to come here tonight.'

'Would she be the young miss who served the cakes with you?'

'Yeah. The one I served the cakes with.'

'A pretty little creature,' he observed, standing up and buttoning his shabby coat. 'I advise you not to lose that one.'

'I'll do my best,' I replied, getting up as well. There was something in Percival's manner that I warmed to. He was a good man who had fallen on hard times. I reached into my pocket and found a banknote. I only meant to give him a fiver or a tenner, but my fingers pulled out a £20 note and I could hardly plead student poverty and ask for change. I thrust it towards him before I thought too much about my credit card debt.

'Here,' I said. 'Take it. Find yourself somewhere to spend the night.'

He ripped it from my grasp as if he were scared that I might be teasing him and suddenly snatch it back. Recovering himself, he touched the rim of his fedora.

'Thank you, sir,' he said. 'You have a good soul.'

And with that, Percival sauntered away, hopefully to spend his new-found wealth wisely on a decent sleeping place, but more likely to blow it on cigarettes and super-strength lager.

I looked round for Summer. She was still talking to the man in the tracksuit who seemed to have calmed down. I could tell now that he was of Asian descent so perhaps they had found some common ground. I started to walk over to them and as I did he pulled out what looked like a piece of paper from his sweatpants and handed it to Summer. I noticed that she had a pen in her fingers. She scribbled something on the paper and gave it back.

'Are you going to introduce me to your new friend, Summer?' I laughed as I approached.

The man put the paper back in his pocket and scowled at me. He had black, greasy hair and a flabby face, and his lower lip sagged unfortunately, revealing a gap in his discoloured teeth where one of his upper canines used to be.

'Summer?' he said, thrusting his snub-nosed face towards me. 'Is that your name? Nice.'

Summer's hands grabbed my arm.

'Let's go, Ben.' She sounded anxious, but I was in charitable mode.

'Hey,' I smiled at the man, 'did you enjoy the cupcake?'

'Cupcake?' he said disdainfully. 'She owes me more than a cupcake.'

'Manu, please. Leave us alone.' Summer's voice was strained.

'Why? Why should I leave you alone?' He stood with his legs apart and his fists clenched, and spoke the words in a low, menacing whisper.

'I'm sorry,' I tried to step in as the peacemaker, 'is there something we can do for you?'

The man sneered at me.

'Careful of this one,' he said, 'she's a snake. Poisonous.'

He turned back to Summer and patted the pocket of his sweatpants.

'Thanks for this, mishti.'

Summer stiffened and her lips curled in obvious distaste. I pushed her forward and he spat on the grass as we passed, muttering under his breath, 'A snake. A King Cobra of a snake '

My patience snapped and I turned round, wanting to give him a mouthful. He stood his ground, grinning at me with his lopsided teeth, daring me to have a go.

'Ben, come on,' Summer urged. 'He's nothing. Leave him.'

She was shaking and her breath was coming in short bursts, so I decided it was best not to aggravate things. I put my arm around her shoulders and we walked away. By the time I risked one further glance behind, the man had melted into the crowd.

We left the square by the south-east corner with the High Court Buildings ahead of us. When we were out of sight of Lincoln's Inn Fields, her body relaxed.

'Summer, did you know that guy? What did he call you?' I was curious. Something had not been right about the encounter.

'Mishti. It means 'sweet', an Indian term of affection.' Her voice was cold.

'So who was he?'

'He was nobody,' she said, quickly, 'just a homeless guy who needs help.'

'And what did you give him?' I pressed.

'Does it matter?' she asked. 'I saw you handing something to the old man with the hat. What was that?'

I mumbled, embarrassed. I didn't want to admit I had given away twenty quid. She stopped, took the basket from my hands and set it down.

'It was nothing, Ben. Nothing important.'

'But I saw...'

She leant over, pushed her scarf to one side and kissed me. I couldn't resist. I pressed my tongue to her lips and she opened her mouth so that our tongues entwined and we were locked together. My hands fell gently down her back and her body slackened as she gave in to my embrace. I held her tight in my arms and pulled her closer. Lavender and orange. When we finally came up for air, she buried her head into my neck and I felt her warm breath against my skin.

'Please, can we forget that man?' she mumbled.

I gave her a hug which I knew she would take as a 'yes' answer. She lifted her head and her face glowed in the light from the streetlamps.

'Let's go to the river,' she said. 'I want to see the lights shining on the water.

Flashmob Iftars

An iftar is the evening meal eaten by Muslims to break their daytime fast during Ramadan. In 2008, Miqdad Asaria, a twenty-seven-year-old computer scientist set up a Facebook page to invite young Muslims and others to the first flashmob iftar in Lincoln's Inn Fields on the first Tuesday of Ramadan. His idea was for Muslims who had gone hungry during the day to share their food with those who went hungry all year, in keeping with the Islamic tradition of generosity to the needy. On the first evening, one hundred Muslims turned up to serve hot food to the homeless. By the second week, this number had grown to 150. The initiative has continued since 2008, not only in Lincoln's Inn Fields and other locations in London, but also spreading to other parts of the country, including Birmingham, Manchester, Cardiff, Leeds and Bristol.

Asaria's Facebook page included the statement: 'No agenda, no organisation, no rules, just normal Muslims doing their thing.'

Fleet Street

Thursday 20 October 2011

I was sitting at my desk, unable to concentrate. I hadn't heard from Summer for a week now. No answers to my texts, my phone calls straight through to voicemail. We had gone to the cinema last Thursday – *Restless*, a Gus Van Sant movie starring Henry Hopper – and then spent the night at my flat. She had left early the following morning for work with a kiss, a smile, a wave. No indication that anything was wrong.

And that was it. Since then, radio silence. I should have been used to these episodes by now but they still bothered me. I was worried that something had happened to her. What if she had been run over by a London Routemaster? Would anyone even tell me? I had never met her mother and I was pretty sure she wouldn't know how to contact me in an emergency. Or what if Summer had just decided to leave me? To walk out of my life and never return. I shuddered at the thought.

In the past, Summer had always told me not to worry, that she would always come back, but the fact that she had been true to her word so far didn't reassure me. One day, she would leave me for good. I was certain of that.

I had a quick look to check my boss wasn't about to breathe fire down my neck for slacking before ringing Summer's work number. Summer hated me ringing her at the office, but I decided to go for it, convincing myself that I wanted to check that she was OK. Her landline was answered after two rings.

'Hello,' I said, as confidently as I could muster. 'Could I speak to Summer Meadows, please?'

'Summer Meadows?' a girl answered, whose voice I didn't recognise, but that was not surprising as I had never met anyone from Summer's work.

'Summer Meadows, yes.'

'I'm afraid she's not here. She's on holiday. Can I help?'

'On holiday?' I was stunned. Summer had never mentioned anything about a holiday.

There was a pause. 'Sorry, who's calling?'

'Ben… Ben Richardson. I'm her…' I faltered. What was I?

'Oh yes, Ben.' The girl's voice lifted. 'Summer talks about you all the time. I thought you'd be on holiday with her. She said she was going with family.'

My mind was a jumble. Summer talked about me all the time. She was on holiday with family.

'No, sorry. I had to work,' and then I decided to add, 'I thought she'd be back by now.'

'No, she's not due in until Monday,' the girl continued. 'Unlucky you though. You could be sunning yourself in Dubai and instead you're suffering our miserable weather.'

'Dubai?'

'Dubai, yes. Summer said she had wanted to go there for ages.' The girl's voice turned wary. 'Didn't you know?'

'Yes, of course,' I blurted. 'Sorry. I've been busy at work. My mind's scrambled.'

The girl at the other end relaxed again.

'Tell me about it. We're flat out here. Could have done with having Summer around. Anyway, shall I tell her you called?'

'No, no, that's fine. I'll see her when she's back. Thanks.'

'No problem. Maybe Summer will introduce us sometime. We're all dying to meet the wonderful Ben.'

'Yeah. Sure. That would be nice.'

'Bye then.'

'Bye.'

I put the phone down. If I was the wonderful Ben, it didn't feel that way. Summer had taken off on a holiday to Dubai with family I didn't know and hadn't even told me about it, let alone asked me along.

Right on cue though, Summer texted me early the following Monday, desperate to see me that evening. I never mentioned the phone call or her work colleague, I never asked about Dubai.

Fleet Street

Friday 16 March 2012

My boss was called Andrea. She was in her mid-thirties and unmarried. Her latest boyfriend was a Portuguese artist called Leandro who she met on an internet dating site. She told her PA that with Leandro she was enjoying the best sex she had ever had. Her PA promptly informed the rest of the office, which is almost certainly what Andrea intended her to do.

When Andrea had a new boyfriend and was getting regular sex, she lavished her largesse upon her underlings, praising us for our work, and treated us to rounds of drinks in El Vino's on Friday evenings. When she was going through a chaste phase, she stomped around the office with a face of granite, staring at our computer screens over our shoulders and growling disapprovingly at what she saw. Andrea went through boyfriends like our office guillotine sliced through foolscap and so the atmosphere in our office lurched from paranoid fear to joyful partying with nothing much in between.

For this reason, when Andrea asked me to join her for a coffee in the meeting room, I was pleased that Leandro was proving such a success between the sheets. On a bad day, coffee with Andrea could reduce even the most hardbitten of advertising executives to shivering wrecks. On one infamous occasion, a graduate trainee who miscollated a pile of photocopying was bollocked so mercilessly by Andrea in the middle of our open-plan floor that he was last seen running down Fleet Street in tears. We had to box up his coat, bag and personal effects and courier them to his home address. We dropped in a 'So Sorry You're Leaving' card, signed by all of us – except Andrea of course – because we felt so bad.

The meeting room referred to was actually a branch of Starbucks on Fleet Street. We went there so often we ought to have had a corporate account. Andrea wafted a £10 note and asked me what I would like to drink which was a good sign. I ordered a flat white. She had what she always had: a double-shot Americano.

We sat down in a corner and I wondered what was coming: a pep talk, a pay rise, a reprimand? I had had a run in with one of our more important clients, a fruit importer, the previous week – a frank exchange of views, as they say, with their commercial manager, Bill Hargreaves, a no-nonsense Yorkshireman who knew the value of money in the same way that a farmer knew the value of horse manure.

'You bastards are ripping us off,' he screamed at me down the phone. 'If only your adverts were as creative as your fucking fees.'

'Well, if only your oranges were as juicy as your language, we'd all be OK,' I retorted.

To be fair to Bill, he did laugh at that and I thought I'd got away with it until Andrea forwarded me an email where I was referred to as a 'sarcastic, jumped-up little twerp'. Work was a bit slow that year, with the economy still struggling to recover, and I winced; it wasn't a great career move to piss off a lucrative client.

Andrea included a note: 'Explanation and draft reply needed' – adding one of her standard sign-offs: 'FDIN'. Effing do it now.

Andrea didn't look in a feisty mood though. She sipped her coffee and sat forward with a disconcerting Mona Lisa-like smile threatening to break out between her cherry-red lipsticked lips.

'So,' I ventured, 'what would you like to talk about, Andrea?'

'You,' she said. 'I would like to talk about you, Ben.'

My shoulders tensed. I swallowed a mouthful of coffee and the espresso tasted bitter as it glided down my throat.

'What about me?' I asked coolly.

'Well, Ben. As you know, I think very highly of you...'

I didn't know this, but I relaxed slightly to hear it.

'... even though our clients do not all share the same view as I do.'

I was instantly tense again.

Andrea milked the moment, savouring my unease as she took another mouthful of coffee.

'And as you are aware, business has been somewhat challenging of late.'

Now I was rigid. Was she going to fire me? In a coffee shop?

'Er, I suppose so,' I mumbled.

'So, I am concerned that you haven't had enough quality work recently to get your teeth into.'

'Well, I've been busy, Andrea,' I protested. I thought about reaching for my coffee but I could feel my hands shaking, so I decided to leave it.

Andrea smiled. 'You're just humouring me, Ben. I know inside that you're desperate for more work, to prove yourself.'

Was I? I suppose I was if Andrea said so.

'So I have a solution.' She put her coffee cup down with a bang and leant in towards me, as if she were about to let me into a big secret.

'A solution?'

'A solution, yes.'

'What sort of solution?' I whispered the question.

'I have arranged for a twelve-month secondment for you to our New York office. They need good people like you over there. They have more work than they can handle at the moment and you'll learn a lot.' She paused. 'Plus, it will be a blast for a youngster like you.'

Her bright red lips pursed together in a look of smug satisfaction. I couldn't tell if Andrea had carved out a valuable career opportunity for me at our Head Office or engineered an exit for a troublesome employee.

'Well, what do you think?' she asked irritatedly. 'If it were me at your age, I'd be jumping for joy right now. Instead, you're doing a convincing impression of a constipated goldfish.'

I realised that my mouth was open and shut it quickly.

'I... I don't know what to think.'

'Well,' she leant back in her chair, 'I suggest that you get thinking about it pretty quick. If you don't want to work in New York...' she paused for effect, '... then I'll have to think of another solution for you.'

Her face hardened and I decided to stall for some time.

'I will have to talk it over with Summer,' I said.

'Of course. I had forgotten that you two are...' she took a breath as she pondered how to finish the sentence, '... so attached.'

Despite his sexual prowess, it was obvious that if Andrea were granted such a career opportunity, she would spare no thought for Leandro. He would be history in a flash. Another lover could be easily sourced.

Andrea raised her cup, lifted her head back and drained the last of her Americano. She put the lipstick-stained cup back on the table, picked up a napkin and dabbed her lips. The cherry red stained the napkin which she scrunched up and dropped on the table in front of me. She pushed her chair back, stood up to leave, and fired a final, parting shot.

'You have the weekend. I want your answer on Monday.'

Fleet Street to St Paul's Cathedral

'Wow! That's some kind of ultimatum. Move to another country or lose your job.'

Annie and I are walking along Fleet Street. We pass the Starbucks where Andrea asked me to transfer to New York and I look through the window at the table where we sat that day. I suppose she was giving me an ultimatum, although I am not sure I saw it like that at the time. I was excited at the prospect of living and working in the Big Apple but my main concern was Summer, who was working in government relations for a PR agency and loving it. I didn't know what she would think about a move to America and it was inconceivable to me that we should live apart on opposite sides of the Atlantic. I spent the rest of that day in a cold sweat, thinking about how to present it to her. If Summer said no it would kill me but I would just have to decline Andrea's golden opportunity and take my chances. It was a risk though; I had a hefty mortgage on the flat and simply living in London was expensive. I couldn't afford to be out of work. I went home that night in a fog.

'Oh, look. Do you mind if we stop?' Annie tugs at my sleeve and points to a couple across the road at Ludgate Circus. They both look old enough to be retired. The man is sitting on the pavement, staring at one bare foot, which gleams white under the streetlights. The lady stands next to him, looking down with a concerned expression on her face. Annie walks over and I follow.

'Are you OK?' she asks, sweetly. 'Only, I have some plasters if you need some.'

The lady turns round and her face looks pained.

'Oh, thank you, dear. I'm afraid we came out without any. We're so stupid. We do lots of walking and thought we'd be fine.'

'Oh, don't fuss, Margaret,' grunted the man on the floor. 'It's only a blister. Nothing to bother about.'

Annie kneels down beside him.

'It looks a bit nasty to me,' she says. 'My name's Annie, by the way. And this is Ben.'

'Thanks for stopping,' says Margaret. 'It's good of them to stop, isn't it, Geoff?'

'If you say so,' concedes Geoff.

I take off my rucksack and rummage around inside. I find my first aid kit and hand it to Annie.

'Oh, thanks, Ben. We can use mine if...'

'No, no. Help yourself,' I say quickly, trying not to think about the state of my own feet.

'Look,' protests Geoff, 'it's just a bit of blood. I'm putting this sock back on and I'll be fine.'

'Sorry, Geoff.' Annie gives him a stern look. 'I'm a trained nurse and I'm not going to let that happen. Ben, have you got any antiseptic cream? If not, there's some in my bag.'

Geoff leans back, placated. He might argue with his wife but he is not going to take on a professional. It takes Annie just a few minutes to clean the blood away, apply the cream and fix the plaster.

'There. You can put your sock on now. It should feel a lot better.'

'Thank you. Thank you so much,' Margaret coos over her shoulder. 'It means a lot for us to get round, you know.'

'Are you doing this for someone?'

'Our son,' Geoff says, gruffly. 'He's got Hodgkin's lymphoma. Not a lot that can be done for him.'

'We just feel so helpless,' says Margaret. 'This is our way of doing something to help.'

'I'm... I'm sorry.' I don't know what else to say.

I think back to what Annie said to me at the beginning of the evening. Everyone on this walk has a story.

Geoff struggles to his feet and carefully places his weight on the offending foot. He walks a few paces.

'Much better,' he declares. 'Thanks, young lady.' He shakes Annie's hand.

'No problem,' she says. 'I'm glad we could help.'

'You two carry on,' urges Margaret. 'We don't want to slow you down.'

'If you're sure...'

'We're sure,' says Geoff. 'You push on. Maybe we'll see you at the finish.'

'Nearly two-thirds of the way round,' I say encouragingly, with a broad grin. Well, we are past mile fifteen, so it's almost true, although I feel guiltily like one of the over-enthusiastic volunteers. All I need is a big pair of Mickey Mouse hands to wave Margaret and Geoff on.

Annie wishes them good luck and we walk slowly away, up Newgate Street – site of the old debtors' prison in Dickensian times – and towards St Paul's, its huge silver dome shining ahead of us.

'I didn't realise you were a trained nurse,' I say to Annie.

'I'm not,' she replies, 'I design greetings cards.'

Saint Paul's Cathedral

Friday 21 October 2011

Mary holds her duster self-consciously in her hands, thinking she really should have left it somewhere out of sight rather than bring it to such an important meeting. She is sat on a simple wooden chair along with the rest of the staff in the North Transept. In front of them stands the Dean, grim-faced in his black cassock with its smart, red trim. Behind him, the Chancellor, a jolly man with a round face and protruding ears, smiles and chats to the Treasurer. The Chancellor is well-liked because he appears on *Thought for the Day* and writes for newspapers and is therefore a Church celebrity, although he is a little too modern for Mary's tastes.

They are all overlooked by the figure of Christ with his crown of thorns. His simple robes glow in the light from a lantern held in his left hand, while his right hand is held aloft as if he is pointing out a path. Mary knows that this is the famous painting *The Light of The World* by William Holman Hunt, as she has gazed upon it many times during breaks in her work. Someone told her once that the Chancellor didn't believe in the Bible's version of the crucifixion. Mary can't understand how you can be a Christian if you don't believe that God sent his son to die for our sins.

The Chancellor gives a big belly-ache laugh which bounces off the stone walls of the cathedral and rings in her ears. Mary frowns because she does not think that this is a time for laughing – not with all those people outside.

They call it a peaceful protest but she is intimidated by the demonstrators. For a week now, Mary has tiptoed into work snaking her way through the forest of tents in Saint Paul's Churchyard. It makes her feel nervous and she doesn't care for their chanting, particularly when they use foul language. She shudders at the memory of the word they use to rhyme with bankers. She can't bring herself to repeat it, even in her head, as such language does not belong in a house of God – or outside on its steps for that matter.

The Chancellor with the inappropriate laugh told the man from the television news that the protesters were welcome and Mary wished he hadn't said that. She prays God will forgive her lack of charity, but she finds the protesters dirty and smelly and wishes that someone will magic them away. The rubbish is piling up outside the cathedral and the home-made banners look tawdry next to Wren's graceful architecture. The Chancellor had even told the police to allow demonstrators on to the steps of the cathedral which, as far as Mary is concerned, defiles the very steps where Lady Diana stood in her beautiful wedding gown before she entered the cathedral to marry her prince. In Mary's opinion, buildings dedicated to God should not be hijacked for political purposes and it is wrong to allow the steps to be commandeered by the protesters. The Chancellor disagrees, saying that we should worship God and his values and not the building, and that Jesus himself would be outside with the protesters and not inside the cathedral with the worshippers.

Mary does not know about that, but wonders why the demonstrators can't find somewhere else to pitch their tents. They are angry about bankers being paid lots of money and making a mess of the economy. They are not upset with the Church, so why do they have to camp outside Saint Paul's? Their target is the London Stock Exchange – she knows that from their 'Occupy LSX' banners – but the Stock Exchange is almost 200 yards away across Paternoster Square.

It has also been obvious in the last few days that visitor numbers have dropped off. Worshippers and tourists are too scared to walk through the tents to the cathedral entrance and admission fees and café takings must be well down on normal, which can't be good for the cathedral's finances. In fact, as Mary looks around the cavernous cathedral now, she does not see any visitors.

Mary turns her head back to the front and considers the Treasurer. He is listening politely to the Chancellor but when the Chancellor laughs he just smiles, and then looks nervously down at his feet as if he is concerned that people may feel he isn't taking the situation seriously. Perhaps, thinks Mary, he is worried about the money.

Mary wrings the orange duster in her hand. She hopes the Dean won't take long because there is a lot of bronze and silver to be cleaned and she wants to get home on time. And today, she wants to give the Henry Moore sculpture that stands in the North Quire Aisle a good polish. Mary has always been especially fond of that piece – *Mother and Child* – and it gives her particular pleasure to make its beautiful marble surface pristine for their visitors.

The Dean coughs once, twice and they fall silent. He has short grey hair and a crinkled brow. It may be her imagination but Mary feels sure that his hair is a little greyer now than it was a week ago, before all the unpleasantness started.

'Dear colleagues,' he starts. A murmur goes around the staff. The gravity of his tone does not bode well. The Dean pauses, before starting again.

'Dear colleagues, thank you for being with us today. As you know, this last week has been a difficult one for us here at Saint Paul's. We fully support people's democratic right to protest and we are pleased that, to date, the protest outside our great cathedral has been a peaceful one. Indeed, there is something deeply appropriate that a protest in favour of fairness and equality should be conducted on the steps of this most holy of places. However, the size and nature of the camp brings with it a number of practical issues, issues which I discussed last night with members of the Chapter. It is these issues and their consequence that I wish to speak to you about today.

'We have been advised by our health and safety officers and our fire officers that there are serious risks to the safety of the public, our members of staff and, indeed, the protesters themselves, arising from the current situation. These include a fire hazard from the stoves and fires being used in the camp, combined with the limited access that now exists to and from the cathedral, and the obvious health issues associated with so many people camped in an area without proper sanitation.'

Mary shudders at the thought of the rats and mice and other pests scuttling around the churchyard. At the same time, she wipes away the question of where all those people do their business. It is too disgusting for her even to think about it.

The Dean continues.

'As a result of these reports from our advisers and my meeting with the Chapter last night, we have taken the difficult decision to close Saint Paul's until further notice.'

There is a great gasp among the 200 or so people in the cathedral. The last time Saint Paul's closed was during the war, when an unexploded bomb landed in Dean's Yard.

The Dean looks up, waiting for his audience to fall silent. Mary fancies that his shoulders sag as he scans the dismayed faces in front of him. He returns to his notes.

'We have taken this decision with heavy hearts but believe that we have no lawful alternative. As your Dean, I have written an open letter to the protesters outlining our decision to close the cathedral and the reasons for doing so. This letter was released shortly before this meeting and my colleagues...' he signals the Chancellor, Treasurer and others standing behind him, '... will distribute copies of this letter to you after this meeting. In my letter, you will see that I have requested that the protesters vacate the camp to allow us to reopen the cathedral as soon as possible.'

Out of the corner of her eye, Mary senses a barely imperceptible shake of the head from the Chancellor.

'In the meantime, I have asked the Registrar to implement emergency procedures to secure the cathedral during this closure and to ensure that it is fit for purpose when we are able to open our doors again to worshippers, visitors and other pilgrims.

'Finally, I would like to make one last point, and that is this. It is important for you to understand that all of the Chapter are at one on this difficult decision. As a Church, we sit alongside many of the protesters' aims in seeking greater fairness and justice in the world, and this debate is at the heart of much of what we do here at Saint Paul's. However, today is about our ability to continue our mission and to provide free and open access to this most hallowed place.

We hope that the protesters will appreciate the issues that we face, recognise that their voice has been heard, and withdraw peacefully from the vicinity of the cathedral to allow us to continue God's work.

'Thank you for listening and may God be with you.'

Saint Paul's Cathedral and the Occupy London Stock Exchange (Occupy LSX) Peace Camp

On 15 October 2011, as part of a day of global action, some 3,000 protesters attempted to occupy Paternoster Square, home of the London Stock Exchange. Paternoster Square is private property and a High Court injunction was obtained to prevent public access. The police sealed off the square and as a result, the protesters moved to the nearest public space, Saint Paul's Churchyard, outside the entrance to Saint Paul's Cathedral. The protesters issued the following statement:

At today's assembly of over 500 people on the steps of St Paul's, #occupylsx collectively agreed the initial statement below. Please note, like all forms of direct democracy, the statement will always be a work in progress.

1. The current system is unsustainable. It is undemocratic and unjust. We need alternatives; this is where we work towards them.

2. We are of all ethnicities, backgrounds, genders, generations, sexualities, dis/abilities and faiths. We stand together with occupations all over the world.

3. We refuse to pay for the banks' crisis.

4. We do not accept the cuts as either necessary or inevitable. We demand an end to global tax injustice and our democracy representing corporations instead of the people.

5. We want regulators to be genuinely independent of the industries they regulate.

6. We support the strike on 30 November [public sector workers' strike over pensions] and the student action on 9 November [student march against tuition fees and the privatisation of universities one year on from the 2010 London Student Demonstrations and Riots], and actions to defend our health services, welfare, education and employment, and to stop wars and arms dealing.

7. We want structural change towards authentic global equality. The world's resources must go towards caring for people and the planet, not the military, corporate profits or the rich.

8. We stand in solidarity with the global oppressed and we call for an end to the actions of our government and others in causing this oppression.

9. This is what democracy looks like. Come and join us!'

A substantial minority of the protesters stayed to camp on the first night and by the third night there were 100-150 tents in Saint Paul's Churchyard. On the Sunday (Day 3 of the protest), the Reverend Canon Dr Giles Fraser, Chancellor of Saint Paul's, stated that he supported the peaceful protest. He was interviewed on television outside Saint Paul's where he confirmed that Sunday services were proceeding as normal and explained that he had asked a line of policemen to stand down and allow the protesters on to the cathedral steps. Following this intervention, Giles Fraser became something of a talisman figure to the protesters.

The cathedral's stance shifted, though, over the course of the next few days as the protest continued, and on 21 October, quoting health and safety and fire risks, the Dean of Saint Paul's, the Reverend Graeme Knowles, announced that the cathedral would close to the public until further notice.

In response to this, the protesters made some concessions – in particular, allowing barriers to be erected to permit public access to the side door of Saint Paul's. Consequently, the cathedral reopened one week later on 28 October although the galleries and dome remained closed.

However, by this time, the Cathedral Chapter (consisting of the Dean, the four residential Canons, the Chancellor, the Treasurer, the Pastor and the Precentor, and three lay Canons) had determined to support the City of London in their application to evict the protesters from Saint Paul's Churchyard. The Church insisted that this was a decision based on safety grounds, although some protesters suggested that loss of income from paying visitors was also behind the decision. Saint Paul's Cathedral charges an admission fee to sightseers for entry and operates both a café and a restaurant.

Giles Fraser resigned as Chancellor on 27 October, stating that he feared that a forcible eviction of the protesters could result in violence being perpetrated in the name of the Church. Fraser Dyer, a part-time chaplain at Saint Paul's, resigned the following day for similar reasons. The Treasurer, Mark Oakley, stated publically that he had supported Giles Fraser's stance in Chapter and was reported to be considering his position. In the event, he did not resign his post.

There then followed a backlash against the Chapter's handling of the situation, including its decisions to close the cathedral and to support the Corporation of London's legal action to evict the protesters, and more generally its failure to engage effectively with the issues raised by the protesters. Graeme Knowles subsequently resigned as Dean on 31 October, saying that his position had become untenable.

The protesters were finally evicted by a team of bailiffs and police four months later on the evening of 27 February 2012 after the City of London Corporation eventually secured its court order. The eviction was relatively peaceful; video footage shows one incident of an object being thrown at, and striking, a bailiff, a piece of wood being thrown which did not hit anyone, and one bailiff being dragged from a barrier as he attempted to remove protesters. Otherwise, there were only minor scuffles and chanting, although twenty-three people were arrested by police. Giles Fraser was present in a show of support for the protesters, but failed to gain access to the camp as police cordoned off the area.

In one piece of video, in answer to a specific question from one of the more prominent Occupy London activists, a member of the police is heard confirming that they had permission from Saint Paul's to remove protesters from the cathedral steps.

One year later, Saint Paul's announced that the Treasurer, Mark Oakley, would be promoted to the position of Chancellor vacated by Giles Fraser, with effect from 1 January 2013. Part of the Chancellor's role is to oversee the cathedral's arts programme. Saint Paul's is, and has been, host to a number of works of art designed to provoke thought, including a Yoko Ono installation, an Anthony Gormley sculpture and, in autumn 2013, a bronze statue by Nicola Hicks of a man holding another injured or dead man in his arms. The statue, created by Hicks in 1993 during the Bosnian war, is entitled Sorry, Sorry Sarajevo and was placed in the Dean's Aisle opposite the permanent Henry Moore exhibit, Mother and Child: Hood, a representation of the Madonna and Child in marble.

Saint Paul's to St Martins Le Grand

'Greetings cards?'

Annie ignores me. 'Occupy London sounds like a cause that Summer would have believed in. Was she there?'

'Oh no,' I answer quickly. 'She read about it avidly of course, but Summer was not that predictable. In fact, she was against the protest at Saint Paul's.'

Annie looks bemused. 'Why? It sounds right up her street. Anti-establishment, anti-corruption, pro-democracy.'

'Maybe, but she hated any political activist group that dragged religion into the argument. For her, it was unforgiveable that they made Saint Paul's their base. In Summer's mind, they put good men in a terrible position and forced them to make impossible choices.'

Annie scratches her head as we walk up into the City.

'Now you put it like that...'

'And to give Summer credit, she also thought that the issues were much more complex than the protesters made out. Occupy London seemed to be a mishmash of causes with easy targets, but for Summer it was too simple to bash greedy bankers, or criticise the power of corporations. And the protesters didn't have any answers. Not ones that would work in the real world, anyway.'

'I guess we didn't hear much about their proposals, more their gripes,' conceded Annie.

'Summer would have agreed with you. She thought they were very good at expressing what they didn't like and less good at coming up with their own solutions. They had a form of parliament where they all sat in a tent and had to agree on everything. All that meant was they came up with a bunch of anodyne statements that sounded like rallying calls – Stop Corruption, Fight Injustice, Feed the Poor – stuff that you can't argue against but how do you get it done?'

Annie turns her blue eyes on me. I have worked out

by now that she does this when she is about to ask a killer question.

'And what did you think?' she asks innocently.

I can't stop myself.

'I thought that all they achieved was a few church dignitaries losing their jobs.'

Annie stops walking and stamps her foot.

'Ben, you are hopeless.'

I am laughing.

'Sorry. I knew that would wind you up. Look, there are some things in society that don't seem right and what they did made a lot of people think, which was a good thing.'

Annie punches my arm again. An image of Summer flashes in my head.

'Well, that's a better response.'

'You know,' I continue, 'I was able to get into the library at Saint Paul's once, when I was at UCL. One of their most valuable books is an English translation of the Bible by a chap called William Tyndale.'

Annie looks at me curiously. 'What's so special about that?'

'It dates back to the early sixteenth century. At the time, English translations of the Bible were strictly forbidden. The Catholic Church was worried about the rise of the protestant movement and the only approved translation was in Latin.'

'And? Go on.'

'Well, Tyndale printed English language bibles in Germany and sent them over to England. The Church burnt all the ones they found and now there are only three of his bibles left, including the one in Saint Paul's. He also managed to piss off Henry VIII by criticising his divorce of Catherine of Aragon and remarriage to Anne Boleyn.'

'That must have reduced his life expectancy,' observes Annie.

'Quite. In the end, he was caught in Belgium and strangled to death for heresy. Or he might have been burnt to death. No one's sure whether he was already dead from the strangling when they put him on the stake. His last words were, "Lord! Open the King's eyes."'

Annie looks bemused. 'I'd never heard that story. How sad.'

'Yes, but the point is that only four years later, Henry VIII's eyes *were* opened and he authorised English translations of the Bible based on Tyndale's version. Now you find an English bible in every hotel room in the country.'

'Meaning?' She raises an eyebrow.

'Meaning attitudes change. Maybe in a few years' time, or even 400 years, people will look back on the Saint Paul's protesters and think how they were obviously in the right. How could the rest of us have been so stupid?'

'Mmm.' Annie considers this, but before she can respond, a caterwauling starts up behind us.

We both turn round. The four women with the pink wigs who we had seen at the UCL pit stop are behind us, and they have launched into song. Inevitably, it is '500 Miles' by The Proclaimers.

'And I will walk 500 miles…'

They sound like a hen party at a karaoke evening after a few drinks too many.

'Oh God!' sighs Annie. 'How long are we going to have to put up with this?'

'And I will walk 500 more…'

I smile. I admire their spirit, if not their singing ability.

'Da-da-da-da-dah, da-da-da-dah…'

Oh dear. They only know two lines.

'Come on,' urges Annie, 'let's get a shift on and get away from this. I have sensitive ears.'

'Alright,' I say, my thigh muscles screaming at me as we increase our pace, 'but you're going to have to tell me about the greetings cards thing.'

Annie shrugs.

'It's no big deal. I'm a graphic designer, and that's what I design.'

'Birthday cards?'

'Everything. Cards for birthdays, Mother's Day, Father's Day, Valentine's Day, Christmas, Easter, Get Well Soon, With Sympathy, New Baby, New Job, Retirement, Sorry You're Leaving, Glad You're Leaving, Best Friends, Worst Enemies, Good Luck, Bad Luck, Nice Hairdo…'

'You're making these up now.'

She flicks her ponytail and smiles at me.

'OK, I'm making some of them up. But honestly, there are cards for everything now. It's a wonder we're not sending one to someone for something every day of the week.'

'Please tell me,' I say, 'that you don't write the mushy verses in the middle.'

'You mean, like: "With every beat, my heart is true, and when I sleep, I dream of you"?'

'You didn't write that!'

'No. I didn't write that.'

We laugh together. The girls behind have moved on to Abba now, and Annie's high-pitched giggle tinkles prettily compared to the tuneless strains of 'Dancing Queen' behind us.

We have turned into St Martins Le Grand. I have been here before.

Tuesday 13 May 2008

Summer texted me about meeting for lunch after lectures. It was a warm spring day and she suggested a park in the City, which intrigued me as we didn't often venture east. As always, I went with the Summer flow. The park was just north of Saint Paul's and I brought sandwiches and apple juice for the two of us because I knew that Summer would never think to provide lunch. When I got there, she was sitting on the grass eating cherries casually from a plastic punnet.

'This is a pretty place,' I said, looking around.

The park looked vaguely familiar, but I couldn't remember having been here before. Around us, groups of office workers were taking advantage of the fine weather to spend their lunch break sunning themselves on the grass. There were beds of pink camellias and yellow pansies and neat holly bushes, and a magnificent horse chestnut tree in full bloom provided shade. A red-brick church with a white clapboard bell tower stood in one corner and rows of moss-stained gravestones were lined against the park walls. To one side, what looked like an extended lean-to was propped up against the flat-faced apartment building behind. Under its shelter, I could see plaques on the wall, ignored by the people sitting on the benches below who read papers, played with mobile phones or simply stared glassy-eyed into the distance. It wasn't much more than a garden shed, but it did look familiar.

'It's called Postman's Park,' said Summer. 'I thought you might know it.'

'Can't say that I do,' I replied, settling down on the grass beside her.

Summer reached over and gave me a cherry-breath kiss.

'Why is it called Postman's Park?' I asked.

She pointed to a white marble building that towered over us and formed the southern perimeter of the park.

'That,' she said, 'was the General Post Office headquarters

when the park was opened. Instead of students like us sitting here, there were postmen.'

I chewed a corner of my sandwich.

'OK, interesting,' I conceded. 'How did you find out about it?'

'From the movie, silly.'

'The movie?'

'Oh, come on, Ben. You're being dense.' She bit into a cherry and a trickle of juice rolled down her chin. I made a move to lick it, but Summer was ahead of me and wiped the juice away with a finger. She held her finger to my lips so that I could taste the sweetness of the cherry.

'Come on,' she said, getting up. 'I'll show you.'

She grabbed my hand, dragged me to my feet, and pulled me over to the shelter, abandoning our food and drink. A man in a Superdry T-shirt looked up from his copy of *Metro* as we approached. He could tell that Summer wanted to read the plaques on the wall above him and he slid along the bench to be out of the way.

I saw now that the plaques were made up of ceramic tiles, arranged in rows, some of them cracked and most fading with age. Each of them bore a name, a few words in a mix of fonts, and a date; most had a date in the late nineteenth century. About half of the tiles were decorated with mauve-bud flowers, the other half with what looked like stylised candelabra with green flames shooting from the tops of them. The two middle rows were full, while the top row was partially tiled and the bottom row was empty. It all looked haphazard and unfinished.

Summer took me to one side and pointed at a tablet made up of eight tiles.

'See. Look at that.'

I read it. 'G. F. WATTS'S MEMORIAL TO HEROIC SELF-SACRIFICE.'

'What is this?' I asked Summer.

'G. F. Watts's memorial to heroic self-sacrifice,' she answered, unhelpfully.

I laughed. 'I can read that Summer. But what is it?'

'A Victorian memorial to ordinary people who gave up

their lives trying to save others. Look.' She dragged me back
under the lean-to and pointed out one of the tiles.

'ELIZABETH BOXALL
AGED 17 OF BETHNAL GREEN
WHO DIED OF INJURIES RECEIVED
IN TRYING TO SAVE
A CHILD
FROM A RUNAWAY HORSE
JUNE 20 1888'

'How sad,' I said, inadequately.

I read another about Samuel Lowdell, a bargeman who had
drowned while rescuing a boy who had fallen in the Thames at
Blackfriars Bridge. Apparently he had already saved two others
before the water dragged him to his death. And then there was
Sarah Smith, a pantomime artiste who 'died of terrible injuries
when attempting in her inflammable dress to extinguish the
flames that had engulfed her companion'. It was all terribly
Victorian and yet there was a certain charm and pathos to the
memorial.

There must have been about fifty tiles, each of them
carrying a story of heroism. A surprising number of Victorians
seemed to have died in tragic accidents involving drowning or
being burnt to death. Summer tugged me over to look at one
in the middle row.

'This is what I wanted you to see.' She hopped from one
foot to another with excitement.

It was a tile dedicated to the memory of Alice Ayres, a
bricklayer's daughter, who perished saving three children
from a house fire in Borough. Alice Ayres? I had heard that
name before.

'Come on, Ben. Don't make me have to tell you?' Summer
was testing me.

Alice Ayres. Something to do with a movie.

And then a light flicked on in my head and I remembered.
Last night at the college film club we watched *Closer* with
Natalie Portman and Jude Law. This was the name of Natalie

Portman's character – Alice Ayres – stolen from a tablet she saw on a memorial in a park. Summer had loved that film. She had bounced back to my room afterwards.

'Ahh. I see. From last night. *Closer.*'

'Yes!' Summer shouted and punched my arm. 'I knew you'd get it… eventually.'

She gave me a fake frown to chastise me for being slow. 'This is the actual park where they came in the film.'

Summer put her arms around me and squeezed me so hard I struggled for breath. The man in the Superdry T-shirt gave me a look as if to say, 'What's all the fuss about?' Unlike me, he couldn't smell cherries.

St Martins Le Grand to Leadenhall Market

'When I saw the film, I didn't realise it was an actual London park. I looked it up when I got back to UCL. George Watts was a painter and he proposed the memorial to commemorate Victoria's Golden Jubilee. When it was unveiled in 1900, it only had four plaques.'

'And the rest have been added since?' Annie asks.

'Yes. Hence the different styles. Most of them were added in the early 1900s, but there is one from 2007. A guy who died saving a girl from drowning in the Thames. They might start putting up new ones again now to use up the spare spaces.'

'Well, that sounds like a good thing to do.'

She hesitates.

'I've seen that film though. I thought all the characters were horrible. Why did Summer like it so much?'

'They were. But the film was about truth in relationships. They insisted on telling each other the brutal truth and that generally turned out to be a bad plan. Summer could relate to that. Like I said before, there were parts of her life that were closed doors to me and I just had to trust that it was better that way.'

'Mmm. I'm not sure about that,' Annie replies.

'Well, that was just the way it was. I accepted Summer on those terms or not at all.'

'And I suppose Summer related to the Natalie Portman character?'

I am taken aback by Annie's insight. The Natalie Portman character was different from the others. She lived a lie all the way through, stealing her name from an old memorial, and the film's big reveal is when Jude Law goes to the park and sees the tile with Alice Ayres written on it. Then he realises she was lying to him all along.

'You know, I think you're right. Summer saw a bit of herself in Alice Ayres.'

'Summer certainly sounds like someone who would have sacrificed herself to save the lives of three children.'

I look at Annie with her crème-caramel hair tied back in a simple ponytail, her ridiculous rainbow beanie hat, and her impossibly thin legs that are carrying her for twenty-six miles. A ripple of tenderness comes over me. Annie never met Summer, but she understands her. Instinctively, I put my arm around her shoulder.

Annie pushes me away and even in the darkness, I can see her face go pale.

'I'm sorry,' I stutter, 'I didn't mean...'

'No, no. You're fine.' Her words come out in a hurry. 'It's just...'

We have rounded a corner and are heading down St Mary Axe. To our left is the torpedo-shaped Gherkin building, a phoenix from the ashes of the old Baltic Exchange, bombed by the IRA in the early nineties.

'It's just?' I ask, gently.

'It's just that building is where Peter used to work.' She points at the Gherkin.

'Oh.' I'm not sure what to say. 'I'm sorry. I didn't know he was a banker.'

'He wasn't,' she says, 'he was in insurance. Funny thing really. That was all I ever knew. I never understood what he actually did in insurance.'

She goes quiet and we walk on in silence.

I look at my watch. It is nearly 2.45am and we are past mile seventeen. Within a few minutes, the glass roof and cobbled stones of Leadenhall Market come into view and a string of volunteers are holding out goodies for us. Annie puts her hand on my arm.

'I'm sorry,' she says, 'sometimes I get a bit... sad.'

'It's OK. That's allowed,' I reply. 'Now, come on. My feet feel like they have been cut to ribbons. I need some of your nursing skills.'

★

We spend nearly fifteen minutes at the pit stop. My right sock is now soaked with blood and the blister on my left heel has also come up. Annie takes charge. She cleans up the blood, puts antiseptic cream on the blisters and finds some second skin in her backpack.

'That should be better than ordinary plasters,' she tells me.

I dig out a spare pair of socks from my bag and roll them gently on to my feet.

'Are you sure you're not a nurse?' I ask.

'I'll send you one of my 'Get Well Soon' cards next week,' she says. 'Personally signed.'

She smiles, but before I can think of a good reply we are interrupted by the singing women, who have caught us up in the time it has taken to treat my injuries. They are now onto Wham and 'Last Christmas', which seems unseasonal for September, but at least they know the words to the chorus. As they come into the pit stop, they spark off the volunteers who join in with remarkable gusto.

Annie puts on her backpack.

'Time to go,' she says. 'I haven't liked this song since… well, you know.'

I know. Of course I know.

'And,' she grimaces, 'they'll be singing Barry Manilow soon.'

I tie up my trainers, stand up and stamp my feet a couple of times.

'Good as new,' I announce. 'Let's go.'

We leave the market, heading towards Bank, arms and legs pumping. The City streets are eerily quiet as we walk past the Mansion House and down Queen Victoria Street towards the river. The rain has stopped but the night is getting colder now. Lights blaze in a late night, early morning bar and a group of smoker-drinkers congregated under heat lamps wave and give us a cheer. Annie waves back good-naturedly and receives some politically incorrect wolf whistles in return. She smiles and I can tell that she is a little flattered. I hunch my shoulders against the chill; it is 3am in the morning.

We sweep down to Blackfriars and on to the riverside path. I know from experience that it is a dark and creepy spot after sunset, but tonight we are protected by a phalanx of neon and glow-sticked walkers. There are no homeless people here tonight; perhaps the stream of Shine walkers has persuaded them to move to other pitches.

Ahead of us are the red and ivory rust-stained spans of Blackfriars Bridge, where an Italian banker was once found hanging from scaffolding beneath its parapet, his jacket pockets stuffed with bricks and dollar bills. I picture him now, cold, pale, with his neck snapped sideways by the rope, swaying over the water below. The last thing he saw was the Southbank skyline that I am looking at now.

There are other ways to die here. The river beckons me to jump over the parapet, but I know that if you fall in, accidentally or deliberately, the strong currents will suck you to the bottom, just like poor old Samuel Lowdell from the self-sacrifice memorial. The cold Thames water will flood your lungs and squeeze the life out of you. Your body will lie on the riverbed, until eventually the very same currents that dragged you to your death will expel your bloated and disfigured corpse on to the shore, where an unfortunate boatman or passer-by will discover you. I look at the shore and wonder how many dead bodies have washed up here over the centuries.

★

We pass under the bridge's just-above-head-height rafters that look like giant Meccano. There are fifty metres between the road bridge and the modern rail bridge that carries trains to and from Blackfriars station, and between the two bridges, eight clusters of terracotta columns, four columns in each group, stand like lost souls in the swirling river. Each cluster rests on a partially submerged cylindrical granite base swathed in algae and clinging barnacles. A bottle-green cormorant perched on the capital of the nearest column watches us suspiciously with a yellow eye. It is a non-bridge. The old span that carried the railway was too weak for modern trains and was eventually sliced away, but the pillars remain, marooned in the muddy Thames waters.

As we pass by the non-bridge, a cocktail of guilt, excitement, fear and above all, sadness, bounces around my head. For months now, I have been like the terracotta columns: stranded, aimless, obsolete.

Blackfriars Bridge

Tuesday 23 September 2008

After the flashmob iftar, Summer dragged me down to the Embankment near Blackfriars Bridge. She removed her headscarf and packed it away in the basket. It was a warm evening, but there were few people about. We dropped on to the footpath that ran alongside the river and Summer held my hand as we gazed out over the water. Summer was right: the lights from the offices and flats on the Southbank shimmered in the oily Thames.

Across from us was the Oxo Building, with the letters O-X-O carved into its tower, and to the right, the no-frills concrete of Waterloo Bridge and the National Theatre. The full circle of the London Eye, shining white, was almost directly in front of us, an indication of just how much the river bends. The Thames itself was a hive of activity. A line of barges carrying heaps of sludge chugged downriver towards Tower Bridge, belching diesel fumes into the air, while a police boat screamed past, sending a succession of small waves flapping against the stone wall of the Embankment beneath us.

'Hey!'

I heard a voice behind me, turned round and recognised him immediately. Unwashed, black hair, pot belly, slack lip, snub nose, grimy sweatpants. The Asian man from Lincoln's Inn Fields. A light glinted on glass. He was holding an empty beer bottle which he waved in my direction.

'Hand me your wallet.'

'Manu! Don't!' Summer shouted at him over my shoulder.

'Why?' he hissed. 'This man's messing with you. The least he can do is spare me some cash.'

I hesitated.

'Come on, man. I haven't got all day.'

'Ben, go on, give him your money,' urged Summer. I could feel her shaking.

He took a step towards us and Summer flinched. I stepped across to protect her and growled at him.

'Yeah. And what if I don't?'

'Tell him to give me the fucking wallet, mishti, or I'll cut him.' He bent down and smashed the bottle on the ground, sending shards of glass skittering across the paving stones. When he stood up, the top of the bottle had gone, leaving a sharp, jagged edge at its neck.

'And you,' he pointed the broken bottle at Summer's bracelet, 'you can give me that thing round your wrist.'

'No!' She moved out from behind me.

'It's OK, Summer,' I said, stepping between her and our assailant. 'I can handle this.'

'Think you can,' he snarled. 'Think you can handle this?' He thrust the bottle in my direction and I took a pace back, pulling Summer with me. She gripped my arm and her fingernails pinched my flesh.

'Forgive me for interfering,' a Queen's English accent cut through the charged atmosphere, 'but might I be so bold as to ask what is happening here?'

Percival, the homeless man from the flashmob iftar, emerged from the shadows, clutching his Sainsbury's bags, his fedora tilted at an angle.

'Go away, old man. This is none of your business.' The Asian man flashed him a sight of the bottle and scowled.

'Do I discern that you are threatening my friends, sir?' Percival was not going to be scared away so easily. He dropped his bags and raised his fists, taking up a comical boxer's stance. 'Any man who fights friends of mine must also fight me. Put 'em up, you varlet.'

Our would-be attacker glared at him, weighing up the situation in his head.

He turned and pointed the bottle in Summer's direction.

'Tell the old guy to fucking piss off.'

Summer stood out from behind me and spoke in a voice clear as a bell.

'You know, swearing doesn't suit you, Manu,' she said, firmly.

'Oh, for fuck's sake.' He threw the bottle against the wall

behind him in a gesture of disgust. Splinters of glass arced through the air, catching the lights from the bridge.

'You owe me, mishti,' he growled, then turned and jogged away.

I stared at Percival who touched his hat.

'At your service, sir, ma'am.' He picked up his bags and retreated down the path.

I watched him go, taking a moment to pull my thoughts together.

'Summer,' I said, 'the mugger? Do you know him?'

I turned back to her and as I did so she pushed me against the stone parapet that formed the river wall, planting hot kisses on my mouth, my cheeks, my neck.

'Ben, now,' she murmured. 'I want you now.'

'Summer, that guy...'

'It's OK,' she was breathless. 'He's not coming back.'

Her hand snaked down to my trousers and I was instantly silenced. In one movement, she released my penis and twisted round so that she had her back to the wall. She pressed her lips on mine while her hands fumbled with her skirt. I pushed against her and she slid her knickers to one side, guiding me in. She was so wet I entered her easily. The scent of her lavender and orange perfume and the rush of blood through my veins made me giddy and I swayed, my hands groping for purchase on the wall. I stretched out, lay my palms flat on the parapet and thrust hard. Summer groaned, digging her fingernails into my cheeks, and I screwed my eyes shut to ignore the sting of the scratches. We were panting in unison and my body shuddered as I reached my climax. She grabbed me round the shoulders and pulled me closer to her – she didn't want me to stop – I pushed one more time and then she stiffened as her orgasm swept through her. She threw her head back and let herself fall. Still inside her, I caught her under her arms, and we fell against the wall, our hearts racing.

The roar of cars crossing the bridge echoed in my ears and behind us, a boat sounded a horn. Summer reached up and kissed me on my hot cheeks.

'You're bleeding,' she said, licking pinpricks of blood from her lips.

Blackfriars Bridge to the Tower of London

Annie is laughing. 'What? You did it here?'

I have to admit that underneath the arch of Blackfriars Bridge is not the most romantic spot in the world. I sniff the air, hoping for a hint of lavender or orange blossom. Instead, I inhale diesel and rotten fish.

'It was a spur of the moment thing,' I explain. 'Adrenaline, you know?'

Annie smiles. 'I'm not sure I do.'

But the shine in her eyes gives her away.

'I think you do,' I say.

She punches my arm and we walk on. Towards London Bridge, the Tower of London and Tower Bridge, which will be the easternmost part of the walk. Then we will turn and follow the river back to Battersea. My thighs are seizing up and my blisters are shooting jabs of pain into my feet at every step, but I am strangely saddened by the thought that there are only eight miles to go. I have two and a half hours at most left of Annie's company.

A beefeater stood at the base of the White Tower addressing some twenty tourists. I wheeled Summer up to the group so that we could listen in. It was a hot day, but Summer kept a rug over her thin legs. She wore her pixie-green peaked cap and underneath it, her once glossy hair had been reduced to grey wisps. Sometimes I thought that, without the cap, it would only take a breath of wind to scatter her tufts like seed pods from a dandelion clock.

I was fulfilling a promise I made seven months before, to take Summer to the Tower of London to see the Crown Jewels. I worried that she was too weak, but my concern was outweighed by my fear that if we didn't go now, we might never have another opportunity, and I couldn't break a promise to Summer.

The beefeater was running through his script.

'And this is where the famous princes in the tower – twelve-year-old Edward V and his younger brother, Richard – were held captive in 1483 before they disappeared. We believe that they were murdered on the orders of Richard III so that he could become king.'

Summer shuddered next to me.

'So much of the history of the Royal Family is terrible,' she said.

I let her comment pass and the beefeater continued.

'Other famous prisoners include Anne Boleyn – her headless ghost is still believed to haunt the tower – and Lady Jane Grey, who was queen for only nine days. Both were beheaded here in the Tower of London. And a German spy called Josef Jakobs – the last person to be executed here – who was killed by firing squad over there in the moat in 1941.'

The group turned their heads to where he was pointing.

A handful of children were rolling on the grass, laughing, while their parents looked on. One of the dads was hunched down on his hands and knees, engaged in a play-fight with three boys, who took it in turns to jump on his back and then squealed as he shrugged them off. It was hard to imagine that such bloody events had happened in this place.

A man to one side of us with an industrial-sized camera hanging from his neck raised his hand.

'Yes, sir?' the Beefeater acknowledged him.

'Is it true that the Kray twins were the last prisoners to be held here?'

The beefeater did not seem phased by the question.

'That depends on your definition of the term 'prisoner'. The Kray twins were indeed detained here for refusing National Service. They were held for a week before being transferred to military prison to await court martial.'

Summer leant over to me.

'Who were the Kray twins?' she asked.

'Ronnie and Reggie Kray. London gangsters in the '50s and '60s. Pretty ruthless,' I explained. 'The regiment they were assigned to was stationed here, but after they reported for duty, Ronnie Kray punched the corporal in charge and they went back home to the East End for their tea.'

Summer smiled.

'You've been looking things up again.'

'Well, maybe just a bit,' I conceded.

The man with the camera lifted his hand again, like the class swot.

'And Rudolf Hess?'

The beefeater cleared his throat.

'Yes. You are quite right, sir.' I sensed a degree of irritation in his voice. 'Rudolf Hess, the Deputy Führer, who parachuted into Scotland on a failed peace mission in 1941 in the early days of the war. He was held here temporarily before he was transferred to a secure house in Surrey on a more permanent basis.'

The beefeater paused for a moment, before speaking again. He was going to have the last word on prisoners in the Tower.

'In fact, while the stories of Rudolf Hess and the Kray

twins are relatively well-known,' he glared at Camera-Man, 'you may not know that the last person to be sentenced to imprisonment here was a British army officer called Norman Baillie-Stewart. He was convicted of treason in 1933 and spent four years incarcerated in the White Tower.'

'Ooh, how horrible,' said Summer, beside me, looking up at the tower. 'To be cooped up in such tiny rooms for all those years.'

Summer could never stand the idea of being caged.

'On his release,' the beefeater added, 'he fled to Germany where he broadcast Nazi propaganda on radio and was one of the voices that became known as Lord Haw Haw.'

'Did you research him too?' asked Summer.

I shook my head.

'You should do,' she said. 'He sounds interesting.'

Satisfied that he had trumped the know-it-all tourist, the beefeater began to walk away, his group following him obediently to the next point on their tour. Summer and I let them go and headed for the Jewel House.

The colours did not disappoint: the rich purple velvet in the crowns, the glittering rubies, emeralds and sapphires, the diamonds that sparkled rainbow colours in the glare of the artificial lights. I fussed over Summer, constantly checking that her rug was straight, asking if she wanted a drink of water, or anything to eat; I had brought Jaffa Cakes which were easy for her to chew and had become one of her favourite snacks. Interminable bouts of sickness during her treatment had made her teeth brittle, and a few had fallen out, although as if defying her illness, Summer smiled more than ever now.

After politely refusing a Jaffa Cake for the umpteenth time, she rested a bony hand on mine as we stopped by the cabinet containing the royal orb and sceptre.

'Ben, you know I love you,' she said.

I stroked her hand gently. Her paper-thin skin bruised easily these days.

'I worry about you, Ben,' she went on. 'What will you do after I've gone? I feel as if everything is going to fall on you. I'm scared that you will be crushed.'

I knelt down, desperately fending off tears. I cried a lot

those days – when she was asleep, when I was in the bathroom, when I left the house – but I never cried in front of her, and I wasn't going to start now. I looked into her tired face, with its sallow skin that sagged under her sharp cheekbones.

'You mustn't talk like that, Summer,' I said weakly.

Summer smiled.

'Denying it won't make it go away, Ben.'

I held my head in my hands. It was just not fair.

Tower of London

Monday 23 January 1933

'So, let me get this straight, Lieutenant. You met this girl...' the Colonel pauses and looks at his notebook '... Marie-Louise, when you were on holiday in Berlin.'

'Yes, sir.'

'And you were introduced by...' another glance at his notes '... a man you knew as Herr Obst.'

'I knew him as Herr Obst because that was his name.'

'That was his name.' The Colonel ponders this response. 'Can you describe this man for me?'

'He had a scar that ran down his left cheek.' The Lieutenant runs a finger from his eye down to his jaw.

'Is that it? A scar is all you remember about this man?'

'It was his most noteworthy feature.'

'Our information is that this man's real name is Muller and that he is a major in the German Intelligence Service.'

The Lieutenant regards him with unblinking blue eyes.

'His name was Obst. Otto Waldemar Obst.'

The Colonel scribbles in his notebook. A bird squawks outside the barred window.

'And you claim that you entered into a relationship with this Marie-Louise?'

'It is not a claim. It is a fact. She was infatuated with me.'

'We find that difficult to believe.' The Colonel sucks the end of his pencil and observes the young officer from across the wooden table. The Lieutenant is fresh-faced. Some might think it not inconceivable that an inexperienced young girl could fall for such a man.

'Do you expect me to respond to that?'

The Colonel ignores him.

'And you met...' he pauses again, '... Marie-Louise... on a number of occasions.'

'We went dancing several times. And we used to go to the park in Berlin.'

'Where on at least one occasion, you say you made love together?' The Colonel winces as he poses the question. In contrast, the Lieutenant smiles as he responds.

'It was by a lake. It was very romantic.'

The Colonel's lips tighten at the impudence of the man.

'Can you tell me this girl's surname?'

'I told you before. I do not know. She was twenty-two with blonde hair. She had money and I was grateful to have her attention. I never asked for her full name.'

'You made love to a girl and you didn't even know her name?'

'Her name was Marie-Louise.'

'In broad daylight? In a public park?' The Colonel's voice rises in pitch.

'In a park, yes, sir.' He waits a moment and then adds. 'There were bushes.'

The Colonel leans back in his chair.

'I am trying to help you here, Lieutenant.'

'And I am trying to help you, sir.'

'You would help me if you told me the truth.'

'I am telling you the truth, sir.'

The Colonel gives a sigh of exasperation.

'What was the address of this girl? Where did she live?'

'I do not know, sir.'

'You... do... not... know.' The Colonel repeats the words slowly, while writing them down ostentatiously in his book.

'She always asked to be dropped off a few blocks from where she lived. I understood that she did not want her parents to find out about me.'

'How very convenient.'

The Lieutenant does not reply. The Colonel picks up his book and turns back a few pages. He scans the page and stabs his finger on a particular note.

'You say you were in Berlin on a private holiday?'

'Yes, sir.'

'Yet we have reliable information that when you were in Berlin, you contacted the German War Office.'

'I tried to make contact, yes, sir.'

The Colonel smiles. 'And why did you do that?'

The Lieutenant picks up a glass of water from the table and takes a sip. He replaces the glass and picks at a thread on his uniform. The Colonel's patience is wearing thin.

'Why did you try to contact the German War Office, Lieutenant?'

'Because,' he replies, in an even tone, 'I was a British officer in a foreign country. I felt that it was incumbent upon me to pay my respects to our German counterparts.'

'Do you expect me to believe that, Lieutenant?'

The prisoner leans back, clasps his hands and tilts his head slightly, considering his reply.

'I am asking you to believe that, sir, because it is the truth.'

'Damn it, Lieutenant!'

The Colonel picks up his notebook and slaps it on the table. The slap echoes like a gunshot around the stone walls of the cylindrical room. The Lieutenant's water slops against the sides of the glass, and a drop spills over the rim and trickles slowly down to the tabletop. The Lieutenant does not flinch. He reaches into his pocket, withdraws a handkerchief, and dries the side of the glass. He dabs the table, but the single drop of water has already soaked into the wood.

The Colonel composes himself. He must remain calm in order to marshal the facts for the inevitable court case.

'Let us move on to Holland. August last year. What was the purpose of your visit to Holland?'

'To meet Marie-Louise.'

'To meet Marie-Louise?'

'As I said, she was infatuated with me. I suggested a flying visit to Holland when I left Berlin. It was easy for her to get to.'

The Colonel rubs his chin.

'Were her feelings for you reciprocated?'

'I'm sorry, I don't know what you mean.'

'Were you similarly infatuated with this girl, Lieutenant?'

'Oh, I see. I apologise.' He focuses on a point above the Colonel's left shoulder. 'No, I was not.'

'Lieutenant. Our records show that you visited the Hook

of Holland on 8 August last year, and then again in October and November. You are asking me to believe that you made three separate trips to Holland to meet a girl that you did not care for?'

'I did not say I didn't care for her. I am not entirely callous.'

'You know what I mean, officer,' the Colonel snaps back.

The Lieutenant shifts his gaze to the Colonel's reddening face.

'I told you, sir. She had money. I am embarrassed to admit it, but I also travelled to Holland in the hope... in the anticipation... that Marie-Louise would advance me some funds.'

'Money? How much money?'

'On the first occasion, I received £10 in Dutch Guilder.'

'£10? Is that all?'

'She gave me a further £5 in October. And again in November.'

'So,' the Colonel looks at the ceiling to make a show of adding up the sums in his head, then drops his eyes to the prisoner, 'you received £20 from Marie-Louise in Holland. What, may I ask, was this money for?'

The Lieutenant holds his head in his hands and a tremor of satisfaction rises in the Colonel's chest, but the prisoner's discomfort is only brief. He shakes his head, as if he has come to a decision. When he speaks, his voice is clear and confident.

'For services rendered, sir.'

'For services...' The Colonel cannot finish the sentence. He is stunned that an officer of the British army can possess such a brazen attitude.

The Lieutenant shrugs his shoulders.

'I saw the money as a gift, for the whole of our friendship. I have told you, sir. She was...'

'... infatuated with you. Yes. You have told me that before.'

Outside, the Colonel hears a yeoman barking orders. A new watch must be about to begin. The Colonel wonders what it is like to be incarcerated here, imprisoned by cold stone, with only the ghosts of Britain's bloody history for company.

'Lieutenant, we know that you met Muller when you were in Holland.'

'Muller?' His lower jaw rotates in a small circle, as if he is literally chewing this name over. 'Who is Muller?'

'Do not be obtuse, Lieutenant. The man you knew as Obst. Do you admit to meeting Muller... Obst... in Holland?'

'I met Marie-Louise in Holland. I have not seen Herr Obst since I left Berlin.' He reaches down for the glass of water and raises it to his lips. 'And I do not know your Muller.' He drinks from the glass.

The Colonel pushes his chair back and stands up. The chair legs scrape on the stone floor. He pulls some loose papers from his notebook and walks around the table so that he is standing behind the prisoner. The Lieutenant stares at the now empty chair in front of him.

The Colonel reaches over the prisoner's shoulder and lays the papers in front of him. He takes a few paces back, leans against the wall, and talks to the rear of the Lieutenant's head.

'Can you tell me what I have placed in front of you?'

The Lieutenant coughs and picks up the first sheet, staring at it for a few seconds before replying.

'It is a newspaper cutting. A photograph of a tank.'

'Do you recognise it?'

'The tank? No. I am not an expert.'

'Not the tank, man. The cutting.'

'The cutting?' The Lieutenant's voice lifts in an air of surprise. 'Is it *The Times*?'

The Colonel walks up to him and puts his mouth by the prisoner's ear. He could almost bite the man's earlobe.

'This cutting was found at your flat. Why would you have a picture of a tank?'

The Lieutenant doesn't miss a beat. 'Like lots of people, I keep a scrapbook. Perhaps this was in it, I don't know.'

The Colonel growls, 'What about the other two?'

'These are notes.' The Lieutenant speaks the words slowly. 'They are my notes,' he admits.

'They are your notes, yes,' says the Colonel, trying to hide the triumph in his voice. 'Your notes on the specifications of military equipment. Tanks, rifles, armoured cars. And details of vehicle movements. Am I correct?'

'I do not deny it.'

The Colonel walks back round to face him.

'Why did you make these notes, soldier?'

'I was studying for exams.'

The Colonel looks down on his charge, struggling to prevent his features from registering the scorn he feels. The prisoner continues.

'This information is not classified, sir. It is available from the library at Aldershot. You only have to look in the Army Manuals.'

The Colonel ignores him.

'You passed this information across to Muller, didn't you, Lieutenant?'

'I told you. I don't know any Muller.'

The Colonel leans in towards the prisoner, so that their faces are almost touching.

'This is the information he asked you for, isn't it? This is why you received the money?' He forces the words out through clenched teeth and globules of spit spatter on to the Lieutenant's face. The Colonel feels the heat in his cheeks and forehead. His head hurts from concentration.

The Lieutenant reaches into his pocket again for the handkerchief. He leans away and gently wipes the spit from his face. A spider scuttles across the floor and dives into a crevice.

The Colonel picks up the sheets of paper and tucks them back into his notebook. He retrieves another three pages and lays them on the table.

'Look at these, Lieutenant. Tell me what they are.'

The Lieutenant recognises them immediately. He glares at the Colonel.

'How did you procure these?'

The Colonel ignores him.

'That is not your concern. What are they, Lieutenant?'

The prisoner's shoulders slump and his face sags.

'They are private correspondence,' he says. 'Letters from Marie-Louise to me.'

'Forwarded by Muller.'

'Fowarded by Herr Obst. After our meetings in Holland, Marie-Louise requested that all correspondence be directed through Herr Obst, for reasons that I am sure you can understand.'

The Colonel grunts. 'Oh, I think I understand the reasons, Lieutenant.'

He settles down on his chair again, and puts his hand on the letters.

'What was in these letters, Lieutenant?' He waits a moment. 'Besides ardent declarations of undying love.'

The prisoner smiles, and the vein in the Colonel's temple pulses furiously. He is annoyed that he has allowed himself to be drawn into sarcasm.

'She sent me money, sir. As I am sure you are aware.'

'How much money, Lieutenant?'

'I believe the first letter contained £50, and the second £40.'

The Colonel opens his notebook. He writes down £50 and £40 in thick, black pencil.

'That is £90 in total, sir.'

The Colonel snaps his notebook shut and stares at him.

'I can perform simple arithmetic, officer.'

The Lieutenant looks down at the table and says nothing.

'What is your explanation for why you received this money?'

'Marie-Louise was a girl of some means. As I said, the money was a gift. For our friendship.'

'Are you saying that she paid you to be her... to be her...' the Colonel struggled for the word, '... paramour?'

The Lieutenant raises his eyes again. Baby blue eyes, set deep in his fresh, handsome face.

'I suppose you could put it like that, sir.'

'This third letter,' the Colonel taps his finger on one of the sheets, 'this was written by you, wasn't it? It is your handwriting, is it not?'

The Lieutenant picks up the letter and stares at it for a few seconds, his brow creased in thought.

'Yes, sir,' he says, eventually.

'And this letter is addressed to Herr Obst.'

'Yes, sir.'

The Colonel holds his tongue, waiting for the prisoner to elaborate. He is not disappointed.

'As I said, sir, Marie-Louise asked me to correspond through Herr Obst. The words in the letter were from me to her. Herr Obst was merely an intermediary.'

'And yet, it is signed...' the Colonel gently removes the letter from the prisoner's fingers and turns it round so that he can read it, '... it is signed... Alphonse Poiret. Why is that, Lieutenant? Why did you not sign your own name?'

'That was her private name for me, sir. It was a silly game that we played.'

'How very touching.' The Colonel drops the letter on to the table and sits back. He is unconvinced. 'I will give you one final chance, Lieutenant. The money was from Muller, wasn't it? In return for the intelligence you supplied him. The truth is that you are a traitor, sir. Herr Obst is a fiction and Marie-Louise is nothing but a figment of the imagination. A cover story. Is that not the reality, Lieutenant?'

'Marie-Louise is very real, sir. She is twenty-two. She is blonde. If you met her, I am sure that you would find her very...,' he searches for the word, '... enchanting.'

'Utter rot!' the Colonel exclaims.

'It is the truth, sir. Is it not your duty to discern the truth?'

The Colonel snorts like a locomotive letting off steam.

'How dare you presume to advise me as to my duty?'

He reaches into his pocket and pulls out a pear. He thuds it on to the wooden table, hard enough that it bruises. The Lieutenant's eyes widen as pear juice seeps into the wood.

'Lieutenant, do you know what Obst means in German?'

The Colonel cannot be certain, but he thinks he registers a flicker of alarm pass across the man's face.

'I am sure that you will tell me, sir.'

'It means "fruit". Obst means "fruit".'

'And Poiret? What does that mean in French?'

The Lieutenant mouths the words.

'I didn't hear that, officer. I am afraid that you will have to speak up.'

'It means "little pear",' he says.

'That's right, officer. Little pear. How affectionate.'

The Lieutenant's brow furrows. He is not smiling any longer.

'And do you know what this is?' The Colonel picks up the dappled-green pear in front of him. Juice trickles over his fingers. The prisoner's mouth is open but he does not answer.

'This, Lieutenant, is a variety of pear known as a...' the Colonel counts the seconds in his head – 1,000, 2,000, 3,000, '... a Marie-Louise.'

The Lieutenant shifts uneasily in his seat. The Colonel continues.

'Obst, Poiret, Marie-Louise. Is that not a remarkable coincidence, Lieutenant?'

The Colonel lifts the pear to his mouth and bites into it. It takes just a moment for him to swallow the soft flesh before he holds the part-eaten pear up for inspection. The prisoner is not smiling now. His lips are clamped tightly together.

'Mmm,' says the Colonel, 'Marie-Louise. Particularly sweet. You should try one sometime, Lieutenant.'

Both Rudolph Hess, the Deputy Führer to Adolph Hitler who had flown to Scotland early in World War II on an attempted peace mission, and the notorious East End villains, the Kray twins, were famously held in the Tower of London. Hess was held for four days in 1941, pending a transfer to Mytchett Place in Surrey. The Krays were confined for seven days in a guardroom in 1952 for refusing National Service, as the Tower of London was serving as the barracks for their regiment, the 1ˢᵗ Batallion Royal Fusiliers. The last execution to take place at the Tower was that of a hapless German spy, Josef Jakobs, who was captured by the Home Guard just minutes after he had parachuted into Huntingdonshire, and was killed by firing squad on 15 August 1941.

However, the last person to serve a formal prison sentence at the Tower of London imposed by a British court was Norman Baillie-Stewart, who was court martialled at Chelsea Barracks in March 1933 for contravention of the Official Secrets Act – in other words, he was found guilty of treason – and sentenced to five years' penal servitude. Baillie-Stewart, a handsome twenty-four-year-old lieutenant, was arrested in January 1933 and shortly afterwards was transferred to the Tower for questioning and to await trial. He soon became known as the Officer in the Tower, and members of the public standing on Tower Hill would gather to see him, dressed in his Seaforth Highlanders uniform and escorted by two guards, taking his daily thirty-minute exercise behind the ramparts.

Baillie-Stewart faced ten charges connected with providing information which might be useful to an enemy of Britain. Specifically, the prosecution argued that he arranged a meeting with Major Muller of the German Intelligence Service, which was 'an act preparatory to communicating information prejudicial to the State's interests' and subsequently supplied Muller with details of army equipment and military movements, including a photograph of a Vickers tank and information on a new army rifle.

In return, Baillie-Stewart received £90 in two letters signed 'Marie-Louise' and routed to him by Obst – ten £5 notes in the first letter and four £10 notes in the second. Significantly, at a time when it was difficult for a private individual in Germany to obtain foreign currency, the bank notes were sequentially numbered.

In his defence, Baillie-Stewart argued that he attempted to contact the German War Office in Berlin in order to discuss regimental liaisons and that the military information in his possession was readily available to members of the public from libraries or newspapers. He explained that a newspaper cutting of a tank was for a scrapbook he maintained, and that references to tanks, equipment and an automatic rifle were to settle arguments with his brother.

He also contended that he had met Otto Waldemar Obst (who the prosecution claimed was actually Muller) in a café when he was on holiday in Berlin. Obst had introduced Baillie-Stewart to a twenty-two-year-old, fair-haired girl of some means, called Marie-Louise. The Lieutenant met Marie-Louise on a number of occasions over several weeks (in court, Baillie-Stewart said the two of them were inseparable during this period), including a liaison in a park where they made love by a lake. Despite the supposed closeness of the relationship, he never discovered her last name, or where she lived.

When Baillie-Stewart left Germany to return to England, he said that he arranged to meet Marie-Louise in Holland, partly for adventure and partly in anticipation of financial assistance. He stated that he met Marie-Louise on three separate occasions in Holland when she gave him a total of £20 in Dutch money. This version of events was disputed by the prosecution who claimed that the purpose of his visits to Holland was to meet Muller and provide him with military information. Baillie-Stewart's counsel contended that his client had taken advantage of Marie-Louise's infatuation with him to obtain money from her, leading the Judge to characterise this argument as 'a woman keeping a man'.

British Intelligence had in fact monitored Baillie-Stewart since his time in Berlin, having been alerted by the hotel porter (who, unfortunately for Baillie-Stewart, was a British agent) that the Lieutenant was seeking to establish contact with the German War Office. Consequently, Baillie-Stewart's correspondence was intercepted and the letters containing the money were critical pieces of evidence at the trial, as was a letter sent by Baillie-Stewart to Obst, which he signed as Alphonse Poiret.

Baillie-Stewart claimed that the money and the letters he had received, which referred to the settling of a loan, were from Marie-Louise in consequence of their love affair and to enable him to revisit her. However, the letters were described in court as being 'singularly businesslike', contradicting Baillie-Stewart's assertion that Marie-

Louise was in love with him. Examination of Baillie-Stewart's bank account also showed that he had never had more than £50 in his account at any time and therefore, the prosecution argued, he could not have lent such sums to anybody. Baillie-Stewart also struggled to explain why he signed his letter to Obst as Alphonse Poiret, saying that he objected to his real name going through an intermediary and in adopting a pseudonym he was simply playing along with Marie-Louise's subterfuge. He said he was surprised when told of the connection between the names – Obst being the German word for fruit, Poiret being French for little pear, and Marie-Louise being a variety of pear.

Baillie-Stewart was found guilty of seven of the ten charges against him and served a further four years in the Tower of London. He was released in 1937 at which time he moved to Austria and subsequently to Germany in 1939. He worked during the war as an English language presenter for German propaganda radio and some have argued that his aristocratic accent was the original inspiration for the term Lord Haw-Haw. After the war, he was tried again on a charge of committing an act likely to assist the enemy and sentenced to a further five years in prison, although not in the Tower. The Attorney General decided not to pursue a higher charge of treason which, if proven, would have carried a death sentence.

On his release, Baillie-Stewart moved to Ireland where he died in 1966, reportedly still haunted by the injustice of his first trial in 1933.

For some time after the trial, there were reports of Marie-Louise being discovered. One journalist tracked down a girl called Olga Israel who fitted the description, being blonde and twenty-two when Baillie-Stewart was in Berlin, and who admitted to having gone dancing and boating on the Wansee with the Lieutenant. She denied, however, that she ever had an affair with Baillie-Stewart or engaged in correspondence with him. Another connection was made with a twenty-seven-year-old woman called Marie-Louise Martin, who was arrested as a spy in Finland in late 1933, carrying a Canadian passport but able to speak only broken English while being fluent in German. The true identity of Marie-Louise, however, if indeed she ever existed, remains a matter of speculation.

Tower Bridge to City Hall

'That was the last time she left the flat,' I say quietly.

Annie doesn't answer. There is nothing for her to say.

The vivid blue suspension cables of Tower Bridge stretch out ahead of us and the bridge shines against the inky sky. We are silent while we cross the river, both of us lost in our thoughts. As we turn right into Tooley Street, I shake my head in an effort to jolt myself out of my torpor. I can't keep drowning in the past. At some point, I have to come up for air and start living again.

We are at City Hall, another pit stop. I have not been looking forward to this point on the route, but now I am here I know what I have to do.

'Do you mind if we sit down for a bit?' I ask Annie.

'Do you need new plasters on your blisters?'

'No, no. It's nothing like that. I could just do with a moment.'

'OK. We're not in a hurry.'

We ignore the volunteers handing out treats and head for the river. Annie starts towards a wooden seat, but I grab her by the arm.

'Not that one. Over here.'

She frowns, but doesn't protest, and I guide her over to a bench I have sat on before. It looks out across the river, where the modern City meets old London town – futuristic office blocks standing uneasily next to the ancient walls of the Tower. The view is burnt into my memory.

City Hall

Sunday 18 March 2012

I had wondered how to broach the subject of Andrea's unturndownable opportunity to work in New York all weekend and the point was fast coming where I couldn't procrastinate any longer. I knew I needed to give Andrea an answer tomorrow.

Summer and I had walked lazily along the South Bank, which in recent years had developed into one of the joys of London. Almost in defiance of the backdrop of drab concrete, a colourful community of street vendors, performance artists and skateboarders had descended on the embankment. Relatively new introductions – such as the London Eye, the Globe Theatre, the Tate Modern and the Millennium Bridge – had landed like alien spacecraft and all added to the mix. It was a warm spring day and Summer wore a purple gilet over a lilac blouse, her hair tied back with a matching purple ribbon. She entwined her hand in mine as we meandered along the pavement.

We caught the train to Waterloo and our walk was bookended by Westminster Bridge and Tower Bridge. City Hall – the lopsided sphere that is home to the Mayor of London and the Greater London Authority – is one of the newest developments on the stretch at the easternmost end, sitting next to a suite of steel and glass offices, monuments to twenty-first-century corporate life. Unwary visitors who take a careless step can find their shoes and socks soaked by a designer stream that runs through the complex along a narrow channel cut into the slate tiles. No doubt the architects called it a rill and thought it was a good idea on paper. From time to time, open-air theatre is performed in and around a small, hollowed-out amphitheatre appropriately named The Scoop, but there were no such distractions that day. Summer and I sat on a bench looking out across the river to the Tower of London and I knew that the time was right for me to raise the New York issue.

'Summer,' I said, 'I need to discuss something with you.'

I felt her tense next to me. Summer could always read my moods and she knew I was worried about something. I took a deep breath.

'Andrea has asked me to transfer to New York.'

The words hung in the air like damp washing. A tugboat chugged upriver and blasted its horn, while behind us, a baby started to scream.

'Summer?' I looked at her anxiously. 'I think I have to go. What do you think? Will you come with me?'

She grasped my hand and I saw a sheen of tears in her eyes.

'What's wrong, Summer? Is it that bad?'

'Ben,' she spoke evenly but I could tell that she was struggling to do so, 'I can't go with you to New York.'

'Why not?' I pressed. 'It might be fun.'

'You should go,' she said. 'You're right. It will be fun.'

A seagull screeched as it soared on the breeze above our heads.

'Summer,' a wave of dread swept through me, 'are you saying…' I couldn't finish the sentence.

Summer leaned over and hugged me. She was wearing her Jo Malone lime and mandarin perfume.

'Ben, I have been scared of this moment ever since I met you.'

'What moment? What are you talking about?' I was panicking.

'I don't think we should be together any more. There was always going to come a time when it was right for me to let you go. I think this is it.'

I was dumbstruck. I had half-expected her to baulk at moving to New York, but not to suggest that we should break up. I wriggled out of her grasp and stared straight ahead. Everything suddenly appeared grey: a grey sky over grey office blocks next to a grey river.

'Ben?' She touched my arm and I turned back to her. Now I was fighting the tears.

'Summer, New York doesn't matter. Andrea doesn't matter. If you want to stay in London, that's fine. I can get another job.'

'I know,' she said, 'but I can't hold you back. It's not fair on you.'

I couldn't process her words. Summer had never held me back. She was always the person who made me fly. She caressed the back of my hand.

'Ben, I need to tell you my story.'

The Story of Summer (1)

Sunya loves her father. He is a bear of a man with a wiry moustache that tickles her cheek when he hugs her and cumin seed breath that reminds her of her grandmother's house in West Bengal. Abba has always looked after his daughter. Whenever she visits there is a present: a box of halwa sweets perhaps when she was younger, now a DVD or a new headscarf. She always dresses traditionally when she goes to her father's flat as she knows that he prefers it that way. He has lived in the UK for twenty years, but India is still in his heart. One day, he will go back there, and when he does, she will miss him.

His flat is small, but comfortable. Two bedrooms – she is the only one who ever stays overnight in any case – and a sitting room with a galley kitchen attached. A chocolate sofa, old but comfortable, sags against one wall, with a portable television in the corner, but Abba rarely watches TV. Instead, the centrepiece of the room is a G Plan stereo that he acquired from a neighbour when he first arrived in England, saving the neighbour the task of taking it to the dump. The stereo is Abba's pride and joy; he sits alongside it in his armchair, wearing his ear-muff headphones, listening to records for hours on end.

Ever since the happy acquisition of the stereo, Abba has spent most of his spare time scouring the local markets and second-hand record shops, accumulating an impressive collection of LPs. The rise of the compact disc meant that records were being sold at knockdown prices. More recently, the internet has become a rich source of old vinyl, as ageing music lovers clear out their attics. At first, Abba was driven by economic expediency. Now, he claims to prefer listening to the scratch and hiss of vinyl anyway.

'The imperfections are part of the music,' he announces, 'they give it soul.'

Sunya thinks that Abba loves the ritual of it all. The stacking of the record sleeves along the skirting board in an order that only he can fathom. The holding of the discs carefully in one hand while he uses the other to run a duster over the grooves. The cleaning of the stylus with the tiniest of brushes before lowering it gently on to the vinyl.

Brass bands are his favourite. He loves marching music and sometimes dispenses with his headphones so that he can play along with imaginary instruments. Sunya laughs as he marches in circles around the sofa to 'The British Grenadiers' or 'When the Saints Come Marching In', sawing away at a make-believe trombone or banging a non-existent drum. Sometimes she joins in, high-stepping like a majorette and twirling her own pretend baton.

She was small when her parents split and she can no longer imagine them being together. They live separate lives and now that Sunya is old enough to make arrangements for herself they hardly speak. There is no animosity between them; they are just two people who have drifted apart. Once she asked her mother why she fell out of love with Abba.

'It was harder than I thought it would be,' she said, 'being from two different cultures. In the end, I was always compromising.'

Her mother still wears Asian clothes – Sunya thinks that she likes the bright colours – but while she will go to the cinema, or out to dinner with friends, her father lives a more solitary existence. He works long hours for a local minicab firm, often during the night as he can earn more when rates are at their highest. He has a stash of tape cassettes stuffed in the glovebox so that he can listen to his brass band music while he works. Abba recorded them himself from the G Plan stereo system and he has labelled them all meticulously. Sunya doesn't know anyone else who still plays cassettes in their car.

One day, when she is studying for her exams, her father knocks and enters her room. She is sitting on the floor, her school books spread out on the carpet around her.

'You work so hard, sweetheart. Is it all worth it?'

'I hope so,' she says. 'I need good grades, Abba. To do A-levels, to get to university.'

Her father frowns. He does not understand her desire

for education. Back home in West Bengal, girls left school, married and bore children. What good were GCSEs, A-levels, degrees to a wife and mother?

'I was thinking,' he says, fingering his moustache, 'I would like to take you on holiday this summer, after your exams.'

She looks up, surprised.

'Holiday? Where to?'

'I thought we could go and see your grandmother in Nanoor, and then spend a week in Dubai. I hear it's really nice in Dubai.'

'Dubai!' Her eyes widen. 'Are you sure, Abba? It sounds expensive.'

He shrugs.

'I have saved up some money. Business has been good lately.'

Some of her friends have been to Dubai. It sounds amazing: sunshine, wonderful hotels, water parks. After the hard slog of her GCSEs, perhaps she deserves some relaxation.

'Well…'

'And Thakur-ma would like to see her granddaughter again. She is getting old, as you know.'

Sunya is aware of this. She has only been to India twice in her life: once when she was too small to remember, once when she was eight years old. It is time for her to make another visit. She comes to a decision and beams at her father.

'I think a holiday would be lovely,' she says, 'if you are sure you can afford it.'

Abba kneels down and gives her a hug. She smells the spices on his breath.

'We will have a wonderful time, sweetheart,' he says.

★

She doesn't remember much about the flight. Abba slips a couple of pills into a glass of water just before they take off and hands it to her.

'To help you sleep,' he says, softly.

She has never liked the feeling of confinement that she gets squashed into an aircraft seat and drinks the water happily.

The pills must have been strong, as she only wakes up when the plane starts its descent and her ears begin to pop. The Captain announces, 'Twenty minutes to landing,' and a map appears on the screen above their seats.

Next to her, a man lowers his head and whispers in her ear.

'Are you well, sweetheart?'

She is still groggy from sleep but she recognises her father's voice and the smell of his skin. She pictures his flat, with the raggedy sofa and the old stereo, and she hears the strains of marching music playing in the background.

'I shall take you on holiday, sweetheart. As a reward.'

A reward. Yes. For working hard at her exams.

'I shall take you on holiday, sweetheart. To Dubai. I will arrange it with your mother.'

Dubai. They are going to Dubai, with its sunshine and swimming pools and white sands and deep blue sea. Her heart lifts a little at the thought.

She shakes her head to focus. The little white plane on the screen is hovering over a big green triangle of land that she recognises instantly as India, heading for a white spot labelled Kolkata.

Of course. Before Dubai, they are going to see Thakur-ma – her grandmother.

'Sweetheart, are you looking forward to your holiday?'

She turns her head and smiles at Abba, with his bushy moustache and intense, brown eyes. She does not need to say anything.

Abba reaches into the pocket in the seat in front of him and pulls out a hijab, dull-grey.

'I have brought this for you to wear in your homeland.'

He thrusts it towards her and she hesitates.

'Abba, my home is London.'

He looks pained.

'If you say so, sweetheart, but wear it for me. Please.'

She takes the hijab and wraps it around her head. She knows that her father will always struggle to accept that his child is a daughter of Britain, not India.

Thakur-ma lives in the town of Nanoor, a three-hour drive from Kolkata. Abba has organised a taxi, a rusting blue Nissan driven by a boy who hardly looks old enough to shave, let alone to drive. He greets them outside the terminal building with a stupid grin and bows several times in her direction before loading their luggage into the back. Their cases form an unsteady tower and the boy straps the boot lid to the bumper to hold everything in. As a result, he can see nothing out of his rear window, but she notices that the Nissan does not have a rear view mirror in any case.

She sits in the back seat with Abba gazing out of the open window, while her father makes idle conversation with the driver in Bengali. She is hot and the hijab feels scratchy against her skin. She thinks about removing it to let the breeze cool her face but decides against this as she does not want to upset her father. They make good time along the Durgapur Expressway, their driver weaving around ox-drawn carts carrying mounds of potatoes and maize and honking his horn at overloaded buses until they veer off the road to let him pass. The crumbling concrete of the city soon gives way to fields of rice and jute with farmworkers gathering crops and sowing next season's seeds.

After two hours, they leave the expressway and their speed slows. The taxi bounces through potholes and the fields are replaced by plantations of Sal trees with paddle-shaped leaves, and bursts of jasmine bushes, their flowers wilting in the heat of the day. She remembers collecting sprigs of jasmine with her grandmother from the woods at the back of her house.

'Jasmine is the tree of sorrow,' Thakur-ma had told her.

'Why do they say that?' she had asked.

'Because the flowers appear overnight and at first light they are bright. But then it is as if they become sad, and they fade during the day, until at night time they are gone.'

'I don't think they are sad,' she said. 'I think they are happy to be so pretty, even for one day.' Her grandmother had smiled.

Sunya has no memory of her first visit to Nanoor. She could barely walk, but her mother showed her old photographs, curling at the edges, of her playing in the dust outside Thakur-ma's house. She recalls more from her second visit when she was eight years old. The bright colours of the saris – pinks and greens and turquoises – and the rich smells that escaped from the clay pots on her grandmother's kitchen stove and steeped the house: sweet saffron, orange-peel turmeric, fresh coriander. She also remembers being permanently tired, the suffocating heat and the uncomfortable mattress on her small wooden bed combining to deprive her of sleep. She would lay awake for hours, bathed in a film of sweat, the mattress springs pricking her back, following the shadow of a gecko as it danced across the mud-plaster wall.

When the mountains come into view, their lower slopes covered in conifers, she knows that they are getting close. She wonders how long they are to stay here. She feels guilty at even thinking it, but while it will be nice to see Thakur-ma again, she is more excited by the prospect of a comfortable, air-conditioned hotel room in Dubai with lazy days by the swimming pool than cooking and cleaning with her grandmother in the stifling heat of a breeze-block house, the men drinking and smoking outside. She half turns to ask her father, but as she does so their driver starts to chatter, pointing at a battered sign that says 'NANOOR' in capital letters and underneath, in italics, 'The Birthplace of Chandidas'. They have arrived.

The town is as she remembers. The rest of the world may have moved on eight years since she was last here, but time has stood still in Nanoor. A skeletal cow wanders undisturbed along the dusty main street, picking its way through the dregs of the day's market. Yellow mangos are laid out on a rickety wooden table and a display of necklaces, bracelets and beads sits on a grey tarpaulin. A group of men lounge on plastic chairs outside a café, the dog-ends of cigarettes glowing between their fingers. She smiles as they pass the confectionary store with its corrugated iron roof, remembering how Thakur-ma used to take her there to buy sweets and fresh yoghurt. Between the houses, she catches glimpses of the ponds, green with algae, where the men of the town farm fish and the women wash clothes.

She catches the eye of a policeman, wearing aviator shades like Tom Cruise in *Top Gun*, who waves to her and she smiles back. There has been trouble in Nanoor recently; eleven people were killed over a land dispute and the murderers await trial. Her father knew some of the victims and raged to her one night about 'the bloody government scratching their balls and doing nothing'.

The taxi slows down as they come up behind a rickshaw crawling down the middle of the road. The rickshaw driver, blissfully unconcerned as to their presence, does not deviate from his course. The taxi driver shouts and pulls down hard on the steering wheel, so that she bangs her elbow against the side of the car as they lurch round a corner into a side street.

Some children are playing in the road, bare-footed and dressed in rags, and they scatter as the taxi comes through, jabbering to each other. She waves at the smallest one, who immediately hides behind his friends. The taxi makes one more turn and she recognises her grandmother's street: a cul-de-sac of four simple cottages, arranged in a crescent, with a communal collection of cheap tables and chairs scattered outside. A pair of mangy dogs scrabbling for scraps in the dirt lift their muzzles as the car approaches, before returning to their scavenging. An old man with a nut-brown face and a half-closed eye drinks from a mug and regards them suspiciously.

Her father throws open his door and shouts.

'Mama!'

She steps out of the taxi, shading her eyes from the sun, and through the glare she sees her grandmother, her hair woven into a tight ball, drying her hands on a cloth and shuffling from her house in a purple sari. She is tiny – no more than 5 feet tall – and her skin is wrinkled like an elephant's hide. When she sees her granddaughter, Thakur-ma's mouth opens in a gummy smile and she holds out her pencil-thin arms.

She walks over and, suddenly weak with exhaustion after the long journey, falls into Thakur-ma's arms.

'Oh, my dear.' Thakur-ma hugs her back. 'It is so good to see you at this special time.'

⋆

She wakes the following morning and instinctively reaches for her phone on the bedside table. It is not there. She looks around the simple room, but there is no sign of it. While she has been asleep, a suitcase has been set on the floor underneath the window, although she does not recognise it as her own. She jumps out of bed and unzips the suitcase. Inside are colourful saris, headscarves, sensible sandals, but she ignores these and flings the clothes from the case until it is empty. No mobile phone. She didn't expect to find it in this strange case that is not hers but she had to look. Her head pounds. Without a phone, she has no contact with her mother or her friends at home. She takes deep breaths to calm herself. Her father must have taken it from her for safekeeping.

*

Thakur-ma has made pancakes for breakfast. She sits down with her father and eats, while her grandmother fusses around them. Abba points at his mother with his fork and speaks through a mouthful of pancake.

'You should learn from your grandmother, sweetheart. A good Indian girl knows how to look after their husband's stomach.'

She ignores him.

'Abba, do you have my phone?' she asks.

He does not answer immediately, continuing to chew on his food.

'Only I can't find it in my room,' she adds.

He swallows hard and wipes his lips and moustache with the back of his hand.

'Why do you need a phone, sweetheart?'

She tries to keep her voice from rising. 'I don't know. To speak to Mum, my friends maybe.'

'But you are on holiday. There is no need to worry about what is happening in England.'

Thakur-ma sets another plate of pancakes on the table and lays her hand on her wrist.

'You should eat, Sunya. You are too skinny. Your husband will prefer more meat on your bones, I am sure.'

'Thank you, Thakur-ma.' She turns back to her father.

'Abba, do you have my mobile phone?'

He frowns, pushes his chair back and stands up.

'Sunya, you have no need of a phone here. Please do not mention it again.'

He grabs a pancake from the plate, and strides out of the room.

After breakfast, there is no sign of her father, and she decides to take a stroll around the town. She needs to clear her head after the strange conversation over her mobile. He has never bothered about it back home, so she cannot understand why he is making such a big deal of it here. Her grandmother is sweeping the floor as she leaves.

'I am going for a walk, Thakur-ma. To the temples.'

Thakur-ma leans her broom against the wall and wrings her hands.

'Are you sure, Sunya? Will you not stay here with me?'

'I won't be long. I just need to get some fresh air. I feel cooped up inside.'

'The rains are coming,' her grandmother says flatly.

She opens the door and looks at a cloudless, blue sky.

'I think it will be fine for a little while.'

She walks over to her grandmother and kisses her cheek.

'Please don't be long. I will be worried about you.'

'I won't, Thakur-ma. I won't.'

As well as her phone, she is missing her Western clothes – no jeans, no tops, no trainers or high heels. She supposes her father has hidden her own suitcase away and provided her with the Indian clothes, no doubt aided and abetted by her grandmother. She is irritated but she understands that he would want her to dress in traditional outfits. She chooses a tangerine sari that she finds in the case, and simple leather sandals, but she decides against a hijab, partly to signal her annoyance with Abba. The people of Nanoor shall see the whole of her face.

She follows a dusty track outside her grandmother's house which soon gives way to a cratered tarmac road that runs through the centre of the town. She stops at a craft stall where a man in a pointed white hat smiles broadly with two remaining brown teeth and blackened gums.

'These very good luck,' he says, in broken English,

handing her a necklace made of a series of black and silver beads threaded on a thin rope of leather. She runs the necklace through her hands before she rests it on the table and shakes her head.

'You not want good luck?' he asks.

She laughs. 'Good luck would be nice,' she says.

He reaches out to clasp her hand in his and she feels the rough callouses on his fingers.

'I think you need good luck. Ten rupees. Deal?'

She smiles.

'I am sorry. I cannot pay.' She withdraws her hand from his and holds both hands palm up to show her lack of money.

He picks up the necklace, unclasps it, and fixes it around her neck. He smells of sweet tobacco.

'For you,' he says. 'A present for pretty lady at wonderful time.'

'I, I can't...'

He holds a finger to his lips.

'Every time you pass, you smile for old Ganesh.'

'Thank you very much... Ganesh. You are very kind.'

He opens his two-toothed mouth. 'See. Ganesh's smile not beautiful. But yours. Your smile very beautiful.'

She can't help but break into a wide grin.

'Ha!' He claps. 'Like that!'

She holds out a hand.

'My name is Sunya. Pleased to meet you, Ganesh.'

She continues along the road and it is clear that she is an object of attention. A group of women carrying laundry baskets whisper to each other as she walks past and two men drinking coffee from chipped mugs in front of an iron shack break off their conversation and stare at her. She lifts her chin and walks confidently forward.

A collection of terracotta temples huddles at one end of the town and she spends an hour or so walking around them. Some are ornately decorated, others are simple affairs, such as the three-arched stone temple where the fourteenth-century poet, Chandidas, worshipped Saraswati, the Goddess of Literature.

The ghost of Chandidas runs through Nanoor like a seam

runs through rock. There is a mound that marks out the site of his house and a shrine to his memory, but it is his story of forbidden love that is his real legacy. Her grandmother told her the tale when she was last in Nanoor.

'Chandidas was a priest,' she said, when Sunya asked about him, 'and he fell in love with a beautiful girl called Rami.'

'Did they get married, Thakur-ma?'

'Yes, yes. They got married. But Rami was a Rajkini, a washerwoman. She was below his caste and Chandidas was excommunicated.'

'Excommunicated?' It was a long word for an eight-year-old.

'Cut off. Excluded from his religion.'

'Urgh! People are so mean.'

Her grandmother shook her head. 'Yes, they can be. But Chandidas stayed true to his love. He wrote many poems about Rami.'

'I like Chandidas,' she had said, stoutly.

As she walks amongst the temples, she reflects that not much has changed over the centuries. The women of Nanoor still line the edges of the pools that lie behind the houses, scrubbing and beating their daily washing as Rami would have done, and as their ancestors have done for generations since.

The sun is high in the sky and she realises that it must be close to lunchtime. The air is clammy and black clouds are rolling towards Nanoor from the west. The rains will come soon so she sets off on the return journey to her grandmother's house. On the main road, she stops by the old sweet shop where Thakur-ma used to take her. Although she has no money, she is curious to see through a window into her past, so she pushes aside the bead curtain and steps inside.

The heady smell of sugar takes her back to her childhood. On the counter are plates of cheesecake-like sandesh, with toppings of mango, raspberry and chocolate, next to bowls of syrupy roshogolla. On the shelves behind, delicately coloured sweets sit on greaseproof-papered trays, freshly made that morning – little balls of pink, lemon, lime green, cream.

The shopkeeper peers at her over *pince-nez* rimless spectacles. He has a round face and a stomach that bulges proudly over his trousers, a testament to the quality of his own confectionary. Like Ganesh before him, he recognises her as English, despite the sari.

'You want to try some, miss?' he asks.

'I'm sorry,' she says, 'I don't have any money. I was just looking.'

'Nonsense, nonsense. A lovely lady must try one of Madhur's sweets. Once tasted, never forgotten.'

'That's very kind of you, but...' She turns to leave the shop, embarrassed, but the shopkeeper steps out in front of her and thrusts a tray in her direction.

'Here, kiwi fruit. My latest creation. Delicious.'

His bulk bars her exit and it would be both rude and difficult for her to refuse. She selects one of the little green balls and takes a small bite. The dough melts between her teeth and she tastes the kiwi fruit – subtle, but unmistakable.

'See. Is wonderful, yes?'

She nods and eats the rest of her sweet.

The shopkeeper picks one for himself and tosses it whole into his mouth. He goes back behind the counter, replaces the tray on the shelf, and then hands her a paper bag.

'For you,' he says, 'for a special time. A selection of Madhur's favourites. Lemon, strawberry, chocolate.' He puts his fingers to his lips and kisses them.

'Oh, I can't.'

'No, no, I insist. You pay with a promise. You must visit Madhur and his sweets whenever you are in town.'

'Well, I don't know how long I will be here, but I promise,' she says, taking the bag from him.

He looks at her quizzically over his glasses and his smile fades.

'You are very nice lady,' he says, 'I hope everything will be good for you.'

*

The first fat raindrops are falling as she reaches Thakur-ma's house. Despite the rain, her father is standing outside, stern-faced, hands on hips.

'You are not wearing a hijab.'

'No. I don't wear one at home. I don't see why I should wear one here.'

'This *is* your home.' He speaks from the corner of his mouth, clearly agitated. 'And you will wear a hijab because I say so.'

She feels anger rising within her but she holds her tongue. There is something wrong.

'Where have you been?'

'Why? What does it matter?'

Her father's face tightens.

'Damn it! You are my daughter. I demand to know where you have been.'

'If you must know, I went for a walk into town. To the temples.'

His chest heaves as he draws himself to his full height.

'What is wrong with that?' She glares at him. 'I wanted to get some air.'

'You have no business going into town, do you hear?'

'Why?' She stamps her foot irritably. 'Am I a prisoner in the house?'

'Do not disrespect your father!' He clenches his fists and his eyes bulge as if the pressure inside his head is forcing them from their sockets. 'Show some manners.'

She holds out her palm and catches raindrops.

'It's raining. I'm going to my room.' She pushes past him to go inside but he grabs her arm and holds her back.

'We have guests tonight. Thakur-ma needs help with the preparation.'

'Ow. You're hurting me.'

He loosens his grip.

'Help your grandmother, Sunya. You need to learn how to be a wife.'

She shakes him off and runs into the house, past her grandmother who is rolling out dough on the kitchen table. She doesn't stop. She can feel tears swimming in her eyes and needs to reach her room. If she is going to cry, she will cry alone and unseen.

It is early evening when she is woken by her grandmother. The rain has stopped and the last of the day's sun filters through the window. A pair of drongos serenade each other in the cotton trees that stand behind the house and the scent of mustard seeds drifts into her room.

'It is time to get ready.' Her grandmother holds up a sari of duck-egg blue, embroidered with swirls of silver. 'Here. I have chosen this for you.'

She rubs her eyes and sits up, hoping that it is not obvious that she has been crying.

'It is very pretty, Thakur-ma. But what am I to get ready for?'

Her grandmother lays the sari carefully on the bed.

'We are to have visitors.'

'Visitors? Who?'

'Your Uncle Thani and Aunt Hasina,' she hesitates for a second, 'and your cousins.'

'My cousins?' She has vague memories of a family get-together when she was last in Nanoor. Children of all ages filled the clearing in front of Thakur-ma's house, playing tag, throwing rubber balls to each other, skipping with ropes. The adults sat on the plastic chairs eating grilled fish from a barbecue, while the teenagers – too cool to join in the games with their younger siblings and too young to enjoy conversation with their aged parents – skulked inside the house, playing cards and reading magazines.

Bewildered, she sat on her mother's knee, speaking only when spoken to, which fortunately was not very often. Occasionally, her mother would remove the skin from a fillet of catfish, pick out the needle-like bones, and scoop the pink flesh into her daughter's mouth with a teaspoon. Thani Ventrakam was actually her father's cousin, so his offspring were not relatives of hers, but in India everyone in an extended family was referred to as a cousin. She couldn't recall any of their names, but she remembered Uncle Thani. He was a local celebrity, a wealthy businessman who owned a milk distribution business and a large brick house on the edge of town. At home, when her father met someone new, particularly if they had recently arrived from India, it would not be long before he mentioned Uncle Thani.

'Thani-ji,' he would say to anyone prepared to listen, 'is a rare combination. He is both the most successful and the most generous man in West Bengal.'

She reasons that something important must be afoot for Uncle Thani to grant them a visit. Perhaps the return of her father with his daughter is more of an event than she realised. Her grandmother kisses her on the cheek and stands up to leave the room.

'Thank you for your help this afternoon,' she says.

'My help?' She is confused. She has been asleep for hours.

'With the cooking.'

'But I...'

Thakur-ma lifts a finger to her lips to shush her.

'It is good for all of us that you were of assistance. And now you should get dressed.'

★

Uncle Thani announces his arrival with an ostentatious toot on the horn of his Mercedes. He lives barely half a mile away on the edge of town and could easily have walked. Abba stands up from his chair and she thinks the expression on his face betrays both admiration and jealousy as his cousin climbs out from behind the driver's seat. Uncle Thani is a tall man, with sleek hair the colour of crude oil. She thinks he must use dye, as his eyebrows and beard are burnt charcoal-grey.

'You like my silver bird?' He gesticulates towards the car.

'Very much, Thani-ji,' says my father. 'It is a fine motor vehicle.'

She recognises that it is an old model, but even so it seems out of place in the small, dusty clearing in front of her grandmother's cottage. Behind Uncle Thani, his family emerges from the car like peas being shelled from a pod and she counts six of them – her Aunt Hasina and five offspring, three boys, two girls – who line up for inspection in height order. The smallest is a girl of some ten years old while the tallest is a boy in his early twenties, who stares at the ground and makes circles in the dust with the point of his shoe. They are all dressed up for their visit. The boys wear white shirts buttoned to the neck; the girls wear matching lilac dresses and grey pumps.

Aunt Hasina is dressed all in black, from her headscarf down to her sensible shoes. She approaches with her arms outstretched and gives her a bear hug that sucks the breath from her lungs.

'Sunya, my child. How charming you look.'

'Thank you, Aunt Hasina,' she gasps. 'And how are you?'

'Your aunt is on top of the world,' roars Uncle Thani, 'just for seeing you.'

She blushes and looks down at her feet.

'But, Thani-ji, where is Manu?' her father asks.

'He will be here presently, cousin. He will be here. He left before us, to find some courage.' Uncle Thani winks.

'Ahh.' Her father nods. 'I understand.'

Thani turns to his family. 'Come on, Hasina, children.' He addresses them in English which she realises is for her benefit. 'I am sure Thakur-ma has a wonderful meal for us. We must go inside.'

Thakur-ma has laid out bowls of chutney and pickles next to piles of bread on two tables that have been pushed together. Eleven uncoordinated seats – a mix of plastic and wood – have been sourced from various parts of the house and she fusses around the children as they troop in, showing them where to sit.

'Sunya, over here.' She points to a chair in the middle of the table on which she has placed a purple velvet cushion with gold tassels. None of the other seats have a cushion.

'Grandmother,' she protests, 'surely Aunt Hasina should sit here.'

'Nonsense, nonsense,' booms Thani. 'This is for you as guest of honour. And my boy, Manu, will sit here.' He pats the seat next to her. She vaguely remembers Manu now. He was a thin, gawky looking sixteen-year-old when she was last in Nanoor, with a pig-like nose and an unfortunate drooping lower lip that made him look like the village idiot.

'Vani. No!' Uncle Thani barks at his younger daughter who has already torn off a mouthful of luchi bread with her teeth. The girl puts the bread down, but continues to chew guiltily. Her father frowns at her, but says no more.

When they are all sat down, Thakur-ma brings out steaming bowls of fried fish, curried mutton and mixed vegetables. She hands round her best china dinner service with the willow pattern which she keeps in the dresser in the sitting room, and at a nod from their father, the children begin to scoop the food greedily on to their plates.

Abba circles the table pouring glasses of milky-white sweet lassi from an earthernware jug. When he reaches his cousin, Thani regards him with an air of contempt.

'Have you nothing stronger, cousin?' Abba bows and retreats to the kitchen, returning a minute or two later balancing three bottles of beer in his hands.

'That's better,' Thani announces. 'A real drink for real men.' He thumps the beer on the table and froth erupts from the top, which he licks happily from the side of the bottle. The white foam catches in his beard like snow on the branch of a pine tree.

Abba sets the second bottle down at Manu's place and takes the last one for himself.

'What a feast, Thakur-ma,' booms Thani. 'Fit for a maharajah.'

'Thank you, Thani-ji,' her grandmother replies, 'but I cannot take all the credit. Sunya was of great help.'

She looks questioningly at her grandmother who raises her forefinger to warn her from saying anything.

'Excellent, excellent,' Thani continued. 'A toast to the cooks. To Thakur-ma and Sunya.'

He takes a deep gulp of beer, while the rest of the table raise their glasses sheepishly and sip their drinks. Aunt Hasina beams at her from across the table.

Manu arrives fifteen minutes later with greased black hair like his father and wearing an ill-fitting brown suit. He has filled out since she last saw him and he now has round cheeks and a protruding belly, although his lower lip still sags noticeably.

'I am sorry I am late, Father, Uncle, Grandmother.' He speaks in a monotone that suggests he is not sorry at all. Abba stands up to indicate his seat, which is an unnecessary gesture as there is only one empty chair at the table. Manu smirks and sits down, clumsily. She thinks that he has already been drinking, and he looks at her with glassy eyes. She turns away and he slaps his thigh in amusement.

'Ah ha. I like a girl that is hard to get.' He tries to whisper, but he mistakes the volume of his voice so that the whole table hears. Uncle Thani bangs the table.

'Another toast,' he announces, raising his bottle of beer. 'To Sunya and Manu.'

Everyone picks up their drinks again and garbles their response.

'To Sunya and Manu.'

She looks at her father who takes a swig of beer and grins back at her. Manu slips his hand under the table and rests it on her thigh. Startled, she brushes him off and he throws back his head and laughs.

'All in good time, hey? All in good time.'

★

After Uncle Thani and his family have left and she has helped her grandmother to wash and dry the dishes and stack the willow pattern plates back into the dresser, she makes her way outside where her father is smoking.

'Abba,' she asks, 'what is going on? Why are we here?'

Her father waves his hand.

'He is a fine boy, is he not?'

'Who?' She is being deliberately obtuse.

'Manu. Your half-cousin.'

She gives her father a cold stare.

'No, Abba, he is not a fine boy. He was drunk and he tried to grope me.'

Her father grinds the remains of his cigarette into an ashtray.

'He was nervous, that is all. Nervous at meeting you.'

'Me? Why should he worry about me?'

266

'Because, sweetheart,' he leans back on his chair and steeples his fingers, 'you are to be married to him this Saturday.'

Abba reaches across and pulls another cigarette from the packet on the table next to him. Dumbstruck, she watches him as he rolls it from his index finger and thumb, across to his pinkie and back again. After doing this a few times, he replaces the cigarette in the packet, leans forward again and holds her face in his hands.

He smells of mustard seeds and chillies, beer and ashtrays.

She tries to pull herself away from him, but his grip is firm.

'Do you love your father, Sunya?'

He loosens his hands and she nods once. Slowly.

'If you love me, you will marry Manu. You will do this for me.'

He sits back in the chair and folds his arms, while she struggles to find the breath to speak.

'But, Abba, I do not know this man. I do not love him. Why am I to do this?' She is shaking with fear and desperation.

'Because…' he tips his head back and breathes in deeply, '… because you do not need to love Manu if you love me. You will do it for your father, not for Manu.'

'But, why? Why do you…'

'Enough!' He jumps from the chair and grabs his packet of cigarettes. 'You are to be married on Saturday and that is the end of it. Thakur-ma will help you with the arrangements.'

He strides away from the house, through the clearing, following the track into town. She watches him go, her body numb with shock. Her grandmother appears in the doorway and she makes to get up to go to her, but as she pushes her chair back, her legs buckle and she stumbles and falls in the dust.

'Oh my God! How awful!' Annie claps her hand to her mouth. 'And she had never told you any of this before.'

'No. It was all news to me. I felt so bad. Like I should have known.'

It was true. I remember the guilt seeping through me as she spoke until I was soaked in self-loathing. How could I have been so insensitive? How did I not realise that she had something like this in her past?

'Do you mind if we carry on?' I indicate the riverside path. Sitting on the same seat that I had sat on with Summer had seemed appropriate at first. Now it was making me feel sick.

'Sure. Absolutely.'

We pick up our rucksacks and start walking again, past the modern glass office blocks and *HMS Belfast*, towards London Bridge, following the route that Summer took when I sat rooted to the bench and let her go. I remember staring after her, open-mouthed, as she walked unsteadily away from me, her purple gilet gradually fading into the distance. I could have caught up with her easily enough, but something made me stay.

'You couldn't have known, Ben,' says Annie, quietly. 'You said yourself. There were parts of her life she kept from you and you had to accept that.'

'I could have asked her more questions. I should have picked up on things.'

'No,' there was a sudden firmness in Annie's voice, 'you allowed her to choose when to tell you. That was one of the reasons she loved you so much.'

The moonlight is reflected in the Thames, a long streak of silver that shimmers in the oily water. My nausea is easing and I feel better now, comforted by Annie's words.

The Story of Summer (2)

She lies awake for most of the night, her thoughts lurching from cold fear and desolation to white-hot anger. Above all she feels desperately alone, trapped in a country that is not her own. All she wants is to be home again in North London with her mother, living ordinary days going to school, dance lessons, shopping with friends at Westfield, and yet she has a horrible sense that her ordinary life is now in the past. The pain of loneliness gnaws at her stomach as she lies in bed, the occasional foray by the resident gecko her only distraction, but by the morning she has composed herself sufficiently to determine a course of action. She will confront her father; he cannot expect her to marry an Indian boy eight years older than her who she hardly knows. Apart from the fact that she simply does not love him, there are also practical difficulties. Where will they live? What will happen when she goes to university?

She must also contact her mother who surely is not aware of her father's plan. If she can find a phone in town she will speak to her this afternoon, as it is Thursday already and only two days before the planned wedding. Although they have been separated for a decade, her mother is still the one person who can talk sense into Abba.

Red-eyed from lack of sleep, she eats breakfast in silence with Thakur-ma. Her father is nowhere to be seen. After they have eaten, her grandmother leads her into the living room where a scarlet and gold sari has been laid across the back of the sofa.

She looks at the sari, then at Thakur-ma, then back at the sari again. Is she supposed to try it on? Her grandmother picks the sari up, and holds it in front of her.

'You will look beautiful, sweetheart.'

She turns to see her father in the doorway.

'Abba, we must talk.'

His smile turns to a frown.

'If you say so, but talk will not change anything.'

Thakur-ma gathers up the sari in her arms and backs out of the room leaving her alone with her father. He sits down on the sofa but she stays standing, so that she has the physical advantage of height. A scooter engine whines outside.

'What do you want to say, sweetheart?'

'I cannot marry Manu. I do not love him.'

He fingers his moustache.

'I told you yesterday. Your feelings for him are of no consequence. If you love me, you will marry him.'

She folds her arms in annoyance.

'What about you loving me? Allowing me to choose my own husband?'

He stretches his neck. 'This match is for the best. It is a good match. You should be pleased.'

She ignores him and tries another tack. 'And where are we to live?'

He smiles.

'Manu has a house in Nanoor. It is a fine house. You will be comfortable there.'

She catches her breath. The scooter revs up outside and the two-stroke engine squeals as the bike leaves the clearing.

'Nanoor?' She struggles to say the word. 'You expect me to live in… Nanoor?'

'Why not? It is a beautiful town. You can see the mountains.' He wafts his hand in the air, but all she can see is the bare, plastered wall of her grandmother's living room.

'Why not?' Her voice rises like the wail of the scooter. 'Why not? What about my friends? School? University?'

Her father is unmoved.

'You will make new friends here. And you are old enough to leave school. No more studying. Is that not good?'

Her chest is tight like a drum.

'No! It is not good. I am going to university. Why do you not understand?'

Her father reaches for her hand but she pulls it away. She is desperately trying not to cry.

'Sweetheart,' he says, 'I have arranged for you to marry a nice boy. A good boy who will make you happy. That is what a father should do for his daughter. We will have a fine wedding and you will look beautiful. You will make me proud.'

The tears begin to drip from her eyes and she rushes out of the room before the drops become waterfalls.

★

The rains come again in the afternoon and it is not until early evening that she creeps out of her room. She can hear Thakur-ma busying herself in her bedroom but her father is not in the house. She walks determinedly into town, the dust road now turned to mud that sucks at her sandals, but when she reaches the main street, she falters, unsure what to do. The town is quiet – the market traders packed up and fled the rain hours ago – and a light wind drifts through the town. She hears a cry and sees Ganesh perched on a wooden bench in a bus shelter by the side of the road, waving to her, his pointy hat sitting at a jaunty angle on his head.

'Hey!' he calls. 'Beautiful lady. You have no smile for Ganesh today?'

She is suddenly aware that her lips are clamped tightly together and half opens her mouth in an attempt to smile, but the dark clouds in her head make it difficult. She walks over to Ganesh who doffs his hat to her theatrically.

'I am sorry, Ganesh. I am sad today.'

'Ganesh does not like to hear that,' he says, replacing his hat on his head. 'And what makes my beautiful lady sad?'

'I…' she has difficulty with the words, 'I… I am just sad today, Ganesh. Maybe it is the rain?'

Ganesh frowns and she knows that he is unconvinced.

'The rain washes away bad things and makes everything new again,' he says. 'You should not be sad about the rain.'

'Well…' She sits down next to him on the bench. He stares at her and she feels the urge to trace the deep etches of the lines in his parched skin with her fingers. There is something comforting about Ganesh. It is as if he has been in Nanoor for a hundred years and if you came back in another hundred years, he would still be here, selling his necklaces from his simple stall and grinning at people with his two brown teeth.

'Ganesh thinks it is not about the rain. Ganesh thinks it is to do with a boy.'

She adjusts the folds of her sari and gazes at the mountains in the distance. In different circumstances, it would be a beautiful view.

'Ganesh, do you know where I can borrow a phone?'

He shrugs his shoulders.

'You could try your friend, the sweetman.' He gestures towards the shop opposite, where the bead curtains shiver in the breeze.

★

Madhur is arranging rainbow-coloured sweets into little pyramids when she walks in.

'Ah ha.' His face lights up as he sees her. 'I saw you across the street. I thought you had forgotten your promise. That you were not coming to visit old Madhur.'

'The sweets look wonderful,' she says. 'They are so pretty.'

'You want one? I have a new blueberry flavour one. It makes your tongue go blue, like that girl in *Willy Wonka*.'

'No, no thank you. You must save some sweets for paying customers.'

He picks up a cloth and rubs sugar from his hands.

'So, if you will not eat sweets, what can Madhur do for you today?' he asks, inclining his head to one side and observing her over his glasses. 'Is something wrong? There is melancholy in your face.'

'I'm sorry. Is it that obvious?'

'It is obvious to Madhur. Are you homesick? Have you had enough of Nanoor already?'

'No, no,' she says hurriedly. 'Nothing like that. It's… it's…'

'Family matters?' he suggests.

'Yes.' She looks down at the floor. 'It is family matters. You are right.'

'Then family matters are your business. Madhur will not ask any questions. But I do recommend a blueberry bonbon. I believe they are a cure for sadness.'

He reaches over to a tray, picks up a violent purple sweet, and holds it out to her in his fleshy palm.

She gives in and takes it from him.

'Do you mind if I save this for later?'

'As you wish. But you must return and tell Madhur how you found it. And how long your tongue stayed blue.'

She sees a paper napkin on the counter and wraps the sweet in it, a little parcel that she closes her fingers around.

'Madhur, can I ask you a favour?'

Madhur pushes his glasses up his nose.

'Of course. How can I be of assistance?'

'Do you have a telephone that I can use?'

He considers this request for a moment, taking the opportunity to pop a lemon doughball into his mouth.

'Do you want to ring England?' he mumbles, through a mouthful of sweet. 'That will be expensive.'

'I want to speak to my mother, yes. In England. I am sorry. I have no money and I'm desperate to talk to her. I wouldn't ask but...'

He holds his hand up, tips his head back and swallows his sweet with a loud gulp.

'The telephone is over there.' He points to an old grey dial-phone in the corner which she has not noticed before. The dull-coloured phone shrinks into the walls compared to the vibrant colours of the confectionary that shout from the counter and the shelves. 'It is all yours but...' he smiles '... five minutes only.'

'Thank you, Madhur. Thank you.'

She rushes over to the phone and starts to dial. The dial takes an age to circle back from each number, but finally she hears the ringtone. Two long beeps, followed by a second of silence. Then two long beeps again. The international dialling signal. She prays that her mother is home.

On the third set of double beeps, someone picks up the phone at the other end.

'Hello.' A surge of relief floods through her at hearing her mother's voice.

'Hello, who's there? Sunya, is that you?'

'Oh, Mum. It's me. I'm so glad to speak to you. I don't know what to do.'

'Sunya, where are you? I've been so worried.'

'Mum. I'm with Abba. I'm…'

And then a continuous beep sounds in her ear, like the sound of a heart rate monitor flatlining. The line is dead. She turns and her father is standing over her, his fingers pressing on the cradle of the phone. He holds out his hand and she drops the receiver meekly into his fingers.

'Sweetheart, it is time to go home.'

He replaces the receiver, grabs her arm and leads her out of the shop. She risks a glance towards Madhur, who puts his hands together as if he is praying. She knows he is praying for her.

★

Friday morning is dull and grey. Her father is sitting outside, smoking, when she approaches him. Another night lying awake in bed and going over events has stiffened her resolve. That and Madhur's blueberry bonbon that she ate before she got dressed. Abba has tricked her into coming to India to marry someone she does not know. She loves her father but this is not fair. She cannot let it happen.

She pulls up a chair as her father blows a plume of smoke from his nostrils.

'Sweetheart, are you looking forward to your big day?'

She leans forward, letting his words float away with the smoke from his cigarette.

'Father, I am not going to marry Manu. I do not know him. You can't make me go through with this.'

Abba flicks the ash from his cigarette and it falls on to the ground amidst a ring of burnt-out cigarette butts.

'I know,' he sighs. 'I cannot make you marry Manu.'

She rocks back, surprised by this concession. Her father's shoulders slump and he seems to collapse into his chair.

'I was hoping,' he says, 'that you would do this for me. I need you to do this for me.'

'For you? Why? Why do you want me to marry someone I do not love?'

'Because…' He pauses and drags on his cigarette. His

274

fingers are stained yellow from the nicotine. He is smoking too much these days.

'Because Manu is family. And family matters above all. I hoped that you would understand that.'

The leaves of the cotton trees rustle in the wind and behind her, a dog barks. She hears the rhythmic slicing of a knife inside the house: her grandmother chopping vegetables for lunch.

'Am I not family, Abba?' She rests her hand on his knee. 'Do you not want me to be happy?'

'I do not think you understand love, sweetheart. You are young. Manu is a good boy. He would make you happy. Is that not enough?'

She squeezes his knee and stands up from the chair.

'No. It is not enough. Not for me.'

She walks a few steps towards the house, before turning round to contemplate her father from behind. His fraying hair lies thin on the top of his head and one arm hangs over the side of the chair, the cigarette slowing burning down to his fingers. With his other hand, he wipes his face. She is not sure, but she thinks she can hear the sound of sobs. She has never seen her father cry before.

By the time she is inside the house, she is shaking. Thakur-ma looks up from her cooking, tucks a grey hair behind her ear, and returns to her chopping without saying a word.

★

She lies on her bed, not knowing what to do next. She should feel elated that her father has relented, but instead a sensation of emptiness eats away at her insides. Will her father tell Manu and Uncle Thani and all the guests that the wedding is off? She imagines that Uncle Thani will not take the news well. What will happen then? They will have to leave, back to the UK, which means booking a flight. Will Abba organise that?

The gecko emerges from behind the wall lamp and flicks out his tongue. She watches it scurry across the plaster until it disappears into a crack. As it does so, a pale, bony hand curls around her door and Thakur-ma enters. She sits down on the end of the bed, examining her granddaughter and dabbing at her rheumy eyes with a lace handkerchief. The air in the room is thick and hot; the rains are on their way.

'Is he alright, Thakur-ma?' she asks. Her voice sounds thin and reedy.

Thakur-ma lowers her gaze and shakes her head. A hornbill hoots outside the window.

'Thakur-ma?' Her grandmother looks up. 'Why does he want me to marry Manu?'

'It is a question of honour, child. Your father is a proud man. If you do not marry Manu, you will break his spirit.'

'Why? I do not understand.'

Thakur-ma sighs and wrings the handkerchief into a tight cigar-shaped roll.

'Your father owes Thani-ji a debt. You are his way of repaying that debt.'

Her grandmother speaks quietly but the words hit her with the force of a jackhammer. She is still reeling as Thakur-ma continues.

'When your father was young, he was always in trouble. I could not control him. He messed around with his layabout friends. Smoking, drinking, anything but work. One day, Deepak the policeman knocked on the door. Your father had been arrested in Bolpur.'

Her grandmother's fingers twist the handkerchief into a knot.

'Arrested? What for?' she asks.

'They said he was part of a gang. A gang that paid boys like your father a few rupees to steal videos, televisions, that sort of thing. He was being used.'

'So what did the police say?'

'Deepak said they would have let him off with a warning, except they had caught him with a radio. Something he had stolen for himself and not given to the gang. In the old days, they would have cut off his hands.'

'A radio?'

'He wanted to listen to music. He loved music.'

Images of her father cleaning shiny, black vinyl discs with a duster, before setting them on the turntable of his G Plan stereo and lowering the needle into place. The crackle and hiss of the record before the music came in. Always loud, triumphant. Brass bands. Her father loved brass bands.

'What happened, Thakur-ma?'

'Thani-ji spoke to some people and got him released, but he said he wouldn't be able to help your father a second time. Abba said he wanted to get out of India anyway and that was that. Thani-ji saw to everything: a passport, a visa, a flight to England. Without your uncle, your father and mother would never have met. You would not have been born. Your father owes Thani-ji everything.'

A terrible thought explodes in her mind like shattering glass. Surely not?

'And in return…'

Her grandmother turns her head and looks out of the window. She picks at the knot in her handkerchief. Thakur-ma speaks so quietly that she can barely hear her reply over the pitter-patter of the first drops of rain, bouncing off the jasmine bushes outside.

'You. In return, you were to marry Thani-ji's son.'

★

She finds him sitting under a cotton tree at the back of the house. The rains have stopped but his clothes are soaked and his wet hair sticks to his scalp. She sits down in the sticky mud next to him and raindrops fall on her head from the leaves above and crawl down her forehead and cheeks.

He does not acknowledge her but picks a stone up from the ground and hurls it into the bushes.

'Abba…' she begins.

He stops her before she can go any further.

'You know, I would never do anything to hurt you, sweetheart.'

'I know.' She leans against his shoulder. 'We were never going to Dubai, were we, Abba?'

He lowers his head and takes a deep breath. 'I'm sorry, sweetheart. I'm a fool. I should never have brought you here.'

She squeezes his arm reassuringly.

'So, what do we do now, Abba?'

'I need to get you home.'

'And what about you? Are you not coming home too?'

He stares straight ahead into the trees.

'No. I must stay here. I owe your Uncle Thani and I must find some way to repay him. This is my home now. This has always been my home.'

'But what about me? And Mum? What about Mum?'

Abba buries his face in his hands and his shoulders begin to shake. She has never seen her father like this before. The sun breaks out from behind a cloud and the shadow from the tree falls across them. In that moment, she makes a decision.

'Abba,' she says softly, 'if it means so much to you, I will marry Manu.'

He lifts his head slowly and rests his finger under her chin.

'Sweetheart, are you sure?'

'No, but I will do it for you, Father.' She blurts out the words before she changes her mind.

★

The priest closes his book, lays Manu's hand on hers and with a sweep of his arm invites them to sign the marriage papers. Thakur-ma has draped a cotton cloth over a wooden table on which she has placed a vase of orange and yellow marigolds. A closely typed document sits on the cloth with a ballpoint pen set neatly alongside. A petal has fallen from a marigold flower and glows sunshine yellow against the whiteness of the paper.

There are two plastic chairs behind the table waiting for them – red and blue – with twisted metal frames. She recognises them as chairs from outside the house, where her father drinks and smokes the evenings away. She steps gingerly over to the table and feels Manu's hand on her waist guiding her. A shiver of revulsion ripples through her.

The day has passed in a flurry of activity. Thakur-ma woke her early and helped her dress in a sari the colour of milky custard. Aunt Hasina and her two daughters were already in the house, hanging crepe paper lanterns and streamers from the walls and ceilings and arranging the tables for the wedding feast. The sofa and armchairs had been moved out of the sitting room to make way for an enormous hardwood table that Uncle Thani had arranged to be sent over the day before. It is almost as long as the room, and the backs of the chairs at each end are rammed against the walls. There were too many chairs for her to count.

When she emerged from her bedroom, she was greeted with whoops and squeals and clapping hands. Aunt Hasina produced a tub of turmeric paste and she sat dutifully while the two girls daubed this on her forehead and arms, jabbering to each other in Bengali as they did so. The paste is supposed to make the bride's skin shine, but instead she looked as if she had bathed in mud.

'This reminds me of my wedding day,' said Aunt Hasina. 'I was so nervous. And then when I saw Thani-ji, he was so handsome, I almost cried.'

That was the first time she had met him, she thought. She did not even know her husband before they married.

By lunchtime, the house was all decked out and Aunt Hasina and the girls had left, replaced by an army of cooks who poured out from a battered van as it parked behind the house. They laid piles of coals outside the back door, which they would light up later. Huge black cauldrons sat in the back of the van, alongside boxes of spices and pallets of meat and fish. Two of the pallets were placed at either end of a flimsy picnic table, and four of the men started to scrape and chop and fillet.

She spent all afternoon with Thakur-ma getting ready. She washed her hair with amla powder mixed in water, and her grandmother braided it as it dried. She painted her nails with pearl-white varnish and, on the backs of her hands, Thakur-ma piped a henna design of an intricate stylised sun with finely-wrought leaves and flowers that curled along her fingers. The henna looked like melted chocolate and smelt of green tea.

For her eyes: thick, black mascara, peach eye shadow and coffee-coloured eyeliner.

Rose-pink blusher on her cheeks.

A blood-red stripe of lipstick.

She dressed in the red and gold wedding sari, and her

grandmother clucked and circled around her, tucking, smoothing and folding it into place, checking from every angle.

Thakur-ma produced a tray of glittering bangles, and she slipped a dozen gold rings over her wrist, but she refused an elaborate gold pendant for her neck; instead she wore Ganesh's necklace of black and silver beads. She knew it would look rustic and out of place amidst the finery of the rest of her outfit, but it gave her a sense of comfort. Finally, her grandmother placed a gold chain around her head, with a ruby centrepiece that fell over her turmeric-stained forehead.

When they were finished, Thakur-ma ushered her in front of the mirror that had been stuck crookedly on to the back of the bedroom door. They stood side-by-side assessing the final effect and her grandmother beamed her gummy smile.

'Sunya, you are beautiful. This is the happiest day of my life.'

But she didn't see a beautiful young woman; she saw a fragile china doll gazing back at her with scared eyes.

And now the wedding party is crammed into Thakur-ma's front room and everyone is watching the final part of the ceremony. Manu is dressed in a cream sherwani embroidered with gold stitching at the neck. He wears his black hair slicked back with gel. She has kept her head bowed throughout the ceremony, trying not to look at him, but now, sat next to him on a plastic chair, she catches his eye. He tries to smile, but to her it seems more like a smirk. He picks up the biro, signs the papers with an extravagant flourish, and pushes them across the table. She takes the pen from his hand and lets it hover over the page. In the front row of seats, Thakur-ma smiles and Abba strokes his moustache.

Sensing her hesitation, the priest puts his finger on the page, showing her where to sign. She cannot delay any longer. She lowers the pen to the paper and writes her name next to Manu's. Her fingers are numb and she struggles to apply any pressure, so that the black ink barely registers. By comparison to Manu's thick, bold strokes, her signature looks like the strands of a spider's web.

Southwark Cathedral

Friday 6 September 2013

'A few of the old gang are meeting up for some beers. Come along. It'll be fun.'

I had finally answered my phone after ignoring several previous calls and texts. Chas meant well, but his words didn't fool me. I knew this was for my benefit, to get me out and wrench me from the malaise I had fallen into, and I could imagine them all talking about me in concerned tones.

'Ben's in a bad way. We need to help him out.'

I couldn't think of anything worse than being 'helped out' but in the end I agreed to go, more to stop Chas from bugging me than from any desire on my part to spend the night in stilted conversations tiptoeing around a painful subject.

I had discovered that sleeping was a good way to lose time and had slept for a couple of hours that afternoon. I kept the bedroom curtains closed all day now, so that I could flop into bed at a moment's notice when the seconds started to drag. Sleep wasn't easy though. I owned a king-sized double, but I still slept on one side of the bed and sometimes I would roll over, stretch my arms out like I used to and wake up with the shock that her warm body wasn't there. And if I found that my head was too full of bitter thoughts to sleep, I would reach for my old scrapbook and relive the good times; I could picture it now with its faded red cover on the bedside table, next to the silver photo frame that still lay face down.

Buster usually slept with me, curled up on the sofa at the foot of the bed like a deflated balloon, his ears resolutely flat against his head. He lay on my discarded jeans and T-shirts, covering them in dog hair, but this was preferable to putting my clothes away in the drawers and wardrobes and facing the sight of Summer's bright outfits that would never be worn again. For a while, I couldn't escape the feeling that Buster blamed me for his mistress going away. He would look at me accusingly with his black eyes and finally, not being able to stand it any longer, I had attached the letter 'S' from her charm bracelet to his collar. He had nuzzled my hand with his wet nose as I did so, as if saying, 'Thank you,' for the gesture. Things had been better between us since.

When I dragged myself from the bed, I slouched into the kitchen, dunked a teabag in boiling water and surveyed the debris from the last twenty-four hours. A pizza box and four empty beer bottles were waiting to be recycled, while a carton of cornflakes and an open packet of Mother's Pride white sliced sat on the formica work surface by the toaster, surrounded by crumbs, sticky dollops of jam and greasy butter. A day's worth of washing up was piled in the sink and my shoulders sagged as I realised that I hadn't bothered to stack the dishwasher since breakfast the day before.

I put some food down for Buster and left him scoffing eagerly with his clacking jaw to wander into the sitting room. The floor was strewn with newspapers and music magazines, and the coffee table was covered in circular stains from mugs and beer bottles. I half-heartedly rearranged the cushions on the sofa and winced as this revealed a slice of congealed pizza squashed on to the upholstery. I peeled the pizza off with distaste and laid it on the coffee table, which at least hid one of the stains.

Turning my back on it all, I walked along the corridor to my tiny second bedroom-cum-study and tapped away on my computer while I sipped my tea – my usual aimless internet surfing, just seeing what was out there. Chas had arranged for us to meet at the Anchor Bankside pub in Southwark, so for want of a better idea, I typed in 'Southwark' and went from there.

And so there I was, half an hour early for Chas and the rest of them, looking up at the great arched ceiling of Southwark Cathedral, feeling guilty that I had left early to avoid having to clear up the mess in the flat and depressed that it would still be there when I got back. I don't know whether it was coincidence or simply that in my current state my eye was drawn to such things, but I had come to Southwark Cathedral off the back of one particular event almost sixty years ago.

I imagined her sitting where I was standing, in a simple wooden seat, lost in her thoughts as a great hubbub surrounded her. Despite the crowd and the altogether different scale, she would have been lonely, just like me at Summer's simple service at Putney Vale Crematorium. No one else present had suffered the same loss or could understand how she felt, and when the service was over and everyone returned to their lives – the relatives, the friends, the colleagues, the well-wishers, the Bishop, the organist, the choir, the cathedral staff, the journalists – she would be left alone, with nothing but memories and an empty space in her life.

My thoughts rattled around my head as the murmured voices of visitors echoed around the cavernous cathedral. I wasn't ready to face Chas and my uni friends. I would bale out and retreat to my darkened flat with the closed curtains and a soppy old mongrel dog for company. At least I had Buster.

Win sits on her wooden fold-up chair and contemplates her surroundings. The thick stone columns give way to gracefully curved arches and high, high above her head, so high that it makes her dizzy to look, the vaults criss-cross the ceiling in perfect geometry. It is all a long road from their soot-bricked end of terrace in Blackburn. Kaff would have laughed at the ridiculous grandeur of it all and Win can hear her now. 'Lucky Kaff,' she would have said.

In front of her, the Bishop stands in the middle of the aisle in his white cassock with red piping, appropriately solemn-faced. Occasionally, he gives a little nod, acknowledging someone in the congregation. Win knows that there will be hundreds of people filing in behind her – Bernie had been very efficient with the invitations – but she dare not turn round for fear that the sight of such a large crowd will send her into hysterics and force her to run from the cathedral. She always suffered from stage fright at school; she could think of no torture worse than being compelled to perform on stage. It is funny how two people cut from the same Lancashire cloth could turn out so different. Kaff was always at her best when she had an audience. Well, she would have a big one today, that's for sure.

She wishes her father could be here to comfort her and then instantly regrets this selfish thought. Poppy would have been destroyed to see his beloved Kathleen die before he went to his own grave. Bernie will sit down next to her after she has ushered everyone to their places, but for now Win feels horribly alone, small and fragile in such an enormous building. She attempts a smile at the Bishop, but his gaze is focused beyond her, to more interesting people taking their seats for the service.

She imagines who will be here today. Bruno will be towards the front, she knows, preparing for his reading and trying to retain his composure. She remembers the telephone call when she told him that Kathleen had passed. Bruno had screamed so loudly down the receiver that Win's ear rang for hours afterwards. The Barbirollis, of course, J.B. and Evelyn; she must talk to them after the service. Bert would probably be here as well, sitting discreetly towards the back in a neat, dark suit, minding his own business. Bert would have been too sensitive to bring the new Mrs Wilson.

In her most fanciful thoughts, she had hoped that Her Majesty would make an appearance. It was over a year ago that Kaff had sung for the young queen at her uncle's house, but Kaff never stopped talking about what a sweet poppet she was. Who would have thought it? The two most famous women in England staying next door to each other for a few summer days in an obscure Hertfordshire town. And Kaff is asked round one evening. Just like that. A rousing version of 'Land of Hope and Glory', a few cups of tea and Bob's your uncle: Kaff is friends with the Queen and gets a CBE six months later. Klever Kaff.

Kaff knew she was ill then of course, and the Queen had been especially concerned because of what had happened to her father. They say he died of heart trouble, brought on by the strain of office, but everyone knew the truth: that it was the cancer that did for him like it did for Kaff. Win wonders why people don't talk about cancer, as if the disease is too despicable to mention. Perhaps she ought to do something about that, in Kaff's memory, but without her sister Win was a nobody, just a little girl from a northern town lost in the bright lights of London. What would she be able to do? And besides, Kaff herself never liked people talking of her illness. She was always desperate to hide it from her public.

'I have wonderful camouflage, Win,' she said.

She shudders at the memory of Kaff's last performance. The doctors had warned her to take it easy, but Kaff would never listen. She insisted on keeping her schedule going as long as she could, but *Orpheus* at Covent Garden was the final straw. In her nightmares, Win still hears the dull crack of her sister's thigh bone when Kaff's leg disintegrated on stage. No one knew what had happened and Kaff just kept on singing – even now, Win has no idea how she finished the performance – and in the dressing room afterwards, she carried on taking well-wishers, resting her leg on a chair and wincing through the pain.

'Just snipped a bit of bone in mi 'ip,' she said to anyone that asked afterwards. ''ad to limp for the rest of the evening.'

Stopped her going to the Palace of course, to pick up her ribbon. Instead, a parcel came registered delivery and Win had to sign for it at the post office. They had to conduct their own private ceremony in the hospital, but it didn't stop Kaff being 'pickled tink with mi little gong'.

Something hisses and crackles above her head and Win looks up. There are speakers attached to the columns and she recognises instantly the delicate strings that introduce Mahler's *Das Lied von der Erde*. It is Bruno's recording, of course. And then her sister is singing, her clear, unwavering, glorious voice soaring through the cathedral rafters, piercing her to the spine. Win closes her eyes and she is no longer in Southwark anymore, but back in the concert hall in Salzburg, hearing Kaff sing the Mahler for the first time, wearing her favourite rich green brocade dress that Win had made for her. Kaff before she was ill, a shining star, her voice like ice, achingly sad, the whole audience rapt, held rigid in its grasp.

The last movement of *Das Lied* is 'The Abschied' – 'The Farewell'. It finishes with the word 'Ewig' sung over and over as the music fades to silence, and sometimes Kaff would be so lost with emotion that she couldn't sing those last words. Ewig. Ewig. Ewig. It means 'forever' in German. Bruno knew, of course, that Kaff was dying, and that was the very reason he made the recording, so that she would live on forever. Her sister: beautiful, wonderful, unlucky Kaff. The service today is her *Abschied* – her farewell. She will sing for the angels now.

Kathleen Ferrier (1912-1953)

Kathleen Ferrier was an English contralto singer who, at the time she died of breast cancer at the age of forty-one, was described by one commentator as possibly 'the second most celebrated woman in England after the Queen'. Indeed, the opera critic Rupert Christiansen observed that Ferrier's death on 8 October 1953 'quite literally shattered the euphoria of the Coronation' which had taken place four months earlier in June.

Kathleen Ferrier (known to herself and her family and friends as Kaff) was brought up in Blackburn, Lancashire, with her older sister, Winifred ('Win'). She often described herself, somewhat ironically, as Klever Kaff, or self-deprecatingly Not So Klever Kaff. This epithet derived from an incident in her youth when she sewed a button back on to the coat of a young boy, signing off with a flourish as if finishing a piano piece. The grateful boy, Peter Hetherington, called her Clever Kaff which, in its corrupted form, stuck.

When she left school, she started work as a telephonist for the General Post Office, marrying Albert Wilson, a bank clerk, when she was just twenty-three. Their union did not work out, however – it is reported that the marriage was never consummated – and when Albert left for the war five years later in 1940, their relationship was effectively over. The couple were granted a divorce in 1947.

It was after Albert left for military service that Ferrier's singing career began to take off. After hearing her sing at a concert in Blackpool, the conductor Malcolm Sargent recommended her to the London agents Ibbs and Tillett, who agreed to take her on as a client. In December 1942, Ferrier relocated to London with her sister, the two of them taking a flat in Frognal Mansions, Hampstead. Win took a teaching job at a school in Chiswick and in her spare time, as clothes were rationed, she made outfits for Ferrier to wear on stage, one of her favourites being a green Liberty brocade dress.

There followed a decade of increasing fame and success for Ferrier, and a hectic schedule that encompassed tours of America, the Netherlands, Germany, Austria, Switzerland and Italy, as well as the UK. Ferrier's staple pieces were arias, but she endeared herself to a wider audience by also singing versions of traditional folk songs, the best loved being 'Blow The Wind Southerly', which was regularly played on radio. Win was too busy to accompany her sister on most of these

287

trips, but in 1949 she did see Ferrier perform Orfeo ed Euridice in Amsterdam in front of Queen Juliana and Prince Bernhard, and two months later, sing Mahler's Das Lied von der Erde under Bruno Walter in Salzburg.

In January 1951, Ferrier's father died at the age of eighty-three and less than two months later she discovered a lump on her left breast, or as she described it, 'a bump on mi busto'. Ferrier fulfilled a week of engagements in continental Europe before she visited her doctor. Tests confirmed cancer and on 10 April 1951 she underwent a mastectomy at University College Hospital, after which all her immediate engagements were cancelled.

Ferrier went to great lengths to keep her illness from the public – at the time, it was not common for cancer to be openly discussed – and returned to the stage after only two months. Over the summer and autumn of 1951, she fitted hospital appointments in between concerts and tours, culminating in a stirring rendition of 'Land of Hope and Glory' at the reopening after war damage of the Free Trade Hall in Manchester, a performance that the conductor John Barbirolli, who had become one of Ferrier's closest friends, described as 'moving everyone, not just the conductor, to tears'.

After this concert, however, Ferrier undertook a course of radiation therapy and was forced to rest for another two months. She returned to the stage in January 1952 for a series of concerts with Benjamin Britten and, despite being in increasing pain, undertook a heavy work schedule for the rest of the year, including travelling to Austria in May to record Das Lied von der Erde with the tenor Julius Patzak, the Vienna Philharmonic and Bruno Walter. Walter and Ferrier thus preserved their partnership on disc and this recording is Ferrier's most celebrated work.

An unusual episode occurred during the year when, on staying at a friend's house in Hertfordshire one July weekend, she was asked by their neighbour to come round and sing one evening. The neighbour was Queen Elizabeth II's uncle, David Bowes-Lyon, and the young Queen just happened to be visiting for a few days. In a letter to her Canadian pianist, John Newmark, Ferrier wrote: 'sang for about half an hour – then chatted with her for another on all subjects – sweet poppet, she is. Wasn't that lucky, eh?' It is thought that one of the subjects touched upon was Ferrier's illness, the Queen having lost her father to cancer earlier that year.

On New Year's Day 1953, Ferrier was made a Commander of the British Empire in the Queen's Birthday Honours List and she commenced rehearsals for Orpheus at the Royal Opera House, Covent Garden, fitting these in between continuing radiotherapy treatments which weakened her greatly. Four performances of Orpheus were scheduled and the first on 3 February was hailed as a triumph by the critics. However, at the second performance three days later, disaster struck. During the second act, the femur in Ferrier's left thigh cracked and splintered. Despite the pain, she completed the performance, immobile and using the scenery as support. Afterwards, she received well-wishers in her dressing room, with her leg strapped and propped up on a chair. When everyone had gone, her sister Win asked her if there was anything she could do. Ferrier responded by saying: 'Get me a stretcher.' This was Ferrier's last-ever public performance.

The remaining shows of Orpheus were at first rescheduled and then eventually cancelled, although the awful truth of Ferrier's illness was still kept from the public. An announcement in The Guardian read: 'Miss Ferrier is suffering from a strain resulting from arthritis which requires immediate further treatment. It has been caused by the physical stress involved in rehearsal and performance of her role in Orpheus.'

Ferrier spent two months at University College Hospital and missed her investiture. Instead, the CBE was brought to her hospital bed. In April, she left hospital for a new ground-floor apartment in St John's Wood that Win had rented for them, as her sister could no longer manage the stairs in Frognal Mansions. However, Ferrier's stay in her new home was short-lived as she returned to hospital at the end of May where, despite further operations, her condition deteriorated.

In early June, she received the news that she had been awarded the Gold Medal of the Royal Philharmonic Society, the first female singer to receive the honour for nearly forty years. Her letter, dated 9 June 1953, to George Baker, the secretary of the society, in which she wrote that the 'unbelievable, wondrous news has done more than anything to make me feel so much better' was probably the last letter she ever signed herself. From that point on, she weakened steadily, seeing only Win, her devoted secretary Bernie (Bernadine Hammond), and a few close friends.

Probably the last person to hear Ferrier sing was John Barbirolli, who visited her just two days before she died. Ferrier sang parts of

Chausson's 'Poème de l'amour and de la mer', a piece which Barbirolli had encouraged her to take on in order to stretch the range of her voice higher. The conductor said afterwards that although her body was wasted, her 'voice had lost none of its radiance'.

Ferrier died peacefully on 8 October 1953 at the age of forty-one. Her death was a shock to the nation, as the public had remained in ignorance of her illness. A memorial service was held at Southwark Cathedral one month later. Of the many tributes, perhaps the most memorable was from Bruno Walter, who said that 'the greatest thing in music in my life has been to have known Kathleen Ferrier and Gustav Mahler – in that order'.

For the rest of her life, Win Ferrier was active in preserving the memory and legacy of her sister. She published a book, The Life of Kathleen Ferrier, in 1955, and became the first President of the Kathleen Ferrier Society which she helped to establish in 1993. She was also instrumental in establishing the Kathleen Ferrier Cancer Research Fund which in 1984 helped establish the Kathleen Ferrier Chair of Clinical Oncology at University College Hospital, and the Kathleen Ferrier Memorial Scholarship Fund, which awards music scholarships and runs an annual competition for young singers every April in the Wigmore Hall. Win was a regular attendee at this week-long event and often presented the prizes, as she did for the fortieth competition in 1995. She died six months later at the age of ninety-one.

The Story of Summer (3)

He rolls off her, snorts and flops on his oversized belly. She turns away and bites the end of her pillow, determined not to cry. Manu drank so much at the wedding that he had to be helped into Uncle Thani's silver bird Mercedes that drove them to Thani-ji's house. She had hoped that when they got to bed he would collapse, thus sparing her the ordeal of sex with her new husband for at least one more night. Unfortunately, in the bedroom, Manu recovered himself sufficiently to force himself on top of her.

She lay there, limp, her eyes closed as he sawed away. After the first stab of pain when he entered her, she felt nothing, turning her head to gain some respite from the beer and whisky fumes that soaked his breath. This was not how it was supposed to be in her dreams.

She moves into Manu's house in town the following day. It is a simple brick-built, two-up two-down structure, with a kitchen and sitting room on the ground floor, and a bedroom and a bathroom on the upper floor. Manu leaves the house at lunchtime and she is glad to be on her own. She busies herself tidying and cleaning, picking Manu's clothes up from the bedroom floor and scrubbing mould off the bathroom wall.

In the afternoon, Abba brings round her clothes and the few possessions she has and she makes him a cup of fragrant tea. Thakur-ma has sent a box of freshly baked roshogolla, which she hides in the pantry before Manu can see, and some rohu fish wrapped in paper.

'For you to cook something for tonight,' her father explains.

She hadn't thought about food, but Abba is right; she will be expected to cook for her husband. She places the fish in the fridge while her father takes her cases upstairs.

'How are you, sweetheart?' he asks, when he comes back down. 'How is being a wife?'

She ignores him.

'You must learn to be a good wife, sweetheart.'

She puts her teacup down and draws breath.

'I agreed to marry Manu, Abba. I made no promises as to what sort of wife I would be.'

'If you are a good wife, Manu will be a good husband.'

'I think your definition of a good husband is very different from mine,' she says coldly.

He creases his forehead.

'You know, I only want you to be happy, sweetheart.'

She takes his cup off him, pushes her chair back and stands up.

'Would you like some more tea, Abba?'

★

Manu returns early in the evening. He grunts at the tidiness of the house, but otherwise makes no comment. She has prepared a rohu fish curry with mustard seeds and rice that she found in a kitchen cupboard, and as they eat together in the kitchen, she considers her new husband.

Without the oil, his dark hair sticks up in unruly tufts. He has a boyish face, with a snub nose and the beginnings of a double chin, and she thinks that he will grow large in middle age if he is not careful. She shudders at the thought that she will still be with him to see that outcome. He wears a striped shirt with a wide collar and loose cuffs, over brown corduroy trousers. The shirt is horribly creased with yellow sweat stains spreading underneath the armpits.

He bolts his food down as if he hasn't eaten properly for weeks. A dribble of curry sauce falls down his chin which he scoops up with a chubby finger that he then licks with a mischievous grin. She shakes her head but says nothing.

'Mishti,' he says, 'that was good. Everyone teased me that you would be no good as a cook. They were wrong.'

She picks up the dishes and takes them over to the sink. He comes up behind her and curls his arms around her waist. She stiffens involuntarily.

'What is wrong? You do not like your husband, mishti?'

She takes his hands and removes them from her waist.

'My name is Sunya. And not now, Manu. I must wash the dishes.'

He kisses her neck and she feels the wetness of his saliva on her skin.

'Later then. I am going into town to meet my father. He wants to celebrate finally marrying me off.'

When he returns, she pretends to be asleep, and he stumbles around the bedroom, worse the wear for drink. He climbs into bed and drapes an arm around her, which she shakes off disdainfully. After two more attempts, he gives up. Either that or he has fallen into a stupor. She lies awake listening to his soft snores and thinking of her mother. She must find a way to speak to her.

They have been married for less than a week when he hits her for the first time. She had taken a decision that she would not give herself to him while he was drunk. And as Manu went out every night and came home stinking of beer and cigarettes, they had not had sex since their wedding night. When he was drunk, she found him easy to repulse, as he was too uncoordinated to stop her from pushing him away.

It all changes on a Thursday. He returns from the bar slightly earlier than usual and she is still awake, reading in the front room. This catches her by surprise and before she can get up he has thrown himself on top of her on the sofa. She is momentarily winded, and takes a moment to catch her breath. He fumbles at her sari, grabbing clumsily at her breasts, and manages to place one leg between her thighs, levering them apart. She kicks out and catches him on the shin, causing him to howl in pain.

And then he slaps her. Hard, with the flat of his hand, so that her ears ring and her cheek stings. She is so stunned that she stops still, staring up at him, angry. He takes the opportunity to seize her wrists in one hand, holding them above her head, while he unzips his trousers with the other. She squirms but the weight of his body holds her fast, and without the use of her arms to push him away she is trapped.

He pulls her sari apart and finds her knickers.

'No,' she screams. 'Get off.'

He releases his hand, and for a second she thinks he is letting her go. Bang. He slaps her again and the ring on his finger bites into her cheek. He reaches down again, pulls her knickers to one side, and forces himself inside her. She cries in pain and tries to bite his hand holding her wrists, but he only laughs and begins to thrust. She spits in his face, which startles him, and he stops for a second. Only for a second. He puts his other hand around her neck and starts to push into her again. She feels the pressure of his thumb on her windpipe and wonders if he is going to strangle her, if she is destined to end her life here, on a cheap sofa in a little brick house in West Bengal. He is too excited, though, to last long; he is spent within moments and falls on to her, releasing his grip on her neck and wrists, panting heavily. She feels his semen dribbling down the inside of her thigh and gags.

He lies there for some time, recovering his breath, and when he finally picks himself up, he stands over her, adjusting his trousers.

'That is how to be a wife, mishti,' he says, with a smirk.

*

After the incident, she keeps a kitchen knife with her at all times, and at night, she sleeps on the sofa. Manu seems to realise that it won't be so easy for him to force himself upon her a second time and maintains his distance. On a couple of evenings, when he comes in, she hears the door to the sitting room open slightly and she grasps the handle of the knife tightly, her heart pounding in her ears. But then he closes the door again and she hears him padding up the stairs.

When she walks into town, she wears a hijab which hides the welt on her face. Madhur the sweetman probes her with questions, but she gives nothing away.

'Are you well, Sunya? How is married life?'

'I am well, Madhur, thank you.'

'You do not smile for Madhur like you used to. Are you unhappy?'

'Just tired, Madhur, that is all.'

'Ahh,' he thumbs his nose knowingly, 'not getting so much sleep, hey? Madhur knows.'

It is true she is not sleeping well, but not in the way Madhur thinks. She lays awake on the sofa for as long as she can, to be ready in case Manu comes in, and it is only in the early hours, when she can no longer keep her heavy lids open, that she drifts off into a sleep full of monsters.

She visits her father and Thakur-ma one lunchtime. Abba is agitated, constantly fiddling with his moustache, and chain-smoking. When Thakur-ma disappears into the kitchen, her father speaks.

'Sunya, Thani-ji has been round. He complains that Manu says you are not a good wife.'

She looks at Abba with disgust.

'I married him. That was the agreement. I did not agree to be a... good wife.'

'Sunya, it is important. If you make Manu happy, things will be better for you, I promise.'

'Should he not try to make me happy?'

Abba throws a hand in the air, exasperated.

'What is so wrong with Manu?'

She slowly pulls her hijab to one side. In the days since Manu hit her, the bruise has become the size of a lime, with a centre of ochre surrounded by a blue-black stain. There is a scab where his ring drew blood.

Abba gasps.

'Did he... did he do this to you?'

She nods, replacing the hijab over her face.

Her father's face falls and he stares into his lap.

'What did Manu do?' Thakur-ma stands in the doorway, drying her hands on a towel.

'It is no matter, Thakur-ma,' she says, but her grandmother walks over to her and pulls at her hijab.

She brushes her fingers over the bruise and Sunya flinches. It is still sore.

'I will get some camomile,' she says, and then she turns to her son.

'Oh, Abba. What have you done?'

★

295

The second time he hits her is also the last. He leaves for work as normal, but then surprises her by returning home before lunch. She is in the kitchen, preparing vegetables for dinner that evening, and doesn't hear him enter the house. The first she knows he is there is when he grabs her roughly by the waist from behind and throws her against the wall. She still has the chopping knife in her hand but he pins her arm to the wall and squeezes so hard that she drops it.

'Manu, get off me!' she shrieks.

He clamps his other hand to her mouth, gagging her.

'I want you, now.' His eyes are wide and she wonders if he has taken something. 'You are my wife. You must act like a wife.'

She wriggles to try and free herself, but he is too heavy. He presses against her and she feels his erection through his trousers. She bites, and he yelps in pain as her teeth scythe into the flesh of his palm.

'You fucking bitch!'

He releases his hand from her mouth and shakes it. And then he curls his stubby fingers into a fist and punches her in the chest.

The pain is excruciating. She doubles over, clutching her stomach, struggling to breathe. He jerks her head up again and slaps her face with the flat of her hand. Her vision blurs, but she can feel him fumbling with the folds of her sari. She gulps in a mouthful of air and summons just enough energy to lift her knee sharply into his groin. At the same time, she pushes at his stomach and he stumbles backwards, holding his pelvis.

She shakes her head and runs. Out of the kitchen, through the hallway. She hears him behind her, yelling.

'Bitch. I will beat you black and fucking blue.'

She fumbles with the latch on the door and he jumps on her, tearing at her hair. They fall backwards against the door, which swings open as she lands on top of him. Sunlight floods the hallway and she hears a voice from her dreams.

'Leave my daughter alone.'

She rolls away from Manu and looks up. Her mother stands over them, hands on hips, her small frame filling the doorway, a look of pure fury on her face.

Behind her is Abba, wringing his hands.

She struggles to her feet and her mother gives her a hug.

'You are coming home with me now, Sunya.'

Manu picks himself up and scowls.

'She stays here. She is my wife.'

Her mother looks him up and down with an air of disgust.

'No. You are not fit to be a husband. Sunya is my daughter.'

She takes her hand and leads her away from the house.

Manu makes to follow them, but her father steps in front of him, blocking his path.

They have gone no more than ten paces when Manu shouts after them.

'Your daughter. She fucks like a whore. You know that. Like a whore.'

She turns round, to see her father punch Manu square on the jaw. She hears the crack of fist on bone and sees a tooth spiral into the air as Manu crumples into a heap.

Her mother puts her arms around her shoulders and they walk away.

South Bank

'So what happened then?' Annie urges.

'She came back to England with her mother. Her father stayed in India, worked for Thani and repaid his debt that way. He had to make up for breaking Thani's son's jaw now as well, so that probably added a year's hard labour for him. Summer told me that he passed away a few years later, but I wondered if she just meant that spiritually. That maybe he lived on but that he had died in her heart.'

'And she changed her name?'

'Yes. From then on, she was Summer Meadows. Sunya means sunshine and Meadows was her mother's maiden name, so Summer just fitted. It meant that she could make a fresh start without completely losing her roots. After her ordeal, she was determined to bring a touch of happiness to every day, starting with her name. She was making a statement, I suppose, with her new identity.'

I pause for breath and Annie doesn't reply. Perhaps there is nothing to say. Walkers are streaming past us, heading west along the river, but we seem to be in a bubble of our own. Voices float over our heads, the words indistinguishable to my ears. I am all talked out now and Annie and I walk side-by-side in silence. We have about an hour's walking left before we return to Battersea Power Station and the finish and it feels like the final stretch, as it is pretty much follow-the-Thames-back-to-Battersea now. Around us, groups of tired Shine walkers are chattering in high spirits.

In the time I have been talking, we have been walking along the South Bank from Southwark Cathedral where Win Ferrier bade goodbye to her sister. I had stolen a guilty look at the empty chairs and tables outside the Anchor Bankside pub, thinking of Chas and the others waiting in vain for me to show up that evening, and moved quickly on.

Many of the iconic buildings on the South Bank look

blatantly out of place, parachuted in by over-enthusiastic city planners desperate to create a modern, vibrant riverside walkway. Like the vanilla whitewash and timber structure of the Globe Theatre – a reconstruction of Shakespeare's original that would sit comfortably in a Disney theme park. And the Tate Modern, opened in the year 2000, a renovation of a grimy post-war power station. No doubt worthy trustees toasted themselves with glasses of fizzy prosecco at their success in presenting modern art in the context of an industrial setting.

I like the wobbly Millennium Bridge with its vista across to the dome of Saint Paul's and its steel suspension cables that sweep elegantly across the river, but even so, it looks odd stuck between the peeling paintwork of the more substantial Southwark and Blackfriars roadbridges.

'Peter and I used to come here a lot.' Annie breaks the silence and points at the Tate Modern as we pass, and I realise that I have spent most of the walk lost in my own tale. I have not heard much about Annie.

'Tell me about him,' I say.

'Peter?' She looks round at me. 'He was the best brother a girl could wish for, always looking out for me. He defended my honour at school, helped me find a flat when I moved to London, he was a shoulder to cry on when things weren't going well at work.'

'Your best friend?'

'Yes. I guess so. It was ironic in the end that I had to look after him, when he got sick. He was so tired all the time, and he kept getting infections. It was horrible.'

'What was it, if you don't mind me asking?'

'It's OK.' Although I notice that she is staring rigidly ahead now. This is still painful for her. 'It was leukaemia. He was diagnosed aged twenty-five and less than two years later he was dead.'

'I found the worst thing was seeing the person you love waste away, as if their soul was being stolen away in front of your eyes, and there was nothing you could do about it.' I kick myself as I speak. I am bringing the conversation back to me again, but Annie doesn't seem to mind.

'I had such a feeling of helplessness. I kept doing trades in my head. If Peter gets to live, I will devote my life to the poor. That sort of thing.'

'I used to wish that we could swap places,' I reply. 'That it was me undergoing the chemo, confined to bed, sentenced to death.'

'The trouble is,' she says, finally turning to look at me again, 'there was never anyone to do the trade with.'

'No one who was listening, anyway,' I say bitterly.

'But, you have to move on. You know what Peter's last words to me were?'

I don't need to respond. She will tell me.

'He told me that we came from the same womb at the same time and so a piece of him would always be inside me. That I should live my life for the two of us and make the most out of every day.'

'And do you?'

'I try, but it's not always easy. I couldn't leave the flat for a week after he died so I didn't make such a good start, but I've got better since. I'm doing this walk for one thing. He would have been proud of that.' She smiles and I am sure she is right. And I know that Summer would have been proud of me too.

We have walked past the National Theatre and under Waterloo Bridge now. Approaching us, I can see a posse of bikes, led by the boy with the shades and the beatbox strapped to his panier rack. They must have been cycling around London now for eight hours. He is blaring out Queen as they pass us. 'We Will Rock You.' Some of the Shine walkers join in the chorus, and I am convinced I can hear the pink-wigged girls amongst them.

'We will, we will… rock you!'

The boy lifts one hand from his handlebars and conducts them.

'We will, we will… rock you!'

Caught in the moment, Annie and I raise our voices as well.

'We will, we will… rock you!'

The cyclists move away and the music fades with them. We walk by the graffitied undercroft of the Queen Elizabeth Hall where London's baggy-trousered youth hang out with their skateboards and BMX bikes, and beyond us we see the Hayward Gallery and the Royal Festival Hall.

Friday 4 September 1970

Royal Festival Hall

Konstantin surveys his dancers with a critical eye. They are lined up on stage behind the closed curtain like exhibits in a human zoo, legs together, toes pointing at 45 degrees, hands clasped, chins in the air.

'Olga!' he barks. 'Straight back!'

A ballerina pushes out her flat chest and stiffens her back. She does not acknowledge her Director, instead keeping her eyes fixed firmly forward.

Konstantin is weary of this tour. It is not just the pressure of maintaining the Kirov's artistic standards, but the stress of being on constant alert that takes its toll. He guards his ballet corps as a shepherd watches over his flock of sheep, but it is impossible to be with each of them all the time. A tour to a Western country is like taking a group of children from a ghetto to a sweet factory, allowing them only to look and not to taste. He is under no illusions; the Party expect him to bring all his dancers home, a dictat that was made extremely clear to him at a briefing in KGB headquarters some weeks before they left. Nureyev's defection in Paris nearly a decade earlier was an embarrassment to the Soviet Union, and the Party will not countenance a repeat.

Konstantin hears a commotion in the wings and one of the stagehands gives him a thumbs-up. He claps his hands and his ballet dancers flex their muscles and tighten their postures. As they do so, a thin man with a high forehead and thinning hair steps on to the stage. He wears a dark suit, a stiff white shirt and a black tie. He looks as if he could be attending a funeral, rather than a performance of *Sleeping Beauty*. Konstantin thinks he looks fitter than in the pictures he has seen on the files back home in Moscow. Perhaps the London life agrees with Mikhail Smirnovsky.

An aide behind the Ambassador whispers in his ear and Smirnovsky looks up to identify Konstantin. He contorts his lips into a mean smile and strides across the stage, holding out his hand.

'Your Excellency.' Konstantin takes Smirnovsky's hand and gives a half bow.

'Sergeyev,' the Ambassador's voice is sharp, like vinegar, 'a pleasure to meet you. I am very much looking forward to the performance this evening.'

'We hope that we do not disappoint.'

'I am sure you will not.'

Konstantin senses that it is almost a threat. 'I am sure you will not… or else…'

'May I introduce you to the *corps de ballet*?' He extends his open palm, inviting the Ambassador to walk along the line of dancers.

Smirnovsky obliges and together they proceed, like generals expecting the troops. Konstantin introduces each one by name. The men bow gracefully, the girls lay one leg behind them and give deep curtseys, their hands sweeping the stage floor as they do so. Smirnovsky shakes all their hands, and every so often stops to ask a question with practised ease.

'How are you enjoying the tour?'

'Is this your first performance of *Sleeping Beauty*?'

'Have you had chance to see any of London?'

The dancers chatter back nervously, casting anxious glances at Konstantin, who reassures them with smiles. As artists they are not accustomed to small talk with Party officials, and are concerned not to say anything that could be misinterpreted. Their answers are guarded and where possible monosyllabic.

'Very much, Your Excellency.'

'No. This will be my third, Your Excellency.'

'We have seen Buckingham Palace from the coach, Your Excellency.'

The whole process takes ten minutes and when they reach the end of the line, Konstantin claps his hands again, and the corps flutter away like butterflies.

'They must prepare for the performance now,' he explains.

'Of course, of course.' Smirnovsky pauses, stroking his

pointed chin. 'Tell me, Sergeyev, is Makarova not dancing tonight? I would very much have liked to see her.'

'I am afraid not, Your Excellency. We have a rota so that the prima ballerinas stay fresh. She has the evening off.'

'And she is not here?'

Konstantin shuffles his feet. He had asked Makarova to be present in order for her to meet the Ambassador but she had implored him to allow her to dine with friends. Reluctantly, he had acceded to her request. Natalia was looking a little drawn and had been somewhat distracted over the last few days. The rigours of the tour were getting to her and a complete break from the ballet for a few days would do her good.

'No, Your Excellency. She is not here.'

'Ahh,' he says. 'That is disappointing.'

'I assure you that the performance will be excellent nevertheless,' Konstantin ventures.

Smirnovsky's face brightens and he checks his watch.

'Fifteen minutes,' he says. 'I had better find my seat. So good to meet you, Sergeyev. And your *corps de ballet*. Your dancers are a great credit to you. I will report back that the tour has been an unqualified success.'

'Thank you, Your Excellency.'

The two shake hands and the Ambassador turns on his heels. Konstantin exhales slowly as he watches him go, and his shoulders relax as the tension seeps out of his body. The Director of the Kirov Ballet is relieved – they have passed inspection.

Konstantin Sergeyev

Konstantin Sergeyev became Artistic Director of the Kirov Ballet for the second time in 1960 after a four-year term from 1951-1955 when he was both Artistic Director and Premier Danseur. As a performer, Sergeyev was renowned for his lyrical interpretation of leading romantic roles and his partnerships with Galina Ulanova, and Natalia Dudinskaya, who he married. However, his tenure as Artistic Director focused mainly on classical techniques in the ballet standards. Sergeyev was dismissed from the Kirov in 1970 after the prima ballerina, Natalia Makarova, defected while on tour in London. His dismissal was viewed both as a punishment from the Communist Party, and as an attempt to prevent further departures from a company demoralised by his conservative policies. Despite this black mark on his career, Sergeyev was reinstated as director of the choreographic school in 1973 and awarded numerous state honours, including the Lenin Prize.

Royal Festival Hall

Saturday 18 August 2012

I sat nervously in the third row of the auditorium, which seemed to be the appropriate row for family and friends. I wasn't sure that I qualified as either, but nevertheless I was there. Summer was next to me, holding my hand. Neither of us spoke.

On stage a group of eight-year-old girls were being put through their ballet paces by a stern-faced woman in Lycra and legwarmers. My attention was focused on only one: a skinny girl with dusky skin and a tangle of caramel hair that fell to her shoulders. All the other girls had their hair tied back, but not this one. Her hair defied a ponytail. It was like seeing an old photograph of Summer when she was a child, for this was Rae – Summer's daughter – and today was the day when she and I would meet for the first time.

I had bought her a cute, cuddly lion as a present. Summer had laughed. Perhaps eight-year-olds are beyond cuddly toys, I didn't know. Surely they are not into make-up and clothes at that age? The lion sat on the chair next to me.

The woman clapped her hands and the girls floated off the stage with little ballet steps, their practice session over for the day. *The Nutcracker*, Summer told me, had been specially adapted for Rae's age group and was to be performed at the Royal Festival Hall in front of adoring parents in two months' time, proud as punch at their daughter's achievement.

I wanted to be there, with Summer, watching Rae. I wouldn't count as a bona fide father, but I would be the next best thing, if I was acceptable, if I passed the Rae test. I knew that Summer would only move in with me if Rae was happy about it. I was under no illusions; Rae's wellbeing came before mine and in truth that was how it should be. There is no bond stronger than that between mother and daughter, and Summer herself was testament to that. I needed to be on sparkling form, though, but I had no experience of eight-year-olds. What did they talk about?

Summer eased herself up from the seat and looked down at me. I was paralysed. Was this it? Surely I had more time to compose myself. We couldn't be going backstage now, could we? I rubbed my palms, greasy with sweat, on my jeans, exhaled sharply and stood up. My legs wobbled and I reached out to lean on Summer for support.

'It will be fine, Ben.' She smiled at me. 'Just be yourself.'

I didn't know what that meant. Be myself. The geeky bloke who dabbled in history. Who made up stories about what might have happened. Who had let her mother walk away from him five months before. Who almost abandoned her mother in hospital to hop on a plane to New York.

Summer leaned over. 'You love me, Ben. That will be enough for Rae.'

We left the auditorium and were shown to the wings, where a small line of parents had formed, waiting to collect their daughters. I was the only idiot clutching a cuddly toy lion.

One or two girls wandered out, to be greeted with smothering kisses and cries of, 'Well done, Esme, you were wonderful,' and, 'Beautiful, Isabella, you looked so beautiful.'

And then a bundle of olive-skinned energy bounded from backstage, leapt into Summer's arms, and hugged her as if she hadn't seen her for months. The two of them stood there holding each other while I examined the scenery. After the longest minute in my life, Summer spoke.

'Angel,' she slowly peeled Rae's arms from around her torso, 'there is someone I would like you to meet.'

Rae pulled away and stared at me with deep brown eyes just like her mother's.

'This is Ben, angel. You know. I told you about him.'

Rae's face tightened as she looked me up and down.

'Are you Mummy's boyfriend?' she asked, calmly.

'I... I suppose...'

Summer saved me.

'Yes. He is Mummy's boyfriend, and he loves Mummy very much.'

'Hmph.' Rae seemed unconvinced.

'Here,' I thrust the lion in her direction, 'I brought this for you. I'm sorry if it's a bit young for you, but I thought he looked cute.'

Rae reached out and took the lion from me, holding it to her chest. She cuddled it for a few seconds and then seemed to have come to a decision. She held out her hand.

'I'm Rae,' she said, confidently, 'and I am very pleased to meet you, Ben.'

Annie turns her pale face towards me.

'Summer had a daughter?'

'Yes. When Summer got home from India, she found out she was pregnant.' I breathe in heavily.

'And you never knew?'

'I never knew. Not until she told me on that bench by Tower Bridge. How dense was I?'

Annie rests her hand reassuringly on my shoulder.

'And that was why she left you?'

My cheeks are burning. 'That's why I let her go. I couldn't cope with it. It was my fault.'

Annie pats my shoulder. 'It was understandable, Ben. Finding out your girlfriend is married with a secret daughter would be more than enough for anybody.'

Her words are kind, but I regret that moment every day. If only I had had the courage to call her back.

'She's nine now,' I say. 'Her name is Rae, short for Raeleah. It means ray of sunshine. She was Summer's little ray of sunshine.'

'Do you see her?' Annie asks.

'Yes. She splits her time between my place and her grandmother's. After all, Fiona helped to bring her up so that Summer could go to university and then get a job, so they're very close. But when Summer moved in with me after her operation, Rae came to live in the flat with us. Rae says she loves having two homes.'

'And I bet she reminds you of Summer.'

'Every time I look in her eyes. Dark chocolate, just like her mother. It's scary sometimes.'

We are approaching twenty-three miles now. Annie is striding along as if she has just started, and I feel lighter, despite my aching thighs. I hadn't spoken about Summer since she died. Perhaps I needed to.

Ahead, I can make out the glowing white circle of the London Eye.

Saturday 29 September 2012

London Eye

The sun wrapped London in a yellow glow of late summer light as we stepped into our capsule. The little bubbles attached to the wheel of the Eye reminded me of paracetamol tablets, but there was no need for drugs today. The three of us were shining as brightly as the sun above our heads, especially Rae, who danced around in a vibrant blue Hollister top and a pair of skimpy denim shorts.

The doors to the capsule swished shut leaving us encased with one other family. The father leant on the rail and stared blankly out over the Thames, while the mother tried in vain to stop her two children from careering around the confined space in a game of tag.

'You're it,' screamed the boy.

'Homey!' countered his sister, clinging on to her father's legs.

'That's not Homey!' howled the boy in distress.

'Kids! Calm down.' Their mother made a grab for her son but he evaded her grasp easily and staggered back into Summer, knocking her off balance. Instinctively I put an arm out to steady her, and Summer flashed a smile at me.

'I'm sorry, love. Full of beans they are, the little terrors.'

'It's OK.' Summer waved a hand. She liked to see children having fun.

In an effort to calm things down, the husband scooped up his daughter and held her to the window.

'Sweetheart, look over there. That's where the Prime Minister works.'

I felt Summer flinch next to me at the sound of the word 'sweetheart' but knew it was best to ignore it. The little girl must have been four or five. I had missed out on that stage of Rae's upbringing, but instead of regret, I felt that I had come into her life at the best time. Rae was a mini-adult now, and since she had moved into my flat with Summer last month, we had steadily become closer. I found myself watching Disney and Pixar movies while we sipped milkshakes and ate microwaved popcorn together on my threadbare sofa. It was a source of never-ending amazement to me how often Rae could watch the same movie. We could almost recite the screenplay to *Monsters Inc.*

Our favourite line was when Mike Wazowski – the one who looks like a green eyeball on legs – shouts: 'What can I say, the camera loves me!' Rae and I would bellow this in unison and copy him by preening ourselves in front of the TV. It was stupid, but it was fun. Summer usually went to bed early as she got tired, so often it was just Rae and I on the sofa, but when Summer did join us, I was at my happiest. Mother and daughter cuddled up to each other – two peas from the same pod, with their brown eyes and knife-edge cheekbones.

As we climbed slowly above the muddy waters of the Thames, all of London lay spread out like a carpet. Buckingham Palace sat in front of us and I smiled at the memory of Summer sitting on the Queen's throne. The big, green space of Hyde Park lay beyond and if I squinted, I could just make out the boating lake where Buster once destroyed a model clipper.

I picked out various other landmarks that brought memories flooding back. Parliament Square and Whitehall just below us, where Summer ran amok on a student protest. The Tate Modern where we visited the Brian Haw and Henry Moore exhibitions; I can picture Summer in her lemon-coloured coat sailing serenely through the Embankment traffic, and of course I now understood why Summer fled from the *Mother and Child* sculpture. In the distance, I could see University College where we first met and the British Museum where Summer dragged me one day to see the Elgin Marbles. Despite Summer's efforts, the marbles still resided in the museum's Duveen Gallery. Closer to us, Covent Garden and the Royal Opera House were to our right and I had a sudden vision of Summer at the ballet in her scarlet dress. A little further on was Lincoln's Inn Fields, where we handed out cupcakes and pastries at the flashmob iftar. Summer lived in every corner of this city for me.

I felt a tug on my hand and Summer dragged me over to the window facing east, where we could follow the curve of the river to Tower Bridge and the Tower of London.

'The Crown Jewels,' she said, matter-of-factly.

'Sorry?'

'I should see the Crown Jewels. I can't believe I haven't been before.'

'Why? What's so amazing about the Crown Jewels?'

She looked at me as if I were mad.

'The colours, Ben. Emeralds, rubies, diamonds. You will take me one day, won't you?'

Stupid me. With Summer, it was all about colour. I nodded and made a mental note.

We were close to the apex of the Eye now and Rae started to bounce around.

'I want to take a picture. Mummy, Ben. Come on!'

She grabbed my camera off me and pulled me back towards the central window, so that the Houses of Parliament formed the backdrop. The father set his daughter down and moved obligingly to one side, allowing Summer to stand next to me and slip her arm around my waist. Rae dodged the two kids as they lurched around the capsule one more time and started to frame the photo. Their mother ignored them and grinned at me.

'Ready?' shouted Rae.

Summer leant over to me and whispered in my ear.

'I can see Blackfriars Bridge from here. Do you remember what we did there?'

I beamed a massive smile and Rae pressed the shutter.

'That was only a year ago.' I say my thoughts out loud as we pass the London Eye and make our way on to Westminster Bridge.

'Yet it feels like forever, I know,' Annie replies, looking out over the river.

Only twelve months ago, I was full of optimism. Our American boss had flown across the Atlantic the week after my aborted trip to New York and summarily fired Andrea for being, as he put it bluntly in a staff meeting, 'a complete pain in the ass', and our new office manager promptly gave me a pay rise. More importantly, Summer was recovering from her operation, and now Summer, Rae and I were living as a happy family, doing all those things that happy families do: outings, trips to the park, watching movies, playing games, laughing.

But the dream only lasted so long, because the cancer came back worse than before and there was nothing I could do to prevent the inevitable. I was gripped by a sense of hopelessness, sitting for hours at a time in my armchair, playing various scenarios over in my head. Scenarios that weren't pretty. And all the time I felt guilty. Guilty that it was Summer suffering and not me. Guilty that I had let her walk away along the Embankment that day when she told me about her past. If I had stopped her, if I had called back, perhaps this wouldn't all have happened. Maybe if she had been with me, we would have discovered the lump earlier, or I might have persuaded her to see the doctor sooner.

It was Rae who dragged me out of it.

She sat on the sofa next to me one evening, while Summer was asleep upstairs.

'You love Mummy, don't you?'

I was taken aback by her question.

'You don't need to answer,' she said. 'I know you do. You

look at her in a gooey way and you do things for her all the time.'

I started to rock to and fro in the chair, as if that might make Rae stop her line of questioning, but she was Summer's daughter; she wasn't to be deterred.

'We need to help Mummy.'

Forwards, backwards. Rae's words coming at me through a haze.

'Ben?'

I stopped the rocking and nodded. Rae dropped down from the sofa and knelt in front of me.

'We should make the rest of Mummy's life happy.'

Rae was nine years old, yet so much braver than me. She was facing up to reality, while I was drowning in it.

'Will you help me do that for Mummy?'

I knew exactly what she meant. That I had to be stronger for Summer's last months. I reached across and held her hand. My mouth was dry and I was finding it hard to form any words.

Rae looked at me anxiously. 'Mummy doesn't want us to be sad.'

I pushed the strands of her hair to one side and stroked her face. Her skin was hot to my touch.

'Let's be happy for Mummy, Ben.' She was imploring me and just as I could never resist Summer, I knew that I would never be able to resist her daughter either. I croaked out the words.

'I promise, Rae. I promise.'

★

'She's a strong girl, then?' Annie interrupts my thoughts. 'Did you manage to keep your promise?'

I shrug. 'I did my best, but it was tough. We did as much as we could together as a family and Rae and I laughed and smiled like village idiots. Summer never allowed herself to get down, either. She was amazing. We used to say she was brave and she would tell us, "Nonsense."

'"People are brave when they make brave choices," she would say, "but I never had a choice, so I am not brave."'

313

'I found the hard part was trying not to look shocked at Peter's appearance. I couldn't let him see how worried I was as he got thinner and thinner.'

And I realise that Annie must have had a similar experience to me – and not just Annie. Most of the 16,000 other people exhausting themselves on this marathon walk will have been through the same things, and that tonight, it is about fighting back, in our own little way, not allowing ourselves to be beaten, honouring the memory of the people we have lost, making them proud.

'It took me a long time after he died,' Annie continues. 'That was worse somehow. When he was alive, I had a purpose: to make Peter's life better. When he was gone, it was like living in a black hole of nothingness.'

'God, yes. Tell me about it,' I say. 'Without Summer, there doesn't seem much point to living anymore. I hardly go out, and when I do I'm like a soaking wet sponge of misery. So most of the time, I mope around the house, vegetating in front of crap on the TV, or lying in bed waiting for sleep. The only bright spot is when Rae comes to stay, but I can tell that even she is getting tired of me.'

'It does get better,' Annie says. 'It just takes time. After a while, you realise that they would want you to get on with your life, to be happy again, but you're allowed some time to wallow in self-pity. People understand that; it's normal.'

I reach out and touch her hand, which makes her jump.

'What was that for?'

'For listening,' I say. 'Just for listening.'

We are back in Parliament Square some eight hours since we passed through it early on in the walk. It seems a lifetime has passed since then. We cross the square in silence. There are a few walkers around us, with names and pictures of people on their backs.

'I am walking for… Chris.' I read the note pinned on the back of the T-shirt of a middle-aged man who edges past us, hobbling slightly after over twenty-three miles, but still keeping up his pace.

He turns round and grins at us.

'Keep going,' he says, sticking his thumb in the air. 'Nearly there.'

Across the street, I see the green where the TV crews interview MPs, with the Palace of Westminster in the background. A sculpture I recognise as a Henry Moore has been placed there, like two warped bookends that have been dumped next to each other, but there is something pleasing about their gentle curves and irregular form. Summer would have appreciated it, I know. I can hear her now.

'At least it isn't another bloody *Mother and Child*!'

Keep going, Ben. Nearly there. Into Millbank and on to Lambeth Bridge, the dreaded Horseferry Road to our right. Time to face up to my ghost.

Horseferry Road

Sunday 19 May 2013

The address of the Westminster Public Mortuary is 65 Horseferry Road. Fiona and I spilled out from the taxi, stepping gingerly on to the pavement, my skin itching in trepidation. Inside, a glum-faced receptionist directed us down a linoleum-floored corridor that smelt of antiseptic, where a woman police officer stood with a pale-faced man in a white coat.

The WPC gave us a weak smile.

'Mrs Chandra. Mr Richardson. Thanks for coming. I am WPC Smethwick and this is Dr Craven.'

Fiona shook her hand. I caught the eye of the doctor who looked away and scanned the polystyrene ceiling tiles. Dealing with grieving relatives was clearly the least favourite part of his job. Dr Craven would be much happier slicing open cadavers and extracting hearts and livers for forensic analysis – although Fiona and I were not exactly grieving relatives; in my case I was not even a relative.

'How did you find us?' asked Fiona.

'When the deceased fell in the water, he left his jacket on the embankment. He had a mobile phone in it. That's unusual. We don't often find homeless people with mobile phones.'

'I can imagine,' I muttered. I had a good idea who might have given it to him.

'Anyway, there was only one number in the contacts list. He also had a photograph. It had the same phone number on the back.'

'A photograph?' I gagged.

'Here.' Dr Craven held up a plastic bag. In it was a faded photograph of a girl with honey skin and cascades of brown-black hair, dressed in a scarlet and gold sari.

I held the bag and ran my fingers along the plastic, feeling the photograph inside. She was younger and wearing heavy make-up that made her look like a china doll, but it was unmistakably Summer. Her lips were clamped together in a joyless, thin line. It was unusual to see pictures of Summer when she wasn't smiling or laughing. I turned the bag over and saw her phone number scribbled in biro on the back. There were some words written above it in Summer's handwriting.

'In case of emergency.'

I thought back to the call I took on Summer's phone the day before in my kitchen. I supposed you could argue that death was an emergency, only Manu hadn't been able to make the call himself. I handed the bag back to Dr Craven and stared at my feet.

'Do we know whether he fell or...' Fiona stopped. Or whether he jumped. I completed the sentence for her in my head.

'We don't know,' WPC Smethwick said quickly. 'The body was washed up by Blackfriars Bridge and his jacket was found a hundred yards or so upstream, so he probably entered the water somewhere near there, but we have no witnesses, I'm afraid.'

We stood in silence, breathing in the smell of disinfectant. Dr Craven examined the ceiling once more. After a few moments, WPC Smethwick indicated a pair of swing doors leading off the corridor.

'Shall we?'

'Yes, best to get it over with.' Fiona held my arm and we stumbled through the doors into a room of harsh fluorescent lighting and stainless steel surfaces. A row of filing cabinets lined one wall, but I knew they weren't filing cabinets. They were more like left luggage lockers, but the luggage left behind here was nothing anyone would ever want to collect.

Dr Craven walked over to one of the drawers.

'I must warn you that the body was in the water for some time. It is somewhat decomposed and bloated.'

'I am afraid you may find it disturbing,' added Smethwick. 'Are you sure you're both ready for this?'

'Go ahead,' said Fiona, grabbing my arm.

Dr Craven pulled open the drawer and folded the sheet

back so that we could see the head. Manu's cheeks were puffed up and his skin was blotched black and cormorant-green, but I recognised the double chin and the snub nose. It was the man who threatened us with a broken bottle at Blackfriars Bridge. His lower lip drooped as ever and his upper lip was pulled back revealing his teeth clenched in one final gap-toothed grimace. It reminded me of the grin he gave me as we left Lincoln's Inn Fields, as if he was still laughing at me even in death.

'That is Manu,' whispered Fiona, and I nodded.

Panic swept through me as the doctor replaced the sheet and pushed the drawer back. I would have to go home now and tell Summer.

'So Manu had come to London?' Annie asks.

'Yes. He was married to Summer so he was able to live in the UK. It didn't work out though. Drink got the better of him and he couldn't hold down a job, so he ended up on the streets.'

'And you bumped into him at the flashmob iftar?'

'Where Summer felt sorry for him and gave him her number. In case of emergency. He still carried a photo of her from their wedding day, the poor bloke. She wrote the number on the back. I suppose at some point she also gave him a phone.'

'And he pestered her a lot, did he?'

'Not really. Every so often when he was in real trouble. Like the day we went to the Opera House. Apparently, Summer had to bail him out of jail that day after he'd been arrested. He'd punched an American tourist who'd given him a dollar bill. Said it was bullshit money that he couldn't spend.'

Annie laughed and then covered her hand with her mouth. 'Sorry. I imagine it wasn't funny at the time.'

'The thing is,' I turn to her, 'Summer was agonising over Rae and what would happen to her after she died. She was worried that Manu would reclaim his daughter.'

'And so when Manu's body was found...'

'Exactly.'

I could tell that Annie understood. When Summer knew that Manu was dead, she could finally let herself go, safe in the knowledge that Rae would be looked after by Fiona and me. I toyed with the idea of telling Summer that it wasn't Manu lying in that stainless steel box, that we had seen the disfigured body of some other unfortunate, but I couldn't lie. And deep down, I knew that it would be a merciful release.

Tate Britain

Wednesday 14 March 2007

We skipped lectures because Summer wanted to go to the Tate on Millbank. Mark Wallinger had a new installation there: a painstaking recreation of Brian Haw's Parliament Square demonstration. Summer was a big supporter of Brian Haw and my protest that 'we have seen the real thing so why do we need to see a copy' fell on deaf ears.

'It's a principle,' she explained. 'Blair and his cronies lied to get us to fight an American war. They need to be reminded of that every day.'

The detail in the work was impressive. The placards and banners and teddy bears with 'Peace' T-shirts were exact replicas of the originals, even down to the drip marks hanging from the bottom of the red-painted slogans and symbols.

It was clear that Wallinger had a lot of admiration for Haw; he referred to him as the last protester. Most people made a lot of noise initially, took part in a march, maybe even delivered speeches, but then they drifted back to their normal lives. Whereas Haw kept going; he was tenacious.

Later we were in the Tate café, drinking coffee and sharing a blueberry muffin.

'I think I'll write to the government again. We should have a proper inquiry into the Iraq war, not the establishment whitewash that we have had before.'

I loved this about Summer. Like Brian Haw, she never gave up. She didn't stand by and wait for others to take action. Instead, she took responsibility herself.

She wiped a crumb from her lips. Summer was wearing minimal make-up today, just black eye liner – no lipstick, no blusher, no eye shadow. She looked fantastic.

'Ben, what would you write to the government about?'

'I don't know,' I mumbled.

'Come on. What's the one cause that you feel passionate about? Famine in Africa, global warming, what is it?'

I sat back to think, feeling under pressure. The truth was I let most things wash over me. Any protest I made would be like throwing a pebble in the ocean, a few tiny ripples that would never make the shore. Summer's passion for action always made me feel inadequate.

'I don't know.' I stalled for time. 'Perhaps medicine. There are so many diseases in the world that destroy so many lives, I think we should invest more in medical research. The big drug companies are more interested in profits than in finding cures. They need people to get sick so they can sell them their products.'

Summer cocked her head to one side. 'That's an interesting perspective. So we need government to invest more and not rely on the private sector?'

'Yes.' I was warming to my task. 'Like cancer. One in three of us will get cancer. Surely we can find a cure.'

'Well, there you go.' She swallowed a mouthful of coffee. 'Something for you to write to the Health Minister about.'

She looked around. On the table next to us, a middle-aged lady was reading a book on Turner that she must have bought in the Tate shop. She lifted her head, aware of Summer's gaze, and grimaced. Summer flashed a disarming smile back and the woman returned to her book.

Summer leans over to me.

'I don't want to be nasty,' she said, 'but let's hope that she's the one.'

'She's the one?' I was confused.

'You know,' she punched me on the arm, 'the one out of the three of us that gets cancer.'

Millbank to Albert Bridge

Approaching the final mile now. My thighs are in knots and I know that when I take off my shoes my socks will be soaked in blood from my burst blisters. Despite this, there is a bounce in my step. We are nearly finished and somehow it seems to make it more worthwhile to have a degree of suffering and pain.

Annie keeps up the pace next to me, her ponytail swinging pleasingly from side to side beneath her cap. I have been pouring my words out to her now for nearly nine hours and I am going to miss her company.

'Great job, people. Great job. Nearly there now. Coffee and cakes at the finish.'

A volunteer waves us onwards and I feel a grudging sense of admiration for her efforts and those of her colleagues who have given up a whole night to shepherd us round. We will have the satisfaction of completing a marathon, a medal to recognise our efforts, a sum of money generated for Cancer Research. Their contribution will be less tangible, but vital nonetheless.

'Did you do it?' Annie asks.

'What?'

'Write the letter. You know, to the Health Minister.'

I laugh. 'No, I didn't, now you mention it. Ironic really. Another thing to be guilty about. Maybe if I'd written the letter, the government would have allocated a few more pennies to researching breast cancer.'

Annie frowns.

'Now you're beating yourself up again.'

I shake my head. 'It's OK. I'm not being serious. But I should have written the letter, you're right.'

I look at my watch. It is coming up for 5.30. The sun will not rise for another hour or so but the coal black of night has given way to an early Sunday morning of ash grey. Shadowy boats chug along the Thames and the occasional car drives past on the Embankment at a speed that rush hour commuters would find inconceivable.

Chelsea Bridge, with its red suspension cables and white Cleopatra Needle-style towers glows ahead of us, lit up by strategically placed floodlights. This is the finishing line, where we turn off the Embankment, cross the river and return to Battersea Power Station.

Annie points ahead.

'Looks like you have a reception party.'

I look up and see them. Fiona, dressed in a mauve headscarf, clapping her hands and smiling a huge smile. Rae, hanging on to Buster's lead, her tousled hair belying the fact that she has just crawled out of bed. And Buster, ears pointing to the sky, straining so hard at his leash that his front paws are raised from the ground.

'Ben!' Rae shouts, taking one hand off the lead and waving. 'Ben!'

Buster barks and she lets him go. He careers down the pavement and jumps at me, knocking me backwards.

I take a moment to steady myself and then I kneel down and pat his neck while he slathers his wet tongue across my cheek. Summer's silver 'S' swings jauntily from his collar.

Annie laughs. 'Looks like someone is pleased to see you.'

Rae and Fiona join us and Rae gives me a big hug.

'Brill, Ben. You must be zonked.' She steps back and grabs hold of Buster's lead.

'Come on, boy. Give him space. He's just walked a very long way.'

Fiona leans over and kisses me on the cheek.

'Summer would be proud of you,' she whispers.

I am finding it hard not to dissolve into tears. I had no idea they would get up so early to see me home. My family.

I recover myself and remember my manners.

'Fiona, this is Annie. We have walked all the way together.'

Fiona holds out a hand and Annie shakes it.

'He has told me all about you,' Annie says. 'And your wonderful daughter.'

Fiona smiles. 'I can imagine,' she says. 'You probably needed twenty-six miles to hear everything.'

Rae stamps her foot petulantly, irritated at not being introduced. 'And I'm Rae.'

'I know,' Annie responds, 'and don't worry. He talked about you too.'

Rae grins and looks at me.

'He'd better have done,' she says.

Fiona rests her hands on her granddaughter's shoulders.

'Come on, darling. Ben still has a bit to go. We will see him at the finish.'

Rae wriggles away from her and reaches up to give me a kiss.

'See you in ten. Gran will buy us some hot chocolate, won't you, Gran?'

Fiona smiles and nods her head.

They leave us at the south side of Chelsea Bridge to fetch the car and bring it round to the Power Station, while Annie and I turn off onto the path that runs along the river. Shine volunteers have strung themselves out to create a funnel to welcome us to the finish, shouting and waving encouragement. The Battersea Power Station chimneys soar above us and I put my arm around Annie's shoulders as we cross the finish line.

'Thank you,' I say.

'For what?' She looks bemused.

'For listening.'

'Ahh,' she says, 'I told you at the beginning I was good at that.'

We enter a marquee throbbing with people where a volunteer hangs medals around our necks – silver discs suspended from turquoise ribbons – and we fight our way through the crowded tent to the wasteground where we first met, nine hours ago, cringing at the antics of impossibly upbeat Lycra-clad presenters on a temporary stage. I have come a long way in that time, more than just twenty-six miles.

We stand there awkwardly, not knowing what to say, and I am conscious that Fiona and Rae and Buster will be appearing any time soon.

'Can we give you a lift anywhere?'

'No, no,' she says. 'I will get the train. I'm heading back into town. Islington.'

'Oh, you live in Islington?'

She nods and I realise that I hardly know anything

about her. If our conversation over the last nine hours had been analysed like a football match, I would have dominated possession.

'Well… thank you again.'

'That's OK.' She looks at me with her soft blue eyes. 'It was fun. Thanks for keeping me company.'

She stands on tiptoe and kisses me on each cheek.

'Good luck,' she says. 'Remember. Summer would want you to be happy.'

And then she turns and walks away.

I am motionless. I watch her walking away on her thin legs and an uneasy sense begins to flow through me that I have made this mistake before. That I have stood by and allowed a girl to walk away when I should have run after her and begged her to stay.

My phone beeps and I rescue it from my pocket. It is a text message from Rae.

'We r at the entrance. Buying hot chox.'

I close the message and then a thought occurs to me.

'Hey! Annie!' I start running, pushing people unceremoniously out of my way.

A few disgruntled souls bark their disapproval.

'Oy, watch out, mate.'

I ignore them.

'Annie! Wait!'

I see her twenty yards ahead and she stops and turns round.

'Annie,' I catch up with her, breathing heavily, 'sorry, I forgot.'

I show her the picture on my mobile phone. The two of us, smiling cheesily for the camera in Lincoln's Inn Fields, the Cancer Research logo shining on the wall behind us.

'If you give me your phone number, I'll send you the photo.'

Annie says nothing. She shakes her head and I worry that I am being too forward. She probably wants to forget that she ever met the self-obsessed guy who bored her rigid with his depressing story for twenty-six miles.

'Or your email address,' I say quickly, 'if you prefer.'

'Ben,' she says, 'I thought you were never going to ask.'

Battersea

Saturday 19 October 2013

I examine myself in the mirror and allow myself a grunt of approval. I am wearing a jacquard shirt that I bought today and I even ironed out the fold creases that are the tell-tale giveaway of a recently-liberated-from-its-box new shirt. It is a bold shade of purple, but I feel it is right in the circumstances. A smart shirt for a smart West End restaurant. Besides, now that I have finally taken all Summer's clothes to the charity shop – or at least the ones that Rae didn't snaffle – I need some bright colours in my wardrobe.

I put wax in my hair and tease out some strands for a manicured unkempt look, before dabbing a few drops of aftershave on to my newly shaved jaw. Not too much – I don't want to reek like a Lush store – but enough for me to smell fresh and clean. I smooth out the duvet on the bed and as I do so, I take a moment to look at the photo on the side table of Summer and me laughing on the London Eye.

'Love you forever, babe.' I whisper the words.

I walk into the kitchen and check the clock on the wall. I don't need to leave for a quarter of an hour. The dishwasher has finished its cycle, so I while away a few minutes emptying it and putting the contents away neatly into their designated cupboards and drawers. When I have finished, I survey the kitchen with some satisfaction. The surfaces are sparkly clean and even the unread magazines and newspapers have been gathered up and stacked neatly on the side.

My eye is drawn to the table and an envelope sitting next to my open laptop. I have time. I pull out the letter from the envelope and read it again.

Department of Health
Richmond House, 79 Whitehall, London SW1A 2NS
Telephone: 0207 210 4850 Email: info@doh.gov.uk

Mr Ben Richardson
112 Warriner Gardens
Battersea
London SW11 4DU

Dear Mr Richardson

Thank you for your letter dated 2 October 2013 regarding research into the causes of cancer and the development of new treatments for the disease. The Department of Health strongly agrees with your view that cancer research should be a priority area for investment by the National Health Service and I can assure you that the Secretary of State for Health takes a personal interest in ensuring that a significant proportion of the annual £1.2 billion NHS research budget is allocated to cancer. The Government takes great pride in the fact that the United Kingdom now leads the world in many areas of cancer research.

You may be interested to know that the Secretary of State will be speaking at the Britain Against Cancer conference on Tuesday 12 December 2013 at Central Hall Westminster, organised by the All Party Parliamentary Group Against Cancer. Although this conference is aimed at professionals in the field of cancer treatment and research, I would be delighted to arrange a delegate pass for you. I am sure that you would find the day informative. If you would like to take up this offer, please contact my office using the telephone number or email address above.

I would also like to take this opportunity to

congratulate you on completing the Shine Walk in aid of Cancer Research UK. Here at the Department of Health we are very supportive of this annual event and extremely grateful for the funds it raises for such a worthy cause.

Yours sincerely

U– O– CB
Permanent Secretary of the Department of Health

I feel a sense of achievement rising in my chest. My first response from government, and instead of a complete fob-off, I have an invitation to a conference. I replace the letter and turn my attention to the laptop. A document is open on the screen and I read the first few words.

Friday 3 December 1976

Kent

Eric picks up the phone and dials the number of the police station. His herd is going beserk out there and he is hot with rage. After three rings, a man answers and Eric can't hold himself back.

'Are you the guy looking for a pig? 'Cos if you are, I've found it for you. It's in my bloody field scaring my bloody cows to bloody death.'

★

I smile, save the document as 'Pink Floyd Pig', and close the laptop. I am finally bringing my scrapbook into the modern age and will finish the first entry of the new, electronic version tomorrow. I glance at the clock again. It is time for me to leave for the restaurant. I don't want to keep Annie waiting.

A Few Final Words...

The first spark of the idea for *A Scrapbook for Summer* came to me on a beautiful spring day in April – St George's Day in fact – when, with time to kill, I walked across London from a lunch appointment in Mayfair to evening drinks with a few friends in Southwark. On the way, as well as groups of patriotic revellers dressed in chain mail and dragon costumes looking forward to a Friday night of partying, I passed many landmarks from my twenty-five years in the capital which brought back a host of memories. The thing was, they were all in jumbled up chronological order, and the germ of a novel took seed.

Fortunately for my future novel, while my own recollections were vaguely disappointing, stirred mostly by unremarkable events that took place in branches of Starbucks (I have bought a latte of some description in almost every Starbucks in central London) or public houses (ditto for pints of lager and pubs), Ben and Summer enjoyed a much more varied experience of life in the capital. I couldn't resist, though, allowing Ben a few mouthfuls of coffee in a Starbucks I have frequented often in Fleet Street, although I treated him to a flat white on the basis that my own preferred tipple of a caramel latte felt embarassingly poncey and metrosexual.

The seed sprouted two years later when I took part in the phenomenal Shine walk in aid of Cancer Research. Suddenly, I was walking around London again, along with 16,000 others, and I realised that I had found a reason for a character to trek twenty-six miles overnight past many of London's most iconic landmarks. Special thanks to Helen Webster, for being my Annie that night, and to Cancer Research UK, for allowing me to reference the Shine Walk in the book.

If you have got this far, then presumably you have read the book, in which case you will have picked up on the format.

The story of Ben and Summer is interspersed with fictional recreations of real life events and then, in italics, an attempt to set out the facts behind those events.

All the real-life events referred to in the book truly did occur but probably not in the way Ben imagines them in his scrapbook, although I do harbour a faint hope that Lieutenant Baillie-Stewart's interrogator possessed enough appreciation of the dramatic to produce a Marie-Louise pear at the end of his interview. In any event, to the extent that real people are referred to in the book, be they still living, long dead, or somewhere in between, I hope that I have not offended any of them or their relatives and friends with my characterisation. It was certainly not my intention to do so.

I made every effort to be factually accurate in the sections in italics, although it is interesting how difficult this can be. There are many different versions of the truth out there, even when it seems that the truth should be relatively easy to ascertain, and the determination of right and wrong, truth and fiction, is one of the themes of *A Scrapbook for Summer*. Nevertheless, any factual inaccuracies in these sections are my responsibility and mine alone.

I can't remember who I had lunch with that St George's Day (well, actually I can but I don't think they deserve a mention), but I will reference my friends, Slippy, Gareth and Phil who were waiting for me in the pub at the end of the walk. Somehow, after many years of me being a complete plonker and captain of the golf tour cock-up, they still manage to give me the time of day. Thanks boys for the happy memories.

There are others who deserve a mention in relation to the book. Anyone – too numerous to recall them all – who has shared a drink with me in Starbucks or a London pub; all those who sponsored Helen and me on the Shine Walk; Nicola Arnold, for being my University College London tour guide; Steph and Tawnee for putting up with terrible drafts and making the final version so much better; Megan, who always has a smile on the dial, and Nicola, who each read through early drafts of the full manuscript. All the team at Troubador who made it happen, especially Rosie who was with me all the way from the beginning; and Anne

Aylor for her fantastic writing courses. If you want to write, then what are you waiting for? Sign up to an Anne Aylor course.

There are many more who have kept me going through the years of thick and thin and only room to mention a few. From university, my friend, Bob, who I was privileged to act as best man for – something he probably regretted afterwards – and, Dave, one of the most brilliant, funny and genuine men I have ever met, who memorably gave me my acting debut and definitely regretted that. Dave represents all that was best in Cambridge. And Sue, who flies the flag for the north and keeps my feet on the ground.

From work, Sal, Mary, Jonesie – I will never forget our week in New York – and, of course, Trouble. The double-breasted boys now wearing Lycra, Smithy and Gazza, who ran the New York marathon some way ahead of me and will no doubt find this book much more of a struggle than another Étape. The Lads Night Out crew, who have kept going for a quarter of a century due largely to the efforts of Mark Ballantine and occasional vice-captain Mark Elliott, and the Dream Leaguers, who have been kind enough to let me win our version of fantasy football a few times.

Also, Ilene in New York, Suzanne in Houston and Louise in Putney who always encouraged me to write, Shona Matthews who started it all, and the Fairweather-Barnets who provide me with endless support and entertainment. And the teams at Ascot and Cardiff who gave me some fantastic times and who I was indescribably sad to leave behind, and Hurlingham, who along with the Elliott girls (Margaret, Nicola and Zoe) all contributed to the cover design. Sorry Hazel, for abandoning the swirly font.

To my Mum, my Dad, my sister, Alison, who I have probably made proud and exasperated in equal measure through the years – thanks for being there and I apologise especially for the terrible haircuts in the seventies and eighties.

This book is for those I have known who have battled against cancer, some successfully, some sadly unsuccessfully, including Karen Copeland who gave me undeserved credibility at school and whose life was cut short far too early,

Louise Barnes who we all miss terribly, and my father, who has simply refused to give in. A portion of the proceeds from every copy of *A Scrapbook for Summer* sold will be donated to Cancer Research UK.

But most of all, this book is dedicated to Emma, member of Ferrier House and who is a far better Alexis than I am a Richard Castle, and Alison, who has stuck with me through good times and bad, and who was always the one.

Alan Flitcroft

London
September 2015